THE
MOURNING
EMPORIUM

ALSO BY MICHELLE LOVRIC

The Undrowned Child

MICHELLE LOVRIC

THE MOURNING EMPORIUM

A YEARLING BOOK

Text copyright © 2010 by Michelle Lovric
Cover art copyright © 2012 by Kurt Huggins and Zelda Devon

All rights reserved. Published in the United States by Yearling, an imprint of Random House Children's Books, a division of Random House, Inc., New York. Originally published in hardcover in Great Britain by Orion Children's Books, a division of Orion Publishing Group Ltd., an Hachette UK Company, London, in 2010.

Yearling and the jumping horse design are registered trademarks of Random House, Inc.

Visit us on the Web! randomhouse.com/kids

Educators and librarians, for a variety of teaching tools, visit us at RHTeachersLibrarians.com

The Library of Congress has cataloged the hardcover edition of this work as follows:
Lovric, Michelle.
The mourning emporium / Michelle Lovric. — 1st U.S. ed.
p. cm.
Sequel to: The undrowned child.
Summary: "It is 1900, and the evil traitor, Bajamonte Tiepolo, is back, his baddened magic spreading across the globe. Now Teo and Renzo must save both Venice and London, before it is too late."—Provided by publisher.
ISBN 978-0-385-74000-5 (hardback) — ISBN 978-0-375-89862-4 (ebook) —
ISBN 978-0-385-90815-3 (glb) [1. Orphans—Fiction. 2. Good and evil—Fiction. 3. Prophecies—Fiction. 4. Venice (Italy)—History—1866—Fiction. 5. Italy—History—1870–1914—Fiction.]
I. Title.
PZ7.L95949Mou 2012
[Fic]—dc23
2012009510

ISBN 978-0-375-86598-5 (trade pbk.)

Printed in the United States of America

10 9 8 7 6 5 4 3 2 1

First Yearling Edition 2013

Random House Children's Books
supports the First Amendment and celebrates the right to read.

Contents

A little about the past . . .

Less than two years ago, eleven-year-old Teodora and her adoptive parents left their home in Naples to visit the exciting city of Venice. Soon after she arrived, Teo discovered *The Key to the Secret City*, an old book that revealed an ancient prophecy commanding Teo and a boy named Renzo to save Venice from Bajamonte Tiepolo, or *Il Traditore*, a murderous traitor back to seek revenge centuries after his death. Teo also learned that the reason she felt so at home in Venice was because she had in fact been born there. Her natural parents had been killed by Bajamonte, and Teo had escaped the same fate only because she had been saved by mermaids.

With the help of some new friends and a bit of magic, Teo and Renzo *were* able to stop Il Traditore before he destroyed the city. But when it came time to say the part of the spell that would kill him once and for all, Teo's kind heart stopped her. As a result, Il Traditore was merely vanquished until the time when he would summon enough strength and baddened magic to return once more. . . .

1. Only one person to blame

Venice, late afternoon, Christmas Day, 1900

A small girl stood on the ice that crusted the edge of the lagoon.

The storm was over. But the temperature was still falling. The girl shivered, wrapping her arms around her narrow body.

This was not the kind of cold that makes your nose glow, nor the kind that makes you look forward to sitting by the fire with a nice warm cup of something. It was that hopeless, heart-dragging kind of cold that makes you feel like an orphan.

Particularly if you are one.

Like this girl, Teodora Gasperin.

As far as the eye could see, way out on the islands of the lagoon, droplets of fog had frozen into a crystalline haze over the skeletal branches of the trees. It looked as if the leaves had been replaced by diamonds, glittering like angry teardrops. Ice strangled the shore; long white arabesques of it reached into the black water.

As she turned to trudge back home, Teo's eye snagged on something glinting just below her, embedded in the frozen water. She bent down, lifting her pinafore out of the way for a better look.

Then she screamed.

For what she had glimpsed was a white eel, thick and long as a young tree trunk, with red gills sprouting like coral from its muscular neck. At the sound of her cry, the creature slowly lowered one translucent eyelid and winked at her.

"Vampire Eels!" Teo shuddered. "They're back. And Venice all but drowned under the ice. It can only mean one thing.

"Renzo!" she whispered to herself. "I must tell Renzo! And the mermaids. And Professor Marìn and the other Incogniti . . ."

A black-backed gull flapped past, cawing "Ha! Ha! Ha!"

Teo winced at its mockery. Her nose pinkened, and she blinked rapidly. Then she stamped her foot.

"Yes, I know. I know. *I know.* If Bajamonte Tiepolo has come back, and brought all his vile creatures with him, and baddened magic too, then there's only one person to blame."

The girl lifted her head and cried out over the icy tracts: "Me."

2. Signor Pipistrelly

Osborne House, the Isle of Wight, Christmas Day, 1900

When the news of the disaster was brought to Queen Victoria, she did not lift her dimming eyes from the soft-boiled egg in her golden egg-cup.

"Venice?" She frowned.

"The island city, Ma'am. In Italy, Ma'am—it has been destroyed, they say."

"Is this Ve . . . ?" The Queen stopped, her lip trembling.

"Venice, Ma'am," the nurse reminded her gently.

". . . a part of Our Empire?"

"No, Ma'am, Venice has never been one of ours. Won't you try a little egg? It is exceedingly lightly done."

A sudden shadow darkened the window. A cormorant stood motionless on the sill, its ink-black wings spread out.

"Another one!" The nurse grimaced. "I do so hate those birds. Uncannily like bats, they are." She turned back to her patient, "Now, Ma'am . . ."

But the Queen had fallen asleep again, the teaspoon still clutched in her tiny, wrinkled hand.

Queen Victoria of England was very, very old. She had reigned for sixty-three years, six months and five days. She had outlived her husband, three of her children, several of her grandchildren and one hundred and thirty-eight of her dogs.

She was the most famous woman in the world.

Everyone knew her drooping round face, her toadish eyes, her pursed-up mouth, her sharp parrot-beak of a nose, her silver hair pulled back under a widow's cap, her fussy dresses of dull black silk. Everybody knew that, even though she owned plum-sized diamonds, Queen Victoria preferred to wear just two items of jewelry: her wedding ring and a bracelet made from the hair of her beloved—but deceased—husband, Albert. She had been in deepest mourning for him for almost forty years.

Albert's death was only one of the many things that made Queen Victoria look as if she'd just swallowed a long draft of something exceedingly nasty. She was famous for *never* smiling.

These are just a few of the things that Queen Victoria particularly disliked: jokes, warm rooms, typewriting machines, bishops, weddings, magic, mysteries and, most of all, her own distant cousin Lord Harold Hoskins.

Queen Victoria also disliked the general public, which is why she spent a great deal of time tucked away at Osborne, her vast private estate on the Isle of Wight. If she absolutely *had* to mingle with her subjects, then Queen Victoria carried a parasol lined with chain mail, as several of those subjects had shown a tendency to aim pistols at her at close range. Undoubtedly, most of these would-be assassins had been stirred up by Harold Hoskins, who had the gall to pretend he'd more right to rule Britain than Queen Victoria herself.

So many times, Queen Victoria would have liked to say, "Off

4

with his head!" But Harold Hoskins was, after all, family, and these were, after all, modern times. So the Pretender to the British throne was now lord of the sand and flies on the island of Hooroo in the South Pacific, where he'd been conveniently dispatched as governor of a penal colony five years before.

And what did Queen Victoria like? She liked suet pudding very much indeed. Queen Victoria was partial to dining off gold plates, even at breakfast. She liked ruling an empire as wide as the world, even if it seemed to her that many of her subjects were savages, heathens or even Australians. She heartily enjoyed ordering her family around and criticizing their personal habits—in spite of the fact that some of them had countries of their own to rule.

So there was a very big to-do when the news got out that, on December 25, 1900, Queen Victoria had not got out of bed, nor put on her black dress, nor read the dispatches from her ministers. For the first Christmas of her long reign, she had not criticized a single member of her household. Her memory wandered. She could not manage even a lightly boiled egg.

She wasn't sick; she had simply worn out.

"Not much longer," squawked the spy, flying away from the windowsill with ice in its black feathers. "Our time is coming. South, south!"

On a remote island off the Australian coast, where Her Majesty's convicts toiled in the pitiless sun, Harold Hoskins stroked his neat sandy beard as he watched the dark cloud of birds cruising into the belfry of Hooroo's bleak little stone church.

How convenient it was that his guest had taught him magical means of communicating with them.

"And what perfect timing," he gloated, after the birds had delivered their news. "The Venetian operation a complete triumph! And now *she* can't last much longer, the old bezzom!" Harold Hoskins, the Pretender to the British throne, could never bring himself to refer to his cousin Queen Victoria by name or title.

The spies had also brought happy news of their specially modified *Vampyroteuthis infernalis*, recently dispatched to London on a mission for his guest.

"Nasty little creatures," thought Harold Hoskins fondly. They were, after all, his firstborn experiment in baddened magic. "I must tell him!"

He hurried carefully—for he could not risk a fall—down the passageway that led to a secret lagoon on the farthest and wildest edge of the island. He would be sure to find him there, gazing north as always. Anyway, it was time to check on their latest little project.

They had been testing certain spores on the local South Sea dolphins. Harold Hoskins didn't see the harm in the fish himself, but his guest was most insistent that they should be treated "like the traitorous vermin they are."

The blackened corpses of five dolphins lay on the beach. They were being drained of their marrowfat by a select band of yet another *almost* perfectly successful experiment, the Ghost-Convicts.

Who'd have thought it would be so simple to resuscitate the corpses of two hundred convicts who'd tried to escape the island back in 1835? The men had promptly driven their boat straight into Hooroo's deadly reef. All perished. Now their ghosts, unattractively shark-nibbled, had been raised from the seabed and were turning into quite promising pirates. The Pretender's faithful Lieutenant Rosebud had taught them all the villainous arts. The Ghost-Convicts were still slightly defective in function, however, with an inconvenient tendency to steal sheep.

Lately, the forces had been swelled by stripping the well-stocked graveyard on Hooroo for men who'd been hanged for bushranging or murder. Finally, there were the living criminals he'd bribed with pardons. Of course, the most dangerous—living and undead—had already been dispatched north on that satisfactory little mission to Venice, with Lieutenant Rosebud himself and *the lady*. His guest had insisted that she too be given a pardon, despite her crimes. "She'll be perfect for the work in hand," he'd rasped.

Down on the beach, the Ghost-Convicts sang gruesome sea shanties as they drained the dolphins. The dreadful noise masked the baaing of several sheep they had hidden under an upturned dinghy.

"Nice to see them so jolly," thought Harold Hoskins. "And they'll be happier still to take revenge on the Old Country for years of subjugation and snobbery."

Now the Pretender could start topping up their high spirits with mentions of the jewels that would be worn by the world's royalty, who'd soon be gathering in London for Queen Victoria's funeral.

What a shame that metal was in short supply on Hooroo, mused Harold Hoskins. They had to use bullets made from pollywaffle—pellets of compacted parrot dung.

A deep shadow of black glided along the distant foreshore.

Harold Hoskins knew better than to call out. No, better to let him come in his own time.

The Pretender's guest favored a long black cloak. It emphasized the deathly pallor of a face Harold Hoskins still found it hard to look at for long—although *the lady* obviously hadn't been able to drag her eyes away from it. Given that long black cloak and that upsetting face of his, it had been easy for Harold Hoskins and Lieutenant Rosebud to coin a code name for their guest when he was first washed ashore, all those months before.

"Signor Pipistrelly" was what leapt simultaneously to their lips.

"Signor Pipistrelly"—Mr. Bat.

Harold Hoskins was not entirely sorry to realize that Signor Pipistrelly would be rushing north too, just as soon as he heard the birds' news. A barn had been prepared for him outside Calais, conveniently close to the English Channel.

At the same moment, but half a world away, two men stood high up on the bell tower of San Giorgio, gazing down on the ice floes in the lagoon. The older of the two drew respectful bows from the other Venetians who'd hurried up the terrace to behold the full scale of the disaster from the best vantage point in the city. Professor Marìn was the famous author of such excellent volumes as *The Best Ways with Wayward Ghosts* and *Lagoon Creatures—Nice or Nasty?*

The other man, quite unreasonably handsome, was nevertheless oblivious to the admiring glances of all the ladies. The circusmaster Sargano Alicamoussa was too distressed: not just at the devastation of his beloved Venice, but at the news that schools of South Sea dolphins were perishing from a mysterious disease in the Pacific.

He lamented, "Is a hair-erecting horror! First the ice. Now this! Can it be coincidensical that the dear dolphins that helped us in the battle are suffering so? Colder than goanna's blood is a villain who destroys such noble beasts, yes."

Signor Alicamoussa was a native Venetian, but had passed much of his life roaming the Antipodes in search of rare Australian beasts. So his vocabulary was sometimes alarmingly exotic.

Now he wiped a tear from his brilliant blue eye, causing three ladies to rush forward with their handkerchiefs. When they had retreated, the circus-master continued, "The brave dolphins perished too close to the island of Hooroo. Youse'll know I was there last year, Professor, for to collect some bare-eyed cockatoos. I don't trust that knack-kneed dingo Harold Hoskins any more than I'd trust a dog with a butcher's bucket. Is something crook going on there, yes. My oath!"

He lowered his voice. "Reckon that Harold Hoskins has got himself a snoot of baddened magic."

"Impossible!" cried the professor. "Young Teodora put an end to all that for us."

Signor Alicamoussa confirmed joyfully, "And the sweet girl's safe from the ice, bless the beetles. And is surely sure that dearest Lorenzo . . ."

An egret alighted on the railing and tiptoed on its star-shaped feet toward the two men. It bent its graceful neck toward them and chirped a few sad notes before it flew off.

"No! Poor Renzo!" breathed Professor Marìn.

"I'll be there"—Signor Alicamoussa was already striding toward the stairs—"quicker than three jumps of a fleck-eared flea."

"Godspeed, Sargano," called the professor. "You know where I'll be. I've got a ship to shape up."

Just across the water, at the Hotel Danieli, a lady with a row of kiss curls on her forehead sat at her dressing table, admiring her beautiful face in the mirror.

She'd had the luck—or the foresight—to insist on a room on the third floor, well above the ice flood. She'd just finished dabbing her wrists with perfume and was tucking a pistol into the belt that cinched her waist, when she was summoned to the window. A seagull was tapping on it with his yellow beak.

"You have news for me?" she asked, drawing on her gloves. Her voice was cold and clipped.

She opened the window and let the bird in. "Is there news of the insufferable Studious Son?" she demanded. "And of the accursed and as yet Undrowned Child?"

3. The Worst Christmas

what had happened the previous night

On the night before Christmas, the city had been caught by surprise: a brutal, murderous surprise.

Venice was used to floods. Fifty times a year, several feet of water tumbled into the great square of San Marco and other low parts of the city.

"So?" the Venetians asked, and shrugged. "What's a bit of water?"

The next tide always pulled it out again. People usually managed to extract some fun from this practical joke played by Nature. Gondoliers would pole people straight into cafés and they'd drink a glass of wine at the bar, still standing in the boat.

But on Christmas Eve, 1900, the sea had risen swift and silent in the night. The hydrometers of the Brenta Canal were simply swept away, so they could warn no one. Coils of gray water snaked deep into the city. Venice had never seen floodwater like this, slithering on its cold belly through the streets, carrying on its back flotillas of cruelly sharp miniature icebergs and ice floes in jagged sheets.

Many Venetians had been to midnight Mass; others had sat up late, enjoying the Christmas Eve feast of fried fish and reminiscing over Christmasses past. Everyone went to bed overfed, overtired and very happy.

So no one heard the poor tethered dogs of Venice barking until the water closed over them. As the sea crept up the walls, a few Venetians who lived on the ground floor woke. They were the unlucky ones. Alerted by a slapping noise, they innocently opened their doors. A mountain of water gushed in and swept them away.

The ice floes clanked as the waves surged higher. The snake of water lashed its tail. The ice nudged, scraped, rattled and finally shattered the windows of houses, shops and churches. Suddenly, the narrow streets were flowing with a shocking soup of food and furniture, Christmas wrappings and baubles, baby carriages and chamber pots, children's toys and human beings. Rings and necklaces tumbled from the jewelers' windows. Coffins floated out of funeral chapels to jostle among the icebergs. The jaws of the water snatched the dead fish from their baskets at the Rialto Market and bore them away in limp shoals down the Grand Canal.

The next people to be woken were the staff of the Accademia Galleries, home of Venice's finest paintings. With the water rising over his knees, the night watchman telephoned for help. Soon all the museum curators came sloshing through the city in the thigh-high boots all Venetians kept for flood times.

But it was too late to save the paintings of Venice herself: portraits of the city painted by Bellini, Carpaccio and Canaletto. The priceless masterpieces floated through the smashed windows to join the thickening soup.

The sorrowful light of Christmas dawn revealed a drowned city. The ruins of gondolas lay like the skeletons of slender whales. In front of the shops, the remains of their wares, sodden and black with mud, were heaped in funeral pyres, waiting to dry out enough to burn. Venice looked like an enormous flea market, one that sold only pitiful damaged goods.

The first outsiders the Venetians saw were photographers and journalists, who called comfortably from their safe, dry boats, "Are you Venetians freezing and wretched? Have you lost your mothers? Any babies swept away?"

Mute with misery and cold, the Venetians stared back at them. The journalists jotted furiously while swigging hot whisky-and-orange from their flasks.

"Row on, man!" they ordered their boatmen. "This lot aren't wretched enough. See if you can find a motherless child crying, will you?"

Everywhere Venetians were asking each other one question: "*Why?*"

After all, Venice was famous for her great seawalls, the *murazzi*. How had the *murazzi* failed the city, just when they were needed the most? A party of fishermen set off in salvaged boats to see what had happened, and to forage on the islands where Venice grew her food. As they approached the Lido, the men paled. The *murazzi* had been flung around like toy building blocks. And the orchards of Sant'Erasmo were sad ghosts of themselves: bleached, flattened and poisoned with salt.

From a distance, the fishermen glimpsed swollen bodies on the shoreline of Pellestrina.

"More dead," they sighed, unrolling blankets. "Will it never end?"

But as the fishermen approached, the bodies emitted loud honking sounds. Those icy beaches were now home to some new inhabitants. The ice storm had swept a colony of monk seals north from Croatia. The seals cried their fear and loneliness in the unfamiliar environment.

And now snow was falling in thick threads, weaving a white blanket over the town. Fragile roofs sagged under quilts of snow; churches were folded away in blank curtains of ice. It was as if the city had died, and now lay pale and otherworldly in a soft white shroud.

And so it was, on the afternoon of Christmas Day, that Teodora Gasperin came to be standing on the frozen water that jutted into the lagoon. Until the moment she'd encountered the Vampire Eel under the ice, Teo had been wondering about her adoptive parents, a mile away across the water.

While Venice froze and drowned, at least those two must have been safe at work in their beautiful new laboratory perched high on the island of the Lazzaretto Vecchio, where they were the proud directors of the new Lagoon Museum. Knowing them—Teo smiled fondly—Leonora and Alberto Stampara probably hadn't noticed the icebergs sweeping past the island. Their eyes would have been glued to their microscopes.

"They didn't even come back for supper last night! Christmas Eve!" Teo grumbled. "I know they're on the verge of a breakthrough, but really, how can the locomotion of the common squid be so interesting that they forget to come home and watch me open my presents?"

She sighed indulgently. "Well, it's not the first time."

And when they did come home, she knew they'd be their usual affectionate selves, liberal with hugs and praise. She couldn't have asked for kinder adoptive parents. And a little absentmindedness on their parts meant that she and her friend Renzo were free to explore the city and islands to their hearts' content.

All was also dry and snug back at their third-floor apartment near the Fondamente Nuove, where the family's housekeeper, Anna, was boiling cauldrons of soup and roasting slices of pumpkin. Teo had spent her day trudging through the streets to deliver buckets of soup and trays of pumpkin to neighbors whose ground-floor rooms were still pitifully damp and whose ovens were clogged with mud. The hours had passed in a steamy haze of onions, hot water and the grateful tears of the people Teo visited. She imagined Renzo doing something similar where he lived, over in Santa Croce, on the other side of town. Renzo's mother was just the sort of woman to tuck up her sleeves and throw herself into helping those less fortunate than herself. Teo pictured her busy in her blue shawl, bringing as much comfort to people with her lovely face as with her kind, swift hands.

"Of course Renzo's safe," she told herself. "*Of course* he is."

But she still asked everyone she met, "Do you have any news of Santa Croce?"

They shook their heads. Teo had glimpsed the lists of the dead on the walls. They were so miserably long that she could not bear to study them. In tiny Venice, everyone knew everyone else, or was related to someone who did. The names of people Teo knew and loved were bound to be written on those sheets of paper.

There was no doubt, fortunately, that their friend Maria was out of harm's way: the convent school where she boarded was on high ground over on the island of Giudecca. A neighbor told Teo that the nuns were taking in people made homeless by the flood. Maria would be in her element, sorting out warm clean clothes for everybody, choosing the prettiest dresses for the saddest girls who needed them the most.

And Teo too had tried to bury her own worries in hard work. All day, the sun had hardly dared to show its face, as if it knew that it was irrelevant to the desolate city. The orange glow of Teo's hot pumpkin was a cheering sight in the bitter mist and inside houses lit only by stubs of candles.

At last, when everyone possible had been comforted with soup and hugs, Teo had slipped away for a little time to herself. Standing on the lonely shore at the Fondamente Nuove, she finally allowed her shoulders to sag. She was tired to the marrow of her bones. She'd slept fitfully the previous night, tortured by a nightmare.

Some of it had already come true.

In her dream, shadows had flitted through black water. There had been tails with jewel-like scales, and pale, slender arms bearing away flailing humans and tumbling paintings. A black ship with cobwebbed sails had cast nets down into the water where drowning souls thrashed and screamed. There had been images of giant squid pushing children into their thorny maws, and of a dead Venice trapped and perfectly preserved beneath a hundred feet of crystal ice. Over these scenes had floated a gray eminence, not quite man-shaped, not quite bat-shaped. It had swooped to whisper in Teodora's flinching ears: "Death, and worse, to all Venetians."

The distant honking of the lonely monk seals brought her back to the present.

"Poor seals," she thought, "swept away from everything they know."

And that was the moment when Teo had looked down and seen the red gills and the winking eye of the Vampire Eel, and known for certain that Venice herself, and not just the unfortunate seals, now stood in the loneliest and most terrifying kind of danger.

Under her knitted cap, the cold suddenly gripped her, as if wrenching the hair off her scalp. She whispered, "Oh, Renzo! Where are you?"

4. Mud

a dank and dismal Christmas Day afternoon, 1900

Renzo carried the bucket into the dark house and threw its contents over the terra-cotta floor his mother had always polished to a shine. Each pailful loosened a little more of the stinking mud that slimed up to his ankles. Renzo's mind was blank, but his feet automatically followed the path to and from the well in the courtyard. His numb hands sent the bucket plummeting down through the ice. Then his aching arms lifted the dripping pail and carried it into the ruined kitchen.

Upstairs, his mother's body had been laid out on her bed by two kind neighbors. The funeral gondolas were busy with dozens of victims of the ice flood. The rich and noble were buried first. Renzo's mother had to wait her turn. In this raw cold, the bodies of the dead remained perfectly preserved. Renzo's pretty mother looked as if she had fallen asleep. There was only a small cut under her hairline to show where the iceberg had struck as the swiftly rising waters lifted her up. Unconscious, she had drowned while Renzo flailed through the black water, screaming her name.

After every hundredth bucket, Renzo allowed himself to warm

his hands by the brazier for the count of twenty, and to climb to his mother's bedroom and stroke her hair, pick another strand of wet tinsel from it and clasp her hand. Then he returned to sluicing out their home.

Against his will, a sweetly sad image invaded Renzo's mind: the cemetery on the island of San Michele. He saw the cypresses pointing to the heavens over the pink brick walls, just across the water from the cavern under the House of the Spirits, where the mermaids dwelled. Yes, he would bury his mother alongside his father, who had been taken from them by bronchitis. His friend Teo's real parents were buried at San Michele too. During this last hot summer—the mere *thought* of warmth comforted Renzo for a moment—he and Teo had rowed across in the gondola to take daisies to his father's grave and roses to her parents'. Then they had shared a ferociously spicy piri-piri pea pie with the mermaids.

"We're both orphans now, Teo and I," Renzo realized.

Bajamonte Tiepolo, Orphan-Maker.

The words brushed across Renzo's brain for a second. Then he exclaimed, "No! I won't even think it. We got rid of him!"

But memory throbbed painfully in his ribs, two of which had been broken in single-handed combat with Bajamonte Tiepolo eighteen months before. And with that memory came questions: How had the mermaids fared in the ice flood? Was Teo with them now?

The latest bucket of water had dislodged a tinkling object from the mud. Renzo knelt to pick it up. He cradled the small china money-box against his chest, even though it was clotted with dirt.

One corner had been smashed, and all the money had washed out. Renzo ignored the coins scattered underfoot. Tenderly, he

wiped the mud off one side of the money-box, revealing A PRES-
ENT FROM LONDON stamped beneath an etching of Tower Bridge's
Gothic ramparts. The money-box had been a gift from his father,
a souvenir of a short visit to London made with Renzo's Uncle
Tommaso, just after the splendid new bridge had opened on the
Thames.

"I'll take you to London, for your thirteenth birthday," his
father had promised six-year-old Renzo, handing him the china
box. "You can use this to save your pocket-money for that trip!"
And he had gone on to talk of London's narrow cobbled streets,
the quaint bookshops in Paternoster Row and the graceful gray
cupola of St. Paul's.

"And the Londoners!" Renzo's father had enthused. "Fuller of
purpose than an egg is full of goodness!" But he coughed the last
word. The coughing soon got worse.

Last summer Renzo and Teo had argued about London. Renzo
couldn't wait to go there and was saving hard.

"Imagine," Renzo said dreamily, "the attics full of scribbling
poets, the historic London rain beating softly on their roofs—"

"Rain is not historic, Renzo," Teo had interrupted.

"And the picturesque London urchins . . ."

"You mean poor children, Renzo?"

Renzo continued, "The cozy Inns of Court, where white-
wigged lawyers . . ."

"Strip people of their inheritances, according to Mr. Dickens,"
Teo pointed out.

"Teo, do try to understand. Remember how you felt about Venice before you even saw her? Well, that's how I feel about London.
Just from seeing them in books, you loved the palaces and canals

of Venice. Well, I already love the Houses of Parliament on the Thames, the flowerbeds of Kew Gardens . . ."

Flowers! Renzo thrust the broken money-box into his pocket. How and where, in this deadly cold, would he find flowers for his mother's funeral? She loved violets. He had to salvage and wash her best dress for her to wear in the coffin. He must remind the priest of her favorite hymn. And above all, he had to clean the floor. His mother would have been horrified to see their spotless little house in such a filthy state.

What would happen to Renzo himself did not concern him at all. He seized the bucket and ran back to the well.

Unfortunately, just at that moment, someone else had Renzo's destiny right at the forefront of his not notably excellent mind.

5. A quick word about the Mayor

the Town Hall, Venice, Christmas Day afternoon, 1900

The Mayor of Venice wriggled toes clad in silk socks in front of a cozy fire. His sumptuous second-floor office was cheerfully lit by a four-hundred-year-old candy-colored chandelier burning fifty candles at once. He dipped an almond biscuit into a glass of sweet Malvasia wine. You would never have guessed that a city lay broken and suffering outside his sparkling windows.

While Venice struggled with the flood's aftermath, the Mayor had passed happy hours designing a new form in triplicate for anyone who was homeless or needed blankets and food. That was when he wasn't on the streets, elbowing the firemen and policemen out of the way when photographs were taken.

For the Mayor of Venice had just two ambitions: to bring more rich tourists to the town, and to get himself photographed in a smart top hat for as many newspapers as possible. True, the ice flood was a sore setback to tourism, but it had allowed the Mayor more photographic opportunities than ever. He'd already kissed a dozen muddy babies for the cameras that very day, making them cry with his stiffly greased mustache.

And now, by the glitter of his chandelier, the Mayor of Venice was signing a document that bore the name Lorenzo Antonello at the top. The Mayor's mustache twitched as he handed the paper to one of the police officers who always protected him. Since June 1899, when he'd misled the world about certain dangerous events in the town, the Mayor had not been the most popular person in Venice.

"See that it's done immediately!" the Mayor ordered Officer Gianni.

The officer read his orders and a queasy expression came over his face.

As the policeman went trudging down the stairs, an officer of the Carabinieri—the policeman's cousin, as it happened—hurtled past him toward the Mayor's luxurious office. Pausing, he panted, "Gianni, there's been a kidnap! The Lagoon Museum Director and his wife—snatched! Too clever for their own good, that pair. Knew too much about underwater loco-moco-thingy-you-know. Now they've got press-ganged into service for a foreign power, that's what they're saying!"

Officer Gianni showed his cousin the document he'd to deliver to Renzo. The water officer raised his eyebrows. "Did the Mayor eat an extra bowl of stupid this morning? Lorenzo Antonello? Isn't that the gondolier's widow's kid? Signora Antonello's on the drowned list—*che tragedia*, that was one sweet woman. Now, to send the boy away to a floating orphanage . . . !"

Officer Gianni stammered, "The—the *Scilla*'s a kind place. They look after the boys, don't they just?"

His cousin growled, "That old crock, in this weather? Have you seen the sky? Have you looked at the barometer?"

Gianni pulled his collar up and wrapped his scarf tightly around his neck. But he stopped in the act of donning his hat: "Those scientists kidnapped from the Lagoon Museum—don't they have a daughter? Adopted, wasn't she?"

Teo had been born in Venice. When her real family died in a mysterious shipwreck, only the infant Teo had survived, the Undrowned Child of an old Venetian Prophecy. The Mayor had not wanted journalists poking around, asking questions about why nine Venetian lives had been lost in the lagoon waters. For the Mayor, it would have been more convenient if the *entire* family had vanished without a trace. So he had the baby Teodora Gasperin sent away for adoption in a city in the south. For eleven years, Teo had lived in Naples without knowing who she really was.

Then the kind scientists who adopted Teo had brought her to a symposium in Venice. She had found *The Key to the Secret City*—or rather, the magical book had found *her*, by falling on her head. And Teo had gone "between-the-Linings," becoming invisible to all but ghosts, magical beings and other children. The book had led her to Renzo, the Studious Son of the same prophecy that named her the Undrowned Child. Together, they'd befriended the Venetian mermaids, and the *Incogniti*, the Unknown Ones, a secret society that protected Venice from baddened magic. Teo's real parents had been members. It had cost them their lives.

That baddened magic had been wielded by the spirit of Bajamonte Tiepolo, a noble Venetian who conspired to seize power in 1310. After his plot failed, he was secretly strangled by a state assassin. For nearly six hundred years, the restless spirit of *Il Traditore*—"the Traitor," as he was known—had simmered hate and revenge. Finally, the summer before last, his ghost had grown strong enough to turn that hatred into deeds.

Had he but known it, the Mayor had every reason to be grateful to Teo and Renzo. The two of them had joined with the mermaids, raising an army of ghosts and good creatures against Bajamonte Tiepolo. Renzo had taken on Il Traditore's own savage spirit in a fierce battle of wills. And finally, Teo, using ancient skills born into her family, had used his own Spell Almanac to curse Bajamonte Tiepolo back to death. A deep whirlpool in the lagoon had sucked him away.

That is, Teo had cursed him *almost* to death. To oblivion, anyway. There had been one last, unspeakably horrible imprecation that she'd not been able to force herself to utter.

Of course, the human population of Venice had remained entirely unaware of the true danger. Adults—including tender-hearted policemen and stupid, vain Mayors—simply could not see ghosts, mermaids or supernatural creatures.

The four-hundredth bucket came up with more ice than water.

Over the clatter of mop and bucket, Renzo did not hear Officer Gianni tapping at the open door. Nor did he see the stricken look on Gianni's face as he took in the boy's pitiful attempt at clean clothes, the chipped cups and saucers he had carefully washed and placed back on the dresser, his mother's best dress rinsed and fluttering in the thin column of warm air above the brazier. Tears came to the policeman's eyes when he saw the damp Christmas wrappings already carefully folded, the ruins of a cake lying in a bowl of mud, and a bunch of violets carved out of wood, Renzo's last present to his mother. The purple paint had not yet dried.

"What a Christmas for the lad!" Officer Gianni thought. "What a Christmas for Venice!"

At that moment, Renzo was thinking about Teo. Where was she? Surely she would know that his mother was among the drowned: new lists were fixed hourly to every wall in town. He could hardly bear to walk down the street, forced on every corner to confront his mother's name next to the word "dead." And below it, he'd just seen the name Tommaso Antonello, his beloved and only uncle. Renzo's classmate Augusto was also listed, next to "missing, presumed drowned," like dozens of other boys and girls.

So why had Teo still not come? Wasn't she supposed to be his best friend?

Renzo longed to see her, but he dreaded it as well. He had very bad news; the worst, in fact. There'd been another victim of the flood: his most precious possession, apart from the money-box. And it wasn't even really his: technically, it was merely on loan from Teo. Now that Renzo had sluiced the entire house, he had to admit it was true: there was no trace of *The Key to the Secret City*. It must have floated out of the house along with all the other books in Renzo's collection.

"Lorenzo Antonello?" The policeman's voice was gentle.

Renzo spun around.

The officer repeated, "Lorenzo Antonello, I'm hereby ordered to conduct you to the *Scilla*, where you shall be apprenticed for a sailor."

26

"My mother . . ." Renzo's voice was as blank as his face. "She's not buried yet." .

"That will be taken care of. The Mayor has already arranged it."

At the mention of the Mayor's name, Renzo scowled ferociously. "So you're that foot-licker's henchman? I'll have nothing to do with you."

"Boy has a cheek!" Officer Gianni marveled. He could not but sympathize, nevertheless. It was despicable to drag a grieving boy away from home without letting him attend to his dead mother.

"But orders is orders," Gianni thought regretfully. He reminded himself that he was lucky to have a safe job in these hard times.

He said, "It's out of your hands, son. You ain't of legal age. You're a ward of the state and you've got to go where the Mayor tells you. Come, put your things together, boy. The *Scilla*'s not bad. Not for an old warship, anyways. She's a proper boat, lad, painted wood and canvas sails! Your family's menfolk have been gondoliers and sailors for generations, haven't they? Sea's in your blood."

"Lorenzo! Dearest chap! I just heard!" a melodious voice fluted from outside the door. A strikingly handsome man with piercing blue eyes hurried in. He gathered Renzo in a powerful hug that smelled of warm hay and lemons. "My precious boy, my poor, poor child. Are you hurt, yourself? How's every rib in your dear body?"

Then he held Renzo away from him and peered at the boy's pinched white face. "What, no tears? Are youse entrapolated in your grief still? But Lorenzo, you must cry, let us weep together for your sweet mother, and for Venice too."

At this Sargano Alicamoussa burst into noisy sobs. "An

adorable woman!" he wept. "Our incomparable city! And the darling dolphins too! My heart's dropping off in lumps with the sorrow of it."

"I carved some violets for my mother," said Renzo dully. "With my penknife."

"What a skill you have, dearest boy! Now, I am quite decided—youse shall come live with me and my wife, Mercer. We shall adopterate youse, yes."

Unheard, the policeman murmured, "Err, sir . . . ?"

Signor Alicamoussa looked deep into Renzo's deadened eyes, whispering, "We Incogniti take care of our own."

The policeman stepped forward, holding out the Mayor's order. "Uncommon decent of you, sir, however the boy's already signed over to the *Scilla*. The boat's been notified. They'll be expecting him aboard any minute."

"Beg yours? The *Scilla*? Feather me, *there's* a coincidence! Pearler! Wait till . . . But no, no, no, no, no, dear Lorenzo has no need to be an orphan sailor. He shall have a loving home! My charming lady wife to cherish him! Lions and wildebeest as his pets! Signed over, you say? Without so much as a 'Do you fancy a naval career?' to the boy himself? Says who? Upon my word, what outrageous outrage is this? I shall frankly not permit it."

"It's too late, sir. Look—the Mayor's signature."

"The Mayor? That dilapidated dog! Only my wife, who is Irish and has the gift of the gabble to an amazing extent, can curse the fellow to my full satisfactioning, and do so quicker than a laxative through a koala bear.

"But of *course* the Mayor wants to hide dear Lorenzo away from the world. This boy's heroism is too glorious a mirror for his own jellyfish heart! And no doubt he'll be ravening after our little Teodora next. With her parents kidnabbled—I just heard the news. Reckon it looks in the altogether poorly for them."

Renzo turned to Signor Alicamoussa. For the first time, a spark flickered in his eyes. "Teo? What's happened to her?"

6. Despicable deeds

Venice Town Hall, late afternoon, Christmas Day, 1900

Teo hadn't even made it home after she saw the Vampire Eel. The policemen were waiting for her on the shore. Dragging her through the ruined streets to the Mayor's office, they had not wasted any tact when describing the state of Leonora and Alberto Stampara's laboratory in the lagoon: the smashed pipettes, the crabs and shrimps left gasping in shattered tanks, the diagrams ripped off the walls. Of her adoptive parents there had been no sign at all, except a fragment of a silk dress and her father's pipe, still fragrant and faintly warm.

Now a tearful Teo paced up and down the Town Hall's grand vestibule. The two policemen had not been amused by the teethmarks she'd left in their wrists. Their eyes followed her back and forth, their arms folded over their barrels of chests.

Despite being fully twelve and a half years old, Teo could not resist sticking out her tongue at her captors.

"After all," she reasoned, "they work for that perditioned rat, the Mayor. What's he up to in that office? Certainly nothing to help my parents. He's making a boffle of everything again!"

Step by step, Teo paced her thoughts into order.

The last thing the Mayor would want, she realized, was the publicity that would follow an announcement that a young girl called Teodora Gasperin had for the second time been left without parents, and under the most dramatic circumstances.

"He's going to send me away again!" A bitter chill coursed down the back of Teo's neck. "That's what he's going to do, the dismal cockroach!"

The Mayor's voice now fussed from inside his office, "Blotting paper! My signature is smeared!"

As the Undrowned Child of the old Prophecy, Teo was the lucky—or sometimes unlucky—owner of a number of unusual gifts. One of these was that when people talked, she could see their words in their own handwriting in the air. The style of that hand-writing revealed a great deal about them. As the Mayor's voice boomed out of his office, Teo saw smug lettering with absurd flour-ishes in gushing purple ink floating down the corridor.

"All done!" the Mayor said with a triumphant smirk. "A good day's work. Got the Antonello boy off my hands, and now we'll not be troubled by *that* young lady again. Fortunately, there's a shortage of children in Norway."

"You potato-witted absurdity!" yelled Teo at the top of her voice. It should also be mentioned at this point that Teo, like Renzo, was a rabid bookworm and consequently endowed with a vocabulary that could sever a steel cable. The policemen tried in vain to suppress smiles.

The Mayor's curled head appeared around the door, wafting perfumed pomade into the hall. Even though he'd stolen her life not just once, but twice, the Mayor, by careful calculation, had

31

never actually laid eyes on Teo herself. Now their eyes—hers, an unusual sea-green and his, moist and puppy-brown—met for a single quivering second.

Teo couldn't help it; the words leapt out of her mouth: "Poor Venice, stuck with a futile fop of a mayor! Your mustache has more brains than your head! Don't you understand? You can't send me away now! This is just when you and Venice need me the *most*."

The Mayor took a step backward, as if someone had punched him on the nose. It was evident that in the flesh Teodora Gasperin was everything he'd been afraid she would be. His face grew greasy with an awkward emotion that jiggled between fear and shame.

Teo took the opportunity to crouch down and bolt between the legs of the policemen now doubled over in helpless mirth. Then she hurtled down the stairs, three at a time, as if she was flying.

Teo skidded through the muddy streets toward the one place where she'd surely find the answer to the question she could hardly bear to voice.

A sob tore from her throat. "It was *him* who sent the ice storm, wasn't it? *He* kidnapped my parents, didn't he?"

It was not the Mayor's mustachioed face Teo carried in her mind as she virtually skated on her heels through Campo San Bartolomeo. The Mayor's foolish vanity made him nothing more than an unwitting tool of the real enemy. That was how it had been last time: the Mayor putting all Venice at risk, without the least idea of what was really happening. No, as she pounded over the Ponte dell'Olio, what Teo was recalling was the pointed face shimmering like half-boiled egg white, the pale lizard eyes and the sharklike nose of Bajamonte Tiepolo, Il Traditore, staring down at her with a centuries-old hatred. She remembered him striking a sickening blow to Renzo's cheek. Renzo! Surely he was thinking the same thing she was? Perhaps he was with the mermaids already?

Never had the House of the Spirits seemed so far: it felt as if someone had moved it two miles away from its original location at the Misericordia. A stitch clamped Teo's side and she stumbled over a pile of sodden postcards. All the gaily colored photographs of Venice had turned black.

"Even the pictures of Venice—ruined!" she mourned breathlessly.

By San Felice she had shrugged off her heavy-footed pursuers, who were still forced to pause and laugh every so often, remembering what she'd shouted at the Mayor. Finally, Teo stopped, sniffed the air and looked around her.

"Strange," she muttered. "It doesn't *feel* as if . . ."

At the basin of the Misericordia, she threw herself into a boat, clambered over four more and then grabbed a drainpipe to lever herself on to an ornate gate. This she scaled with her customary lack of grace, dropping on all fours into the garden below. Teo galloped through the sodden grass and into a small chapel, where frescoes glowed above a pool of water. She reached down into the still wetness to grasp the handle of a door almost hidden by floating seaweed, lifting it with a grunt.

The water parted like a curtain and a mouth-tingling fume of curry wafted up from the light-filled staircase below. It was underlaid by a faint smell of squid ink from the Seldom Seen Press, the mermaids' printing machine.

"Eating, as usual!" An emptiness stirred in Teo's own belly. All she'd managed since the flood was a bowl of lukewarm soup and a nibble at a rind of cold pumpkin. She took the stairs two at a time, finally tumbling through an archway to a gilded cavern in which nestled a deep pool of black water rimmed by a sturdy walkway. The first thing she saw was a tattered Christmas tree bedecked with silver seaweed and living fireflies in tiny filigree cages.

"I'd almost forgotten it was Christmas," Teo thought, struggling to catch her breath. "Doesn't much feel like it now. Renzo!" she puffed hopefully. "I'm . . . here!"

No answer came back. A prickle of worry nipped her spine. At the sight of Teo, the cavern filled with splashing and rough, sweet voices. A hundred blond and tousled mermaids greeted her affectionately. "Why, Teodora!" "'Tis the Undrowned Child!" "Give the little maid a bite o' somefing hot and nicely greasy!"

The Seldom Seen Press stood silent, for the mermaids were presently gathered around floating banquet tables. Their faces showed distinct traces of enthusiastic dining. A flock of melon-sized icebergs eddied and bumped around their blue tails. Above the mermaids' pretty heads, dozens of parrots in rainbow plumage craned their necks toward Teo.

The birds squawked, "Bite! Bite! Bite!"

Teo thought, "They won't be so hungry when they hear what I've got to tell them."

"Sweet maid's all tuckered out! Timber-shiv'ring cold it is! Will ye not have a little sumpin' to warm yer gizzard on this perishin' day?" a mermaid in a chef's hat offered. "There's a lovely plunk o' chicken-that-flew-stew just hottin' up on the griddle. You ain't tried this one yet."

Teo panted, "I thought you . . . were vegetarians, Catalina?" She was one herself. "Wait! I have to . . . tell you . . . Do you know that . . . the Vamp—"

"Who's disputin' yer? Don't ye git yourself in a blue tweak, Undrowned Child. 'Tis veritable vegetablish. Just chickpeas. Sartin 'twere a chickadoodle in da original recipe. But it flewed away. We added more chili, and you'd never notice da lack o' poultry for da fire in your mouf."

Catalina thrust a steaming spoonful between Teo's cold lips before she could get out a single word about the Vampire Eel, Bajamonte Tiepolo or the Mayor. A spicy flame lit Teo's tongue and throat. While she chewed the delicious mixture, Teo's watering eyes searched out Lussa. A glint of gold alerted her to the Queen swimming forward. Since the day of the battle in the lagoon, the mermaid's beautiful face had been lightly embossed with gilded lettering, for she carried on her body the Spell Almanac of Bajamonte Tiepolo. She was its guardian now.

Lussa exclaimed, "Teodora! 'Tis an exquisite Relief to see You."

Her accent was refined, quite unlike those of her mermaid subjects, who had learned to speak human language by eavesdropping on uncouth sailors and pirates.

Now that she finally could get a word in, Teo was too distressed for pleasantries. "He's back, isn't he? Il Traditore. Bajamonte Tiepolo!"

"Say ye not his cursed name!" cried Flos, Lussa's young second-in-command. "'Twould make a weasel weep to hear it!"

The parrots chanted dolefully, "Weasel weep, weasel weep, weasel . . ." For in last year's struggle, the mermaids had been betrayed, and Vampire Eels, their only natural predator, had ambushed them at the sea-entrance to this very cavern, killing a dozen of their number.

"Yar, Teodora," mourned Lussa, "I fear You are right. And now We must . . ."

Teo buried her head in her hands. "How many Venetians have died today, because I was too much of a coward to utter that one last curse when I had a chance to get rid of Il Traditore forever? And my parents . . . and *where* is Renzo?"

Lussa said, "We could not save your Adoptive Parents, dear Teodora, from Whomsoever Scoundrels & Miscreants abducted Them. We arrived too Late. But We saved as many Humanfolk from the Ice Water as We could. Under Cover of Dark, We carried Them to Land."

"I dreamed you doing that," Teo remembered.

"We brought Them warm Sustenance. We treated their Wounds with Venetian Treacle. Of course, when They wake up, They shall have no Recollection of Us."

Venetian Treacle was a magical medicine made of sixty-four ingredients. Teo and Renzo had discovered a secret cache of it at an old apothecary called The Two Tousled Mermaids by the old gates to the Ghetto.

"But Renzo?" Teo's voice wobbled. "Did you . . . ? Is he . . . ?"

Lussa hung her head. "The Victims were too Many, and We were too Few. We were also too Late for dear Lorenzo's Mother. He is now as You are, Teodora, an Orphan Child."

Teo wailed, "Not his mother!"

"Rendered Unconscious by an Iceberg & Smothered by the heartless Waves."

"You mean murdered by Bajamonte Tiepolo! Poor Renzo, I must go to him."

Tears leaking from the sides of her eyes, Teo ran toward the stairs.

"Teodora! Come back! You shall not find Lorenzo at Home. He's been taken to the *Scilla*."

"The floating orphanage?"

"The Human Mayor has signed Lorenzo yonside for a Sailor."

At the words "Human Mayor," a violent hubbub broke out among the mermaids: "Sufferin' seahorses! He doan know Christmas from curried eel!" and "Busy as a cat buryin'—"

"Ladies!" interrupted Lussa in a scandalized tone. "Belay your Indecencies in front of the Undrowned Child! The Human Mayor is truly Destitute of the Bowels of Compassion, but He is hardly worth a Toothful of Scorn. Our True Enemy . . ."

"I hate him," growled Teo.

"Indeed 'Tis your Trade to hate Him," Lussa reminded her. "Whensoever & Whithersoever Il Traditore raises his Ugly Head, 'Tis Ordained that You shall be There to push It down, as the Undrowned Child of the Prophecy."

"I failed before. You'll have to get yourselves another heroine this time," said Teo miserably. "I resign. Everyone dies or loses people around me."

The parrots in their gilded cages took up her words, repeating "Everyone dies, everyone dies, everyone dies . . ." until the echoes of the grim words faded to silence.

"But," mused Teo, "all the way to the cavern, I've been thinking. I don't feel as if he's actually *here*. Bajamonte Tiepolo, I mean. I don't feel him. When his spirit was abroad in Venice before, there was a kind of crackle in the air, something frightening. I had a sense of him everywhere."

It was true. Last time there had been sharks in the Grand

Canal and fountains of poison gushing from the wells. Wooden statues had come to life. A vast creature had stirred in the lagoon, heating the water to a perilous temperature. The ghost of a cannibal butcher had stalked the streets, hunting children.

Lussa mused, "The Fact is that the Whirlpool probably sucked Il Traditore a great Distance from Venice. Maybe even Continents away. Of course He has other Scores to settle too. The English Melusine & Sea-Bishops helped to defeat Him. The poor South Sea Dolphins may have already felt his Wrath. Yet there may be another Reason why He's not among Us. As We know, Il Traditore is *not* Notable for his Courage. In Fact, He's Distinguished mainly by his Cowardice."

The mermaids snarled, "That wibbling wheyface!" and "Beslubbering blue-funking barnacle!"

"Indeed, Ladies," agreed Lussa dryly, "I suspect He would be too Afraid to return to Venice while She is still inhabited by his Twin Nemeses, the Undrowned Child & the Studious Son of the Prophecy. Moreover, his old Allies—the Ghosts of the Dalmatian Convicts, the Serbs, the Dark Elves, the Dwarves—were All thoroughly Defeated & Humiliated in the Battle. Il Traditore, if He is indeed Revived, shall need to look Elsewhere for Friends now."

Teo caught sight of something cat-sized, furry and brown. "Hideous!" she squealed, backing away.

A dozen spiders, each the size of a large cat, were spinning silk around a sorry collection of battered paintings. Cautiously leaning forward, Teo recognized some of Venice's great art treasures—Tintorettos and Titians. The spiders worked industriously, but their movements were slow. They too were hampered by the cold.

Lussa explained, "We saved what Art We could. Now the Sea

Spiders are weaving the Paintings securely into Cocoons, for There is Worse to come by Way of Weather, I believe."

Teo noted anxiously, "These are all Madonnas and scenes from the Bible. Why are there no pictures of Venice herself?"

"You are ever Observant, Teodora. Mayhap Bajamonte plans to destroy all such Paintings, and so too the very Image & Memory of Venice."

"And the postcards of Venice have turned black—it's all part of his plot, isn't it? The books about Venice will be next, won't they? What can we do? We have no ghosts left! They all redeemed themselves in the battle last year . . . who is going to help us now?"

"We still have our Undrowned Child and our Studious Son," said Lussa, but her voice was not quite serene.

Teo knew, from past experience, that Lussa always had some kind of plan prepared for her. "Should I join Renzo? But," sighed Teo, "the *Scilla*'s just for boys. Girl orphans have to go to the nuns."

The only nuns she knew lived in the House of the Spirits, directly above the mermaids' cavern. They were sweet souls. But sedate convent life did not appeal to a girl who'd become accustomed to astonishing adventures on a regular basis.

"Please, please, don't send me to the convent!" she appealed to Lussa. "It would be like being buried alive."

"The Abbess is waiting. She shall help You with What You must do Next." Lussa smiled mysteriously.

Flos called, "Prithee take ye care, Undrowned Child. Remember dat ye is right precious to us."

Teo dragged her feet up to the garden of the House of the Spirits. Night had fallen. In the dense darkness, barely lit by stars, the garden topiary—mostly saints trimmed out of box hedges—looked as if it was carved from licorice. With her head cast down despondently, Teo did not notice the *magòga* waiting on top of a leafy Virgin Mary. But when it saw *her*, the big seagull began to hop about excitedly, shaking its tail as if performing a rude kind of folk dance.

These monstrous gray gulls had once been the minions of Bajamonte Tiepolo. After his defeat, they'd repented, and been forced to eat bitter insects as their punishment. Since then, they'd claimed to be as loyal as the egrets. But Teo still had her doubts about them. Those pitiless yellow eyes had never softened.

The *magòga* now put its head on one side, leaning forward to examine Teo's tearstained face. Then it exclaimed "Caw!" and sped off with great purpose. Teo winced instinctively at the sound and the grim memories it carried, and she gazed fretfully after its departing shadow darkening the frost-whitened grass.

7. Teodora Teodoro

at the House of the Spirits, Christmas Day evening, 1900

The Abbess welcomed Teo with a kiss on the forehead. Her robes gave off a delicious scent of candle wax and lavender as she ushered Teo into her lamp-lit study, where jeweled Bibles and richly tooled hymnbooks glowed on deep mahogany shelves.

In spite of these agreeable surroundings, Teo's shoulders clenched.

This was going to be difficult.

She and the Abbess were old friends. This nun had held Teo in her arms when she was a tiny baby just rescued by the mermaids and still damp from the sea. The convent had been Teo's home for a few months, before the Mayor dispatched her to Naples. And this delicate old lady was a member of the Incogniti too, like Signor Alicamoussa the circus-master and Professor Marìn.

"I'm not really very good material for a nun," Teo began. "I'm always messy and I'm not awfully obedient, and I—"

"Don't fret, child." The nun's lips twitched. "That the mermaids and I had calculated for ourselves. We've another idea."

She pointed to a sheet of blue paper on her desk. "After the tragedy of your real parents' drowning, your birth-documents were lodged here with us. Here you see your original name, 'Teodora Gasperin.'"

Teo bent over the form, intrigued. The paper was speckled with official stamps and scrawled with various signatures. She frowned at the sight of the most ornate one, executed in flourishes of purple ink.

"Do you see with what haste the town clerk scribbled 'Teodora'?" inquired the Abbess. "He barely finished off his letters. Do you not agree that the final 'a' of 'Teodora' looks rather like an 'o'?"

Teo understood immediately. "'Teodoro,' a boy's name. And no one, not even Bajamonte Tiepolo, would think to find me as a boy."

"And as for your original name, 'Gasperin'—what a muddle the clerk's made of that word. The 'G' looks like an 'O.' The 'sp' seems to be 'ng.' In fact, it looks more like 'Ongania,' doesn't it? Especially *now*."

The nun deftly added half a dozen tiny marks to the blotted word.

"Perfect!" exclaimed Teo. "I'm safe!"

The girl Teodora had needed to hide from the Mayor's policemen. The boy Teodoro Ongania could walk—no, *swagger* (That was what Venetian boys did, wasn't it?)—with *his* head held high.

The nun folded the paper into a fine lambskin pouch, handing it to Teo with a smile. "And now Teodoro Ongania can join the *Scilla*."

"And be with Renzo!"

"Indeed—when *Teodoro* is properly outfitted for life on board, of course."

From a drawer, the nun pulled out a neatly ironed pair of bell-

42

bottomed breeches, a sailor's cap, a pea jacket with piping, thick wool socks and some underwear that did not in any way resemble Teo's own lace-trimmed combinations. Teo gulped. "Those too?"

"Sailor clothes will disguise your shape."

"I don't have much of a shape to hide," Teo muttered.

The nun turned her back while Teo slipped out of her jacket, pinafore and dress and into the sailor suit. She quietly decided to retain her own combinations. The boy's underwear was really far too scratchy.

"Ready? Very convincing! I understand sailors don't go in for frequent bathing, so it's rare for them to have to remove all their clothes. In fact, it happens only if they are terribly wounded, and the doctor needs to amputate."

"If it comes to that I s'pose it won't matter too much if they discover I'm a girl. So it's just my hair now."

A pair of silver scissors lay on the Abbess's desk. Eager to complete her transformation, Teo snatched them up to shear off a handful of her own curls. The nun remonstrated: "Enough! Some sailors still wear their hair long, tied in a queue. So." She fastened a narrow black ribbon around Teo's hair, making a neat tail. "Just one more thing."

The nun handed Teo a glass tube. "For . . . bodily functions. It may be necessary to use this, if the 'heads,' as I believe it's called, lacks a door."

Blushing furiously, Teo thrust the tube into the nearest pocket, alongside her sailor cap.

"To the *Scilla*, then, my child."

"There's still one thing," Teo blurted. "How will we account for the disappearance of Teodora Stampara?"

"I believe the Mayor shall be quite gratified to add that

43

particular name to the lists of the drowned." The nun winked. Then she looked sober. "Teodora, there's something you should know. We've just heard that there has been one other casualty of the ice flood."

She explained that when the waters subsided, it was discovered that the Column of Infamy, erected to the eternal dishonor of Bajamonte Tiepolo, had disappeared without a trace.

"He's erasing history again," Teo whispered, "just like before."

The Abbess escorted Teo to the street door, clasping her hand tenderly all the way. Neither noticed the gull, who had returned and sat watching them with evident satisfaction.

"Be kind to young Lorenzo," the nun urged. "The loss of his mother . . . Teodora, you know how that feels, for you have lost not just one but two mothers."

"My adoptive parents may still be alive. They must have been kidnapped for what they know. So they're too valuable to kill, aren't they?"

This was the thought that had kept Teo's hopes afloat over the last hours. The Abbess said gently, "They cannot help you, child, wherever they are. You're to have new companions now. I have often thought a ship full of sailors must be rather like a convent full of nuns. It is a true miniature of the world itself: a select, enclosed gathering. You may not leave. There is nowhere else to go."

Suddenly, Teo was less certain that the *Scilla* was where she wanted to be.

"But Renzo will be there," she reminded herself.

"On a ship," continued the nun, "as in a Venetian convent, you are safe from all enemies, except one—the sea—which can snuff out your life on a whim. And yet the ship, like the convent, is a thing that most inhabitants learn to love. Perhaps we humans always long for a mother, be it a church or a ship, to hold us safely to her bosom, and comfort us."

"Don't worry! I shall look after Renzo," Teo promised. She turned to kiss the silky cheek. Then she stepped out into the pitch-black street.

As the door shut quietly behind her, a large hessian sack was thrust over Teo's head, and a hand closed over her shrouded face, choking the breath out of her. Through the coarse weave of the cloth, she smelled the sour stink of rum, and felt the grip of sharp, malicious nails.

8. Aboard the *Scilla*

on the Zattere, Christmas Day evening, 1900

Signor Alicamoussa kissed Renzo warmly upon both cheeks. "I would not for thirteen worlds agree to leaving youse here, my precious boy, except that I know youse'll be in the handiest of hands. Belonging as they do to an old friend, in factiest fact."

At this, a familiar voice saluted them from the deck above. Over the rail appeared the kind, creased face of Professor Marìn. "Young Lorenzo! You and I join the *Scilla* at the same moment, son! I, as her new captain and director of studies, and you as our next top boy, I've no doubt."

Sargano Alicamoussa agreed, "You're not wrong, Professor. Young Lorenzo's tremendously nifty with the noodlework, yes. This boy takes the cake—no!—he confiscates the *macaroon* for brains!"

For the first time since his mother died, Renzo's face opened into a smile. "Professor Marìn!" he exclaimed. "Captain of the *Scilla*! But I thought you were writing another book?"

"I've just finished my *Meticulous Maritime Manual for Young Salts*. It's time to put it into practice. Where better than on a training ship for young Venetian sailors? And sadly a new captain was

46

urgently needed. The *Scilla*'s captain was ashore last night. He was one of the ice storm's victims."

Professor Marìn's voice softened. "Lorenzo, I'm so sorry for your loss."

The policeman saluted Professor Marìn with a click of his heels. He would not have been so matter-of-fact about it if he had realized that the celebrated author was also a leader of the Incogniti, the secret society of protectors of Venice, and friend of mermaids, good ghosts and talking beasts.

The circus-master asked the professor, "Youse'll have heard about young Teodora's parents? And what of the dear girl, her dear self?"

"It's a bad business, Sargano. The parents are both gone, all their notes and equipment too. Teodora was taken to the Mayor's office, but she escaped. The Mayor's men are hunting for her."

"Suffering stink-beetles!" exclaimed the circus-master. "What a confloption!"

The policeman looked up in not-altogether-disappointed surprise. "Lost that girlie, did they? Let's hope she didn't slip on the ice and drown."

Signor Alicamoussa growled, "Drowned? Any more of that drongo tanglemongering, and I'll land youse a right fericadouzer on the chops, sir! Our Teodora's a peppery little party, not to be sherry-trifled with. Feather me! She's plainly playing possum where your tallow-gutted Mayor cannot find her."

Renzo knew exactly where Teo would have run. Suddenly, he wished he was there himself. He turned to the circus-master. "Signor Alicamoussa, will you look for Teo? Could you ask . . . our *particular friends?*"

Renzo did not judge it safe to mention the mermaids in front of the policeman. The only adults who could see mermaids were all members of the Incogniti, like Signor Alicamoussa, Professor Marìn and the Abbess at the House of the Spirits. Anyway, the policeman worked for the *Mayor*.

"Certainly, certainly," the circus-master cried, "'twill be the doings of the utmost urgency! Darling Teodorina! Dear little bandicoot she is! In fact, I'm off upon that errand now, quicker than a bare-eyed cockatoo to a water hole, yes. Smackeroo kisso, one and all!"

Another pair of kisses and first Signor Alicamoussa's fragrant mustache and then the man himself whisked away.

"My mother . . . ?" Renzo's voice quavered against his will.

"I'll go to the funeral myself," promised the policeman. "I'll see it's done proper, lad." He eased the bunch of carved violets from Renzo's hand.

"Now come aboard, Lorenzo," urged the professor. "Oh, and there's a most important personage for you to meet. That's it, up the ladder, son. Here is Sofonisba come specially to welcome you."

A large gray tabby cat strolled across the deck just as Renzo's head reached that level.

His eyes flew to the furry sides to check for wings. Some of Venice's most beautiful and luxuriant cats were of the Syrian species, which not only grew to outrageous size but also kept discreet furry wings tucked up against their flanks. Syrian cats had in the past delivered Renzo from certain death at the beaks of a thousand seagulls. They had helped to save the lives of dozens of gondolier children during the final battle in the lagoon against Bajamonte Tiepolo.

"Or *was* it the final battle?" Renzo could not keep this dismal question out of his head any longer.

If the cat Sofonisba had wings, they were very well concealed. She stopped dead and looked Renzo straight in the eyes: "Oh, another dirty little boy. Worse luck!"

Renzo had come across several talking cats during the campaign to save Venice from Bajamonte Tiepolo. None were overly respectful. However, none had been quite as rude as this.

"I was promised something better," lamented Sofonisba.

"I'm awfully sorry." Renzo smiled.

"You will be," said the cat.

9. Thaw

dawn, Boxing Day, December 31, 1900

When Teo awoke, it was to the sounds of water dripping and waves surging.

Hours must have passed since the sack was thrust over her head, for the first glimmerings of dawn were visible and her hair was stiff with frozen water. An intense and painful sensation of cold slid down her spine. She was still wearing the sack in which she'd been kidnapped. Its bottom end had torn so that her head stuck out. She tried to sit up, but found that her neck, arms and legs had been tied with sturdy cords. She was lashed to an iceberg the size of a small carriage.

There was not a soul in sight: not a fisherman, not even a bird. As the iceberg wallowed in the dark hollows of the heaving water, Teo felt like the last living creature on earth.

Above her was a strange apparatus consisting of a magnifying glass and a compass balanced on a tripod. Wires jerked the magnifying glass to follow the compass toward the strongest rays of the rising sun.

"That's what's causing the dripping," Teo thought. "The magnifying glass focuses the sun's heat on the ice, so it will melt."

A slight tapping from below drew her attention. She swiveled her neck around to see what it could be.

"*Uffa!*" Teo shrieked. She was not alone after all. Frozen into her iceberg were two Vampire Eels, staring up at her hungrily. The tapping noise came from their powerful tails, impatiently beating against their increasingly fragile case of ice.

"That settles it," moaned Teo. Whoever had done this to her was in some way connected to Bajamonte Tiepolo, for no one else had ever harnessed the savage appetites of the Vampire Eels to their purpose.

Teo wished she did not know quite so much about the lifestyle and feeding habits of the Vampire Eel. "So when the ice melts, the Eels will be free to eat me. First they'll suck my blood. They prefer to do that while their victim is still alive. The blood is tastier that way. Oh!"

Teo was distracted from her dismal prospects by a sound like a cow lowing and a sudden stench of burning.

The source of the scorched smell was easily identified: the magnifying glass was now trained on a piece of the sack that swaddled her. Down by her feet, the heat had dried out the fabric, and it was starting to smolder.

"So." Teo grimaced. "I may be the first person ever to burn to death on an iceberg."

She jerked her sack-clad foot out of the beam of the magnifying glass. As she did so, the glass moved infinitesimally toward her again.

"I am not going to be able to do that for much longer," she realized. "If only I had *The Key to the Secret City*, I could use a sharp corner of it to break the ice under my hands. Then I could untie these ropes. On second thoughts, no. It's better that the book's safe with Renzo."

51

The mooing sound came again, quite close to her ear.

"A *cow?*" she asked. "In the middle of the lagoon?"

The noise came a third time, a definite cowlike sound. But now it was accompanied by a chorus of chirruping and quacking.

With an effort, Teo twisted her neck. To her left, a number of water birds had gathered in a semicircle, each with its head on one side and a concerned expression on its little pointed face.

"Good morning," she offered politely. "How do you do?"

A merry clacking and quacking answered her.

Then Teo remembered the two Vampire Eels. "Go away!" she bellowed at the birds. "Look below me! Those Eels will eat you too! They'll be absolutely famished after all this time trapped in the ice."

The birds merely stared at Teo, and then at the Eels, and went back to chirruping, quacking and nodding among themselves. Some flew up to the iceberg, hopping along the cords that bound her, inspecting them with their blackcurrant eyes.

Teo ached, but was too polite, to say, "Shoo! The warmth of your bodies will melt the ice even quicker."

A sandpiper lifted his beak in a sympathetic chirp.

"Oh," groaned Teo, "I know you'd help me if you could. But someone stronger than you wants me dead."

The magnifying glass had spun so that Teo's foot was again feeling the heat. Her bonds were tight. This time she could move her foot only one inch away.

"An inch. That gives me how long?" she wondered. "Perhaps another fifteen minutes?"

Tiny sharp batterings vibrated through the iceberg. The birds were pecking at the cords on Teo's sacking. Others flapped their wings against the magnifying glass so that it toppled and dangled at an angle from the tripod. The morning sun no longer beat through it. The sack had stopped smoldering.

The red-rimmed eyes of the Vampire Eels gazed through the ice at Teo and her feathered helpers with expressions of greed and longing.

Even as the birds frayed the ropes, Teo's mind was leaping beyond hope and into the next abyss. From the jerky movements of the iceberg, she detected powerful currents below. The black water must be glacial. Even if she escaped the Eels, she'd not survive twenty minutes in its bitter embrace.

Between pecks, the birds appeared to be arguing among themselves. Finally, the whole flock of *alzavole* rose into the air and swept off across the lagoon. The rest of the birds resumed pecking at the cords, pausing to grumble occasionally.

A few minutes later, a sad honking ruffled the air. Led by the ducks, a dozen monk seals were swimming toward the iceberg.

To Teo, lying flat on her back, the seals looked fearsome, easily twice her length and ten times her girth. "And they eat living creatures," she worried. "Fish. In their normal habitat. All the way up here, perhaps they can't find any fish to suit them. Perhaps they are so starving, so desperate . . ."

The herd of seals surrounded the iceberg. Their faces were kind. She could have sworn that one of them nodded at her. They peered into the iceberg with their intelligent eyes.

At the sight of the Vampire Eels squirming inside, they snuffled with alarm.

But one female seal, with a pup in tow, placed her flippers on the ice. Her whiskers tickled Teo's face. Teo was relieved to smell fresh fish on her breath.

The mother seal honked to her pup, who pulled itself up on to her back. The mother gave Teo a significant look. The pup slid off, and the mother seal arched her back invitingly. At the same moment, one of the tufted ducks nipped through the final filament of the bonds on Teo's right hand. She reached out to stroke the seal's damp fur. She could feel its heart pounding beneath the warm softness.

"Thank you," she breathed.

By now Teo's left hand and both her feet were also free. She sat up. The Eels, sensing that their meal was escaping, thrashed inside the ice. A cymbal-clash of shattering made all the seals and birds back away. A fissure forked through the center of the iceberg. One of the Eels was wriggling up inside.

Teo looked desperately at the mother seal. A tender baby monk seal would no doubt be a delicacy for Vampire Eels. If the mother seal helped Teo, her pup would be left vulnerable.

A black tongue flickered through the fissure. The whole iceberg shook.

The mother seal still hesitated, staring at the black tongue with an appalled expression. Then the tongue suddenly disappeared and a terrible rumpus broke out inside the iceberg. The second Eel was furious that the first one had broken through ahead of it. It had clamped its jaws around its companion's tail, nearly separating it from the rest of the body. The first Eel retracted its head in order to deliver a savage bite to the lungs of its assailant.

The fissure was widening.

Teo made a gesture of cradling to the mother seal. The creature seemed to understand. She slid alongside the iceberg and nudged her pup toward Teo, who took it in her arms. Then Teo herself slid onto the mother seal's back, using one arm to cling to her neck and the other to wrap around the pup.

The iceberg exploded into glassy arrows, white lumps and slush.

But Teo was already hurtling away from the Eels, who were fortunately intent on fighting each other to the death. The seal herd sped through the archipelago of tiny islands that made up the outer reaches of the Venetian lagoon. Teo bounced up and down on the mother seal's back, occasionally submerging completely as the creature plunged below the waves. Her mouth and nose were burning with cold salt water. The rest of the seals kept pace, packed in tightly around the mother, and helpfully nudging Teo back up whenever she began to slide off her perch.

The baby seal wriggled, uttering its milky soft cries.

"I'm sorry," murmured Teo, kissing the top of its head. "Thank you for sharing your mother with me."

Finally, the herd of seals slowed. Teo, wiping her waterlogged eyes on the mother seal's fur, saw the bell towers of Venice in the misty distance. By gripping, and pointing with her head, she guided the seals to the Zattere, where the masts of the *Scilla* stood ghost-like, her sails folded up like long loaves of unbaked bread.

"I'll never forget this," Teo told the seals, sliding off the mother's back on to the seaweed-fronded stairs of the *fondamenta*. "If I can do anything for you in the future, you can be sure I shall."

Teo sloughed off the ragged remains of the sack. Running toward the *Scilla*, she stopped dead. Fixed to a lamppost was a fresh list of victims of the ice storm. For the first time, she forced herself to look. Her eyes slid down to the "S"s, dreading to see the names of her parents. Instead of Leonora and Alberto Stampara, she read her own name: *Teodora Stampara—missing, presumed drowned.*

"That dandypratt the Mayor didn't waste any time," she growled. "Couldn't wait to pronounce me dead as a nit again!"

Then she remembered—her papers! The ones that proved she was a boy! They must be ruined! Teo reached into her soaking pockets and pulled out the document that the Abbess had given her. The spidery writing had remained dry and safe inside the lambskin packet.

She pulled her sailor hat out of the pocket where she'd wedged it and set it, wet and cold as it was, at a jaunty angle on the side of her head.

Even half drowned and freezing, Teo had every intention of making the best possible impression upon her new shipmates.

10. A sad reunion

aboard the Scilla, *Boxing Day, 1900*

"**H**alt! Who goes there?" demanded a boy's voice as Teo laid her hands on the ladder. Even though she could not see the boy, Teo saw his writing in the air above—swift and cheeky.

"The way a monkey would write. If a monkey could," she thought.

"Teodoro Ongania," she answered, trying to keep her voice deep and confident, "reporting for duty on the *Scilla.*"

"You're not on my list," shouted the boy. "Get lost. No cake for you."

"But I'm an orphan. Come to be a sailor."

"Stop bothering me. You're giving me a headache with that whining. If you don't go, I've got some veg peelings for you and a slop-pail for afters."

Teo was taken aback. But after all she'd just been through, she simply wasn't having it. "Who are *you* to say that I am not an orphan and can't come aboard?" she demanded. "I'm coming up now."

"I'm the first watch, aren't I? Go teach your granny to griddle goats! Now, I warned you."

A pile of rotting carrot peelings landed on Teo's head.

"Pooh!" she shouted, pushing them out of her eyes.

"You can have some of *that* next, if you don't toddle off sharpish."

Help came from an unexpected source.

"Ow! Ow! Ouch!" cried the first watch. "That hurts. Stop it, do!"

He was answered with angry yowling. His footsteps pattered hastily away.

Teo brightened. Of course there would be a ship's cat. She adored cats.

A gray striped cat duly poked its head over the railing. "I've dealt with that little excrescence, otherwise known as Sebastiano dalla Mutta," the cat announced graciously. "That's the worst of boys. You give them a bit of a job and they think they're God creating the universe. Sofonisba, the ship's cat. Pleased to meet you. Do come aboard, Miss."

"But I-I-I'm a boy," stuttered Teo. "Teodoro . . . Ongania."

"If you say so," replied the cat, smirking.

"No, really," Teo urged, "it's got to be a secret. If they find out I'm a girl, I'm in big trouble."

"Indeed. Well, I won't betray you. I'm happy to have a civilized female on the boat. Not one of these young tykes has any talent for ailuromancy. How's yours, by the way?"

"My ailuromancy?" Teo loved large words, the larger the better. But she'd not come across this one before.

"Predicting the weather by observing the behavior of the ship's cat, particularly the motions of the tail, that being the most communicative part."

Teo smiled diplomatically. "I can't wait to learn it."

"Takes a lifetime," said Sofonisba ironically. "Excuse me, there's a rat by the water barrel. Must attend to it. I'll send the captain along to you. Ah, here he is, a good fellow. Knows his ailuromancy, anyway."

A familiar voice greeted Teo joyfully. "Young Teodora! We've been worried to death about you. I had a message from the nuns. We expected you last night! Signor Alicamoussa has scoured the town, fruitlessly. Dear child, you're soaking wet! Come to the mess: it's warm there. We'll get you some dry clothes and something hot to drink."

"Professor Marìn!" Teo almost choked on her delight. Her old friend was the perfect person to run a school for sailors, and the kindliest.

Hugging the professor, she asked anxiously, "How is Renzo?"

"He's safe, at least. But what of you, Teodora? Where have you been all night?"

Dry and freshly dressed in a new sailor suit, Teo explained her adventure in the lagoon. Professor Marìn knitted his white brows. "This is bad news, child. Bajamonte Tiepolo may not be here—and I personally agree with your theory about that—but there are minions of his abroad in Venice. And they know who you are, unfortunately."

The cat had followed them into the mess, and sat cleaning rat blood off her whiskers in a pensive sort of way. She remarked, "The *magòghe* have turned—that's the word in the alleys. The cormorants too, this time. It's being put about that the seagulls spied on the gondoliers' sons when they buried Bajamonte's bones in those separate secret places. All six graves have recently been disturbed.

Now, someone had better tell the nuns and the handsome circus-master that their Undrowned Child is safe. I suppose that someone had better be me."

Nimbly, Sofonisba scaled the companionway. Through a porthole, Teo watched the cat jump down to the *fondamenta* and disappear in a westerly direction.

Teo tugged the professor's sleeve. "The Mayor has already written me off as 'presumed drowned.' My death was designed so that there'd be no trace of me. The Vampire Eels were to see to that. So whoever tried to murder me will not suspect I'm still alive. Or that I have come aboard the *Scilla*."

"But, my dear, you must have been wearing that sailor suit when they kidnapped you."

"It was pitch dark. Whoever it was, they were waiting outside the House of the Spirits. The *magòghe* must have told them where I was. But I was attacked from behind. They couldn't have had a good look at me. The first thing they did was bundle me into a big sack. I was still wearing it when I woke up on the iceberg."

Professor Marìn reflected, "That's true, Teodoro, young *man*. If they think the Undrowned Child is dead, they won't be looking for her anymore. You shall be under my protection from now on, child. Come, meet the rest of the sailors. They are at elevenses on deck. And young Lorenzo *needs* to see you."

Professor Marìn led the way, calling, "How chear ye, fore and aft?"

He winked at Teo. "That means 'How fares all the ship's company?' I'm getting them in the mood for sailoring."

All the young sailors were sitting cross-legged on the deck, swigging warm chocolate milk from Murano glass bottles and eating big pieces of cinnamon chocolate cake. Teo's eyes scanned the party for Renzo, hoping that he would not give her away as a girl.

She was at first afraid that she might see some of their friends, for their presence here could only mean one thing: that their parents had been drowned. Rows of sailor-suited boys looked at her curiously. They were all strangers. When Sebastiano dalla Mutta, the erstwhile first watch, was introduced, he stuck out his tongue. But his brown eyes were smiling. Teo returned the courtesy in kind, crossing her own green eyes for further effect.

Renzo was sitting by himself, away from the other boys. He looked trim and handsome in his sailor suit, but he might have been a shop dummy for all the life in his face. He gazed out across the Giudecca Canal. He had not touched his milk or cake. He was turning a little penknife over and over in his hands. Years before, Renzo had carved its handle into the shape of a gondola's tailpiece. He had once used this same *ferro* penknife to save Teo from the ghost of the child-eating Butcher Biasio.

Teo dropped to her knees in front of him and took his hand. "Renzo! I am so sorry about your mother. So very, very sorry."

He stared at her sailor suit and cap. "What . . . ?"

Teo quickly hugged him hard, taking the opportunity to whisper in his ear, "Shhh. No one's to know I'm a girl."

He mumbled into her hair, "Where have you been?"

Teo whispered at a furious speed, "I was kidnapped, and tied to an iceberg with Vampire Eels inside. I escaped with some seals. . . . Now we need to look at *The Key to the Secret City* and find out what to do. It's obvious that Bajamonte Tiepolo is back."

Renzo pushed her away, blurting, "*The Key* got taken by the ice flood."

The news struck Teo like a fist in her stomach. Without the book, Venice would have fallen to Il Traditore the year before last. More than that, *The Key* was like a living thing, like a friend. But, looking at Renzo's stricken face, she found it in herself to lie. "It doesn't matter. It's only a book."

Renzo shook her off. "Don't patronize me, Teo. *The Key to the Secret City* is *not* 'only a book.' You know better than that. I couldn't save it. I couldn't save my mother. I am utterly useless."

Then, looking thoroughly ashamed of himself, Renzo suddenly clamped his mouth shut and stared fiercely at the deck, thrusting his penknife into a plank. It stood quivering between them.

11. School for sailors

aboard the Scilla, *Boxing Day*

Sailing school was more demanding than land school. For a start, living on a ship meant learning a whole new language.

The professor would point to various parts of the sail or rigging, and then pick a boy, who was expected to shout, without hesitation:

"That's the gooseneck, sir, at the end of the boom!"

"That's the jigger tackle for hauling the bunt of the topsail, sir!"

"That's the shoulder-of-mutton sail, sir!"

"What is the measure of the cat-harpins?" the professor would ask.

"One-eighth the hoist of the topsail, sir!"

They learned to read charts, taste the winds for danger, and to diagnose the tug of a current. They applied fresh coats of best Stockholm tar to the rigging. The *Scilla* creaked out into the lagoon each day to give the boys practical experience of life under sail. Every evening, the old boat returned to the safety of the Zattere, and moored for the night.

Then, after a hearty supper, there was the language of flags to be mastered, and a hundred different knots, from the tiny monkey's fist to the formidable sheepshank.

Meanwhile there were also things to *forget*, sailoring being a highly superstitious profession. The boys had to banish from their vocabularies all the words that must never be uttered aboard ship. Teo and Renzo had a head start there: the mermaids had already taught them that at sea one must never mention any part of a rabbit. Also banned was any uttering of the names of goats, hares and pigs. As the professor explained, "A boat is easily bewitched. And witches are particularly inclined to turn themselves into such beasts in order to wreak their mischiefs."

All the orphans were obliged to throw any item of green clothing overboard: that too was supposed to bring bad luck. And whistling was absolutely forbidden, lest it conjure a gale.

"You must treat your ship like a goddess," warned Professor Marìn.

"Or a cat," added Sofonisba. The boys had quickly ceased to marvel that she could talk: they were more interested in learning how to read her tail.

An unusual feature of shipboard life was teaching the *Scilla*'s parrots to speak, using mirrors. Each boy would hide his face behind a mirror and patiently talk to his parrot. The bird, staring at a parrot face reflected in the glass, would believe another of his own species was engaging him in conversation, and would answer in kind. Although easily tricked in this way, they were otherwise highly intelligent birds and seemed to rejoice in increasing their vocabularies. Professor Marìn's trained parrots were in great demand for transmitting messages: the telegraph office and the telephone exchange in Venice were both still submerged in mud.

The young sailors had ordinary lessons too, but in roundabout ways. Mathematics was taught by stacking and measuring supplies. They studied geography by poring over charts. They learned how to mend ripped sails, darn nets and, finally, to sew shrouds. That last lesson was accomplished in a subdued mood, with several boys—those freshly orphaned by the ice storm—quietly weeping while Professor Marìn explained how the last stitch was to pass through the nose of the corpse. This was done in order to avoid any chance of throwing a body overboard while life still remained in it.

"Remember, boys," urged Professor Marìn, "the pain of having a stitch passed through the nose can be depended upon to rouse a barely living sailor."

Rosato demanded, "Why can't you take a dead person home to his family?"

"A ship with a corpse aboard will always sail more slowly," responded Professor Marìn gravely. "A dead body is thought to bring bad luck. Crews have been known to mutiny if one is kept aboard."

Fresh air and physical activity made the young sailors strong and rosy-cheeked. Luncheon and dinnertime found them hungry as piranhas. Even over the well-laden mess table, lessons continued. They learned the names of the traditional naval dishes prepared by Cookie, the *Scilla*'s jolly chef, an old merchant sailor too plump for active duties these days. Most often requested were schooner-on-the-rocks, a joint of meat with roast potatoes around it, and bloodworms-in-the-snow, which consisted of thin and extremely tasty sausages with creamy mashed potatoes. Cookie's galley calendar was splattered with gravy.

The more frightening lessons took place late at night, by

candlelight. Then Professor Marìn gathered all one hundred boys (and one girl) together to hear him read from his own stories of pirates' devilry and murder. These savage tales were somewhat softened by being delivered in the professor's kindly voice, and accompanied by deep mugs of hot chocolate and thick slices of Cookie's excellent spicy ginger cake.

Sometimes Professor Marìn read to them in English, explaining, "Queen Victoria's Royal Navy rules the seas—it behooves us to understand her language, though we must never lose our own Venetian tongue. Our words are ourselves, and they must survive flood, ice and loss."

The young Venetians nodded gravely.

And it wasn't too strenuous or boring to learn English from such exciting volumes as Captain Mayne Reid's *Ran Away to Sea*, and Captain Marryat's *Mr. Midshipman Easy,* or the general favorite, Marryat's masterpiece, *Rattlin the Reefer.*

Other nights, Professor Marìn read from his own books about the monsters of the deep, including the giant squid and its even bigger cousin, the colossal squid. He also taught the boys about every kind of shark. At these lessons, Renzo and Teo drew instinctively closer together, for they knew what it was to come face-to-snout with one of those ruthless monsters.

Teo didn't truly relish it when Renzo's high scores in astronomical calculations nudged her own out of first place. Renzo found it ever so slightly irksome to be trounced in an exam on Venetian sea-life by a girl who hadn't even been brought up in Venice.

With an amused eye on the young rivals, Professor Marìn taught a special lesson on the more subtle aspects of shipboard comportment. "It is by no means enough that a sailor should be a capable mariner; he must be that, of course, and also a good deal more. He should be, as well, a gentleman of unfailing courtesy and with the nicest sense of personal integrity. A Venetian sailor should care more for honor itself than for carrying off the prize in petty competition."

Then Professor Marìn introduced singing lessons. Apparently, any sailor worth his salt had to know a great many sweetheart songs and sea shanties. In this, Renzo, with his beautiful voice, shone. He was never embarrassed at how romantic the words were. When they listened to him, all the young sailors fell silent. Teo was defeated. Her own voice might be compared, unfavorably, with an untuned piano.

Renzo was also best at the wheel, and indeed took his place there unquestioned for every excursion into the lagoon. He had a natural coordination of hand and eye, always kept his weather eye to the windward side of the ship and seemed to know instinctively when to meet and when to slide against a wave. Everyone jumped to when Renzo called, "Give that keel a bite of water."

And Professor Marìn would lay a proud hand on Renzo's shoulder, saying, "Well done, son."

And so the first five days aboard passed in a blur of cold, salty busyness. Professor Marìn had a way of making the young sailors regard sailorliness, shipshapeliness and spick-and-spanness as points of pride and not a chore. At night, they slept like dormice: even Teo. Her night-nagging dream seemed to have washed away.

As, perhaps, had the bodies of the missing children and men

of Venice. The *Gazzettino*—now in print again and delivered daily to the *Scilla*—mused gloomily, **All the adult female victims of the ice flood have been recovered. But the children's corpses, being lighter perhaps, must have floated away on the tide. However, we cannot explain the loss of at least three dozen men.**

The *Gazzettino* wrote of funerals held for the lost children, with flowers and their favorite toys buried in their empty graves. With so many missing, the disappearance of Teodora Stampara rated only the barest mention. Teo noted indignantly, "All it says is that my funeral was conducted at municipal expense!"

The Mayor had also succeeded in hushing up news of the kidnapping of the two scientists from the island of the Lazzaretto Vecchio.

Fortunately, the *Scilla*'s sailors were too absorbed in their tasks and homework to notice when Teo stole away to a quiet part of the boat to wash and change in privacy. The heads had a door, so Teo was spared the dread embarrassment of the glass tube. She tried to keep her voice low. And she never, never cried, no matter how much it hurt when, with her native clumsiness, she got tangled in a bowline bridle or skidded on a slippery deck.

The worst thing about keeping her cover was that she had to sleep in a hammock in the forecastle cabin putrid with snoring boys who were under no compulsion to wash their socks, and whose favorite after-hours conversations were about the stupidity, vanity and general uselessness of girls. Renzo, she noticed, never said anything to defend the species—or to help her out.

"Sorry, can't be gallant. You're supposed to be a boy," Renzo whispered, when she sprawled flat on her face in front of him after yet another mishap with a mop and a bucket of water.

"Don't need your help," declared Teo. "Thank you very much all the same."

"For now," remarked Sofonisba, who happened to be passing.

On the fifth night in her hammock, Teo lay awake, trying to work out the tune for "Bobby Shaftoe" and a way to anchor her voice to the melody.

That was how she came to hear what she would only later understand was the noise of a bullet meeting human flesh, just above her on the deck. And then a faint, low scream. She lifted her head and sniffed the air—what was that acrid smell like burning metal?

"Cookie must be preparing something new for tomorrow," she told herself. "Not one of his better efforts, I'd say. Hope there's ginger cake for afters."

With that comfortable thought, sleep at last overtook her. And once more it happened, after the welcome peace of the past five nights: her dreams were invaded by that dreadful night-nagging voice breathing hotly in her sleeping ear.

"Death and worse to all Venetians. Death to Venice. Blacken her very image. Death to her memory."

12. Miss Canidia Uish

morning assembly, aboard the Scilla, *New Year's Eve, 1900*

"**I** never met a child I didn't want to slap."

Teo saw sharp staccato letters slashed in the air above the beautiful lady. It seemed impossible that such unpleasantness could issue from those rosebud lips. The woman's skin was downy as a white peach. Her big brown eyes danced with pretty mischief under glistening curls piled high above her head.

The beautiful lady now smiled like an angel. Then she reached out and slapped the nearest child, Alfredo.

"Stop making those big, round, wet eyes at me. You look like a kitten on its way to the bucket." An impish giggle intruded; then her voice flattened back to harshness: "No one cares. Do you understand?"

Alfredo bowed his head and bit his wobbling lip.

The smile sparkled like sunlight, but the cut-glass English accent was as cold as the frost on the *Scilla*'s rigging. The woman was dressed at the height of fashion in a sharp tailored jacket with naval trimmings. From her shell-like ears dangled earrings in the shape of tiny iridescent hummingbirds. Leg-of-mutton sleeves sprouted from her shoulders. Beneath the dress, her willowy body was encased in a corset that bent her back into an S-shape. Below the cruelly cinched waist, her skirt stuck out, rigid as a mountain.

Professor Marìn was nowhere to be seen. Sofonisba crouched by the water barrel, swearing terribly at the interloper.

"Miss Canidia Uish," the woman introduced herself. "It is pronounced like 'wish' in English."

"As in 'wish we'd never met you,'" muttered Teo inaudibly.

"Henceforth," continued the woman, "you will address me as 'ma'am.' Or suffer for it."

The faces of the assembled boys expressed one single thought: "Who *is* this unpleasant female landlubber, and *what* is she doing on the *Scilla?*"

"Brats," recommended Miss Canidia Uish, "it has come to Queen Victoria's attention that there are some poor wretched Venetian orphans who need taking in hand after the ice flood that devastated your city. So Her Majesty has decided to extend her patronage to those unfortunate orphans who exist outside the benevolent protection of her great Empire."

She beamed. Then her expression changed dramatically, a vicious glance clattering down like a guillotine upon the young sailors' feelings. "Stand up straight when I address you, you insignificant pieces of offal!" she shouted. "Where's your gratitude? Don't you know that you are *privileged* to be under my protection?"

They shook their heads humbly.

"I have been sent here on the express instruction of the prime minister of Her Majesty's government, Robert Arthur Talbot Gascoyne-Cecil, ninth Earl and third Marquess of Salisbury, who is my personal friend and a great favorite of the Queen herself.

Which means, brats, that I represent Queen Victoria's interests"—
she looked around her disparagingly—"in this dismal corner of the
globe. Do I not, Malfeasance?"

An ill-favored man of middle years stepped out of the shadows.
Dark stripes of discontent furrowed his cheeks.

"Malfeasance Peaglum, my second-in-command, and now
yours too," announced Miss Uish. "Disobey him at your peril."

"Where's Professor Marìn?" asked Teo boldly. She refused to
add "ma'am."

"History does not relate." Miss Uish gave another of her
strangely poisonous yet radiant smiles. She bent her head to stare
at Teo. "Write that boy's name on my list, Malfeasance. What a
poor specimen it is too. In England we have a name for weaklings
like him—we would call him the Nestle Tripe, or runt of the litter."

Peaglum produced a black notebook from a crevice in his
greasy waistcoat. He sidled up to Teo, nudging her with his elbow.
"Well?"

"Teodoro Ongania," she said proudly, trying to keep her voice
low. He scribbled it down with a grin. "You don't want to get put
on this list again," he snarled, "Teodoro Ongania, Nestle Tripe."

"Venice," Miss Uish continued, "is a backwater now. A Nestle Tripe among cities, as it were. Her glory lives only in the dim
past. What pantaloons the Venetians are, preening and thinking
that everyone admires them still! Believing that anyone cares
about their flood? About their so-called history? Their gaudy art?
Hardly!"

Peaglum sniggered, a disgusting sound like someone treading
fatally on a toad. Miss Uish pronounced, "Everything around here
has to be tightened up, shipshape, British-style. Starting with the

younger Venetians, who might have a hope of reform. The older ones," she sneered, "are too idle and decadent to bother with. If they're not drowned already. Queen Victoria is gracious with her charity, of course, but personally Her Majesty feels that if Venice had not deserved her present calamity, it would not have happened to her. Queen Victoria does not believe in magic, but she certainly believes in just deserts."

She giggled and whispered something to Peaglum that sounded strangely like "That old bezzom!"

The young sailors were dumb with shock. Queen Victoria was known to be a bit of a dragon, but could she really be as cruel and unfeeling as that?

Miss Uish rapped, "Now, stop pouting. Abandoned orphans cannot always have all things to please them. You think sympathy and sugared Earl Gray tea should be brought to you in china cups for free? Just because you're *orphans*? Do you think life owes you a favor because you were so stupid as to have parents who floated out of your houses and drowned?"

The hummingbird earrings quivered on Miss Uish's earlobes. Teo realized: "They're real! Or were. Poor little stuffed birds! How cruel."

Having silenced the *Scilla*'s crew, Miss Uish consulted a fob-watch attached to her left shoulder by a fleur-de-lis picked out in black brocade.

"I must attend a reception at the Town Hall. On my return, I shall expect to find that mast revarnished in its entirety. Am I understood? First, a word about feeding arrangements."

"Feeding?" thought Teo. *"Like animals?"*

"Cake is henceforward banned," announced Miss Uish. "I'm

imposing a dietary regimen much more suitable for unwanted orphans. Have the cook brought forward!"

Peaglum frogmarched Cookie in front of Miss Uish. The poor man shook uncontrollably. His waxen face was distorted, as if he'd been punched. He could not bring himself to look at Miss Uish, or to speak.

"Here's your new recipe book for feeding these whelps." She threw a slim volume at his head. He ducked and knelt humbly to pick it up from the deck.

"I believe you already have some idea of what might happen if you don't follow my instructions?"

He nodded wordlessly, clutching the book. Teo saw a tear slide down his plump cheek. "What's she *done* to him?" she raged silently.

Miss Uish fastened on her head a hat that looked like a tea tray with a vast meringue on top. Then she stalked away, slipping down the gangplank with grace, and leaving in her wake a cloud of expensive-smelling yet slightly metallic perfume.

Over her shoulder, she called, "Malfeasance, count the brats and write down all their names. And what they're good for, if anything."

While Peaglum busied himself bullying boys with his notebook, Teo and Renzo rushed to Professor Marìn's poop-deck stateroom. There was no sign that he had ever occupied it. It was now overflowing with Miss Uish's considerable wardrobe of clothes and accessories. An ornate black cuckoo clock ticked menacingly on the wall.

The colors of Miss Uish's clothes were strident: electric blue, magenta, purple, arsenic-green, acid-yellow. She favored shiny checks and stripes, made up into costumes with a faint naval flavor, grandly ornamented with frogging.

Renzo's eyes popped open wide at the sight of the stiff rows of corsets, all black, yet decorated with pink stitching and jaunty pink satin bows. The hooks and lacing grommets almost seemed to strain with the hidden presence of their owner. He did not feel comfortable turning his back on them.

An open box on the dresser revealed a large heart-shaped locket on a chain, a link bracelet fastened by small heart-shaped padlocks; even her gloves had four heart-shaped celluloid buttons. Somehow, the effect was the opposite of romantic.

"She said she was 'Miss' Uish," Teo commented.

"She wasn't wearing a diamond solitaire engagement ring either," added Renzo. "Mind you, I can't imagine any man in his right mind wanting to marry *her*. In fact, I'm not even sure she's *human*."

"Do you think she's a ghost? But she doesn't make you feel cold around her."

"How can we tell? We're always cold since the ice storm."

The desk was littered with magazines: *The Ladies' Gazette of Fashions*, illustrated with color plates, and the *Court Circular*, which described Queen Victoria's daily engagements.

Piled in one corner were boxes labeled FINEST AUSTRALIAN LAMINGTONS and HOADLEY'S FRUIT JELLIES.

"Where's Professor Marìn?" lamented Teo. "He wouldn't just abandon us."

Renzo, visibly thinking of his mother, murmured, "Unless something . . . happened to him."

Teo threw him a sympathetic look. "He certainly wouldn't leave us to a creature like *her* by choice. I think she's raving mad! Did you see how she changes from second to second: one minute acting sweet as pie, the next minute, like a wolf?"

"And how can we be sure she's even qualified to run a sailing school? I don't see any certificates or official papers here."

"What about the school inspectors and the magistrates?" demanded Teo. "If she's an impostor, surely they will see through her? And the mermaids? Won't they have seen all this in the turtle-shell?"

The mermaids' turtleshell showed moving stories. They used it to see beyond their cavern, and sometimes even back into past events. Via that shell, Teo had learned the whole history of the wicked life and sorry death of Bajamonte Tiepolo.

"It seems not. Well, there's still Signor Alicamoussa. He won't let this happen. He'll find Professor Marìn."

"He *has* to. And Renzo, I'm worried about Cookie," Teo added. "Did you see how strange he looked? So pale, too. And he didn't speak."

"Go and see him. Maybe he knows something. I'm going to sneak ashore and see if I can find Signor Alicamoussa."

Then they jumped in terror, for the cuckoo clock suddenly struck the hour. Instead of a wooden bird, a black bat shot out of its carved chalet. It did not sing. It spat tiny droplets of black ink that smelled strongly of ancient, rotten fish into a chamber pot positioned below.

In the galley, Cookie was hunched over a saucepan, one hand nursing his jaw. He shuffled through cooking pots tumbled ankle-deep on the floor. The gravy-stained calendar hung askew.

"What's happened in here?" asked Teo. "Do you know where Professor Marìn's gone?"

Cookie shook his head despairingly.

"How did *she* get on board?"

More head shaking, and a pair of tears trembled on Cookie's swollen eyelids.

"Why don't you *say* anything?" cried Teo, in exasperation.

At this, Cookie's face crumpled completely. Teo put her arm awkwardly around the man. He smelled of boiling water and blood. Sobbing, he opened his lips and showed her what was inside.

Someone had rammed crude wooden casings over his teeth, upper and lower. The contraption was welded with wires so that Cookie could not open his mouth more than a quarter of an inch.

Teo backed away in shock. His gums were lividly swollen where they were not covered by the tight wooden casings.

"The pain must be unbearable!" she cried. "You poor dear! If only I had some Venetian Treacle!"

But The Two Tousled Mermaids Apothecary, where the medicine was to be found, was far distant, at the old gates of the Ghetto, just about as far as it was possible to be away from the *Scilla*'s mooring on the Zattere.

Now Teo remembered the night before: how she had heard a scream and smelled burning. Could that have been Cookie's poor jaws being welded together? And the other noise—now, in retrospect, she was *sure* that it'd been a pistol shot she'd heard just as she slipped into sleep. Was that what had happened to Professor Marìn? Had Miss Uish shot him and thrown him overboard?

If she could torture Cookie, then murder was not beyond the woman.

"Did she shoot Professor Marìn?" she asked Cookie. "Miss Uish?"

He made inarticulate sounds of distress.

"Write it down!" Teo ripped the galley calendar from the wall and pulled a pencil from her pocket.

Cookie shook his head helplessly.

The unwelcome face of Malfeasance Peaglum inserted itself through the galley door.

"Is this piece of scum interfering with you, Cookie?" he demanded in a threatening tone. "Teodoro Ongania, isn't it? The Nestle Tripe! You're already on Miss Uish's list, skinny boy."

"Cookie can't do his letters," Teo improvised quickly. "I've come to read him the new recipes."

The cook nodded eagerly. Teo had no idea if this was true or not, but she had an instinct that it might prove useful.

"As you were, then," snapped Peaglum, "and be sharp about it. Here's the new provisions for the job."

He dumped a bloodstained sack on the floor and scuttled off. The sack stank of old fish and putrid meat. A thin line of blood ran from it across the floor to Teo's feet.

Teo opened the recipe book. *"Mock fish soup,"* she read aloud. *"Take ten loaves of old bread and boil in water alongside a sailor's boot for flavor.*

"Cod sponge: take ten loaves of old bread and ten cod. Let one codfish lie on top of each loaf for a few hours to drip. When the fish is dry,

remove. Save the skins. The cod sponge is to be served cold. The fish is to be sautéed with thyme and butter for Miss Uish's supper with an accompaniment of rosemary potatoes, and a marmalade pudding to follow.

"'Cod jelly: take one paper of Nelson's Opaque Gelatine (supplied) and pour boiling water over day-old cod skins. Leave to set.

"'As a special treat, pork heart soup: take the heart, lungs and liver of a young piglet, preferably with the organs still attached together with nerves and veins. Boil with sailor's boot until the heart dissolves. Strain and serve.'"

Teo wailed, "Utterly revolting! And there's nothing at all for me. I don't eat meat or fish, as you know."

When Professor Marìn was with them, Cookie had prepared a thick pea soup for Teo, and spaghetti with *intingolo* of walnuts and cream. "Will you save me some bread, before the fish gets put on it?" she begged.

He was nodding as Renzo ran into the galley, brandishing a rolled-up newspaper. Before he could speak a word, Teo cried, "Something really dreadful has happened here."

She turned to Cookie: "Please open your mouth and show Renzo."

Renzo blanched and grasped the man's hand. "I'm so sorry, Cookie."

Teo said soothingly, "We'll have Signor Alicamoussa bring a dentist . . . or a blacksmith for you."

"No, Teo, that won't be possible." Renzo sighed, handing her the *Gazzettino*. The headline read:

CIRCUS-MASTER ARRESTED ON SUSPICION
OF RELEASING DANGEROUS ANIMALS

Signor Sargano Alicamoussa, Venice's famous circus-master, is today cooling his heels behind bars after several lions were allegedly seen roaming around the city. A deliberate release of the man-eaters is suspected. The Mayor issued this statement: *I hope Alicamoussa will serve a long sentence. I cannot think of anything more calculated to keep tourists away than the sight of those beasts strolling around our San Marco. Shame on the circus-master!*

"Lies! 'Allegedly seen,' my foot! This has been set up by the Mayor! Who will look after the poor animals," breathed Teo, "if Signor Alicamoussa is locked up?"

"His wife, Mercer, is more than capable," Renzo reminded her.

"What are *we* going to do without him? First Professor Marìn, now Signor Alicamoussa. It's as if someone is hunting down the Incogniti. And the same people must have taken my parents. . . . And *what* doesn't she want Cookie to tell us?"

A clack of heels above their heads announced the return of Miss Uish.

"We mustn't be seen talking together," warned Renzo. "We don't want her to know we are friends. She'll find a way to use it against us."

That evening, the young sailors sat down to their cod sponge in shocked silence. They were too hungry not to try it, especially as they'd been tortured by the smell of Miss Uish's delicious supper being cooked. At least she ate it away from their covetous eyes, in Professor Marìn's stateroom.

Evidently, Miss Uish dispatched her food with the crisp efficiency of a lizard eating a fly. For it was a very short time later that she appeared in the mess, smoking a Cuban cigar and blowing smoke in everyone's faces.

"So you're not hungry, whelps?" Miss Uish asked. "Delicate appetites? Perhaps a little bilious this evening?"

To Peaglum, she sneered, "I would say that these boys look worm-ridden, wouldn't you?"

"Riddled wiv 'em, ma'am. Crawlin' wiv 'em. Disgustin' they are, ma'am."

"And so it would be a kindness to dose them, don't you think?"

"You are too good to these wretches, ma'am," simpered Peaglum.

"Get the bottle."

BUMSTEAD'S WORM SYRUP, announced the label on the tall green bottle Peaglum produced from his pocket. And the contents were unspeakably bitter. The sailors were still coughing and retching when he approached them with a second bottle, this time blue. From that, he forcibly administered two drops of DR. C. MCLANE'S VERMIFUGE.

"Give the Nestle Tripe an extra dose," ordered Miss Uish, "and perhaps it'll think twice about opening its impudent mouth in future."

13. Influence

a bad beginning to the year, Venice, January 1–6, 1901

Miss Uish wore a row of lacquered kiss curls across her forehead. On January 2, when the school inspectors came aboard the *Scilla*, Teo noticed with wonder how grown men fixed on those curls. And how they stared at Miss Uish's eyelashes, which curled like palm fronds. And how they followed her swaying walk with their eyes on stalks. And how every one of her radiant smiles apparently detonated their brains, until there was nothing but bewildered liquid swishing about inside their grinning heads.

Most certainly, these men came aboard with the best intentions. Venice was proud of the *Scilla*. And the men from the school board were known to be fastidious about how their orphanages were run, by land or sea. They had questions prepared. Their notebooks were flipped open eagerly.

Miss Uish deflected every difficult question by flirting until they were weak at the knees.

As for the little sailors, they were silent as the grave. When a mustachioed inspector inquired jovially, "So what do you think of your charming new captain?" they answered in a tight chorus, as if they'd been drilled, "Very nice, thank you, sirs!"

What the four inspectors could not have known was this: for the occasion of the inspection, Miss Uish had singled out Sebastiano dalla Mutta, the boy who'd been so impertinent to Teo on her first day. Gagged and bound, he'd been hung in a weighted cage above the icy water below the forecastle, so he could not be seen. To the assembled sailors, Miss Uish had announced, "Any one of you brats utters a word of complaint in front of our guests, or makes any sniveling mention of your Professor Marìn—and Peaglum will cut the ropes. If the plunge doesn't kill your friend, the cold water underneath will. Is that understood, you warts?"

With downcast eyes, the sailors had nodded.

So now the crew stood in tense, silent ranks while Miss Uish guided the inspectors around the polished decks, the immaculate galley, the sleeping quarters and the provisions store. Cookie had been set to preparing a particularly delicious-smelling fish stew. The perfume of roasting butter, onions and caraway seeds floated over the deck. Alfredo drooled.

"An idiot-child," remarked Miss Uish, kicking him discreetly. "He shall be receiving special treatment." Alfredo shuddered.

The inspection went superbly. The inspectors pronounced themselves fully satisfied with discipline, cleanliness, educational excellence and comfort aboard the *Scilla*. They snapped shut their notebooks, beaming at Miss Uish. The most senior of the men concluded, "Queen Victoria may be proud to be represented by such a fine woman as Miss Canidia Uish. And how kind of you to step into the breach . . ."

"When Marìn irresponsibly deserted his post," Miss Uish inserted crisply.

"And she a mere slip of a lovely girl," his deputy added tenderly.

"Too kind, too kind," she murmured, dimpling. Each dimple was a visible bullet to the heart of the deputy. Then she opened her mouth and buried him entirely: "One does one's best for the little dears, yet I still long to do more, bless them. All cruelly orphaned at such a sensitive age. My heart goes out to each one."

"I'd not object to being an orphan," joked the second inspector, "if I had a vision like *you* to tuck me into my hammock at bedtime!"

Miss Uish purred, "That reminds me, there *is* one boon I crave for my darling boys. I fear that they are very cold at night. Shipboard life tends to dampness, and it is difficult for me to keep all their little sailor suits warm and dry, try as I do. May I request an extra supply of heating oil, so that I can keep their cabin cozy?"

While the inspectors took their leave, saying, "You are kindness itself, madam," Renzo was muttering, outraged, "But she has taken the oil stoves out of our cabin. What does she want that oil for?"

The inspection accomplished, the *Scilla* became a very different kind of place. Instead of studying sailoring, the crew was put to work on what Miss Uish described as "profitable enterprises."

First, they wore their fingers raw unraveling the warm sweaters that Professor Marìn had given them, and knitting the good bits of wool into neat socks. Those who had skills at scrimshaw, like Renzo, were set to carving pieces of ivory with skulls-and-crossbones. Speaking-parrot production went on in shifts, twenty-four hours a day. Peaglum dragged crates of birds up on deck. Rosato and Alfredo fashioned birdcages with pagoda-like turrets out of wood threaded with cruelly cold wire pillaged from the ship's chicken coop.

Meanwhile, Miss Uish lost no opportunity to ingratiate herself with the English community in Venice, or at least its upper crust. On Sunday, she attended the English Church of St. George at San Vio, dressed in one of her strident silk dresses with naval piping and a cape frill trimmed with Vandyke ribbon velvet. She clearly made a favorable impression. By Monday, there arrived an invitation from Lady Layard, widow of the famous archaeologist, to attend her *soirée musicale* at Ca' Cappello. After that, new invitations arrived daily for Miss Canidia Uish: to an "at home" at Horatio Brown's Ca' Torresella, and even to exclusive teas in the home of the Eden family, set like a fairy-tale cottage in a frozen garden on Giudecca.

British high society in Venice had no idea that their new favorite, Miss Uish, left behind her on the boat a tribe of young people who were quite literally starving, whose legs were bruised from her casual kicks, and who slept with ice crusting their hair in the damp hold of the unheated boat.

On January 6 came the feast of the Befana, when all Venetian children were accustomed to receiving gifts and sweets. Miss Uish, dressed in purple-and-red-striped silk, presented her orphans with giftwrapped boxes. Inside were new scrubbing brushes. Down in their cabin the sailors fantasized about Befana feasts of the past

when their parents were still alive: stockings full of toffee and cara-
mel, foaming hot chocolate and crunchy fried *galani* biscuits dusted
with sugar.

Miss Uish gave them stone-hard lard sandwiches on stale bread,
a dose of BUMSTEAD'S WORM SYRUP, and a slap in the face.

14. "A Gristly Gizzard for a Heart"

Teo and Renzo passed every unsupervised minute searching the ship, quietly calling out Professor Marìn's name belowdecks and in the passages that led to the cargo hold. All they heard in response was the dejected creaking of the *Scilla*'s timbers.

"Perhaps he escaped," Renzo said hopefully.

"If he had, he would have done something about Miss Uish. He would have told the mermaids."

"We have to get to them somehow."

"Here's how . . . ," whispered Teodora.

On the afternoon of the Befana, Miss Uish was attending a party at the Palazzo Barbaro and Peaglum was to be seen waltzing around the deck, cradling a bottle of BEST NAVAL RUM in his arms.

As arranged, Teo, hiding in the shadows of the forecastle, stuck out her booted foot. Peaglum reeled forward, hit his head on a stanchion and collapsed like a dead spider. A moment later, heavy snores suffused the air.

"I'm off. Cover for me," whispered Renzo.

"But I thought we'd both go." Teo was surprised. "The Undrowned Child and the Studious Son together."

"Two is too risky," Renzo argued.

Sofonisba, passing by, observed, "The smaller the boy, the less he'll be missed."

"That'll be me, then," said Teodora. Renzo opened his mouth, but closed it as Sofonisba walked up to him and stared him in the eye, waving her tail. Teo slid down the ladder and headed west.

"That was unkind of Sofonisba," Teo thought. She would have been glad of Renzo's company as she thudded through the lonely streets. Venice was a ghost town, inhabited by miserable ghosts. Laundered sheets hung like frosted glass, not drying but solidifying. Each bridge, each windowsill, carried its pillow of hard snow. The flowers and vines wavered crystal white on delicate stalks, as if pure essence of cold had replaced their sap. Even though it was only late afternoon, the lamps shone like the eyes of clustered creatures hiding in the dark. And the tops of the buildings were licked away by greedy tongues of fog, the chimneys dimming first and then the pediments slowly unbuilding in the blankness.

The mist took all the smells and rubbed them with its white fingers, extracting even keener stinks from the dead fish and seaweed thrown up by the ice storm. It hurt Teo to see beautiful Venice look and smell so depressingly like something not just dead but rotting.

Ahead of her, Teo caught sight of an insubstantial figure carrying a black tin. He wore a battered felt hat from which corks dangled improbably. She drew back into a doorway when she saw a shark's tooth embedded in his back. "A ghost!" she shuddered, as he bent over a doorknob. "What's he up to?"

Baddened magic was abroad in Venice again. Even without seeing the ghost, Teo would have known it, from the prickling between her shoulder blades and the dragging feeling around her heart.

"Hark! 'Tis the Undrowned Child at last!" cried Flos, as Teo flew down the stairs and into their chamber. The mermaid's blond hair crackled with ice as she swam eagerly in Teo's direction.

"Teodora!" Lussa greeted her. "We've worried greatly about You!"

Marsil, one of the smaller mermaids, observed, "Lackaday! She's in poor fig, the little maid! The flesh has dropped offa her. Thin as a rasher of wind! And where's the Studious Son? Is he also in a parlous state? Give her some warm sea-cow juice! Roundly!"

Breathlessly, over sips of hot sweet milk, Teo asked, "Is Professor Marìn with you? Is he with the nuns?"

Flos shook her head glumly. Crushed with disappointment, Teo sorrowfully explained the disappearance of the professor and the arrival of Miss Canidia Uish.

"But did you not see her in the turtleshell?" she asked. "Look now!"

At a motion of Lussa's hand, two butler-mermaids held up the polished shell. Teo winced to see Miss Uish reflected there, dimpling and smiling in purple-and-red-striped silk under the unmistakable chandeliers of the frescoed ballroom at the Palazzo Barbaro.

"That's her." Teo pointed with distaste. "But what about inside the *Scilla*? Haven't you seen what she gets up to there?"

"Sweet fadoodle on da *Scilla* since New Year's Eve!" lamented Flos.

Lussa explained, "When We try to summon the Ship, the Shell gives Us Nothing but a Black Emptiness & the Sound of Children's Tears. It shows your Miss Uish only when She ventures upon Dry Land. And now You say the good Professor has disappeared? Yes, Child, I see It in your Face: You are Right to suspect Baddened Magic. The Woman Uish has Access to It. 'Tis my Guess that She has cast some Kind of Field-of-Excluding around the Ship."

As Lussa spoke, the Mayor strode into view inside the turtle-shell. Miss Uish curtseyed to him with perfect grace, her face illuminated by a coquettish smile.

Flos muttered, "Undrowned Child, dat's da clinchpoop's what's mistreating ye? We'll knock her bandy-legged!"

"Savin' her grace, of course," added Cara, generally milder than her sisters.

"God's elbows, that's an ugly woman," cried Pianon, one of the butler-mermaids. "Ugly to the core."

"Sink me, wot a bagger!" cried Flos, explaining to Teo, "Face like dat should be covered with a paper bag."

Marsil insisted, "Two-bagger, more like! Needs second bag in case the first one falls off."

Teo explained, "Well, the school inspectors think she's a raving beauty. They go weak at the knees when she flirts with them."

Marsil cried, "Looks like da Mayor's gone da same way. He's makin' da goggly eyes at her."

Lussa observed shrewdly, "Yet I fear that the Captivating Miss Uish has but a Gristly Gizzard for a Heart."

"If he's not here, where can the professor be? You see"—Teo gulped—"I might have heard a pistol shot. But I didn't want to believe it. I didn't want to think . . . And what about my . . . ?"

Lussa shook her head gravely. "And I am sorry, Teodora, We have not been able to locate your adoptive Parents either. Which makes Me believe They have been taken Away beyond the Lagoon."

"And Signor Alicamoussa?" asked Teo. "What is happening to him?"

Lussa pointed. The turtleshell showed the dashing circus-master sitting despondently on a bare plank inside his jail cell. Even in his despair, the glossy curls on his head fell unerringly into the most fetching arrangement on his handsome brow. Suddenly, he shook his shapely fist, and shouted, "That scorpion spawn, the Mayor! Reckon he's done me like a dinner!"

"'S a dirty shame!" cried Marsil. "That gorgeousness shut 'way where nobody can see 'im or 'ave the use of 'im."

"Aye," sighed her companions. "Prithee put me down for some of that!" and "Always does a body good to see them blue-blue eyes, and that pretty-kissin' mouf. . . ."

"Ladies!" warned Lussa. "Such Expressions are *not* appropriately Uttered by any Female other than Signor Alicamoussa's own Estimable Wife."

At the word "wife," there was a quiet hubbub of disappointed mutterings. The turtleshell showed an earnest young woman, evidently not Venetian, passionately scribbling a long letter while the tears ran freely down her pale cheeks.

Lussa leaned forward eagerly. "What does *The Key to the Secret City* tell You to do, Teodora?"

Teo groaned. "Renzo says the book was taken by the flood."

Silence fell on the cavern. The parrots hung their feathered heads in misery.

"That," sighed Lussa quietly, "is a sad Blow to all our Hopes."

She looked more closely at Teo. "Child, 'Tis true, you are much Diminished in Substance & Spirits."

Teo quickly recounted what had happened to the young sailors' rations in the last seven days—everything down to the cod sponge.

"Dat'll put da woefuls in yer gormy-ruddles rightaway!" exclaimed Flos.

"Pore mite!" cried the other mermaids. "No wonder she's a whittled stick o' herself. Bring food alongside, Catalina!"

A platter of fragrant curried seaweed was placed in front of Teo, whose eyes watered with hunger. Catalina implored, "Put that in yer breadbasket, girlie. And have yesself a taste o' these 'ere rib-stickin' jerk split peas wiv turmeric mash. . . ."

"And our Kitchen shall prepare some nourishing Eatables for You to take back to the poor Boys on the *Scilla*. Swallow sparingly, Teodora," warned Lussa. "Do not gorge. After Malnourishment, 'Tis Perilous to fill your Belly with rich Tidbits."

Teo's nose hovered ecstatically above the dish, reveling in the exquisite odor. She tried to nibble slowly, but the spicy leaves were too tempting. She surreptitiously filled her mouth again and again while Lussa ordered, "Bring *The Book of Enemies*!"

A sandalwood skiff was floated in across the cavern. On it

reposed a book bound in black seaweed and glinting with green wax seals. Lussa consulted the pages with a slender gold-embossed finger. "No, a Miss Canidia Uish is not listed Herein as an Enemy of Venice. We have not encountered Her, or Her Like, before."

"Perhaps it's not her real name?" wondered Teo. "And anyway, what can an Englishwoman, who says she's a representative of Queen Victoria, have to do with Bajamonte Tiepolo? And where is *he*?"

"Teodora, I am as Mystified as Yourself. You must do All You can to investigate this Miss Canidia Uish. The Seldom Seen Press shall meanwhiles alert all Good-Hearted Venetians to the Young Sailors' Plight. By Dawn, It shall be Done."

Teo emerged from the cavern into a molten lagoon sunset. A satchel slapped against her side, heavy with parcels of food and clinking bottles.

The sky and sea coalesced into a vivid orange glaze, with the skeletons of buildings spindly and black against it.

There was no doubt that Teo had overindulged on the curried seaweed. The bilious colors of the sunset merged with the vivid sensations inside her belly. She felt rather faint, somewhat removed from the world.

It was then that she noticed the cormorants. There were hundreds—no, thousands—of them, clad in their severe glistening livery, perched on top of palaces, churches and masts, and on the nets out in the lagoon. Each bird stood in the same posture, hanging out its gaunt, ragged wings, its slim beak pointing to the sky.

The birds looked too much like bats for Teo not to think of Bajamonte Tiepolo. He had taken a batlike form when he was between human and ghostly states. Teo tried to reassure herself with page 354 of Professor Marìn's *Winged Creatures*: "Cormorants spread their wings to dry, because their feathers are not water-proofed with oil like those of other seabirds." Yet it still seemed menacing: this infestation of motionless black birds, staring up with their small black eyes as if into a bleak future. Teo hurried on.

A narrow street took her uncomfortably close to a newsstand on which perched another cluster of cormorants. A headline below the birds caught Teo's eye. For the first time since the ice flood, Venetian newspapers were showing an interest in the outside world.

STRANGE CREATURES FOUND DEAD IN LONDON! screamed the headlines. **MASSACRE OF "EXTRAORDINARY" SEA MONSTERS!**

Teo bent to look at the blurred illustration. Corpses were shown floating down London's River Thames. They might have seemed extraordinary and monstrous to the Londoners, but these poor dead creatures were all too familiar to Teo. They were her friends and allies, the English Melusine, a two-tailed kind of mer-maid, and the Sea-Bishops, man-sized jellyfish with pointed human heads. As far as Teo could see from the picture, the Melusine and Sea-Bishops had been attacked by something that had left great sores and weals on their bodies, and had somehow deflated them, as if all their blood had been sucked out.

"And the poor South Sea dolphins too!" Teo recalled the sad news that had arrived in Venice on the same day as the ice flood: that schools of these gentle creatures had been found floating life-less in the Pacific Ocean.

The South Sea dolphins, the Melusine and the Sea-Bishops had one thing in common, apart from their dreadful deaths. All had come to the aid of Venice, when Bajamonte Tiepolo tried to destroy the city two summers before.

"So," Teo groaned aloud, "these murders can mean only one thing."

And where was the murderer now?

15. Lamingtons and Hoadley's Fruit Jellies

early evening, aboard the Scilla, *January 6–7, 1901*

As Teo had run off toward the House of the Spirits, Renzo had stared after her retreating figure, his hands clenched in frustration. He would not let Teo outdo him in daring! He quickly decided to sneak back into Miss Uish's stateroom.

A lovely fug of warmth hit him as he opened the door. He'd left Emilio posted outside as watch. The rest of the *Scilla* was icy, but in her stateroom, Miss Uish had allowed herself the luxury of a handsome Rippingille's enameled oil stove.

Despite Miss Uish's immaculate appearance, her cabin had quickly descended into chaos. The walls and floors were festooned with clothes; the floors were strewn with confectionery wrappings.

"'Hoadley's Fruit Jellies. Best Australian Lamingtons,'" read Renzo, picking up a handful of crumpled papers. They were all written in English: "'Lightest sponge-cake enrobed in rich chocolate and rolled in succulent Pacific Ocean coconut.'"

Renzo sniffed the empty wrapping appreciatively. But how to find anything useful in this midden of silk and waste paper? Taking a step toward the disordered bed, he noticed that there was something strange about the far end of it. Miss Uish slept not on a pillow, but on a slender wooden box.

"A pillow box!" he exclaimed. Renzo, whose knowledge of history was encyclopedic, knew that this long, thin object came from China. Such boxes were used by travelers, who slept with their heads upon their most precious possessions in order to protect them from thieves. Miss Uish's pillow box was beautifully decorated with a swirling design of flowers, white serpents and graceful black bats, in ebony and mother-of-pearl inlaid in green lacquer.

Renzo was reaching a shaking hand toward the lid when Emilio poked his head around the door. "She's back from her party! Get out of there!"

Renzo fled, crashing into Teo, who was sliding down the booby hatch into their sleeping quarters, her arms full of packages and a greenish look on her face.

That night, at least, the sailors dined famously well in the privacy of their cabin. The only one who showed a meager appetite was Renzo, whom Teo quietly told what she'd learned from the mermaids and about the poor dead Melusine and Sea-Bishops. He was also embarrassed at the lack of success of his spying mission to Miss Uish's room.

"But I did notice that there are bats and white snakes on her pillow box," he whispered to Teo.

"White snakes or Vampire Eels?"

"Exactly."

Few of the sailors could manage more than a mouthful of cod sponge for breakfast the next morning. Miss Uish castigated them, "Think you're too good for your rations, whelps? Or are you sickening for a dose?"

With their mouths still pleasantly a-tingle with chili flakes, the young sailors submitted almost cheerfully to BUMSTEAD'S WORM SYRUP, with VERMIFUGE for afters.

Venetians who rose at dawn on January 7 found a notice printed on sea-scented paper pinned to the breast of a certain statue in the Campo dei Mori in Cannaregio.

The statue was of a man with a sharp iron nose and an irritable look to match. His name was Signor Rioba. At moments when something was amiss or being hidden by those in authority, he traditionally "spoke" to the Venetians in angry antique lettering printed on slightly damp paper. Signor Rioba had been most vociferous when Bajamonte Tiepolo tried to destroy Venice, reserving particular and eloquent scorn for the Mayor, who had tried all along to pretend nothing was wrong. Signor Rioba's missives were, of course, printed by the mermaids on their Seldom Seen Press.

The new notice read: *Venetians! Do ye not know that there's a sack of Venetian children being tortured and starved on board the Scilla? A thousand shames on ye snibbling buffers that ye leave 'em there to perish of cruelty. The Mayor will tell ye all is well, of course. Shame on his lying mouth!*

More copies of the same notice were to be found in baskets floating down canals in every part of the city.

Although the Mayor knew nothing of the mermaids and the Seldom Seen Press, he was far from delighted to hear that his old enemy Signor Rioba was up in arms again. "That ruffian Rioba," he was heard to say with a sniff, "has such a coarse way with words. And such an inconvenient tendency to bother the general public with matters that should be handled discreetly by their betters, such as myself."

The Mayor expanded on this theme for the evening paper:

Under our present calamity, naturally troublemakers seek to draw attention to the most far-fetched and crazed notions. It is ever thus. How dare Rioba insult and libel Queen Victoria's adorable representative, such a loving mother to our orphans? If the shining masts of the *Scilla* had tongues, what happy tales they would tell. Lucky, lucky children!

And polite Venetian society merely tittered at the rudeness of Signor Rioba. No one in Venice took the notice seriously.

The conditions on the *Scilla* were not reinvestigated.

16. A shark smelling blood

momentous news, January 7, 1901

Queen Victoria's health had taken a lurch for the worse. She lay in deathly silence upon her bed at Osborne House, too weak to raise her head.

The end of Queen Victoria would be the end of the world as most people knew it. And so the world held its breath, waiting for the blow.

But there were also people observing Queen Victoria's decline with happy excitement.

To the island of Hooroo, to a black-rigged ship in a remote part of the Venetian lagoon and to a dark northern barn, relays of cormorants brought daily bulletins of the Queen's failing health.

Harold Hoskins, the Pretender to the British throne, turned his thoughts toward Osborne House with the glee of a shark smelling blood. As a member of the royal family, he was entitled to be present at the old Queen's death. It was on January 7 that he stepped aboard the new boat that would carry him back to the old country.

"Just in time, with luck," he gloated, stroking his sandy beard.

As the *Kingmaker's Dame* glided over the waves—at four times the speed of any ordinary vessel—the Pretender kept a notebook of comforting statistics by his side. It recorded the number of new warships sliding into the docks at Hooroo's secret lagoon. And he reread the letter of his subtlest and most secret spy, Lieutenant Rosebud, who was currently commanding that black-rigged ship in the Venetian lagoon.

Travel appears to agree with Signor Pipistrelly. Since the interesting events of Christmas Eve in Venice, and his journey to Calais, our Signor Pipistrelly has grown in strength, wrote Rosebud. The birds tell me he will be ready to sail for our rendezvous on the Thames as soon as we ourselves get there. Meanwhile, thanks to that clever device of his, our own Bombazine waits undetected in the waters just outside Venice, and our two new recruits are feeling very motivated—shall we say?—to share their researches. Our colossal comrade has, with due encouragement, developed a taste for the soft sweetness of human flesh. Indeed, we shall be hard put to satisfy its appetite if things continue as they do.

And our colleague in Venice continues to expand her field of influence with the highest and noblest. The lady will shortly be in a position to remove the Scilla to a place of convenience without drawing any suspicion whatsoever.

The Pretender smiled. His pale blue eyes sparkled with delight. He would have danced about the deck, but he knew he must be careful. The sea was swollen, and he must not risk jolting against the taffrail. In his case, given the family malady, the slightest mishap could be fatal. No, the future King of England must take care of his health. Harold Hoskins took up the letter again.

Everything's coming up roses, quipped Lieutenant Rosebud, unless you are unfortunate enough to be a Londoner or a Venetian. Or a Studious Son.

17. English lessons and earrings

out to the lagoon, January 7 and 8, 1901

"There shall be no more vulgar Venetian spoken aboard my ship!" announced Miss Uish, as the *Scilla* creaked out to the lagoon mud-flats for what she had described as "a most interesting training exercise."

"My ship!" thought Teo indignantly.

"*Vulgar Venetian?*" spluttered Renzo.

Miss Uish bestowed one of her most toxic smiles upon the bewildered crew. "From now on, all lessons will be conducted in English, the language of Empire. Punishments shall apply for failure to obey."

Teo and Renzo exchanged apprehensive glances. Both of them had always got excellent marks for English, but what about the others? Professor Marìn's bedtime stories were unlikely to be the kind of English lessons that Miss Uish meant.

"This could turn out uglier than the food," thought Teo.

Miss Uish added, "And as of today all parrots are to be trained in English, even as you are. I daresay some of the birds shall show more aptitude than you brats, as they certainly have better brains."

"Maybe that's 'cos they're better fed," murmured Giovanni behind his hand.

Peaglum had set up a blackboard on the deck. Now he drew the frozen chalk shrieking across the surface, writing out words in Venetian and then English.

The *Scilla*, with a nervous Renzo at the wheel, edged her way through the pockets of water and tufts of salty land known as the *barene*. As each Venetian species, be it plant or animal, hove into sight, the sailors were obliged to chant its name in English.

"*Lattuga di mare*—sea lettuce!"

"*Zostera marina*—grass wrack!"

Even Teo's clever tongue tripped up on those English words. One of her talents as the Undrowned Child was that her memory functioned like a photographic apparatus, taking pictures of whole pages at a time. For her, to see a word was to memorize it—she wasn't afraid of that. Yet how to pronounce them? Unlikely consonants were all jammed together with snipped-up vowels, like a painful tangle of hair in the teeth of a comb. The other sailors stood peering at the board in perplexity, tears sneaking into their eyes.

"Enough greenery!" barked Miss Uish. "And now we shall be concerned with marine creatures. The ones that are fat and greasy are of particular interest."

"Why?" Teo could have kicked herself, but the word had slipped out.

"History does not relate. However, it shall relate that the Nestle Tripe holystones the deck tomorrow. You vermin speak only when asked a direct question, understand?"

For an Englishwoman, Miss Uish was astonishingly well informed about which birds wintered in the Venetian lagoon.

"*Tuffetti*—grrrrebes!"

"*Lombardella*—white-frrrronted goose!"

Miss Uish mocked their pronunciation. "Don't roll your 'r's like waiters, you offal! And stop waving your hands around. Proper British people keep their arms to themselves when they speak. Malfeasance, get the cat-o'-nine-tails out of the bag. Anyone who rolls their 'r's gets a stripe. Hands out, ready!"

Peaglum drew a large whip with nine plaited ends out of a baize bag and dipped it in a flagon of vinegar.

"*Fòega*—coot!"

"*Svasso maggiore*—grrrreat crrrrested grrrrebe!"

That earned them all a stripe of the cat. They also realized why Peaglum dipped the whip in vinegar. When their skin broke, the vinegar sent a fiery thread of pain through the cuts.

At four o'clock, the light was already dim over the lagoon. The *Scilla* was surrounded by the evening flocks of birds, chirping and calling through the mist.

Miss Uish ran nimbly up the companionway, dimpling that impish smile they had learned to fear. She pulled a slender black pistol out of her belt, and shouted, "Examination time!"

The sailors gasped and took a step backward.

She laughed with delight. "Oh, the pathetic little cowards think I'm going to shoot them if their tongues get twisted! Let me tell you now, brats, just at this moment, you are worth more to me alive than dead. Now, what's that?" she rapped, pointing to a *svasso maggiore* in the mud.

"Grrrreat crrrrested grrrrebe!" rang out the voices of Teo and Renzo, the only two who never forgot a word once it was learned. Unfortunately, the same could not be said for their pronunciation.

Miss Uish aimed the pistol and shot the bird with deadly accuracy. "I *told* you not to roll your 'r's," she remarked casually.

Teo began to weep unashamedly. She, who never ate living things, had now caused the death of an innocent bird.

There was a creaking of davits and then Peaglum was to be seen approaching the lifeless creature in a coracle. He tossed the corpse into the boat and looked back up toward his mistress, calling out, "A fine plump one, mistress! You'll get a whole cup of marrowfat out of this one!"

"A second chance, brats. Now, I do declare, what a surprise. What's that?"

A monk seal swam into view, making a slipstream through the water.

"*Una foca . . . ,*" cried Massimo, quickly drowned out by the other children who screamed, "No! You have to say it *in English!*"

Teo leaned over the taffrail. She was sure she knew that motherly whiskered face. Sure enough, a pup was swimming behind the seal.

Miss Uish cocked her pistol and stared at the sailors with a triumphant smile.

"It's not fair, we haven't learned that poor creature's name in English yet!" called Massimo.

"Who said anything about fair?" inquired Miss Uish, taking aim. "Full of marrowfat!" she remarked joyfully.

"No!" cried Renzo, raising his hand toward Miss Uish's wrist. She sent him flying with a blow to the side of the head.

The shot rang out through the blank white lagoon. The baby seal squealed in terror, and rushed to the inert body of its mother, snuffling desperately around her motionless head.

"The baby will die without its mother," whispered Teo.

"Fair enough," chuckled Miss Uish, and shot the baby seal too.

Then there was silence, except for the oars of Malfeasance Peaglum, sculling toward the corpses of the seals, a dagger in his belt and a rope coiled in his lap.

All through the night, great cauldrons were set over the fire in the galley. The sailors' throats burned with the sickly, sour smell of marrowfat being pummeled out of the dead birds and animals by boiling water. Cookie's miserable face was seared scarlet. The corpses were gradually reduced to bones and pots of grease, which were stacked neatly in a locked compartment that Peaglum had constructed in the hold.

The smell of death clung to every board of the boat, every sail, and to the clothes of the sailors.

Teo and Renzo woke next morning to flashes like lightning and the sound of sniveling on deck. Rushing up, they found Miss Uish forcing Alfredo, whose head had been roughly shaved and whose ear was bleeding heavily, to pose in front of a black device consisting of a dark box with a black-shrouded concertina beak, apparently standing on two human legs and three wooden ones.

"It's a monster!" cried the boy as he wept. "It will explode the eyes out of my head!"

Renzo called out, "Don't worry, Alfredo, it's only a photographic apparatus. It won't hurt you."

Malfeasance Peaglum's monstrously ugly head emerged from under the black cloth, and Renzo almost revised his opinion.

"Why are you taking our likenesses?" Teo dared to ask Miss Uish. "Ma'am."

"Put Teodoro Ongania's name on my list again. Not that I owe your impudent Nestle Tripe curiosity an explanation, but I need your pictures for the school records. Malfeasance, do this pair immediately and then deliver the pictures . . . *you* know where."

Their eyes were still dazzled by the photographic apparatus when another scream drew Teo's and Renzo's attention to the aft deck. More sobbing shaven-headed boys were lined up there. A bat-faced nurse pulled Giovanni close to the rocky breast of her pinafore. Then she plunged a needle unceremoniously through his earlobe. Once the hole was made, she shoved a thin gold earring through it, paying absolutely no attention to Giovanni's pleading and sobbing. Then she sheared off his hair, finishing the job with gray suds and a dirty razor.

Miss Uish explained, "I can get good money for that hair. And these earrings will pay for your funerals if your worthless dead bodies get washed ashore in a shipwreck. Don't want you being a burden to some poor foreign parish, do we?"

Teo was gazing at the nurse. Where had *she* appeared from? And why was that craggy face familiar? Beside her, Renzo whispered, "Where is Peaglum going in the coracle with those photographic plates on his lap?"

The nurse departed midmorning, by which time each of the sailors sported a gold earring. Teo's curls were gone and her head was bleeding from a dozen small razor cuts. And now she knew where she'd last seen that gargoyle of a woman—in the hospital in Venice, eighteen months before. The nurse had helped Bajamonte

Tiepolo infect the children of Venice with bubonic plague. And Il Traditore had used an emerald earring to drip poison into the ear of Teo's friend Maria, turning her into a spy. Were these earrings also poisoned? If this same nurse was assisting Miss Uish, surely that *proved* that Miss Uish was somehow in league with Bajamonte Tiepolo?

As they scrubbed the deck together, Teo confided her fears about the nurse and the earrings to Renzo.

"Too cold for our ears to get infected," he reassured her. "Miss Uish just wants to humiliate us, make us look like cutthroat pirates instead of civilized Venetians." He pointed to his shaven head with shame.

They fell against each other as another iceberg thudded against the *Scilla's* prow.

"The ice is eating up the lagoon," breathed Renzo.

It was true. That afternoon's excursion into the lagoon had been slow, impeded by the ice floes. Out there, even the *barene* were decorated with icy ruffles sculpted by the wind. The delicate stems of the reeds were thickened with frost. The saltwort and sea lavender struggled to unfurl leaves weighted down with daily falls of snow. Even the sand on the shoreline sparkled with freezing crystals. Wisps of mist rose above the violet shadows and green frozen depths.

The *Scilla's* rigging looked like fairy necklaces, decorated with miniature gleaming stalactites. The sails might have been carved from white marble, so stiffly frozen were they.

It would have been almost picturesque, if the cold had not been so cruel, and the boys' sailor suits had not been so thin.

"And Vampire Eels are waiting under that ice." Teo picked up her scrubbing brush and started working again. Renzo caught the glitter of a cold eye on the forecastle.

"Shhh, *she's* looking at us. Move away from me!"

That night, Renzo and Teo whispered while the other boys slept.

"It's baddened magic, I just know it is. And I'm sure *she* has something to do with it. We have to see inside that pillow box of hers," insisted Teo. "It had better be me this time."

"It wasn't my fault she came back just as—"

"I didn't mean that. I mean I can memorize any documents in there."

"I'll cause a distraction tomorrow," promised Renzo.

"You mean you'll get yourself flogged? Have you lost your ballast, Renzo?"

"Well, she always comes to enjoy that event, doesn't she? And it'll be a pleasure and relief to tell her what I think about what she did to those poor seals. And it'll be worth it, Teo, if you find out what's going on."

The lantern swung over them as a wave unsettled the *Scilla*. Teo recognized Renzo's mother's favorite blue shawl inside his hammock and the little money-box that was A PRESENT FROM LONDON. She reached across the space between them. For the first time in days, Renzo smiled at her properly, and took her hand. They fell asleep like that, their fingers linked.

18. Inside the pillow box

aboard the Scilla, *January 9, 1901*

The whine of the cat, Miss Uish's tinkling laugh and Renzo's grunts were painfully audible as Teo crept down toward Professor Marìn's stateroom the next morning. She refused to call it Miss Uish's, even though everything pointed to the fact that its rightful occupant had been murdered. She lifted the latch of the door and let herself in. A dismal gray light flowed through the mullioned windows, falling on the bed and its unusual pillow.

Expecting to find it locked, Teo was surprised to feel the pillow box respond to her tugging hand. The arched lid lifted easily. She peered inside.

There were a great many bottles of a black liquid that looked like ink. Teo unscrewed one lid and breathed in a fishy smell.

"Squid ink?" she thought.

Below the bottles was something that astonished Teo: a technical drawing of a colossal squid. She was used to seeing such things, at home. Her adoptive parents always brought their work back at the end of the day, and the dining table was frequently buried under diagrams of marine creatures.

The thought of Leonora and Alberto Stampara made Teo's eyes water. But, absorbed in the drawing, she failed to notice the light footsteps behind her. She felt the blow to the side of her head, and she heard Peaglum's triumphant snigger as she fell.

Teo looked up dizzily. The first things she saw were Miss Uish's calf-high spats rising over her lace-up shoes. Then she raised her eyes higher. Miss Uish's face was distorted with anger. For once, she seemed unable to speak.

Peaglum deftly trussed Teo in tight coils of rope.

"Spy on me, would you?" sputtered Miss Uish eventually. "I know just the thing to cool the curiosity of an impudent Nestle Tripe. And as for the Nestle Tripe's crony, the St—the boy Renzo, let us search his hammock! I've seen them whispering together. They're up to something. Summon the boy! This Ongania brat can bear witness before we . . . dispose of him."

Bound and gagged, Teo was dragged below. Renzo was already in the cabin, facing a corner. Teo's eyes filled with tears at the sight of the stripes of red on his right hand behind his back.

"Stand beside your hammock, boy!" When Renzo was in place, Miss Uish ordered Peaglum to upend the canvas. Renzo cried out, reaching with his damaged hand. It was too late. There was a dull thump and a shocking explosion of china. The painted money-box that had been A PRESENT FROM LONDON lay in fragments on the floor.

Miss Uish poked at the wreckage with her shoe. Then she picked up Renzo's mother's shawl and ripped it in half and then quarters.

"Rags for swabbing the deck." She thrust them into Peaglum's arms. "Now take the Nestle Tripe . . . you know where!"

"Teo," Renzo whispered down to her. "Stay awake! You have to stay awake! It would be madness to fall asleep in the icehouse!"

"Why?" she yawned. "Miss Uish isn't going to let me out. Ever. She wants me to die here. She'll probably boil my body up for marrowfat."

"She wouldn't dare!" hissed Renzo. "The school inspectors have our names."

"And mine is an invention. I don't exist, officially anyway. No loss."

Teo had no feelings at all in her hands or feet. For the first hours, she had kept awake in the narrow pit by sucking ice, and nibbling on pieces of bread that Rosato and Sebastiano had furtively dropped down the hatch.

But then she had stopped even feeling hungry. The silver-tongued waves around the *Scilla* seemed to whisper "Sleeeeep, sleeeep." An almost pleasant torpor had stolen over her. Teo was happy to lapse into half-dreams in which her adoptive parents warmed her with hugs and a pink cashmere blanket. She even dreamed that her real parents came to visit her, and that her mother's sweet breath wafted down the icy shaft to warm her cheeks.

"Darling Teo," whispered Marta Gasperin, "let me read you a story, my love."

Teo was almost angry when another crust of bread fell on her head, shattering the image of her mother's face.

Miss Uish was attending a gala at Lady Layard's. That evening, Peaglum, left in charge of the boys, had roped them together in their hammocks and locked himself in his cabin, from where the clinking of bottles could be heard. As soon as snores reverberated through the ship, Renzo slit his bonds with his *ferro* pocketknife.

"Where are you going?" whispered sharp-eyed Fabrizio as Renzo slid out of his hammock and crawled along the floor.

"Going to get help for Teo," he hissed back.

When he'd taken her the bread he'd saved from supper, she had not even seemed aware of his presence. He suspected that she did not know who he was. Teo had crouched on the floor of the icehouse, talking softly to people who weren't there. "Mamma," she'd whispered, "tell me about the Gray Lady at the Archives, your friend in the old days. Did you know I met her too . . . ?" Peering down, Renzo had seen that Teo had removed her boots and stood barefoot on the ice.

"Help from whom?" Fabrizio was incredulous. "Miss Uish has got everyone in Venice eating out of her hand."

For a moment, Renzo toyed with the idea of telling Fabrizio the truth. Fabrizio was a child—that meant he would be able to see the mermaids. It would be nice to have a companion on the long tramp through the ice to the House of the Spirits. It would be even nicer to share with someone their worst fears—that the vengeful spirit of Bajamonte Tiepolo was once more abroad.

But if they were caught, the punishment would be dire. Fabrizio was thinner than any of them, slender as a weasel. Renzo could not bear the thought of what the whip would do to him.

"Will you cover for me?"

Fabrizio nodded. He pulled the blanket off his own hammock and leaned over to tuck it into Renzo's so it looked as if someone were still inside. There was a tinkle of broken china. Renzo had sewed the pieces of the PRESENT FROM LONDON into his pillow.

"Thank you," Renzo whispered, creeping out of the cabin. He climbed up on the deck and slid down the ladder.

The iced paving stones crackled like broken glass underfoot. Renzo sneaked through the quietest streets, avoiding the late-night cafés like agli Omnibus and Trovatore.

Down in the cavern, Renzo was horrified to find the mermaids busily dismantling the Seldom Seen Press. They were carefully wrapping in dried seaweed the printing machine's struts of fish bones, levers of oyster shells and pearl buttons. While they worked, they sang a sea shanty that sounded odd, until Renzo realized that the words were in English. Other mermaids floated in a torpid state, muttering and snoring, while thin crusts of ice formed around their tails.

"You can't be leaving us!" he gasped.

"'Tis dat giddy kipper, the Studious Son, come among us!" called Flos. "Where's the Undrowned Child, bless 'er 'eart?"

Lussa glided forward, flicking her tail. The ice that coated it shattered and sprayed the gold mosaic walls with shards, ringing out like gunshot. "What has come to pass, Lorenzo?"

He explained about the icehouse and Teo's descent into semiconsciousness, lamenting, "Signor Rioba's handbills haven't worked—no one in Venice believes what is going on aboard the *Scilla*. There's no one to help us against Miss Uish. She can kill Teo if she wants to. No one would ever know."

"Poor Suffering Child!" Lussa grieved. "But Lorenzo, have You petitioned the Ship's Cat? Is the Beast properly Invested?"

"Oh, she's the model of a ship's cat. But Sofonisba doesn't care for any of the sailors, I'm afraid. So no, I haven't asked her."

"Ah, the old Boy/Cat Problem. She might care for Teodora. I presume the Cat has sniffed out her True Sex? Yar. So appeal directly to the Beast. You of all People know that Something in Cats' Higher Natures can come forth in an Emergency."

Renzo nodded, remembering how a cat called the Gray Lady had given her life to protect the precious Spell Almanac from Il Traditore. And during the battle in the lagoon, teams of winged Syrian cats rescued prisoners from cages in the enemies' masts, flying them to safety on Persian carpets. And Venice's winged lions, who'd come to life to defend their city, were nothing if not cats.

"Absolutely. I'll try Sofonisba," Renzo said eagerly, "soon as I can find her."

Since Miss Uish had appeared on the *Scilla*, Sofonisba had kept herself hidden away as much as possible. Renzo explained to the mermaids that Miss Uish took every opportunity to grind Sofonisba's tail with her sharp-heeled boots.

"So," pronounced Flos, "if da estimable feline's da sworn enemy of dat baggin' Uish woman, then it makes sense she'll be pantin' to help one of her victims, woan she jest? No matter how cattishly contrariwise dat Sofonisba's a-feeling! Now this palaver ain't filling da floating portmanteau, is it?" Flos busied herself with inserting the coral letterforms of the Seldom Seen Press into velvet pouches.

Renzo tried to keep the plaintive note out of his voice. "How can you leave at a time like this? Aren't you supposed to be Venice's Protectresses?"

"We are summoned to the North, Lorenzo. And in any Case, We must leave. In this cold, Lorenzo," replied Lussa, "my Pretty Ladies are reduced to a State of Torpor. We cannot be Vigorous Defenders of Venice if We are but Half-Conscious or Dying."

The sleepy voices of the mermaids chanted:

"Bajamonte's gone to sea,
Roasted wraiths upon his knee,
He'll come back and murder me,
Bad old Bajamonte.
Bajamonte's fat and fair,
Eats goat stew and bottled bear;
I'll hate him for evermair,
Bad old Bajamonte."

"I don't believe those are quite the original words," remarked Renzo.

"Yar," said Lussa, and shrugged, "but at least the Frightful Naughtiness keeps some of my Ladies sufficiently Awake to prepare for our Journey."

Renzo asked, "But why north, Lussa? Where?"

"To Britannia herself."

"London?" Renzo leaned forward avidly. Then he paled, "But someone is killing mermaids in London, Lussa!"

"London! London! London!" screeched the parrots, waking up a few of the snoring mermaids, who shouted, "Roasted Wraiths!" and "Bottled Bears!" and "Yoiks!" before slipping back to sleep.

Lussa explained, "Seashells have arrived from our Sister-Mermaids on the Thames. The London Mermaids insist that their Troubles have *a Venetian Flavor* and that We must rush to their Aid. They dare not leave their Cavern after what befell the Melusine. More Shells arrive each Morning, each increasingly Desperate. Yet behold their Script, Lorenzo. Is it not strangely Languid? Almost Drunken?"

Lussa held out a scallop shell scrawled with girlish loops.

116

"We fear that London has already fallen to the same Baddened Magic that threatens Venice."

"London too! Why would Bajamonte Tiepolo . . . ? Why can't her own magical creatures help her?"

"Since the Murder of the Melusine, it seems there's scant other Help for London. For all her Greatness, Britannia's own Magic has been Dulled by Decades of Severe Rationality imposed by her Human Queen.

"London once had more Ghosts per Square Mile than any other Place on Earth. But Victoria was not amused by the Idea of Fairies, Ghosts or Good Spirits. The English Queen's little Mouth has always enjoyed a Sulky Pout more than a healthy Scream of Fright or Wonder. For the Londoners, 'Tis Manifest that Industry works, makes Money, builds Factories. They have mistaken Speed & Grand Scale for Magic.

"So Britannia's own Magic has gradually Stilled to almost Nothing. Her Haunted Houses have been Razed to build Railway Arches. Paved over are her Plague Cemeteries & the Graves of Those who died in the Great Fire of 1666. London's Ghosts have been Dispossessed, & have given up the Ghost, as It were. Now there are just a few Fairies at the Bottoms of Surburban Gardens."

"My father loved London . . . ," Renzo began, but Lussa interrupted.

"Do not fear, Lorenzo. We would wish to take care of London, as we take care of Venice. We have already dispatched Three Dozen of our Incogniti to set up a Business selling Hot Spiced Pumpkin. The Londoners shall quickly come to love It as a Delicacy, just as the Venetians do. Our Incogniti shall ply their Wares on Barrows at populous Corners and so gather Knowledge for Us. They are also to parley with the Thousands of Italian Children who play the Barrel Organ, or exhibit Performing Squirrels, White Mice & Dancing Dogs in London.

"Meanwhile, the London Mermaids' Shells tell Us that the imminent Death of the English Queen bodes no Good for Anyone. . . ."

Flos called out, "Da turtleshell shows dat da Uish woman's gettin' ready for to leave her party. Ye better make with da legs, Studious Son!"

19. Sofonisba's tongue

aboard the Scilla, *January 9 and 10, 1901*

Sofonisba listened to Renzo with a tolerant expression.

"Teodoro, the boy-girl?" yawned Sofonisba.

"Shh. No one's to know that."

"And you want me to help how?"

"Go down to the icehouse and try to warm up her body with your fur. You know Teo . . . is . . . special," wheedled Renzo.

"Evidently," remarked Sofonisba. "Not many girls can turn a boy that red in the face."

"It's just that . . . I . . . ," stammered Renzo.

"Whatever it is you're quite unable to say," remarked Sofonisba, "is likely to be supremely uninteresting to me. However."

Ten minutes later, Teo awoke from her iced stupor to the sound of purring and a tickling feeling in her face. Above her, something heavy thumped across the deck.

She did not really wish to be roused back to the real world, where there was biting cold and cruelty, and no sense of hope whatsoever. It was better simply to fade away. No more floggings, no more hunger. No more fear.

A rasping feeling invaded her left hand. Teo opened one eye. Sofonisba was busily licking the feeling back into her fingers. Teo was not grateful: as the numbness disappeared, stabbing pains ran through each hand.

"Avast licking there!" she implored the cat. "Just let me be."

In answer, the cat set to work licking some pink back into Teo's blue feet.

When it became apparent that the icehouse was not going to kill Teo, Miss Uish freed her.

"I suppose you're faintly more use alive than dead," she said with a sniff the next morning, hauling Teo up by her elbows and dumping her on deck. "You're the orphan with the best aptitude for English, apart from the St—Renzo."

Renzo quietly approached with a blanket, while Miss Uish bent to light one of her bitter cigars with a piece of curled paper she took from a sack on the deck. It was the latest of Signor Rioba's handbills unmasking the true situation of the *Scilla*'s orphans. From the look of the bulging sacks, there were none left in Venice.

Renzo, wrapping the blanket around Teo's shoulders, pointed silently. Teo thought, "No one in Venice knows what's happening to us. She's made sure of that."

Miss Uish's attention had wandered to Rosato and Giovanni, who were struggling to position a large boarded-up crate. "Show me some speed!" she snarled. "Or I'll show you something you won't like."

The thumping noise Teo had heard down in the icehouse was

now revealed as the commotion of ten such crates being winched on deck. She knew better than to ask Miss Uish what those boxes contained. Miss Uish was too happy, purring over the cases, slapping any boy who handled his corner clumsily, all the time urging haste.

Rosato and Sebastiano were set to drilling round holes just under the stanchions of the *Scilla*.

"Ten inches in diameter," shrilled Miss Uish. "Not a fraction more, and not a fraction less. Or there'll be consequences. Bring up the supplies! And pull those chicken coops up now! Faster! We're days behind as it is, you laggards! If I miss my rendezvous because of you . . . !"

Indignant squawking from below announced the arrival of fourteen crated hens, a rooster and several ducks. The "supplies," shrouded in sacks, clinked loudly. There were also sacks of flour and flasks of vinegar.

"Why are we provisioning the ship like this?" Teo asked Renzo. "It's as if we're getting ready for a voyage. We're not going anywhere, are we?"

20. The Half-dead disease

on the streets of Venice and aboard the Scilla, *January 8–10, 1901*

The temperature plunged, freezing the mercury inside the *Scilla*'s thermometer. Stalactites hung from the Rialto Bridge. In the smaller canals, the water no longer writhed under the crust of ice, but lay stilled to the consistency of cold porridge. The crenellations of the palaces were laced with ribbons of frost.

It was not just Venice that was freezing: the Venetians themselves were chilled to their souls. On the morning of January 8, the first person had fallen ill with a mysterious new malady. By that evening, hundreds had taken to their beds, the color draining from their complexions, the skin turning stiffly waxen on their faces and hands.

Someone coined an ominous name for the sickness: the Half-Dead disease.

People with the Half-Dead disease were easily recognized. Their heads nodded pale and frail like snowdrops; they were indifferent to every suggestion, caring not a jot about what happened to them. Sufferers claimed they saw everything through a thick white veil. They hallucinated, whispering of ghosts and mythical creatures. And they were never hungry, or thirsty. Their gums blackened. They just wanted to lie down. Many would never get up again.

The old, the weak and the miserable were quickly carried off by the pestilence. By the third day, it had begun to gnaw on the feelings and the bodies of the healthy too.

The Half-Dead disease was spreading as fast as the Plague that once destroyed a third of the city's population. The Mayor, as ever, tried to play it down. **Piffle!** he scoffed in a newspaper interview. **Some people will do anything to get the day off work, when all they have is a simple head-cold.**

Miss Uish was delighted by the advent of a new way to "toughen" her "lily-livered Venetian blanket-sops."

"Half-Dead disease?" she purred to the boys lined up on deck. "Let me tell you my simple cure. Hard work and a light diet! I want this boat utterly seaworthy and quick smart. Anyone who snivels gets six lashes."

The snivel froze in white trails under their noses.

Just after supper on January 10, a flock of cormorants winged blackly out of the mist and settled on the masts of the *Scilla*. It seemed as if they brought a new shudder of cold with them. Miss Uish walked around the deck, rubbing her hands with pleasure. She murmured to Peaglum, "At last! We'll have our *justification* tonight, if I'm not wrong. If it all works out . . . we'll be there at exactly the right moment!

"And the beauty of it is—the idiot Venetians will be *so* grateful to us for getting their orphans away from the dangerous ice!" She giggled.

The young sailors were ordered to scrub the cormorant droppings off the deck—a thankless, endless task in a rising wind. They went to sleep shortly after midnight. Three hours later, they were jolted awake in their hammocks by a loud crack, like a cannon being fired.

"What's that noise?"

Another low banging noise echoed through the *Scilla*.

"It is the ice, surrounding us," whispered Massimo.

"If the Giudecca Canal freezes over, it will crush the ship," Emilio said in a quavering voice.

"And drag us down to the sea floor with the weight of the ice," added Marco quietly.

Miss Uish's voice rang down joyfully through the booby hatch, "Malfeasance! All is ready! So get those whining laggards on deck!"

"They're sleepin' like lambs, Mistress," simpered Peaglum.

"Then poke them with the toasting fork till they wake. Tie every tenth child to its hammock. Make sure you get . . . *you* know the one. And we might as well keep the Nestle Tripe, as it speaks English so well. And any other remotely useful ones. Send me two strong little brutes immediately for duty. Put the others ashore. We're setting sail!"

21. Skeleton crew

the early hours, the Venetian lagoon, January 10, 1901

The *Scilla* crept out of the *bacino* in the dead of night. Sebastiano and Marco were set to bracing the yards, brailing the spanker and cluing up the mizzen-royal.

Lashed to their hammocks, the remaining sailors exchanged fearful whispers.

"Where are we going? Did Miss Uish tell the school inspectors that we were leaving?" demanded Emilio.

"And why did she put most of the boys ashore?" wondered Teo.

"So as not to have to feed 'em, I s'pose," sighed Giovanni.

"How many of us are left," asked Massimo, "all together?"

"There's you, Teo, Renzo, Emilio, Fabrizio, Rosato, Alfredo and me," counted Giovanni.

"And she's got Seba and Marco up on deck with her. Ten. And Sofonisba," agreed Alfredo tenderly. He loved that cat, and she had come to an understanding with him, sometimes allowing him to stroke her.

"But why us?" Rosato asked.

"I guess we're all good for something," realized Massimo.

"I'm best at net repair and sewing, Teo and Renzo are clever at English, and just about everything in books. Renzo's our wheelman, Giovanni's the top parrot-trainer, Emilio's brilliant at telling the weather, Sebastiano's the master knotsman, Fabrizio's got the sharpest eyes and ears, Rosato is good at woodwork . . ."

"Sssssh! There's her lamp. She's coming. Pretend to be asleep."

"Show a leg, sack-rats!" roared the dreaded harsh voice. Each child in turn felt the rasp of her cold hands as she slit their bonds. "All hands ahoy! Amain! You lot are to be on deck in five minutes. Up the crow's nest, Fabrizio. The others, scrubbing and seaming for you."

"But it's not yet light, is it?" whimpered Emilio unwisely. "Ma'am."

"Will that matter, on your hands and knees? You can smell the dirt that close up. Put Emilio Ghezzo on my list, Malfeasance!"

"Please, ma'am, can we . . . ?" pleaded Giovanni. His growling belly finished the sentence.

"You'll get food when you've done something to earn it."

The faintest dawn light in the porthole revealed that the *Scilla* had already passed into a remote corner of the lagoon. Then the mist opened in pockets to show ghostly jujube trees weighed down with rotted black berries.

"We're heading toward open sea," whispered Renzo to Teo at the water barrel, where they were breaking ice.

They passed islands where ragged nets hung on poles that leaned out of the water at crooked angles. Teo's and Renzo's eyes met sadly: they both realized that the fishermen who once tended those nets must have been drowned in the ice storm.

"Renzo!" exclaimed Teo. "Look at all those books!"

Jostling between the poles were hundreds of Venice's lost volumes, which had been borne away by the flood.

"Can you see *The Key to the Secret City?*" Renzo bent eagerly over the rail.

"Too many of them to know. But look how the books are pushing the poles together," Teo said. "It's as if they are forming letters and words."

"Your eyes are playing tricks on you, Teo," said Emilio. "It's barely light."

"No, I'm sure I'm right." Teo turned to Renzo, and traced the lettering below them with a silent finger.

The other boys saw it too now. They grew as pale as she was.

The poles said TURN BACK NOW. PERIL AHEAD.

Hope faded in ten young hearts in that moment.

"It means she's going to kill us all, one by one," wept Sebastiano.

Miss Uish steered the ship away from the shores of the Adriatic, and as far away as possible from any passing craft. The sea seemed uneasy; sharp waves broke almost vindictively against the prow. Great hollow-fronted rollers snarled around the stern like hungry jaws.

The *Scilla* strained against the swell. Miss Uish showed the poor old ship no mercy. The sailors spent all their time attending to the *Scilla*. They patched canvas, spliced ropes and pumped the bilges. To keep her watertight, they had hacked the old oakum from the seams in the boards with a jerry iron. Then they prodded new oakum into the gaps with the caulking iron, carefully ladling hot pitch to seal it.

Miss Uish ordered Massimo and Giovanni to be lashed about the waist and ankles, then suspended upside down over the side of the ship to tar her outer seams. The boys were eventually hauled back up, soaked to the skin, numb and feverish.

Even when the swell receded, the waves whispered like malicious girls gossiping in a schoolyard. And what was down there, below them? Sometimes there were juddering noises in the water, and a sound like deep, heavy breathing. Teo overheard Emilio and Massimo talking about giant sea monsters.

"Everyone," Emilio insisted, "said that something more powerful than water must have smashed the seawalls on Christmas Eve."

"Quiet!" shouted Miss Uish, coming up behind the boys. "Less talk and more speed." She muttered to herself, "The birds say the old bezzom's fading fast."

At dawn on January 12, a roll of drums summoned all the sailors to the deck. Sofonisba was howling in a cage, her tail puffed up like a feather duster.

"This is how I deal with ill-discipline aboard my ship," announced Miss Uish. "This creature has spurned the rats so plentifully provided, and this evening committed the impertinent act

128

of stealing my roast chicken supper—the supper of the representative of Her Majesty Queen Victoria!"

She brandished a cutlass. "My first thought was to drown the creature in the water barrel. I thought you'd like that, brats, a little extra flavor to your drinking water. But that death would be too quick."

None too gently, Peaglum poked the cat out of her cage with a pole.

"Now, walk the plank!" ordered Miss Uish.

"Throwing the ship's cat overboard is guaranteed to bring on a storm!" Teo spoke desperately and fast.

"Do you think a fine British lady like me would lower herself to believe in such murky feline superstitions?" cried Miss Uish. "Queen Victoria and her Empire are utterly and irreproachably rational!"

Sofonisba looked around at the sailors. Her triangular face was tight with fear. Her eyes filmed over with what looked like tears. Her flanks trembled. Yet even *in extremis*, Sofonisba refused to talk in front of her enemy. Alfredo reached toward her, and Miss Uish cracked her whip once, sharply. Shrieking with pain, the boy tucked his hands under his armpits.

The cat nodded sadly. Alfredo was the only boy she half tolerated. But it was clear that she did not want any more children hurt on her behalf. Slowly, Sofonisba walked along the plank until she reached the very tip. Her weight made the plank vibrate slightly. For a moment, she rocked there. She gave one final long look back, a look that broke the heart of every sailor on the deck; then she lifted her head proudly, stepped off the end of the plank and was seen no more.

There was not even a splash.

"Sofonisba," wept Teo, not caring who saw her.

"Extra scrubbing duty for the crybaby Nestle Tripe," shouted Miss Uish.

The sailors braced themselves for the expected storm. Instead, the sky waxed a deadened gray, with no more wind than would stir a sigh in the sails.

In the absence of Sofonisba, the rat population quickly trebled. The rats scorned cod sponge and mock fish soup. Instead, they took to gnawing on the oakum and the woodwork, apparently finding it tastier than the boys' rations. While the others pitched and sealed, it was full-time work for Rosato and Sebastiano just baiting and emptying the rat-traps. All the rats they dropped overboard disappeared instantly, as if being sucked below by powerful currents.

Other jobs were more mysterious. Why, for example, were the sailors required to spend the next evening blowing on their frozen fingers while they sewed flags of every nation in Europe?

And why was Miss Uish so fretful at their lack of speed, constantly and bitterly bemoaning the lack of wind? They crumbled the increasingly greenish bread for their watery gruel, which, in that pale, sinister light, looked like liquefied ghost strained into a bowl. They snatched sleep in their damp quarters, which stank of hot tar, swampy bilge water, boiled bones and unwashed bodies. And the next day they rose before dawn and did the same again.

It was oppressive, often painful and dismally dull. On their starvation diet, the sailors began to grow vague and dreamy. They

130

had visions of roast beef and sausages, except Teo, who saw chocolate cake and pea risotto. Once, in her delirium, as she plunged a red-hot loggerhead into a bucket of tar, Teo even thought she saw, through the hissing steam, a cat just like poor Sofonisba. Mysteriously, this phantom cat was dashing down the companionway with a pear in its mouth.

She shook herself, whispering, "Hallucinations! Isn't that how the Half-Dead disease starts?"

22. Pirate charter

at sea, the Adriatic, January 15 and 16, 1901

Miss Uish rapped, "Full assembly at five bells and there shall be no more sulky faces. Cookie, you should mark this on your calendar! January 15, 1901, a red-letter day!"

At five bells, the sailors gathered nervously on deck, to find Miss Uish nailing a large notice on the wall of the forecastle.

"Welcome to your Swearing-in Ceremony, brats!" She showed them her sharp white teeth and pointed to the notice.

It was entitled *CODE OF CONDUCT*.

"Read it and weep," said Miss Uish cheerfully. The sailors crowded around the forecastle and peered at the words.

> 1. *The crew shall heed the captain's commands without exception. When so ordered, they shall board other ships, take spoils and capture prisoners.*
>
> 2. *No female, excepting the captain and certain hostages selected by her, shall be permitted on the vessel, on pain of certain, painful and lingering death.*
>
> 3. *Shares of the spoils: the crew shall be entitled to precisely none.*

4. *Punishment for stealing food: to be marooned on the nearest island.*

5. *Punishment for insubordination: infinite, at the discretion of the captain.*

6. *Punishment for attempted mutiny: to have the nose and ears split with a silver dagger, followed by death.*

Teo scanned the list, feeling increasingly weak at the knees, especially at the sight of item 2. Renzo finished reading while everyone except Teo was still on the first clause. He exclaimed, "This isn't a Code of Conduct. This is a *pirate charter*! Pirates are murderous cowards. They attack unarmed vessels. They rob! That is *completely* un-Venetian! And *completely* un-British, by the way! I'm not swearing to this!"

Miss Uish looked down at him with her impish smile. "I rather think you are," she cooed.

Peaglum had set out a black flag and a human skull on a small table. He himself was ceremonially attired in a black frock coat and an eye patch. A row of medals, quite obviously stolen, and a dilapidated black parrot on his shoulder completed his outfit.

"One by one, step forward," ordered Miss Uish, shrugging on a red smock and a feathered hat, and fastening a cutlass at her waist. A silver pistol glinted in a holster at her hip. "Take the skull in your left hand, and place your right hand on your heart, and repeat after me, as I direct you."

No one stepped forward. No one even breathed.

"I see that I shall have to choose a volunteer," observed Miss Uish. "Renzo, were you not the little lord who said he didn't care to sign? What fun! Step forward."

Renzo did so. She boxed his ears smartly. "I said step forward.

recall saying 'quiver like a jelly.' And now—some amus-
playacting! We are going to perform a mock trial, British
miralty–style, to show what would happen to any crew mem-
ers foolish enough to disobey my orders, or so stupid as to get
captured."

Peaglum now produced a canvas swag of accessories—a London policeman's bulbous hat, a truncheon, a shabby lawyer's wig,
a judge's gavel.

"Have you heard of Newgate Prison, whelp?"

Renzo nodded wordlessly. His father had told him of its grim
gates and grimmer history.

"It's the last place most criminals see before they are hanged.
Fine high and spiked walls it has too. It's a stinking, brooding, windowless place. If the Londoners were not so supremely rational,
they would say it was haunted. So many dreadful deaths there!"
Miss Uish smiled sweetly.

One by one, Peaglum played the roles of policeman, Newgate
Prison jailer, lawyer, judge and hangman. Renzo was arrested for
piracy and carried off to Newgate (Peaglum struck a stanchion
with a belaying-pin to convey the dread sound of those fearsome
gates clanging shut). He was then tried, convicted and "carried
out"—right to the point where his head was thrust in a noose.

"So, brats, the purpose of this pantomime has been to show
you what will happen if you are caught by . . . shall we say . . . the
Forces of Order."

Teo protested, "You said you were a representative of Her Majesty Queen Victoria! Why should the Forces of Order want to punish us if we're in your care?" Belatedly, she added, "Ma'am."

"And indeed I did say something of the sort, I believe," Miss
Uish remarked. "But that was when I was still in Venice and needed

to persuade the foolish Venetians to let me take over this ship and her mangy crew. Now I sail under a different flag. Time to show our true colors. Malfeasance!"

Peaglum drew on the flag-rope and unfurled a great smoky-black skull-and-crossbones. Then he moved to the nearest shrouded crate, slit the rope, lifted the canvas and opened a sliding door. Inside crouched a black cannon with an ugly wide snout and a stack of crude gray metal balls.

Massimo asked disbelievingly, "We made the holes in the sides for *cannons?*"

"That boy's powers of deduction are sharp as a dagger," said Miss Uish. "So sharp he might cut himself. If someone doesn't do it for him first."

Although she already knew the answer, Teo couldn't help asking, "What if we don't *want* to be pirates?"

"Do you think anyone remotely cares what you want?"

"So we shall be *punished* if we don't obey you, and yet we may also be executed by the Forces of Order if we do?" asked Renzo slowly.

"Precisely. And in the meantime, you've nowhere to run to, unless you fancy hanging up your hammock on the ocean floor."

Miss Uish unfurled another flag, this one bloodred with a black skull grinning on it. Renzo paled. "That's the *jolie rouge*," he whispered.

"Yes, isn't it a pretty red? What a *studious* brat this one is!" Miss Uish giggled. "And does the clever boy know what it means?"

Teo's and Renzo's eyes met. Why was she using the word "studious"?

"It means no quarter," replied Renzo. "It means that the crew of this ship intend to kill all whom they capture."

"Indeed. And in the meantime we'll be making use of your needlework."

"The flags we sewed, of all nations?" Massimo's voice was eager. His own, in Portuguese colors, had been a masterpiece.

"Nothing to be happy about!" hissed Renzo. "Every time we approach the ship of any nation, she'll make us fly their flag. Until they're close enough to attack."

"And then we put up the *jolie rouge*? That's dishonorable!" cried Teo.

"Utterly," exulted Miss Uish. "And the beauty of it is, we'll not lose a day's progress. We'll just be arriving . . . a little richer."

They took their first ship in the early hours of the next morning. Their victim was French, easily identified by the jib-sails. Spanish and English vessels had one; French boats two.

All through the night, while they stalked the graceful boat, the sailors were kept busy oiling the cannons, learning to maneuver them silently out of their enclosures, and how to load and fire. Teo let go at the wrong moment, nearly losing a leg as the great gun careered into the taffrail. The stanchion creaked, then cracked, and the cannon dropped into the sea.

The sailors stood in silence, gazing at the black waves. They dared not turn around when brisk, furious footsteps bore down on them.

"You weakened that stanchion with your careless holes!" shrilled Miss Uish, holding a lantern over the damage. "Sabotage me, would you?"

The punishment was a promise of "ducks' breakfast"—cold water and nothing to eat the next day. Set to mending the broken stanchion, they were distracted by their painfully empty bellies; Miss Uish, however, had eyes only for the French boat.

Finally, just before dawn, Miss Uish steered the *Scilla* within close range. A fading moon showed the name carved on its escutcheon: the *Rose la Touche*.

"Don't use up all the ammunition, curs!" she warned. "We can't just go to the nearest chandler's shop and buy more! Cutlasses will be of more use to you."

Peaglum laid out an array of curved swords on the deck, sneering, "Choose your toys, babies."

"I will not kill anyone!" insisted Teo. "I am a vegetarian."

"Just as well," said Miss Uish. "I need a hostage."

She jerked her head at Peaglum, who swiftly bound Teo's hands behind her back. Then he drew a noose around her neck, having moistened the rope first by dipping it in the water barrel. He tied the ends of the rope to a hook on the deck.

"You see that noose, offal?" rapped Miss Uish. "As the sun rises, the rope will start to dry. As it dries, it will contract and tighten. Unless you little cowards board the *Rose la Touche* and take her before the sun's fully up—well, your Nestle-Triping little friend will choke to death."

Then she shouted, "Massimo, time to take down that amusing French flag and raise the pretty *jolie rouge*."

While the other boys helped Massimo hoist the flag, Renzo quietly broke a handful of ice from the water barrel and slipped over to Teo. He spread the ice over Teo's noose.

"Ooh!" she protested.

"It will melt slowly; give you more time before the rope shrinks," he whispered. She tried to nod, but the noose was already too tight.

The *Rose la Touche* was sleeping peacefully. Even the second mate dozed at the wheel. No one saw the *Scilla* counter-brace, come to and tie up alongside, or the boys jump the narrow gap between the two decks. They were followed by Miss Uish and Peaglum, who were dressed in hooded black suits that obscured all but their eyes.

The first thing the poor crew heard was Peaglum shouting, "Strike amain!"

Miss Uish herself slit the second mate's throat.

The boys cried out in horror. Alfredo retched.

Peaglum roped the other French mariners together and bound their mouths. Rosato and Emilio were ordered to gather the crew's rifles. At gunpoint, Peaglum marched the *Rose*'s captain and first mate over to the *Scilla*, and then noosed them like Teo, kicking them alongside her.

Teo stared at them. Morning was starting to glimmer in the sky, and the rope was perceptibly tightening around her neck. The French hostages stared back and then up at the *jolie rouge* in silent understanding.

Nimbly, Peaglum rejoined the *Rose*. He hollered belowdecks to all the ship's company, "Anyone want to see a French first mate dance on a rope?"

The *Rose*'s passengers shuffled onto the deck, bleary-eyed and dressed only in their nightshirts. At the sight of the second mate's limp body, the women began to weep. The men looked at Miss Uish and Peaglum, and at the Venetian boys cowering behind them. Miss Uish pushed Renzo in front of her.

"Take a good look at him," she told the *Rose*'s passengers. "He may be small, but I assure you this one's as bloodthirsty a pirate as you'll ever see. Any attempt to resist, and this savage boy shall make sure that your crewmen over on our boat will go the same way as their second mate before one of you can point a gun. Without them, you landlubbers are dead as nails in these seas. Search the vessel. Alfredo, Giovanni—abaft! The others, afore!"

The boys crept through the cabins and staterooms, rifling shamefacedly through jewelry boxes and travel desks. Each brought his haul up on deck and dropped it at Miss Uish's feet. As the pile of gems, fans, snuffboxes and jeweled daggers mounted, she grew almost delirious with delight, raking through the emeralds, amethysts, rubies and opals with her fur-booted foot.

"How he will love me for these!" she murmured fondly.

"Carry the spoils to our boat, offal!" she shouted. "And quickly. Look at the sun rising! Think of your friend, the Nestle Tripe."

When all the loot was safely stored on the *Scilla,* Miss Uish and Peaglum pushed their French hostages overboard. The *Scilla* sailed smoothly away. Renzo rushed to cut Teo's noose with his *ferro* penknife.

"That was fun, wasn't it, brats?" said Miss Uish. "I'm sure you're already looking forward to the next time. Now let's take advantage of that breeze!"

All the seafaring and sailoring they'd learned under Professor Marìn was now used to prey on innocent vessels.

Over the next three days, Miss Uish taught the *Scilla*'s sailors new talents that would have shocked and grieved the professor.

Miss Uish set Renzo to carving sharp bone-jacks in the shape of crows' feet. These were lobbed onto the decks of the ships they preyed upon, causing the poor barefoot sailors terrible wounds, as they ran about in confusion while Peaglum catapulted grenades of burning tar among them.

The gunholes of the *Scilla* were plugged with pieces of wood so as to be invisible to their victims until it was too late. And then Miss Uish had Teo dress up as a girl in a gown pirated from the *Rose la Touche*. A wig of blond curls was crammed onto her shaven head, under a frilly bonnet, and she was forced to parade up and down with a parasol, in full view of any spyglass that might be trained on the *Scilla* from the ships they stalked.

Nothing could seem more innocent than a little girl in a white dress strolling the deck in the shade of a lacy parasol. Miss Uish even had Cookie serve Teo an elegant repast on a bone-china tea set. Of course, the cakes were made of soap and the tea of dishwater.

"Why me?" Teo tried to keep her voice low and boyish. Had Miss Uish guessed her secret?

"You're the smallest and the skinniest, Nestle Tripe. You look harmless from a distance. What a sweet girlie you make! They'd never guess you are a nasty, dirty little boy. If you spill anything on that pretty dress, I'll slap you fore and aft."

Miss Uish thrust her beautiful wild face close to Teo's and laughed. Then she shouted at Giovanni, "Bring me a fresh parrot!"

For Miss Uish had found a way to extract even hidden treasure from the boats they attacked. She took prisoners for ransom. The *Scilla* would be moored a short distance from the defeated vessel, while Giovanni was set to training parrots to recite ransom notes complete with terrible threats.

140

Everyone took the parrots seriously when they perfectly imitated the voice of the hostage crying "Help! Don't! Please don't!" followed by a scream. The families and friends tucked the ransom money into pouches, which the parrots wore around their necks. After she'd counted the money, Miss Uish pushed her victims into the sea, where they invariably disappeared as quickly and mysteriously as the dead rats.

The sailors soon learned to dread the sight of a sail on the horizon. Lateen-sailed poleacres, Danish schooners, Dutch galliots: Miss Uish did not seem to care, as long as they could be taken quickly and relieved of their coins and jewels. For Miss Uish begrudged every hour not spent surging ahead at full speed.

And she always pushed Renzo forward, displaying him to the passengers of every ship they took.

"Did you ever see a nastier piece of work?" she'd ask them. "Take a good look at that face! Is it not the image of a savage pirate? I declare I'm terrified of him myself."

23. Bad blood

The Pretender was on deck shooting gulls when the news flew in from Osborne House.

Queen Victoria had suffered a stroke. The left side of her face was sagging. The cormorants reported that she rarely spoke now, and never lucidly.

Minutes later came other welcome news, this time from the Adriatic Sea:

The lady has commenced her fund-raising activities on her way to our rendezvous. The Studious Son is playing his part famously—also, most visibly and most incriminatingly. Your part of the bargain will be fulfilled to perfection when he is delivered.

Signor Pipistrelly's cormorants arrived on cue just afterward. They carped: *"Your Ghost-Convicts cannot be restrained from stealing sheep, which draws unwelcome attention to our activities. But at least the creatures keep the barn warm. Meanwhile, I have been recruiting most successfully in the prisons of northern France on your behalf. Is the girl delivered yet?"*

Harold Hoskins dispatched a reply. *"She's already aboard the Little Beauty. A matter of hours, not days, till the handover."*

The girl did not matter. For the Pretender, the important thing was that Signor Pipistrelly was mustering the promised human forces on the French border. He breathed a sigh of relief. There had been days, early on, when he couldn't help wondering if Signor Pipistrelly really could deliver all that he had promised.

Now the *Kingmaker's Dame* was speeding through oceans at a rate that could only be described as magical. It was just ten days since they had set sail from Hooroo. Yet already the Spanish coastline lay to their starboard side.

The Pretender had always been a great hunter, burying his nervous energy in the bodies of animals. In the days before his own departure for the north, no wild boar or wallaby on Hooroo was safe from his shooting parties. The Pretender's trigger finger had also itched to dispatch a few braces of those sea-stinking Venetian seagulls that had arrived on Hooroo soon after Signor Pipistrelly, with their beaks weighed down with something that looked horribly like old bones.

Even the Pretender had been afraid of the consequences of that.

But whenever he felt a little uncomfortable about the pact he'd made with his unusual guest, well, then the Pretender had only to think of his hastily managed exit from England to feel perfectly righteous again.

How shamefully the old bezzom's courtiers had treated him! Those weasel words from the Prime Minister: "Such a respectable position guarding Her Majesty's most desperate criminals. A sojourn in the pleasant heat of the colonies would be just the thing for a man of your delicate health. Such an unfortunate disease!"

And the Prime Minister had dared to joke, "I hope there'll be no bad blood between you and our dear Queen over this!"

The cabinet ministers had smirked. And those simpering politicians had given Harold Hoskins an idea.

An idea he had shared with his guest. An idea that had grown into a plan. A plan that was now thrillingly under way.

"They'll be sorry soon," rejoiced the Pretender. "Signor Pipistrelly shall see to that."

Then, despite the sunshine, Harold Hoskins shivered.

Yes, Signor Pipistrelly was a terrifying ally, yet—the Pretender smiled as his rifle butt pointed toward a young albatross—how much worse to have him as an enemy?

24. Wort-cunning and leechcraft

aboard the Scilla, *in the southern Mediterranean Sea,*
January 17–19, 1901

The *Little Beauty* appeared to drift into the *Scilla's* clutches like a particularly negligent fly into a spider's web. The *Little Beauty's* Australian officers put up not one morsel of a fight. Miss Uish waved them all off alive, taking only one captive: a haughty English girl of pale coloring.

Miss Uish seemed particularly delighted at her capture, boasting that the girl was a very rich heiress who'd come straight from a Swiss finishing school. A private interview in her stateroom lasted a very long time. Yet the girl emerged cool and composed, instead of weeping for mercy as prisoners usually did. She had the air of someone born to be petted and served the best of everything.

"This one's a keeper," Miss Uish remarked, presenting the blond girl to her crew. "The longer we keep her, the more she'll be worth. She's called Sibella. *Miss* Sibella to you."

Miss Uish did not lose the opportunity to remind the sailors, "In London, of course, *all* children are as refined as Miss Sibella. None have felt the pinch of poverty. The boys wear moleskin waistcoats, greatcoats with velvet collars, and twenty-five-shilling hats.

The girls are got up in the daintiest dresses imaginable. Everyone carries a silk umbrella, of an elegance that you shabby Venetians could barely conceive."

Renzo's eyes widened. The other boys and Teo stared at the blond girl. Despite being the victim of a pirate kidnap, Sibella had managed to maintain a perfect coiffure and a spotless gown throughout. Her ringlets almost tinkled with the cold. A pair of pale blue eyes swept over the line of boys coolly until they arrived at Renzo. Subtly, she cast her eyes down quickly before raising them to stare him meltingly in the eye.

Teo bristled. "The flirt! Wait till she says something: then I'll see what she's really like from her handwriting!"

But Sibella seemed determined to speak only with her heavily fringed blue eyes, leaving all explanations to Miss Uish: "Our guest is a hemophiliac, so cannot take part in any strenuous activity."

"What's hemo-o?" asked Giovanni. "If you please, ma'am."

"Bad blood. That is, it does not clot properly. She could bleed to death internally from the slightest injury. It is a disease of the upper classes, so you'd know nothing about it, you Venetian vermin. Many of Queen Victoria's own family are sufferers. So you'll be treating Miss Sibella with kid gloves," warned Miss Uish, "like royalty, in fact, or you'll rue the day. And you'll speak English to her at all times."

Finally, Sibella drawled, "I don't wish to be any trouble, I'm sure."

Above Sibella's head, Teo saw the girl's words written in a tense script that seemed to wobble. She thought, "This girl is not what she pretends to be."

Teo turned to Renzo to ask his opinion, but he was gazing at

146

Sibella in awe. When Teo tugged his sleeve, he shook off her hand, in an absentminded way.

"I see," thought Teo. And she didn't like what she saw one bit.

Miss Uish had Rosato and Giovanni clear out a storeroom for Sibella to sleep in. She shared her own luxurious repasts with the prisoner.

Sibella immediately took over Teo's hated role of decoy, apparently with pleasure. She paraded on the deck, taking tiny steps, shaded by a silk parasol decked with more lace than a wedding dress.

All Sibella's clothes were white. Teo had not known that you could get so many shades of white, or that it came in crepe, poplin, batiste, pique and lawn, not to mention mousseline de laine, organdie, voile, gauze, dimity, tarlatan, jaconet and pompadour sateen. The new hostage changed her costume three times a day. As she appeared in each new outfit, Sibella made a point of explaining these terms.

"As if anyone cares," thought Teo, wiping her grimy face with a tattered sleeve.

Even Sibella's dainty shoes were white—satin slippers with a "baby Louis" heel. Her chatelaine bag, her muff and her fur necklet were all confected of the whitest rabbit fur. She wore extravagant amounts of jewelry for such a young girl. Rings flashed on her delicate fingers; pearls glowed at her throat. Pins set with diamonds or pearls secured her collars.

"Maria would love those sparklers," thought Teo. "Even though

Maria's learned her lesson now." Her old friend from Naples had been deceived by gifts of jewelry from Bajamonte Tiepolo. And nearly died as a result.

Maria had also shown something of Sibella's flirtatiousness in the old days, before her final encounter with Il Traditore. Yet Maria had been childish and innocent compared with Sibella, who seemed possessed of some ancient wisdom in the art of making people do what she wanted. Even Miss Uish was strangely deferential toward her. Peaglum bowed to her. The young sailors dared not say a word to Sibella, but they stared at her, charmed, confused and somewhat intimidated.

Only Renzo addressed Sibella directly. Miss Uish had appointed him Sibella's personal attendant. "You're to do for Miss Sibella whatever her heart desires." Miss Uish had exploded into giggles, nudging Peaglum in the ribs. "What larks!"

Renzo accompanied Sibella on her promenades, offering his arm and lifting dirty objects out of her way.

"Look at him playing the courtier," thought Teo resentfully. "How *does* she do it? Belay that Sibella! She's not royalty, even if she acts as though she is!"

The more she saw of Sibella, the less Teo believed in the hemophilia story. Sibella was fashionably pale, yet she did not look sick. There was a niggle at the back of Teo's mind: some teasing, un-pin-downable fact that bothered her about the disease. But she could not remember which of the many books and pages stored in her memory she needed to consult.

To Teo, there was a sinister ring to that glassy laugh of Sibella's. "She's not playing girl-games—this is something much worse."

Was Sibella some kind of enchantress, or even a ghost? Teo

ran through all the species of ghosts she knew. Sibella did not give off an icy aura like the in-the-Cold ghosts she and Renzo had met in the past. Nor was she miserable in their way. In fact, Sibella seemed extremely smug, especially when she was with Renzo.

She was certainly not mutilated like the in-the-Slaughterhouse spirits.

"No," thought Teo, "she's actually repulsively perfect. And she's not in-the-Meltings like Bajamonte Tiepolo." She shuddered at a memory of Il Traditore's not-quite-set skin and his fluid form. "Could she be a witch?"

In all the stories Teo had read, witches and enchantresses were usually wrinkled old women, or at least extremely grown-up.

Yet there *was* a kind of witchiness about the girl, in Teo's opinion. Sibella had some horrible hobbies. She practiced wortcunning and leechcraft, and was often to be seen bending over tiny pots of herbs and a tray of squirming black leeches by the forecastle.

While the sailor boys munched miserably on cod sponge, Miss Uish opened her private stores so that Sibella could mix flour, salt, honey, water and wine into a paste she fashioned into cakes the shape of the crescent moon. These were offered to the leeches and would disappear mysteriously overnight. She carried a little red bag of salt, a stone with a hole in it, also the herbs rue, vervain, paura and concordia. She had a lemon stuck full of different-colored pins: every color except black.

"This preserves good fortune," Sibella whispered confidentially to the circle of boys who had crept up to watch her play with her pets.

"The kind of good fortune that got you kidnapped by pirates like us?" asked Teo quietly.

Sibella appeared not to have heard. She was now busy teaching Renzo the art of "rhapsodomancy," which turned out to be divination by opening books of poetry at random. Sibella had come aboard the *Scilla* fully fitted out with a traveling library of sentimental verse. She and Renzo sat comfortably on deck, surrounded by piles of gold-stamped volumes.

"How vastly dull it is," observed Sibella, "to read a whole book. One should let Fate tell one which poems to read." She lowered her voice to a thrilling whisper. "It is also more exciting. Plus there is more time, then, to talk to interesting people. Like you, Renzo."

Teo, scrubbing the deck near their feet, muttered, "Who'd have thought the so-called Studious Son would ever think it dull to read a whole book?"

Sibella remarked, "There's something detestable about the name 'Teodoro.' I always thought I would give it to a pig if I had a farm."

In her mind's eye, Teo flicked angrily through *The Best Ways with Wayward Ghosts* and *Simple Solutions to Problem Spirits*, looking for a way into Sibella's secret. Professor Marìn's books suggested, "Ask the suspected spirit to name Six Good Things. If he or she cannot do so, then ask for Six Evil Things."

She strode up to Sibella when Miss Uish was below in her stateroom. But Sibella evaded Teo's questions by simpering, "How very banal."

Teo resolved to touch Sibella's chest, hoping that her old skill as a *Lettrice-del-cuore*, a reader of hearts, would reveal something about her. But as she slipped closer to Sibella, saying, "There's a piece of fluff on your gown," the girl turned on her sharply.

"I think you missed a bit of the deck where you were scrubbing. I can see a smudge of tar the size of your fist, Teo."

Fabrizio, detailed to dust Sibella's cabin, reported to the boys that, like Miss Uish, Sibella slept on a Chinese pillow box. When Teo confronted her with this fact, Sibella smiled serenely. "Of course. I keep my leeches inside."

Even Renzo looked somewhat squeamish at this revelation.

"I learn from them while I'm dreaming," she explained, "and they learn from me."

Teo whispered into Renzo's unwilling ear, "Don't you remember how Bajamonte Tiepolo put leeches in the statues so that they bled from their mouths? And don't you remember how those statues tried to kill you?"

It seemed that wherever Teo went, she came across Renzo and Sibella: giggling together by the water barrel, bent over a book by the booby hatch, or, on one painful occasion, whispering confidentially in a niche by the hawse.

"Do you want something?" inquired Sibella in a chilly tone.

"*We,*" reproved Renzo—with an especially deliberate and hurtful emphasis on the "We"—"are talking, Teo. Can't it wait?"

The other boys were jealous that Renzo was so favored by Sibella. They teased him at night while they lay in their hammocks.

"Renzo's in love!"

151

"Did you get a kiss yet?"

"Have one for me."

Renzo maintained a dignified silence. The most he would say was, "You wouldn't understand. Sibella is a lady."

"Like Miss Uish is a *lady*?" Teo asked.

As for the other boys, Teo burned to say, "Excuse me, but in case you haven't noticed, Sibella's a *girl*. Remember what you think about *girls*? I'm not going to forget everything I've heard you say about girls every night in my hammock; how is it that *you* have?"

Teo cornered Renzo alone in the galley, where he was collecting a tray of toast and jam for Sibella, who was served an English afternoon tea in her cabin when there were no vessels to lure.

"You seem uncommonly fascinated by her," remarked Teo, "our hostage."

"Not at all," Renzo replied. "I have to be nice to her. I'm under orders. Now, excuse me, Sibella's toast is getting cold. She likes it just so."

"Miss Uish is right, you make a fine waiter," muttered Teo. "Remember to roll those 'r's.'"

Renzo brushed past her.

Teo called after him, "She's a vile little flirt."

Renzo turned away, "I'm embarrassed for you, Teodora."

"Ssssh! Teodoro, I'm a *boy*, remember!"

"And very convincing you are too. Hard to believe you ever were a girl at all."

152

"One of you worthless wretches has been stealing fruit from my private larder," announced Miss Uish. "It would be better for you all if that creature came forward for his punishment."

Fear, not guilt, spread around the faces on deck.

Miss Uish tapped her fan impatiently. "How tedious you are, with your pathetic little loyalties. Do you know how I intend to repay them? Here's my plan. Each boy shall receive one lash from Mr. Peaglum here. If the offender does not step forward after you've all been lashed once, then we shall go through again. And I'll leave it to your imagination what will happen if someone does not confess after that."

Sibella appeared on the forecastle, delicately munching an apple. The eyes of every child on deck flew to the fruit. But Miss Uish declared, "A girl of this quality has no need to steal. You're all still under suspicion."

"Renzo," hissed Teo, "did you take that apple for Sibella?"

"Don't be ridiculous," Renzo whispered back. "Of course I didn't."

"You'd let us all get whipped for *her*?"

"I told you, I didn't do it," insisted Renzo.

Miss Uish called out, "The Nestle Tripe to be the first one bent over the barrel!"

Fortunately, a Spanish vessel hove into view before Peaglum could give his cat an outing. The boat proved so richly laden that Miss Uish forgot all about the apple and the whipping. She was too busy counting the gold coins and emptying the stolen jewel boxes.

After the Spanish ship had been stripped of its valuables, Fabrizio sidled up to Teo.

"Renzo's s'posed to be your friend, ain't he?" he hissed.

Teo nodded. "S'*posed* to be."

"Just about your *best* friend, I should think?"

"*Once*, he was," she thought. "Before Sibella."

"Well, I happened to be cleaning the keyhole to that Sibella's cabin and I heard her saying, 'You spoil me so, Lorenzo! Delicious! Everyone else is detestable, but you are such a *gentleman*. My family is sure to reward you when I am rescued.'" Fabrizio simpered just like Sibella. His good hearing gave him great skill in mimicking people. In his own voice, he asked, "And what do you think she was thanking him for? I'd say it was something sweet and round and crunchy, wouldn't you?"

He whistled and walked off, leaving Teo to her lonely thoughts.

So Renzo had lied to her, knowingly lied to her? If so, he had lied fluently, without showing a wrinkle of anxiety on his face. He wasn't even ashamed.

Teo's stomach churned miserably. This was worse than hunger. The rest of the day, whenever Renzo spoke to her, she averted her eyes.

That night, the two turned away from one other without even saying goodnight. Curled up in her blanket, Teo felt as if someone had forced a cold, sharp-edged pellet down her gullet. Wide awake, she gulped and gulped, unable to swallow her misery.

Renzo's back twitched slightly, yet he said nothing. He was either not interested in her suffering or asleep—or pretending to be.

And Sibella—did she know that Renzo had been lying to Teo?

Teo's bruised heart lurched. Of course Sibella knew. Sibella and Renzo were thick as thieves. Sibella would be enormously smug to know that at the snap of her fingers, or the bat of an eyelash, she could make Renzo betray the person who had once upon a time been his best friend.

Teo's wretched meditations were interrupted by a clattering in the mast, followed by a glad cry from Miss Uish. Sharp heels tapped across the deck over Teo's head.

"More cormorants," she thought glumly. "More stinking droppings to scrub off."

The birds squawked loudly and Miss Uish's voice mingled with theirs.

"It's as if she's talking to them!" Teo sat up in her hammock, straining to make sense of the eerie caws and cries.

She heard Miss Uish shout to Peaglum, "Failing fast now! We must put on more speed if we're to get there in time for the funeral!"

Now Fabrizio too had woken. Teo detected his eyes glittering with fear in the dim light.

"Whose funeral, Teo?" he asked.

25. Rack off!

Osborne House, the Isle of Wight, January 19–21, 1901

Bertie, Prince of Wales, was the person most immediately affected by his mother's decline. He'd been waiting six decades for his chance at the most important job on earth. But he was not one bit prepared for it. Queen Victoria, who'd never entertained a high opinion of her eldest son's brains, had shooed him out of public life. Bertie took every opportunity to enjoy himself while he could. Now his half-century of playtime was nearly over.

On January 19, the Prince of Wales heard the truth from Queen Victoria's doctor: it was just a matter of time. Next, he had to contend with his sisters, known as the Petticoats, who were rampaging around the great ugly house in a state of twittering outrage. Harold Hoskins, they'd just heard, was shortly due at Osborne. Not only was he deeply unpopular with his family, but worse still, he was a lord! All the delicate protocols would be turned upside down, whimpered the Petticoats, and everyone would be obliged to kowtow to that pompous creature. And how had he known to turn up now? How had he got to English waters so quickly?

Of course, the truth about the Queen's condition could not stay locked up inside Osborne House. Already, the rumor-mill of the British Empire was grinding at a hysterical speed. When Queen Victoria's favorite vicar arrived on the Isle of Wight that night, he was accompanied by the first hounds of the press, sniffing on the trail of the story of the century.

Church attendance was particularly heavy all over the kingdom. The Sunday sermons openly spoke of the great loss that was to befall the nation. The *Times* reported a sense of impending sadness from Calcutta to Cape Town. The *New York Times* headlined with **QUEEN VICTORIA AT DEATH'S DOOR.**

The aristocracy were allowed to vent their feelings by signing a sympathy book at the empty Buckingham Palace. Then they drove straight to the most fashionable emporia in town to order their full mourning outfits.

By the evening of January 19, Queen Victoria was unable to swallow food and barely able to speak. At midnight on January 20, a new bulletin was issued: **The Queen's condition has late this evening become more serious.**

The very stones of London seemed to quiver with unspent tears and ancient frights; the river drew back from its banks in an unprecedented low tide, like a bared grin of terror. Some of London's long-suppressed ghosts began to grow more substantial, though still weak and uncertain of their own existence. They emerged from their hiding places and flitted about Kensington Gardens and Hyde Park, almost indistinguishable from the mist.

An unusually large number of cormorants was noticed in the grounds of Osborne on the night of January 21. The next morning, one sharp-eyed laundrywoman remarked, "If you ask me, them ghoulish birds came flying in with the ship that brought that Harold High-and-Mighty Hoskins here.

"Get!" she shouted at them. "Hanging on my washing line!"

The birds stared at her impassively, until she was forced to lower her eyes and back away.

"Then," she told the other downstairs staff over a wide-eyed breakfast, "then a big devil of a bird that seemed to be the leader, he cawed at all his cronies. And the strangest thing was that bird cawed with an Australian accent, just like that Harold High-and-Mighty Hoskins has grown out in the colonies!"

"'Rack off!' that bird said. I swear he did. And when he said it, they all flew away."

A chambermaid shuddered, pointing out of the window. "Look, they're back now. They seem to have settled in for the duration."

All the servants knew what "the duration" meant. It meant until Queen Victoria was dead.

26. The Bad Ship Bombazine

in the western Mediterranean Sea, January 20, 1901

The *Scilla* plowed on through restless waters. Dim coastlines appeared in the distance. Foreign smells floated across the water. Unfamiliar birds landed on her masts.

On January 20, Teo had stumbled blearily up on deck early for her watch, without waiting for Peaglum to come shouting in his cheese-grating voice, "Rise and shine, rise and shine, show a leg!"

Teo came to full consciousness with a jolt when she saw Emilio and Fabrizio tied, gagged and blindfolded by the companionway. And there was Miss Uish—flashing signals with her pocket mirror to a black ship just a quarter of a mile away. Small explosions of light indicated return signals from the other boat, which appeared to be rigged not with sails, but with swathes of dark cobwebs.

One of Miss Uish's signals lit up the escutcheon carved under a fearful figurehead in the shape of a bat's skeleton. The name read *The Bad Ship Bombazine*.

Miss Uish staggered slightly. In doing so, she swiveled the mirror, and for a single second Teo saw her own terrified face reflected in it.

"Spy on me again, would you?" shrieked Miss Uish. "I'll have your life for that, Nestle Tripe."

She drew the dagger from her belt and swayed toward Teo, breathing heavily. The sickly smell of rum rushed through the air ahead of her.

Teo darted under Miss Uish's outstretched arms, kicking at her ankle as she passed. Miss Uish teetered and fell heavily. Teo dived down the booby hatch, running blindly past the galley and deeper into the *Scilla*, down toward the cargo hold, a place forbidden to the sailors on pain of death, even though it appeared to be full of nothing more precious than barrels of the marrowfat of murdered birds and seals.

There were no pursuing footsteps. Perhaps, hoped Teo, Miss Uish had hit her head in falling. Somewhere between the bilge streaks and the first streaks under the wales, Teo edged along the wall, panting. The darkness was absolute. She held in a scream as a sharp prong speared her shoulder from behind. Was it Peaglum? Was it a pistol? A knife? She froze. The prong did not move. Reaching behind her, she grasped not a weapon, but a smooth bar of metal.

"It feels like a lever," she thought, pressing down on it with all her weight. A panel of wood retracted silently and Teo fell backward. She landed on a pile of something soft yet bony, from which a ghastly smell arose. Muted light flowed through a grimy porthole.

"*Uffa!*" she breathed. "A concealed room!"

"Young Teodora?" gasped the pile.

"Professor Marìn!" Teo extricated herself, kneeling to peer at the man. The floor was sticky with a dark liquid.

She threw her arms around him and hugged him hard. The

160

professor gasped weakly. Hastily drawing back, she saw a wound gaping open above his heart. His eyes were glassy and his hair was matted with blood.

"Miss Uish did this, didn't she?" Teo cried. "She shot you."

"When she came aboard . . . on December thirtieth . . . I challenged her. But she had a pistol. . . . And as I lay dying—or so she thought—she boasted about what would happen . . . to Venice, to . . . Then she had her minion drag me down here to rot. She could not safely dispose . . . of my body . . . in Venetian waters."

"Professor!"

"Teodora . . . I must speak fast . . . don't stop me. Your so-called Miss Uish is nothing to do with Queen Victoria. The woman's an impostor. She was formerly a governess in the royal nurseries of Windsor Castle. . . . Her real name is Whish. Like the noise a whip makes . . . She was caught . . . committing acts of cruelty . . . to the little princes, nearly killed one who had hemophilia. . . . She ended up on the island of Hooroo, the penal colony. Where I believe . . . she met . . . ."

"Harold Hoskins, the Pretender to the British throne! He was exiled there! But she carries on about being an honored appointee of Queen Victoria!"

"That is her cover. She hates . . . Queen Victoria's whole family. She wants to see them . . . brought down. But Teodora . . . she met someone else on Hooroo, too. . . ."

Professor Marìn's mouth opened silently. He trembled with pain.

"Save your breath," begged Teo. "Let me tell you—now it's all starting to make sense. Miss Uish *kidnapped* the *Scilla*! Queen Victoria would never have ordered that! And Miss Uish loves to kill animals! That Harold Hoskins is addicted to hunting, isn't he? I've seen the photographs of his trophies in the newspaper. Mounds of poor dead wallabies. Horrible! So he killed the South Sea dolphins?"

"Hush, child! This may be . . . my last chance to tell you what I have discovered. Miss Uish . . . she is working with the people . . . who kidnapped your adoptive parents. Together, they are putting together some kind of terrible plot. . . ."

"Together? With whom?"

"The Pretender wants the British throne. He could not do it by . . . fair means, so he has chosen foul. And for the foul means . . . he has baddened magic to help him."

"Bajamonte Tiepolo?" breathed Teo. Pins and needles prickled her hands.

"Yes, the woman Uish is in league with Il Traditore, who somehow contrived to survive your cursing."

Teo began to explain, but Professor Marìn held up a feeble hand to stop her. "Avast hating yourself, child. All these days down here alone . . . I've had plenty of time to . . . put together the pieces. The whirlpool in the lagoon sucked Il Traditore all the way down to the South Pacific. He must have . . . finished up on the island of Hooroo, where Miss Uish was confined in the penal colony for her crimes against children. He's allied himself to her . . . and ingratiated himself with the Pretender."

"Three bitter exiles together—they had a lot in common, didn't they?" Teo cried.

"And now . . . Bajamonte Tiepolo's strengthened beyond anything he was two summers ago . . . he may even be almost human now. The seagulls must have . . . carried his bones to him, one by one, after the hiding places were betrayed."

"But Harold Hoskins is only human, surely. . . ."

"Well, yes, but with Bajamonte's baddened magic, he's been able to raise . . . a supernatural army of Ghost-Convicts, as well as living criminals he's pardoned so they'll . . . do his dirty work for him. As soon as Queen Victoria is dead, he'll move against London. And then, my . . . theory is . . . if Bajamonte Tiepolo helps the Pretender with his designs on the British throne . . . well . . . then . . . Harold Hoskins will help *him* destroy Venice."

"And he sent this Miss Uish and his Ghost-Convicts and criminals ahead to cause the ice storm? Why would she agree to do that?" Teo asked indignantly.

The professor took a deep, hurting breath. "I believe Miss Uish has a weakness. She is the kind of woman who's . . . fascinated by anyone crueler and more powerful than herself. They frighten her . . . but it is a delicious kind of fear. . . . Our enemy is just such a man. The way she spoke of him . . . I'm sure of it."

"Miss Uish is in love with Bajamonte Tiepolo?" Teo mused. "They deserve each other! Does he love her?"

"He must have found in her . . . a creature capable of unconscionable cruelty, just like himself. For him . . . that is a priceless treasure. I doubt if he is capable of love, yet he is capable of . . . dissembling it."

The professor clutched his own wounded heart.

"I am convinced, Teodora, that Miss Uish's second act in Venice was to try to murder the Undrowned Child. It would have been a gift for Bajamonte Tiepolo . . . an act of faith. And the reason she has requisitioned the *Scilla* is that it has the Studious Son aboard. She may not realize who *you* are—but she knows who *he* is! Young Renzo . . . is intended as her next gift to Bajamonte Tiepolo. My conscience . . . aches . . . that I have unwittingly helped poor Renzo to his doom."

Bajamonte Tiepolo, Orphan-Maker.

Teo felt dizzy at a depth of villainy that seemed to crisscross the whole world, all because she'd been too cowardly to put an end to Bajamonte Tiepolo when she had a perfect opportunity, and indeed, a duty to do so. Her parents had been kidnapped and Professor Marìn had lain in agony for weeks because of her weakness.

He wheezed. "It's been too many days. I have no feeling in my right side now . . . I can smell the infection of the wound myself. The only reason that I am still alive . . . is that Sofonisba has foraged for me."

"The poor professor is delirious," Teo thought. "Sofonisba is dead."

Yet at that moment a tabby-colored muzzle poked through a small hole in the false wall. In it was a ripe pear. Giving Teo a suspicious look, Sofonisba emerged fully into the room and dropped the pear by Professor Marìn. Around him, Teo noticed, were more pear cores and the pips of cherries and grapes.

"You're alive!" Teo reached out to caress the cat. "We thought you'd drowned. So that's why there was no storm after you walked the plank!"

This single piece of good news in the midst of all the tragedy was the one that moved Teo to tears. Mixed in with the emotion of the moment was the realization that Renzo had not after all lied about stealing the fruit.

"Indeed," replied the cat coolly. She flapped delicate little wings above her flanks. "I simply flew in through the heads." She wrinkled her pretty nose. "I've been—shall we say?—discreet in my appearances since then."

"You kept those wings well hidden! Why didn't you come to tell us what was happening?"

"The professor forbade me. He was afraid of childish heroics on your part! He kept telling me, 'If the boys knew anything, she'd just torture it out of them.' It's true—he's only safe down here because *she* thinks he's already dead."

Teo rose unsteadily to her feet. Shock and pity made her vision muzzy. Her heart was palpitating violently. "I'll get medicine, forceps; Renzo can extract the bullet—he's so good with his hands," she gabbled. "Perhaps there's some Venetian Treacle in the medicine chest."

"Do not waste time on me, child. Save the medicine. You will need it for yourselves, I fear. In London."

"So she's taking us to *London*? Where the mermaids have gone?"

"And you must go. First . . . we must accept that Venice may not survive this new assault . . . by Il Traditore . . . and secondly . . . London will need your help. Thirdly . . . I think your parents may be there. The Undrowned Child and the Studious Son will . . . Teodora, you must be vigilant. If that woman finds out your true identity . . . you will be in even worse danger . . . if possible."

"I'll be careful. And I'll look after Renzo," Teo promised tearfully. She could not bring herself to tell the dying man how she and Renzo were estranged.

"And Miss Uish may not be your . . . only enemy in these waters. The cold undertow will likely bring to the surface many ancient creatures that have for centuries confined themselves to the darkest . . . most freezing zones of the ocean."

Teo whispered, "We've heard something—I'm sure. It takes

165

the rats we throw overboard." She did not say, though she thought, "And the hostages." She would spare the professor the knowledge that his good ship had become a wicked pirate vessel.

"And the *Scilla* was never meant for . . . such a long voyage at sea. The poor old boat is nail-sick. It pains me to hear how she labors. . . . Her rivets are loose and the planks may not defend you from . . . what is below. Go now, child. I cannot talk more. . . . It is best that . . . you talk with the Studious Son and decide on your course . . . together. Explain. . . . You must fight for your lives, for Venice."

"But Venice . . ."

"You did not leave Venice, Teodora, just because you were forced to sail away from her."

Miss Uish was snoring on the deck when Teo crept back up there. Peaglum was at the wheel, singing nasally to himself, his back to both of them. Teo released Emilio and Fabrizio from their bonds and the three of them slipped down to the cabin.

"Wake up!" they whispered, shaking each hammock in turn.

"Professor Marìn is alive!—well, barely. Sofonisba kept him alive by stealing fruit for him. She's alive, too! Miss Uish is an impostor. She shot the professor and imprisoned him down in the cargo hold. And she wants to kill . . . Anyway, we have to take over this ship! We have to mutiny! Then Professor Marìn says we have to take the *Scilla* to London. . . ."

Nine pairs of eyes stared at her, wide with fear. Renzo's flashed with something she could not read. Did he not believe her?

"I don't . . . ," began Rosato.

"How can we . . . ?" whimpered Marco.

Sebastiano dalla Mutta growled, "I'm up for it!"

"I'm thinking, me too!" Emilio balled his fist.

"And me!" Massimo whispered.

"So what should we do with *them?*" asked Marco. "Even if we could knock them down and take them prisoner?"

"Tie 'em up and take 'em back to Venice!" Sebastiano cried out.

"Give 'em to the police," insisted Giovanni.

Teo was stern. "We *can't* take her to Venice, where the Mayor is in love with her and doesn't care a button for the lives of Venetian orphans! Who's he going to believe, *her* or us? One bat of those eyelashes and we'll be the ones thrown in prison. For mutiny on the high seas. And piracy."

"But I don't want to go to London," pleaded Marco in a very small voice. "I want to go home."

Renzo reminded them, "Venice must be frozen solid now. We could not get the *Scilla* within miles of the shore. We could get trapped in ice that would break up the boat. And then we'd all drown."

"Including your darling Sibella, I suppose?" said Fabrizio.

Renzo flushed, but ignored that. He said somberly, "And the Half-Dead disease will surely have put the whole town into quarantine now. If not worse."

Teo jutted out her chin. "We'll have to agree to Professor Marìn's plan. We are trapped on this ship and we must act as one."

"So do we have to kill them? Miss Uish and Peaglum?" Giovanni whispered.

"We have to do whatever it takes," responded Teo.

"Wouldn't we be as bad as them, then?" asked Rosato.

A rat trotted into the cabin and stared intently at Teo, as if it too hung on the answer that she did not know how to give.

Renzo said pointedly, "She said tomorrow it's two lashes each for the stolen fruit. And we can't tell her it was actually Sofonisba who did it, can we?"

"Tomorrow we put an end to the bullying," vowed Teo, meeting his eye. "And the lying."

27. Mutiny at sea

a busy night, January 21, 1901

The rest of the night passed in furious planning.

But first Renzo made his way to the ship's medicine chest in the galley, prising its old padlock open with a fork. He groaned. His first glimpse inside revealed only antique cauterizing irons, forceps and grippers for extracting teeth. Raking through the box, he selected a few items, decanted some brandy and boiled a small pan of water to take down to Professor Marìn.

At the pitiful sight of the professor, Renzo stood trembling and uncertain in the doorway.

"You see me in reduced . . . circumstances, son." Professor Marìn's voice was so weak as to be almost inaudible.

Renzo steadied himself. Using a tooth-gripper, he extracted the bullet, mopped the blood with clean rags and bandaged the wound, having first splashed it with brandy to disinfect it. Then he carefully washed the blood-matted hair, cut off the filthy shirt, and replaced it with a clean nightshirt he'd found in the medicine chest. The professor twice fainted from the pain during this procedure. But he gripped Renzo's hand gratefully at the end of it, whispering,

"Thank you, son. Now go! You must not be caught down here! . . . Spare the boys the awful truth, Renzo, as much as possible. . . . The more they know, the more dangerous it is . . . for them."

The next morning dawned fair, except for the blot of the cob-webbed black ship on the horizon.

The sailors crept up on deck. Sibella never showed herself before midmorning. Miss Uish was nowhere to be seen.

"Nursing a terrible headache in her stateroom," guessed Teo.

Peaglum was bustling about, happily stirring the cat-o'-nine-tails in its flagon of vinegar. He was looking forward to the punish-ments, singing a nasty sea shanty at the top of his untuneful voice. In the lyrics, a young sailor was slowly lashed to death over five verses and finally thrown to the sharks.

So it was relatively easy to sneak up behind Peaglum and run a thin black trip-rope from the hawse to the base of the mast. Hear-ing Rosato's whistle, Peaglum promptly turned and took an ill-fated step. Once he was flat on his face, three boys jumped on his back, just as they'd rehearsed down in the cabin. Fabrizio, Emilio, Mas-simo and Rosato each took a foot or an arm. Peaglum was trussed up like a goat. Teo dipped a rag in Peaglum's flagon of vinegar and stuffed it into his mouth.

Then it was a question of waiting till Miss Uish emerged. The sailors stood warily on deck, alert to every creak from below. An hour passed; a second. Finally, her harsh voice called up the stairs. "Malfeasance! Come clear my room!"

Peaglum grunted inarticulately.

"Malfeasance! Malfeasance! You'll pay for this!"

Miss Uish tottered up into the daylight. Her face was pale, her eyes dull. They fell on the captured Peaglum. Her mouth opened, but before she could speak, Rosato sent the boom spinning across the deck to smack the back of Miss Uish's head. She fell forward like a stone, her revolver hurtling across the planks. Teo caught it and tucked it into her belt.

"Good work!" shouted Sebastiano enthusiastically.

"Is she dead?" asked Giovanni nervously.

"No, just winded. Quick!"

They piled on top of Miss Uish and lashed her feet with bits of oakum. Emilio was attempting to bind her hands when Professor Marìn limped on deck, his eyes screwed up against the sun he'd not seen in weeks. Miss Uish gasped in disbelief. The boys cried out in alarm at the dreadful color of his skin. Renzo rushed to his side, slipping his arm under the professor's to prop him up.

Suddenly, Miss Uish laughed out loud. She slipped her fingers into a pocket of her dress and drew out a tiny pearl-handled pistol. "Here's the weak point in your plan," she chuckled, "a girl's best friend, always willing and able when needed. *Your* best friend, the professor, on the other hand, has turned up at exactly the wrong moment, hasn't he? Distracted you when you should have been tying me up properly! That naughty professor should be punished, shouldn't he, brats?"

She lifted her pistol and shot Professor Marìn through the heart. Then she pointed the pistol at Renzo, who was trying to lay the staggering professor gently down on the deck. Teo stamped her boot on Miss Uish's wrist, pinioning the hand that held the pistol.

The professor lay crumpled and motionless. Renzo leaned over him tenderly, examining the wound, stroking his bloodied hair and hollow cheeks.

"Isn't there anything you can do, Renzo?" pleaded Teo.

Renzo felt for the pulse, and shook his head, white-lipped.

"Is he really . . . ?" Rosato wept.

"Murderess!" Teo whispered. She drew Miss Uish's revolver from her belt, and aimed it with a shaking hand.

"You wouldn't dare, Nestle Tripe," sneered Miss Uish, trying to extract her wrist from under Teo's boot.

"Wouldn't I?" Teo cocked the trigger, as she'd seen Miss Uish do a hundred times in front of a helpless animal. Her voice came out too high, too girlish. Miss Uish stared at her, with too much understanding in her eyes.

"A-are you . . . ?" stuttered Miss Uish. "Could you be . . . ?"

Sibella appeared above them on the forecastle, a vision in white satin.

"If Teodoro shoots her, he'll be nothing but a detestable common murderer himself," she remarked.

Teo took the opportunity to kick the pearl-handled pistol out of Miss Uish's hand. The plan slipped smoothly back into motion. Sebastiano and Giovanni each grabbed one of Miss Uish's arms, and Emilio tied them together behind her. Then Renzo quietly removed the revolver from Teo's shaking fingers and threw it overboard, along with the pistol.

"No! Give them a taste of their own medicine!" screamed Sebastiano.

"Too late. The guns are gone. Treat them the way she treated the cat!" shouted Giovanni.

"Yes! Like the poor cat! Make 'em walk the plank!" agreed Sebastiano.

"That," insisted Emilio, "would be too dignified for the likes of them. Remember Sofonisba."

"Yes, remember me!" Sofonisba herself now leapt up the companionway and looked down on them all from the forecastle, where she commenced a vigorous licking of her tail and whiskers. The sailors whooped joyfully. A look of anger and surprise swept across Miss Uish's face.

"With the ship's cat safe, we'll get our luck back!" cried Rosato.

"Don't count on it," remarked Sofonisba. "Now, where exactly is my master?"

Her eyes lit on the body of her beloved professor. She bounded over to him, licking his face, nudging him with her muzzle. When she discovered the new wound, she keened loudly, laying herself down upon his breast and curling up in pain. The boys' tears overtook them then. For many minutes, they stood around their professor, shaking with grief.

A scornful laugh from Miss Uish reminded them of what they now faced.

"Even if we make it all the way to London, what are we going to do with *them* in the meantime?" Sebastiano gave the two captives a baleful look.

Peaglum struggled furiously. Miss Uish now lay disdainfully silent.

"Hungry!" whined Peaglum indistinctly.

"Well, of course, you must both be absolutely starving," Sebastiano answered. "Do you fancy a nice cup of warm marrowfat, perhaps?"

"Now, that's not an uninteresting idea," purred Sofonisba.

"Perfect!" approved Giovanni, rushing off to the galley. In two minutes, he returned with a jug of swarthy liquid still steaming from the cauldron. The spout was forced into the mouth of first

173

Peaglum and then Miss Uish until each had swallowed a long, deep swig of marrowfat.

Not quite swallowed, it turned out.

For Miss Uish opened her rosebud lips and spat a gush of oil on to the ropes that bound her hands. Her wrists slid easily out of bondage. With one fist she grabbed Renzo's ankle, tipping him backward on to the deck.

"At least I'll have the Studious Son's life!" she shouted, producing a vicious little dagger from a hidden pocket in her skirt.

"The Studious who?" asked Fabrizio.

"Rush her!" shouted Teo. "I'll go for the knife."

"Watch me!" cried Sofonisba. In the scrum of boys, whalebone corset, cat-fur and brown curls, the blade of the dagger caught Teo's fingers in a stripe of pain, but she managed to send it flying through the air. It impaled itself in the mast just as the sailors pushed the professor's murderess and her assistant up against the taffrail, which groaned under their combined weight. Sofonisba leapt to Miss Uish's head and wrapped herself around it like a furry mitten.

"Tie the prisoners together!" ordered Renzo. Over his voice could be heard the sound of metal shrieking.

"That's the stanchion that broke when the cannon went through it," shouted Teo. "Move them to the mast and lash them . . . Oh *no*!"

As she spoke, the weakened stanchion broke neatly away and the taffrail exploded into metal fragments. Sofonisba jumped clear of the widening gap and onto Teo's shoulder.

Miss Uish and Peaglum tumbled into the sea.

The crew stood in awed silence.

"What have we done?" whispered Renzo.

"We didn't do anything!" shouted Sebastiano. "The stanchion smashed, and they fell."

"We can't leave them to drown." Renzo was unrolling the rope ladder. "Throw a barrel down to them. They can swim to that and keep afloat until . . ."

"I ca-a-a-a-n't swim!" The waves had whipped Peaglum's gag off his face.

Miss Uish floated easily on her back, her eyes full of malice. She ignored the barrel that Fabrizio and Teo pitched into the water. Nor did she make any attempt to rescue Peaglum.

Peaglum was mumbling on mouthfuls of sea, screaming and jerking. Finally, his body stilled and dipped below the water.

"Peaglum really truly couldn't swim." Rosato's voice was awed.

Sebastiano whispered, "I thought they were so strong, that they were . . . invincible."

They were wrong. Peaglum was just a man, now a drowned man.

Miss Uish did not sink. Even with her legs still bound, she dipped and bobbed like a sea snake. The sailors watched her kick free of her ropes and pull herself gracefully onto a passing iceberg.

"Let's hope she freezes to death there," cried Sebastiano, "like a codfish!"

"That's not quite gentlemanly," Renzo reproved.

"And what if she did?" asked Sofonisba, erecting her back leg like a spear and giving it a thorough licking.

"Let's vote," insisted Marco. "Hands up who wants to rescue her."

Miss Uish did not appear to be interested in their help. She had gathered her sodden skirts about her and produced a small mirror from a pocket.

Renzo alone lifted his hand. Then he lowered it. "Now we really are outlaws and fugitives. And killers," he blurted.

Sibella appeared on the companionway, her pale blue eyes wide with accusation. "Did you just do what I think you did?" she asked.

28. A bag of the four winds

It was Teo's suggestion to raise the Venetian flag again. And indeed, as Sebastiano unfurled the golden winged lion on its crimson silk, proud smiles returned to the frightened and shamed faces of the boys. The Italian flag fluttered gaily beside it.

Massimo was set to sewing Professor Marìn's body up in their least-patched hammock. He asked Renzo to put the last stitch through the nose of the professor. "You knew him best, Renzo. He was like a father to you, wasn't he?"

All the sailors watched hopefully, but the professor's face did not twitch as the needle passed through his nose.

"He's really, really gone," said Rosato dolefully.

As Renzo tied off that wretched stitch, a black blur skimmed overhead.

"What was that?"

"Someone's firing cannons at us?"

Another black blur collided violently with the mast. A tar-colored parrot slid down the pole to the ground, where it lay feebly flapping a broken wing.

"Whoever it is, they're shooting parrots!"

"Poor thing." Teo stroked the wounded bird. "Perhaps you can set his wing with a splint, Renzo?"

But the parrot then propped itself on its undamaged wing, and delivered a message in such a perfect rendition of Miss Uish's frigid voice that everyone recoiled.

"I have joined a band of Ghost-Convicts from Hooroo on the *Bad Ship Bombazine*," it announced.

"The *Bombazine*," hissed Teo. "That's the black ship that's always on the horizon. Whoever's on board—they must have saved her."

The parrot tapped its beak impatiently against the mast and continued in Miss Uish's voice. "Silence! Expect imminent and fatal revenge. Lieutenant Rosebud of the *Bombazine* is far less tender-hearted than I am. He has a laboratory on board this ship that positively *manufactures* death. Or, what is worse, half-death."

"Like the Half-Dead disease?" thought Teo. "Did the *Bombazine* bring the sickness to Venice?"

They saw the *Bombazine*'s pirate flag looming larger on the horizon even as the parrot spoke. And then, before their eyes, the black skull-and-crossbones transformed into the deadly *jolie rouge*. Worse, the red slowly bruised through yellow to green—emerald-green, the color of Il Traditore's ring and his poison.

Renzo instinctively rubbed his shoulder, the one that had been injured in hand-to-hand combat with the Traitor's ghost. Teo could see what he was thinking: could Il Traditore his terrifying self be aboard the *Bombazine*?

And Teo's own skin prickled at the memory of the green heart beating in his skeletal ribs when Bajamonte Tiepolo had snatched her up inside his cloak.

178

A band of Ghost-Convicts swarmed onto the *Bombazine*'s deck like angry ants from their hill. To crown their pirates' rags, the crew wore black felt hats with corks bobbing from the brims.

Fabrizio, peering into a telescope, exclaimed, "Some of those fellows are half transparent. How could that be?"

The other boys trembled, silent with terror and bewilderment. Teo wrestled the spyglass from Fabrizio's hand. She had a particular reason for needing to see close up what these convicts looked like.

Now, focusing the lens, she groaned. The Ghost-Convicts were spectacularly mutilated, some with deep cuts across their throats, others with the imprint of a shark's jaws in their heads. All carried sturdy black tins with wire handles. The one who seemed to be their leader boasted a shark's tooth curving out of his back. His lusterless black eyes were sunk halfway through his nobbled skull. His white lips seemed merely embossed on the leather of his face.

Renzo asked quietly, "In-the-Slaughterhouse ghosts, I suppose?"

Teo whispered, "Yes, unfortunately. And a few humans who look just as bad. Those ones must be the prisoners Harold Hoskins pardoned. To do his dirty work."

In-the-Slaughterhouse ghosts were a thousand times worse than the more common in-the-Cold ghosts, who had committed a crime in life and wished only to redeem their sins with some heroic act. In-the-Slaughterhouse ghosts were angry to have died, and they wanted to go on behaving as viciously as they had in life.

Renzo urged, "We need something magical from Professor Marìn now, Teo! Can you remember the right pages from *The Best*

Ways with Wayward Ghosts? Specifically, we need one for escaping at high speed from Ghost-Convicts who want to slice us to pieces."

Teo mentally flicked through *Wayward Ghosts* as fast as she could. Two hundred and twenty pages in, she discovered a spell that could help them, but at a horribly painful cost. Reading the page aloud from the memory stored in her mind, Teo told the crew:

" 'If you have need of strong winds at sea, you may summon up a Sea Sorcerer by the gift of an innocent corpse. When he arrives, you should buy a packet of the four winds from him. He will take the corpse in exchange, and be well happy with his bargain. Do not attempt to trick or cajole him of his booty, or he shall see you sorrier than you can imagine.' "

"Professor Marìn's body! We can't! It's too horrible!" cried Rosato.

"He loved us. He'd want us to escape," said Marco quietly.

Silence fell. One by one, the boys nodded, Renzo last of all.

Teo read the spell as she saw it printed on the page:

> *"Come ye, Sorcerer, I entreat ye,*
> *Serve us in the ways of the sea.*
> *For us, four winds to speed our way,*
> *For you, a corpse with which to play."*

There was a short, shocked silence. Then Emilio asked, "Where will the Sea Sorcerer come from?"

"From the sea, I 'spect, stupid," Sebastiano replied.

"What will he look like?" whispered Massimo.

Sebastiano answered with relish, "A horrible monster, I s'pose. With scales and horns and tridents and oysters growing out of his eye sockets. And terrible breath, like dead crabs."

There was another short, tense silence. All eyes swiveled to the *Bombazine*, visibly gaining on them.

"No sign of 'im. P'raps Teo's remembering the spell wrong?"

"Perhaps there isn't any such thing as a Sea Sorcerer."

"Or perhaps he looks a bit like that," said Renzo quietly, pointing.

A translucent white hand with elongated fingers was snaking over the balustrade of the deck. A second hand followed. Then a transparent figure made of gushing water slipped over the rail in front of them. Tucked under his arm was a squirming sack, knotted into four separate compartments.

The white hand gestured at the body of Professor Marìn, now sewn neatly into the hammock, only his face visible under the hood of canvas.

The Sorcerer mimed "Mine?", soundlessly pointing again to the body and then back at himself.

"What will you do with him?" Renzo cried.

"Better not ask," advised Teo gently.

The Sorcerer nodded, drawing his hand across his eyes, as if to block out a painful vision. Teo held out her arms, trembling. The Sorcerer approached, handing her the bulging sack. She had to bear-hug it to stop it squirming away. Before she could say anything else, the translucent phantasm had effortlessly gathered up the body of Professor Marìn and climbed back down into the sea.

The sack churning in Teo's hands was marked with Gothic

lettering. 𝔈𝔞𝔰𝔱, 𝔚𝔢𝔰𝔱, 𝔖𝔬𝔲𝔱𝔥, 𝔑𝔬𝔯𝔱𝔥. Each section was bound with a sturdy constrictor knot. She could hear each of the winds howling quietly in a different pitch.

"Open it!" urged Renzo.

"If I released them at once, we'll just land ourselves in the middle of a great storm. I should let out the exact wind that we need, to push us away from *that*"—Teo pointed to the looming *Bombazine*—"and to get us to London."

"I'm thinking southeasterly, then," suggested Emilio, always weather-conscious. "So prick a hole in the most eastern part of the south pocket."

"Renzo, can I borrow your *ferro*?"

Renzo handed Teo his penknife. Teo slipped the blade into a quarter-inch of sacking. A powerful puff of cool air blew her eyebrows and the stubble on her shaved head into an alarmingly vertical position.

"Is that all?" Renzo quipped. "We don't actually need Teo's hairstyle rearranged, though anything would be an improvement. We want the *wind* rearranged."

But now the puff of air was racing around the mast, filling the sails, even jostling the steering wheel to a northwesterly hold. Then the sea seemed to stop rolling for a second, and to take a deep, deep breath. The *Scilla* bucked and surged ahead, like a clockwork toy ship that had been wound to its fullest capacity and set free in a bathtub.

The sailors set to, working the pumps. They hoisted a new maintopsail. They set the reefed foresail, putting the *Scilla* before the wind. The waves chased her fast.

Too fast. A storm was starting.

"Board the larboard tacks! Bring her close to the wind!" shouted Renzo. The sailors busied themselves cluing up the royals and topgallant sails, each silently thanking Professor Marìn for teaching him these lifesaving skills.

"Look!" shouted Fabrizio. "The *Bombazine!*"

The sea thrashed furiously, surrounding the *Bombazine* with a spume of waves. The pirate flag tore in half. Instead of lagging behind them, the *Bombazine* was being propelled directly into their path.

Two seconds later, the *Scilla* was passing the *Bombazine* at close range. The Ghost-Convicts brandished cattle prods at them. The *Scilla*'s crew was close enough to see the corks dangling from the Convicts' hats, close enough to smell their rank rum-scented breath, close enough to see the cormorants circling over the mast, close enough to take a few very smelly brown bullets in the mast and sails, and close enough to hear a faint plaintive baaing coming from the *Bombazine*'s hold. There was no sign of Miss Uish. Then the Sorcerer's wind seized the *Bombazine* with new ferocity, whipping away her spanker boom and spritsail yard. Enormous surges of green sea swept over her decks, beating her larboard bilge with clamorous blows. The Ghost-Convicts could be heard screaming, "'Strewth! Watch that flaming steerboard!" and "The wheel's come a gutser!" and "In front o' the bloody wind, yer drongo!"

The bow of the *Bombazine* was driven under a great hollow-breasted wave. Miraculously, it rose again, but was caught broadside in the trough of the next wave, and rolled to meet it instead of riding up its towering slope.

"She'll surely broach-to and sink!" cried Renzo.

A towering, foam-lashed rock loomed out of a hollow in the waves. They glimpsed the Sea Sorcerer at its peak, calmly cradling the body of Professor Marìn. With watery fingers, the Sorcerer seemed to be luring the *Bombazine* toward the craggy stone.

29. An ending and a beginning

*Osborne House, the Isle of Wight, and Calais, northern France,
the evening of January 22, 1901*

As the *Bombazine* plunged and rolled at the Sea Sorcerer's mercy, the soul of Queen Victoria was quietly preparing to depart this life.

When it seemed the end was nigh, Queen Victoria's family filed into the room. The Petticoats recounted the names of all present, in case she could hear, although they spitefully left out that of the Pretender.

At that moment, a black cormorant was seen at the royal window, gazing in. The Petticoats swore that it sought out and caught the eye of Harold Hoskins. A footman would afterward insist that the bird had winked, and that the Pretender had silently mouthed a word that looked like "Pipistrelly."

But all agreed on one thing: that at six-thirty p.m.—as Queen Victoria's soul left her body—the cormorant also took flight into a shrewish easterly wind. And that the bird headed southeast.

Five hours later, the black bird soared through the open skylight of a low Gothic barn near Calais and settled on the shoulder of a cloaked figure. It cawed something into an ear that seemed to be not quite made of flesh.

"Good," snarled the figure. "Now it begins! We leave tomorrow for our rendezvous with the *Bombazine*. And then . . . London!"

As he spoke, another cormorant arrived, its wing tips coated with ice. Timidly, it approached the cloaked figure and cawed some less welcome news into that fluid ear. A skeletal hand grabbed the neck of the exhausted bird. A second later, it fell lifeless on the floor of the barn.

The story it had brought was of mutiny and an escape in the remote reaches of the western Mediterranean Sea.

"Summon *Mesonychoteuthis hamiltoni!*" barked Signor Pipistrelly to the cormorants who stood staring at their dead companion. They did not need telling twice, but rose into the sky in a greasy tumble of wet black feathers.

30. Mesonychoteuthis hamiltoni

in deep waters off the coast of Portugal, dusk, January 22, 1901

It was nearly the end of Teo and Emilio's dusk dogwatch. The moon silvered the seam of the wake. Unfamiliar stars punctured the cloudless black sky. The waves breathed softly beneath the prow as the *Scilla* sped north. To starboard was the distant coast of Portugal.

Their bellies were full and round. For what a superior supper they'd enjoyed that night! With Miss Uish gone, Cookie had unlocked the cupboard of fancy foodstuffs stolen from the vessels they had pirated. There'd been ham and tinned pineapple, for which Cookie made a molasses sauce; there were tinned carrots, which Cookie served with preserved ginger. He made a special dish of potatoes and leeks in a chili-lemon-cheese sauce for Teo. The smell of hot cheese still lingered in the air, and Teo and Emilio had a plate of ginger cake to nibble on, should they get a little peckish during their watch.

"It would be a beautiful night," thought Teo, "if Professor Marìn had not been murdered, and if Sibella wasn't here, and if Bajamonte Tiepolo . . ."

She smiled grimly. "Well, it's a beautiful night anyway, and we can all be grateful for a moment of peace."

Emilio, at the wheel, seemed to be thinking the same thing. He murmured, "Lovely evening! This is the safest I've felt since before the ice storm.

"Teo, there was something I wanted to ask you. Did I ever see you in Venice, you know, before all this happened? You weren't at our school, were you?"

"No, I wasn't." Teo was glad to have a bit of truth to tell.

"And I'm thinking your accent isn't quite Venetian; it almost sounds as if you come from the south, or somewhere like that. It's just a bit odd, because there aren't that many boys in Venice, and we all know each other. . . ."

Teo's mind spun. To tell Emilio the truth about her past and about Bajamonte Tiepolo would only endanger him, if Miss Uish caught up with them again, if the *Bombazine* had survived the storm. And what about the other boys? They would not be pleased to hear that she and Renzo had been keeping such a terrible secret all this time. And if they found out that she was a *girl*? That didn't bear thinking about.

"I—I had a tutor at home," she stammered, "and . . ."

Suddenly, the *Scilla* lifted up into the air.

"What the bucket is that?" cried Teo, clinging to one of the cannons. The deck tilted giddily. This was not like the lee-lurches that occasionally tossed the *Scilla* in a high sea. No, this felt as if someone had lassoed the ship from behind. A stink of rotten eggs saturated the air.

Screaming boys in their underwear swarmed on deck just as a pink feeler, the length of a tree, arched over the bow. Teo caught a glimpse of a cone-shaped body as big as a carriage just below the surface of the waves.

She shouted, "I think it's a giant squid!"

Another tentacle appeared at the stern. The squid's body rose briefly above the waves. Four pairs of tentacles were now wrapped around the boat, each a separate monster. A fifth pair, thinner and longer than the rest, was inching up the part of the deck not yet covered by water.

"I'd say that was a *colossal* squid." Renzo's voice shook.

"Renzo!" screamed Massimo. "What do colossal squid ea—?"

Massimo's words were cut off by a tentacle that wrapped around his face. There was a brief, horrified silence and then he grunted in muffled pain. The tentacle uncoiled, seized Massimo's leg and dragged him, screaming, toward the taffrail.

Renzo wrenched the axe from the woodpile. He brought it down on the tentacle, severing it completely. The bleeding stump slithered back into the sea. Massimo slumped onto the deck.

As Renzo bent over Massimo, deftly extracting a black hook from his leg, yet another tentacle slapped over the taffrail by the forecastle. A third seized the mast, while a fourth took hold of the wheel. It was the fifth tentacle that found the cannon behind which Teo crouched, making herself as small as possible. It wrapped itself neatly around her body and pulled her out from behind the gun. Pain seared her arms and sides as its barbed tentacles lifted her into the air and plunged her beneath the boat.

Teo opened her eyes. The water was pinkly cloudy.

"Squid blood," Teo realized. Horribly, she saw the squid's maw chewing and grinding. The squid now brought her close to its own lidless eye. It was the size of a large dinner plate. The cold eye swiveled in its socket, taking in Teo's heaving chest, her fingers holding her nose, her flailing feet.

"It's waiting for me to suffocate," Teo thought, "so it can eat me without a struggle."

Any other child would have conveniently drowned at this point. But this was not the first time a monstrous sea creature had tried to kill Teo. She had certain resources at hand. When the infant Teo had been shipwrecked in the Venetian lagoon, she, alone of all her family, had been rescued in the strangest way. Fish had come from all over the lagoon to tip bubbles of air into her mouth, keeping her alive until the mermaids arrived to carry her away to the nuns at the House of the Spirits. And the year before last, when she'd been forced to hide from a pack of sharks in the depths of the Grand Canal, the kind Venetian fish had once more come to her aid. They'd fed her air and distracted the man-eaters while she swam to safety.

The fish of these northern waters were not Venetian, yet Teo hoped that they had the same good hearts as those of her previous acquaintance. "I am the Undrowned Child." She sent the thought shimmering through the water. "Please, *please*, help me to stay that way."

There was a rustling like someone shaking silver foil. Teo's skin tingled with the vibrations in the water. Then, in a wave of color, they arrived: fish of every species and size. Each swam to her mouth, breathing air into it.

The squid watched impassively. Occasionally, a tentacle snatched a fish and pushed it into the parrotlike maw. Each time that happened, it relaxed its grip on Teo. The barbs retracted from her skin while it chewed the fish, all the while eyeing Teo greedily, as if she was a particularly good delicacy to be saved for dessert.

"I am the Undrowned Child, not the Unsucked or the Uneaten Child." Teo shuddered. One of her shoes fell off, dropping down through the bottomless water. The fish stared at Teo fearfully, their mouths open as if trying to apologize for something.

"They can't do any more for me," she thought. "But if my timing was right, I could wriggle out of my clothes and swim to the surface."

Another mouthful of air, another thought: "*All* my clothes?"

Teo remembered being laid out on a table in the Games Pavilion in Venice, with Bajamonte Tiepolo gradually cutting off the hem of her skirt and petticoats so that he could print the spells that had been embossed on her legs when his Spell Almanac was briefly transferred to her body. There would be nothing gradual about losing her clothes this time.

The squid's eye suddenly bulged. Teo read surprise in the glassy oval.

Again the eye widened, registering unmistakable pain.

"They're doing something up on the surface!"

A long pink tentacle suddenly plummeted past her into the depths. Up on the *Scilla*, Renzo must have hacked it off. A second tentacle followed. The squid's eyes were blazing now, its barbs clawing deeper into her skin.

Then a fine fat grouper arrived, pouring his bubbles into Teo's mouth. He had a resigned expression, nodding sadly to her.

"No!" Teo wept. "Too many creatures have died for me already."

But when the grouper turned slowly, as if to leave, the squid's barbs retracted. One of the tentacles that held Teo unwrapped itself and went in prodding pursuit of the plump fish. The other loosened. Teo took her chance. She left her trousers, jacket and shirt impaled on the squid's barbs, and hurtled up toward the surface, narrowly missing a thump on the head from a third lopped tentacle on its way down to the sea floor.

A feeder tentacle thrashed through the water behind her, hunting its lost prey. A barb caught Teo's ankle, dragging a deep gash through it. As Teo broke the surface, she saw the *Scilla* twenty yards away, already starting to right itself. Renzo was slicing at the remaining tentacles. The other boys were using knives from the *Scilla*'s galley to stab at sections of squid that still clung to the boat.

"Here! Help!" The words came into Teo's head, but she had no breath to utter them. She could hardly hear the hoarse gurgle herself.

She saw Rosato and Giovanni desperately scanning the opposite horizon. She heard Sebastiano and Marco calling her name. Renzo ran back to the wheel, constantly craning his neck toward the water. Sofonisba ran along the taffrail, meowing "Teo! Teo!" Why did none of them look in her direction? The waves were carrying the *Scilla* farther away each moment.

"Save me! Please!" Still nothing but a wet rasp emerged from her mouth. She began to swim toward the boat, dodging and kicking the feeder tentacle that came thrusting up every few yards to find her. At last, weak with gratitude, she felt the rough wood of the *Scilla*'s bow against her arms.

The slender tip of the feeder tentacle surged up just beside her, like a blind snake turning this way and that. Now that she was nearly safe, Teo was overcome with anger. This creature had tried to eat Massimo and to sink the *Scilla*. It was no doubt one of Bajamonte Tiepolo's revolting pets.

She grabbed the tentacle, and in one swift motion tied it into the most complicated nautical knot she could contrive, combining the sheepshank with the bowline and finishing with a tight clove hitch. She threw the writhing lump of tentacle as far away as she could.

Then she hauled herself out of the water and climbed swiftly up the rungs of the ladder, hoping against hope that there would be no one at the top to see her in her clinging lacy combinations and utterly translucent vest.

31. In castigo

a very uncomfortable situation, January 22, 1901

"Well, she can't sleep with us anymore. A *girl*! Ugh! All this time there's been a *girl* in our cabin!"

The deck was darkly slippery with squid gore. The end of one tentacle still lay twitching across the water barrel. Massimo's leg and face were bandaged, and seeping blood. Yet he joined the circle of boys who surrounded her, staring with disgust and fury. The murderous squid appeared to be a mere nothing compared to the horror that was Teo.

Renzo met her eyes, shaking his head subtly. A bitter realization swept over her: "He means I'm not to give away that he knew about me."

The wounds made by squid's hooks began to burn, but not as much as Teo's feelings.

"It's 'cos of him—*her*—that the squid came. Everyone knows girls bring bad luck on a ship." Sebastiano stamped his foot.

"And if Renzo hadn't . . ." Massimo's voice quavered to a standstill.

Emilio suggested, "It's *un-Venetian* for a girl to be at sea."

"But your Sibella's a girl," protested Teo.

Sebastiano maintained stonily, "Sibella's different. . . ."

"Very civilly put together, that one . . . ," added Emilio.

A cool, sweet voice rose above the debate. Sibella appeared on deck. "Gentlemen, given these trying and detestable circumstances, I shall gladly share my cabin with Teodoro, or should one say Teodora?"

The moon shone, it seemed, specially down on Sibella, so that she glowed with an angel's shimmering silhouette. She glided across to the boys as if her delicate boots did not touch the deck. She was the only person not drenched in squid blood. Every blond curl was as perfect, as if spun from golden glass.

Sofonisba asked, "And where was *she* when the squid attacked?"

As usual, the boys were mesmerized by Sibella.

It was only when she sauntered away that they turned back to stare at Teo resentfully; all except for Renzo, whose expression was agonized.

Teo opened her mouth to speak.

"Let's put Teo *in castigo*," suggested Renzo quickly, with the air of someone solving more problems than one. "None of us shall talk to her, or listen to anything she has to say."

He marched past Teo to the wheel, mumbling, "I'm sorry. You and I need to talk when we're alone. But for now it's safer for everyone this way."

"Particularly for you," remarked Sofonisba, gently licking Teo's hand.

Sibella had transformed the storeroom that served as her cabin. Now it was lined with silk like the inside of a jewel box. Exquisite dresses hung on every inch of the walls and spread out on the floor. Teo tripped over an ice-blue mantle trimmed profusely with what looked like white froth.

Sibella lectured, "Do be careful! Pray don't drip blood everywhere! That's guipure lace with crepe ribbon bows, lined with silk. And the hood is of velvet gauze."

Glancing around with wonderment, Teo realized why Miss Uish had exulted in the prospect of a large ransom for Sibella. Clothes like these must have cost a fortune. Sibella had accessories that Teo had never even heard of. A pink box was labeled ACME INFLATED DRESS IMPROVER. She had a bonnet brush as well as a zylonite hairbrush. Her bureau overflowed with bone-topped powder puffs, ivory hand-mirrors, glove-stretchers and nail-trimmers. Another box boasted in copperplate embossing that it contained a Benson's lady's keyless lever watch. Sibella had scarves and skirts and silk stockings in every color of the rainbow. Teo wondered why she always wore white on deck, yet scorned to ask.

The door was rapped once and Cookie came in bearing a pitcher of steaming water and a tube of ointment. He pointed to Teo, and looked sympathetically at the sucker-marks of the squid, the scratches of its hooks tattooed over her arms, and the blood trailing from the gash in her ankle. It was the first truly kind human look Teo had received since surviving the attack, and she bit back tears, nodding a tight smile of gratitude. She was absolutely not going to cry in front of Sibella.

A curtained screen separated off one corner of the room. Teo followed Sibella's eyes there. Kicking aside a porcelain chamber pot, she poured the pitcher into the hip bath. She scrubbed the slime and stink of squid off her body, dried herself with a sheet from a neatly folded pile of fine Irish linen and daubed her wounds with pink ointment. It wasn't magical, like Venetian Treacle, yet it quickly soothed the pain.

From the other side of the screen, Sibella said coolly, "I have some old dresses, which I had planned to give to my maid before I was taken hostage."

"Don't want to wear your fancy clothes," replied Teo, as a gray silk dress was hung over the side of the screen.

"Won't the boys hate you even more, if you go on trying to masquerade as one of them?"

Scowling, Teo snatched up the gray silk dress. Then she sat cross-legged on the floor and ripped off all the lace ruffles. It was good to feel the delicate fabric tearing under her angry fingers. She threw the ruffles over the screen.

"Well, fashion can live without your contribution, Teodora, but decency requires you to at least wear these."

Over the top of the screen was draped a pair of combinations with lace around the neckline and a row of pearl buttons. "Cotton batiste, Chantilly lace," Sibella explained. It was a long time since Teo had touched anything so soft.

A fearsome item was then handed over the screen to Teo. "And you'll definitely be needing one of these corsets. Every woman should possess a perfect and attractive figure. Even the most unpromising shape can be transformed to queenly beauty, superb and fascinating."

The last time Teo had known a girl who spoke like this, it had been one whose vanity and insecurity had pushed her into the clutches of Bajamonte Tiepolo, just because he gave her a bit of finery to wear. True, Maria was now a changed person, a friend, but . . . Sibella was stronger-willed than Maria, more aristocratic and seemingly less insecure. Teo thrust the corset imperiously over the screen.

"I can't work in that," Teo said shortly. She assumed that she would continue with her duties about the *Scilla*. There were barely enough hands to keep the ship afloat. The rats would still be gnawing and the *Scilla* was creaking audibly at every loose seam since the squid attack.

Teo peered around the edge of the screen.

"No, don't even think about it!" She recoiled as Sibella held up a small gray cotton bustle, apparently stuffed with horsehair. "And don't look at me," she implored.

With a mocking smile, Sibella turned her artificially narrow back. Teo rebuilt herself from the combinations up, adding the simplest possible petticoat from the snowy collection on the floor, and completing the outfit with the desecrated silk dress knotted at her waist with a black sash, and a pinafore with handy pockets for tools.

She emerged from behind the screen, carefully avoiding even the briefest glance in the looking-glass on the bureau.

"The Puritan look," commented Sibella, "suits you, insofar as anything might, I suppose. Though even Puritans don't bite their fingernails up to the elbow like you do. Let me at least retie your sash. Some people just don't have the knack."

It was sorely tempting to answer this offer by tearing the sash in two, but Teo forced herself to accept Sibella's deft ministrations. Having lost one of her shoes in the sea, she could not afford to snub Sibella's "patent galoshed brogue vamp" boots, which were snug and warm.

"Thank you," she said gruffly.

Then she climbed on the deck, where the boys were struggling to repair the squid's damage by lamplight.

Every head deliberately turned away from Teo. She took her position at the tar bucket and busied herself with sealing the loose seams of the poop deck. Not a single boy threw a look or a word in her direction, or asked if her wounds still hurt, or came to work alongside the deceitful girl who'd been pretending to be a boy.

After a midnight supper of hot chocolate and ginger cake, at which she was studiously ignored, Teo returned unwillingly to Sibella's cabin. As she opened the door, she became aware that the wind had threshed any remnant of tidiness out of her hair, and that she'd somehow contrived to tear the gray silk dress in three new places.

Sibella smiled icily. "Teodora, there's someone I'd like you to meet. Nail brush, say how do you do to Teodora. And by the way, I've made up a bed for you in the lid of my trunk."

The trunk was so big that Teo could stretch out fully inside.

Teo growled, yet she took the warm flannel nightdress Sibella offered her, closing her ears to the explanation of its "waterfall frills, edged with pink zephyr."

Sometime in the early hours, Teo was woken by singing. Without moving her body, she opened her eyes. Sibella crouched over her pillow box with a candle in her hand. She was chanting quietly to the leeches inside. Teo raised her head. She could see the leeches were churning, waving their heads in a kind of ecstasy. She tried to hear what Sibella was saying to make them so excited, but the words were too faint to be comprehensible.

The letters Teo saw on the air above the back of Sibella's head formed themselves into an antique script. Yet as soon as Teo started to read the words, they disappeared. For Sibella had caught sight of Teo's glowing eyes in her mirror. She closed the lid on her pets, snuffing out the candle.

"You must get your beauty sleep, Teodora," her voice chimed out of the darkness. "I can't think of anyone who needs it more."

Teo's first chance to be alone with Renzo was not until he took the wheel at the beginning of the second watch.

"Teo, at last!" He smiled with relief. But she was quick and blunt.

"Your Sibella is using her leeches to send messages to her friend Miss Uish. When she chants to them at night—it looks like magical spells, Renzo. Miss Uish has baddened magic. What if Sibella does too? What if she's telling Miss Uish that there's a certain Undrowned Child, a girl, still undrowned and on the *Scilla* with her friend the Studious Son? And what if Miss Uish is telling Bajamonte Tiepolo?"

Renzo looked around anxiously.

"Obviously you don't want to be seen talking with me," blurted Teo, "but please hear me out. Don't you see that things have changed? How can we take these brave boys to London on a half-truth? Now we have to tell them about baddened magic and . . ."

"No! Professor Marìn said it was safer for them not to know too much."

"Naturally you want to carry out his wishes. So would I. But Professor Marìn was dying when he said that, Renzo. His mind was clouded by pain."

Teo struggled to keep her voice low. "Put some oil in your lamp! Most of these boys are orphans because of Bajamonte Tiepolo. Including you, Renzo. It's clearly Il Traditore who created the *Bombazine*! For all we know, he might even be aboard her. Who else would summon up Ghost-Convicts in-the-Slaughterhouse? No doubt the colossal squid is his creature too. We have to let the boys choose their own fates. They must decide for themselves if they wish to go on. There will be danger. We may be fighting for our lives, for Venice. For London. For *our world*, if necessary."

The sound of a sharp intake of breath made both of them jump. Looking up, Teo saw Fabrizio crouching like a cat over the booby hatch.

Renzo's face pinched. Teo asked, "Did you hear everything?"

"I should think just about everything." Fabrizio's green eyes were bright with angry shock. He turned to Teo with a remorseful expression. "I am so sorry, Teo. You and Renzo knew all this awful stuff all along? And we've put you *in castigo*! You've not only been alone, you've been worrying about the rest of us and wanting us to know the truth, even when we were being nasty to you."

"And spiteful," noted Teo. "And outstandingly malicious."

"True. We owe you an apology, a really big one."

"Apology accepted," Teo said quickly. "Now let's call everyone together—just the boys, not that Sibella, mind!—and have a *proper* talk."

In the messroom, Teo explained the mermaids, baddened magic, Bajamonte Tiepolo, the Pretender and the Incogniti. She included her theory about Sibella and the leeches. Initially disbelieving, then frightened, some of the boys finally grew angry about being kept in the dark about Il Traditore and the danger that faced not just Venice but now London.

"Didn't you trust us?" complained Sebastiano. "Did you think we were cowards or something?"

"We're Venetians too," Giovanni stated with dignity.

"The professor was afraid what might happen to you if Miss Uish found out you knew the truth."

"Well, now we do, and now we—that's *all* of us—have to make a plan," said Emilio brusquely, waving a rolled-up chart in his hand. "By the way the Sorcerer's winds are blowing us, we'll be in British waters by tomorrow."

"There can be only one plan," said Renzo. "As soon as we get to London, we must find the mermaids and the Incogniti."

"And look for my parents," Teo added in a small voice.

"Of course we will," said Sebastiano generously. "First thing."

And all the while they spoke, the *Scilla* sped toward England on the Sorcerer's wind, magically maneuvering round icebergs that Emilio's charts could not warn them about. When the sailors returned to their duties on deck, no one wanted to mention that the cold was getting more bitter.

In the churning waters of the English Channel, only Teo was happy to see how few fish came to the hooks of their rods. Those

that did were unearthly creatures scooped up by the strange currents. Some waved tentacles with phosphorescent tips. Others had
no eyes at all. Cookie tried to disguise them in a spiced stew, yet
those fish still tasted unpleasantly of the past and of the deep, and
of something better left undisturbed.

"Stinks of baddened magic," said Renzo, pushing his plate
aside.

When sleek Sofonisba—with an air of self-sacrifice—offered
them a pair of freshly killed rats for supper, Giovanni wondered
aloud if Cookie might know a good rat recipe.

That night Sibella chanted once more to the leeches. Teo,
exhausted by her day on deck, was unable to keep awake long
enough to penetrate the mysteries of her companion's archaic
script and strange words. And she was simply disgusted when she
saw Sibella pick one leech out and crush it in a mortar. Then the
girl added the juice of a lemon and, screwing up her face, drank
the mixture in a single gulp.

32. London fog and stone

across the English Channel and up to the Thames, January 24, 1901

It was on the afternoon of the next day that they first sighted the British coast, opening like a grim gray smile in the water. The sea was now cluttered with cutter-rigged oyster-dredgers and Boulogne luggers. A wide estuary beckoned them toward Yantlet Creek, where an obelisk—"The London Stone!" exclaimed Renzo—stood like an old pencil in water that was dead and flat, gray as polished pewter. The sky lurked above it, the same color and seeming just as heavy. The few fishing vessels they passed looked equally lifeless, as did the handful of bleak farms that clung to the edges of the limp marshes fringing the water.

The sailors set the fore-and-aft sail and trimmed the head-sheets down to port. The *Scilla* slid smoothly into the mouth of the Thames. An hour passed and most of another, with nothing more dramatic than gray-green fields and sparsely populated hamlets to be seen on either side. Snatches of woodland, hazy hills and lazy flights of heron punctuated the view.

"Look! All the flags at half-mast," said Fabrizio.

"Do you think," Teo wondered, "is it possible that the old Queen could have actually . . . died?"

"The newspapers in Venice were saying she was on the brink of it, weren't they?" remembered Sebastiano.

A short silence fell.

"If Queen Victoria is dead," said Teo with a shiver, "then whatever Bajamonte and the Pretender are plotting must already be afoot."

The demise of the Queen was confirmed by the deep-black mourning costumes worn by all the populace at the first town they reached. Appropriately, it turned out to be called Gravesend. Its funereal name suited it well: dull brick buildings kept their distance from a joyless pebbled beach. Renzo guided the *Scilla* to anchor a safe distance away from the two barnacled piers.

At Giovanni's urging, they bought ten pints of fresh shrimp and a barrel of silvery pickled herrings from a fishing smack that came alongside, with a cauldron boiling cheerfully right on deck. From another boat, they bought some legs of "York ham," a brace of dressed ducks, and some cheese, pickled cucumber and cresses for Teo. Another boat laden with fruit sold them sixteen pears for a penny. Reluctantly, they used some of their pirated sovereigns to pay for the food. They did not dare moor at a jetty: the *Scilla* was too full of stolen treasure to bear examination by any inquisitive customs officer. Large gulls and unusual crested cormorants circled above the boat. Others floated in the water, their beaks and eyes pointing accusingly at the *Scilla*'s hold.

"I'm thinking we're going to have to stow the pirate loot," said Emilio, as they continued down river, "before we get to London."

"But not here," answered Renzo. Tilbury Docks, vast and swarming with men and boats, was just across the river. "Somewhere quiet."

A few miles past Greenhithe, a deserted jetty tottered into the river. Renzo steered the *Scilla* alongside, and the digging party, led by Sofonisba, went ashore, leaving Fabrizio on watch.

Fear of spying cormorants and gulls forced them to contrive the appearance of a jolly picnic in a field. In fact, they were soon giggling in earnest: after all their days at sea, the sailors had lost their land legs. No sooner had Sebastiano climbed ashore than he flopped on his face. Laughing fit to burst, Giovanni also stumbled into the mud.

"You're like a bunch of drunken monkeys," remarked Sofonisba, sniffing, yet two seconds later she too found herself unexpectedly on her back in a damp hollow.

By a beech tree, and under cover of an outspread blanket, Sofonisba dug a hole in the frozen earth. The small sacks of stolen jewels and gold—all but a modest sum for living expenses—were buried, while they pretended to drink from empty cups and lifted pieces of sponge masquerading as bread to their lips. They flinched as the shadow of a bird passed over the blanket. Fortunately, it was only a duck. Renzo was whittling an image of a cat into the trunk of the tree when Fabrizio called from the boat, "Flock of cormorants approaching from the southeast!"

In spite of the black birds spreading their wings on the masts, the sailors reboarded the *Scilla,* lighter-hearted for dispatching the guilty treasure and the violent memories it carried with it.

They needed all their renewed hope passing Erith Reach, which was haunted by the hulls of ghostly wrecks. Then a prospect of clamorous docks and towering warehouses opened up in front of them.

"Empire Mill, Premier Mill, Spillers' Millennium Mill," read Teo aloud. The other boys set about spraining their tongues by trying to do the same. Before they had mastered the words, the mills too disappeared into the mist. A paddle steamer, the *Hutton*, rushed breathily past them at close quarters a few minutes later, her decks crowded with black-clad passengers.

"The Woolwich Ferry," guessed Renzo, pumping the steering wheel hastily to larboard to avoid one of the dozens of spritsail barges, cockleboats, houseboats, steamboats and naval vessels that had now joined the *Scilla* in this stretch of river. All were heading inexorably west, toward the capital.

They were taken by surprise at the sight of an elegant white palace with pairs of domed towers and gracious low wings clustering around a square.

"This means we are in the part of London called Greenwich," Renzo said, consulting the map. "We are not far from Tower Bridge. The heart of London!"

"If London has a heart," muttered Sebastiano, staring ahead. "It looks as if it's made of fog and stone."

The mist was lifting. They passed an enclosure signposted as *London Docks*, where they glimpsed men unloading puncheons of rum, rolled carpets and sacks of spices, whose scent floated out across the water. Massive doors gaped to show heaps of dyestuffs, and acres of mysterious barrels and bins of horns, sulfur and copper ore. Cork was piled in ribbed sacks. The noise was ferocious. Coopers hammered barrels; sailors yammered in a dozen languages. Clattering carts bore slatted boxes through which spilled vivid tufts of peacock feathers. The water bobbed with heavily laden vessels. A rich smell of coffee was emitted from one; a sour stench of hides from another.

A towering vehicle rolled down a road toward the dock. Drawn by horses, the black box was crammed with tiny people in two layers.

"A *vaporetto?*" laughed Emilio. "A land *vaporetto* with wheels!"

"A London omnibus," corrected Renzo. "My father rode in one once."

"Omblibus!" Sebastiano held his head. "I think my brain just died of one English word too many."

"Never mind that—look at the *horses!*" exclaimed Fabrizio. The Venetian boys crowded to the taffrail: most of them had never seen a living one.

"No," breathed Renzo, "look at that!" He opened his arms.

The heart of London! Retreating into an unimaginable distance, they saw the scribbled outlines of irregular buildings rendered almost transparent by the sighs of a hundred thousand chimneys. Some structures were so tall and narrow, and so closely perched upon the water, that Teo's homesick heart was reminded of Venice. Yet all the great public buildings were on a grandiose scale that made Venice seem like a quaint colony of dollhouses. Even the smallest London warehouse loomed ten times larger than the biggest palace in Venice. Every bridge, chimney and arch seemed of heroic proportions. Between the great edifices, there were glimpses of medieval towers jostling against half-timbered mansions that seemed to be folded from crisp white paper. On higher ground, stone barracks, fitted with a fierce regularity of windows, glared in serried ranks. The Londoners, all dressed in smart black mourning, strode about their business, visibly quivering with energy, even at that distance. Thoroughly intimidated, the sailors fell silent and simply gazed.

Finally, Fabrizio whispered what they were all thinking: "Could human beings have built such a place? Londoners . . . must be *formidable*."

Teo answered, "I see what Lussa meant now—if there was ever any magic here, it must have been crushed by the weight of industry. No wonder the Londoners don't believe in ghosts anymore. They just believe in London!"

The Gothic battlements of Tower Bridge rose in front of them. Renzo was struck silent. Teo, remembering the money-box, stole close and put her hand on his shoulder.

"I'm thinking *that's* from the Middle Ages!" breathed Emilio, but Renzo soon corrected him. "It's only seven years old! They just built it to look that way. Look on the other side, that's the Tower of London, and there's Traitors' Gate. They are *really* old. But the bridge is a marvel of modern engineering."

"It's so low! We'll never pass below it with our mast!"

"Watch and see." Renzo smiled mysteriously. "*Hydraulic* power!" and even as he spoke, the road at the center of the bridge suddenly jerked and then split in two, the two sides rising like a pointy hat. A huddle of tall-masted ships hurried through and then the bridge closed again. On the other side, they glimpsed smaller vessels and barges dodging between the greater ones, and whole clusters of boats moored in floating colonies in the middle of the river.

A small iceberg nudged against the side of the *Scilla*, making everyone jump. Until this moment, excitement had kept their minds off their numb hands. But now Sebastiano blurted, "London's cold is as bad as anything we had in Venice!"

Their eyes were drawn to the white rim of the river: the edges of the Thames were starting to ice over just like the Grand Canal.

In the distance, the dome of St. Paul's rose like a jeweled egg in a pillared cup. Yet even its grave magnificence glittered with a crusting of ice. Ahead of them, a long yellow-brick building boasted gilded-fish weather vanes shimmering with frost.

"Billingsgate Fish Market," said Renzo. "Oh, look, Tower Bridge is opening again. Our turn now!"

The bridge passing was accomplished without incident, thanks to Renzo's quick thinking and firm hand at the wheel. Then they plunged into the maelstrom of river traffic. After weeks at open sea, this was almost as fearsome as a colossal squid, for everywhere fast vessels loomed up at desperately close quarters, their captains yelling threats and insults. The *Scilla* was soon buffeted out of Renzo's control.

As the *Scilla* lurched toward the low arches of London Bridge, Fabrizio cried, "We're *definitely* going to lose our masts this time!"

His words were drowned out by a sound of splintering wood. Teo felt as if her own neck was being wrenched from her shoulders. In a cloud of sawdust, the taller masts crumpled in two, their upper halves hanging down like half-sawn trees.

Then, to the south, just past London Bridge, a slender opening in the river appeared, its gray water lapping delicately almost at the feet of a pretty Gothic church. A sign read ST. MARY OVERIE DOCK. REASONABLE RATES. FOREIGN SHIPS WELCOME.

As one, the sailors nodded. There was something so cheerful about that sign: something that seemed specifically designed to welcome a mortally damaged ship of shivering Venetian orphans, with little money apart from a couple of sovereigns kept back from a few days of involuntary pirating.

Renzo, grunting with effort, pulled the *Scilla* away from the Customs House. By inches, they avoided a Norwegian ship from which an overpowering smell of fish floated.

Zigzagging through barges, square-sterned American half clippers, lumber schooners and men-of-war, Renzo maneuvered the *Scilla* neatly into an empty berth at St. Mary Overie Dock, shouting, "Get the anchors off the bows and let them hang by the cat-stoppers and shank-painters!"

The sailors had not finished hugging each other when an old man appeared. He looked at their flags. "Eyetalian, eh? How long you stay-ee here? You pay-ee now-now in advance, all good, *bene*? You have gold guineas? No? What's that? French coin? Is all right. I take two for now, you decide later how long you stay. Good, yes? Fresh water well there. Clink Street thataway. Horses—gee-gees— thataway. Hatton Garden, all your Eyetalian friends, over river. Food, beer. *La Gazzetta Italiana di Londra* for read! You got barrel organs, *bene*? You got monkeys? You play good? Good, good. Ropes you tie here." He indicated an iron ring on the wharf. He was still muttering instructions as he walked off. The Venetians had not needed to say a word.

Clink Street was a dark canyon lined with warehouses. Dank cobbles threaded with mud meandered drunkenly down the middle. Dismally thin horses clopped down the sides, pulling shabby carts.

Rickety structures, darkly varnished with wet soot, seemed to prop one another up like wounded soldiers returning from a war long past. People hurried back and forth, hunched in threadbare clothes. Several children scuttled in front of the boat. At least, they had the dimensions of children. Their faces were prematurely aged and their limbs wizened.

Renzo lifted the telescope to his eye, searching the grim streets for some sign of the promised wonders of London. "Where are the moleskin waistcoats, greatcoats with velvet collars and twenty-five-shilling hats? And the silk umbrellas that Miss Uish said everyone carried . . . ?"

"Same place as all the other lies she ever told us," answered Fabrizio bitterly. He peered with his sharp eyes into the street. "Look at those bundles of rags lying in the alleyways. Those are people. Beggars! Miss Uish said that even the poor of London lived in palaces. It doesn't look much like, does it?"

"What's that terrible smell?"

Unlike the other London odors they'd briefly picked up in passing, this one seemed to wrap itself around the boat. There was no sailing away from its sourness. Renzo glanced at the map propped by the wheel. "Ah, we're at Southwark. So that'll be the smoke from the chimneys of the brewers, the leather-tanners and the soap-boilers."

"And why has the sky turned that color? It looks like . . ."

"London is famous for its sudden deep fogs. There are different kinds—a cold 'hot-chocolate' fog, a mint-green fog, a turmeric-yellow pea-soup fog."

"You're making me hungry," moaned Giovanni. "Let's go and find some food. Then we'll have the strength to look for those mermaids and Incogniti. Didn't you say they sell hot sliced pumpkin?"

"Any volunteers for a reconnoitering party?" asked Renzo.

Not a single hand was raised.

212

"It have got to be the ones what spake the local lingo the bestest, hain't it not?" suggested Sebastiano in his worst possible English.

Eight pairs of eyes turned to Renzo and Teo.

Renzo pocketed the telescope and shinnied neatly down the ladder to plant his feet on the cobbles.

Swaying slightly, he looked up at Teo. "You coming?"

Teo joined him promptly below. As the two stepped unsteadily into the gloom of Clink Street, an officious-looking man in a serge suit bustled onto the quay.

Renzo whispered, "I don't like the look of that."

He pulled Teo behind a post.

"Eyetalian, is she?" the officer muttered, staring at the broken masts and the *Scilla*'s flags, the green, red and white stripes of the Italian one, and the Venetian winged lion.

"Worse and worser! Venice. Dear me. Oh, dear me. *Tsk tsk tsk.*"

He produced a long roll of tape from his overcoat and proceeded to drape it around the quayside. He announced, "No exit from this ship, or entry upon it."

A small knot of bystanders gathered to hear him intone, "All ships from the afflicted city of Venice—where the Half-Dead disease rages—are to be quarantined until further notice. London must be kept safe from the Venetian sickness."

"Guards!" he called.

And two officers marched to the quayside, thrust their rifles across their bellies and took up their posts in front of the *Scilla*.

33. The Mansion Dolorous

early evening, Southwark, London, January 24, 1901

"**P**ssst!"

They'd hardly walked a hundred yards before four pairs of hands seized Teo and Renzo from behind. Another two pairs of hands covered their mouths and eyes. They were propelled around a low wall, and then pushed to the ground on their bellies. Teo rolled over, escaping the blinding hands for a moment. She just had time to glimpse a sign that said NAKED BOY YARD before her face was slapped hard enough to make her eyes water. She could hear Renzo getting the same treatment.

"This is *our* pitch, unnerstand? Hands off! Sling yer hooks and doan come back. Got it?"

"I thinks they's on a doings. Look at 'em. Sneakin' around."

"Is they on the cadge? They is thin 'nough for to do that."

"On the cadge?" asked Teo.

"Beggars! Is you shipwrecked mariner beggars, or blown-up minin' beggars, or distressed-author beggars, or starved-out bakers' apprentice beggars? Or none of the above?" The boy counted off the possibilities on his fingers.

Teo and Renzo stared helplessly up at their inquisitor, a plump boy of their own age. Their English was adequate for piracy on the high seas, but they were in difficulties with these strange words. Teo's head was jumbled with the uncertain scripts she'd seen above the Londoners' heads. Most of these boys and girls had only a vague grasp of the alphabet, it seemed.

"Or is you thumble-screwers, sawney-hunters, or drag-sneaks?" demanded another boy, this one thin and freckled.

"I cannot be sure," replied Teo, "however, I think it unlikely. Please to explain what those things are."

"Watch-thieves, or bacon-stealers, or robbers what help thesselves to goods wot is on carts?" The boy's voice was stern.

With relief, Teo cried out, "Oh, *definitely* not. We are . . ."

Her voice trailed away as more small figures slunk from the shadows until a circle of a dozen skinny, dirty boys and girls surrounded them, staring with narrowed eyes. All were clad in the deepest black from head to toe, except where dirt and dust had lightened their somber uniform with smudges of gray. Their faces, incongruously, were shining pink and clean.

"Why doan they say nuffink?" asked a girl with overly short arms hanging uselessly from thin shoulders.

"Cat got yer tongues, then?" demanded a boy coated in mud up to his knees.

With dignity and in his very best English, Renzo replied, "We are in full possession of our tongues. The feline race does not in general consume human organs of elocution."

"Wot? 'E's speakin furrin, ain't he?"

"No, that were English, jist pumped fulla pompous."

"La-di-*dah*!"

The muddy boy drew in his breath, wheezing. "Wot if they's *spies* for the mendicity officers?" He poked his finger at Renzo's face. "Or is you truancy officers for the London School Board? Talkin' loik that!"

The Londoners drew back fearfully at the mention of the truancy officers. The freckled boy held out a coin with a pleading look on his face. "Give you this if you doan dob us in to the mendicities. We doan want to go to the Refuge for Homeless and Destitute Children, an' make shoes an' wash clothes . . ."

"We are not spies!" cried Teo indignantly.

"That short-haired girlie speaks plain English anyway," observed the boy who was conspicuously plumper than the rest. "So if you's not spies, what is you?"

"Venetians from Venice, apprentice sailors from the good ship *Scilla*," declared Renzo proudly.

"You doan look much loik sailors, Mister Cyclopeedy. Anyways, I thort Venice drownded under the ice and everybody dieded o' that plague they got there."

"Not everybody." There was a catch in Renzo's voice.

"Renzo's mother drowned," explained Teo in a low voice. "So did his Uncle Tommaso. And his father was a gondolier, but he died from his chest a long time ago. And my real parents were drowned, and now the people who adopted me have been kidnapped."

"Poor show. Hain't the bobbies been able to find 'em?"

"The police," explained a curly-headed girl.

Teo shook her head.

"None of us has got Mas or Pas neither," chorused the boys and girls. "Some of us mothers died. And some dint, but we is better orf wivout 'em."

"I don't understand." Renzo knitted his brows. "We were told there were no poor children or orphans in London."

"Indeedy? Ha!" The Londoners guffawed, and the plump boy was obliged to lie on the ground and hold his belly for some minutes. Then he grinned up at Teo and Renzo, asking, "Now, my treacles, the real question is, has you got any pie? Or giblets wiv gravy and rice an' potatoes an' coffee boiled expressly loik they drinks in Italy?"

"Sorry, we don't have any food," replied Teo earnestly. "If we did, we'd give it to you."

The boy jumped to his feet, his eyes alight with excitement. "Hey, maybe they can git us some hot zooky! They is Eyetalian, they *must* know the zookymen. They talks their lingo anyways. They can interduce us friendly-loik."

"Hot zooky?" asked Teo.

"Only the very latest novelty in savory snacks, innit! A bunch o' Eyetalians is jest arrived in London, sellin' hot spicy pumpkin by the slice."

" 'Zucca' being the Italian word for 'pumpkin,'" said Renzo triumphantly.

Teo's and Renzo's eyes met delightedly. Those pumpkin-sellers—the Venetian Incogniti sent by Lussa—were exactly the people that they desperately wanted to find.

"We'd love to," cried Teo. "Let's go right now! Where can we meet with them?"

"Steady on, girl. Termorrow hafternoon, maybes. It's dark now, not safe on the streets, not for zooky-sellers nor childer. Termorrow mornin' we's got a job on, and after that, well, we's got our own doings to do."

217

"Doings?" asked Renzo and Teo simultaneously.

One by one, the Londoners stepped forward to introduce themselves and their professions.

"Hyrum Hoxton," said the freckled boy. "I sell these 'ere Lucifers"—he struck one of his matches to demonstrate—"an' bootlaces."

Rosibund Grayhoare and Ann Picklefinch, both thin and mousy-haired, told of how they had run away from cruel homes in Glasgow.

"We call 'em the Haggis-munchers." Hyrum explained that they were named after a Scottish confection of sheep's innards held together with grease and oatmeal. The girls' eyes glazed over with culinary nostalgia and their mouths curved upward at the memory of it.

"Now we's snide-blitzers 'n' snide-bubblers," said the one called Ann, showing fingers apparently wrinkled by long immersion in soapy water, while Rosibund jingled her pockets.

"They clean up dirty coins," explained the plump boy, bowing as he introduced himself as "Greasy Ressydew, boy of all trades."

Next, the girl with the short arms edged forward. "Sally Twin-ish," she coughed. "I weren't borned loik this. My ma put me in with the baby-farmers and they shut me in a box so I'd grow up crookedish. They wanted me more pathetical, so they could put me out on the streets to beg. And when I weren't pathetical enough, they whipped me till I were. Then they gave me back to my ma, so she could turn a penny on me. She kept a pin under her dress to make me weep when she carried me round town. So soon as I could walk, I runned away. Now I begs on me own account, and I shares me takin's with me friends, loik. Ta very much!" She smiled warmly at a curly-headed girl who had edged over and now popped a piece of licorice between her lips.

"Tig Sweetiemouth allus feeds me, as me hands doan reach me teef."

Tig smiled shyly at the Venetians and offered them some licorice.

The muddy boy introduced himself next. "Bits Piecer. Mud-lark. I goes in the Thames at low tide and finds stuff." He pulled a much-dented coffeepot from the enormous pockets of his ragged jacket. "Worth a shillin' at the pawnbrokers. Course I hain't saying that I hain't got a power o' work to do on it first." He rubbed it with his thin elbow, producing a slight shine.

A sour whiff preceded the next boy, who did not proffer his hand. "Tobias Putrid, they calls me. I's a tosher. I do wot Bits do in the mud. But in the sewer."

A girl with a scarf wrapped around her lower jaw shuffled up. Her round eyes creased into a smile, yet from her hidden mouth came only inarticulate noises. Teo leaned forward in sympathy. Renzo asked, "Why does she wear the scarf?"

"She were a match girl," said Tobias Putrid, as if that explained everything. "And now she's a cat-gut scraper."

Seeing the questions in the Venetians' eyes, Greasy cut in bluntly, "She's got the phossy jaw, my treacles, doan ye know? Her teeth is gone and her jawbone is rotted by that phossyphorus they use in the match factory. There's dozens loik her. Marg'rit found her dyin' behind the factory gate, put out wiv the rubbish. We doan even know her name, and she can't tell us, can she, so we calls her Fossy. She plays the fiddle—wot's strung wiv cat-gut strings—loik an angel. Show 'em, Fossy."

Fossy produced a shabby little fiddle and played a few notes. It was as if she spoke. The longing and the sweetness were all perfectly legible in her music, like words written on a piece of a paper.

"She's talking about her mother!" exclaimed Teo.

"Who is dead," whispered Renzo.

"Marg'rit Savory has heard her whole story, hain't you, Marg'rit?"

Marg'rit's plump hand crept out to hold Fossy's. "Yes, she's a sweetheart, Fossy. And she would be so pretty if it weren't for the phosphorus. Her ma were a celebrated beauty. Fossy's got her ma's hair."

Marg'rit stroked it, adding, "Of course, Fossy's own barnet fell out when she got sick. So when her ma died, they used her hair to make a wig for her little girl. It were all she had to leave. The quacks had taken all the rest."

"Quacks?"

Pylorus Salt, a towheaded boy with clever eyes, introduced himself and explained, "Them what sell fake medicines on the street corners. It's pure poison, but how them ladies goes for it! There must be summat in it that makes 'em keep comin' back for more, says I."

Next Renzo and Teo were introduced to "the District Disgrace," who lisped: "My mother wath so 'shamed of me that she moved houth wivout tellin' me."

"What did you do to disgrace her?" Teo could not hide her shock.

"No idea. I think I wanted feedin' too often. That's woth she alwayth sayed."

The last boy offered his hand. "Thrasher Geek, general lad-

220

about-town. I say, you doan have any of them Eyetalian barrel organs on your boat, do you? I'd love to have a try. Or dancing mice?"

"Sorry, we had to leave Venice in a hurry. Nothing like that," said Renzo.

Once all the introductions had been done, Greasy Ressydew turned to Teo and Renzo with a huge grinning yawn. "Well, ta-ta then, golden dreams, my treacles. We's off for some pie and shut-eye."

"And where do you repose?" asked Renzo, his own tiredness etched in gray all over his face. Teo too was suddenly stupendously, utterly, overwhelmingly tired. Her shoulders drooped. Yet the quarantine meant that they could not go back to the *Scilla*.

"Yew means sleep? We sleep loik royalty! We lay ourselves down in the lap of looxury each night, my dears," Bits answered with a grin.

"Upon velvet!" Rosibund and Ann seemed always to speak together.

"Upon black velvet 'n' silk 'n' all sorts of lace! So long as it's black, for that is 'the garb of tears,'" quoted Greasy.

"In there!" A dozen smudged thumbs pointed at a somber building in the distance. It was painted black and adorned with large, sober lettering picked out in white and embellished by many curlicues.

Renzo pulled the telescope out of his pocket. He read aloud:

"The Mansion Dolorous
The Family Mourning Emporium
Of Tristesse & Ganorus

All Vestments of Sorrow
Supplied and made to order
Offers Advantages to
the Nobility
And Families of the
Highest Rank
Also to Those of Limited Means."

"It's enormous!" remarked Teo.

"And extremely dolorous," added Renzo. "What are Tristesse and Ganorus?"

"A pair of kind-'earted gintlemen. We works their funerals when we can. But we still keeps our own steady lurks 'n' trades on the side. Ye kint rely on people for to die jest 'cos you want tenpence in fees. They dies when they feels loik it. Meantimes, trouble is, we still gits hungry." The stench of sewers that came off him as Tobias spoke was a powerful reminder of what his trade was.

The boys and girls rustled in their various pockets and produced small card-mounted photographs of themselves posing beside potted aspidistra ferns. Each of them was dressed in fashionable mourning and looking as sad as could be.

"Why do you look so miserable in these pictures?"

"We're in the business of sad, girl! We sell sad. That's what a mourning emporium's supposed to be for."

"The mourning emporium sells photographs of children's faces looking sad?"

"Nah! When Mr. Ganorus goes callin' on the bereaved, he takes our pictures wiv him so people can choose which one of us they want for carryin' the Pathetic Floral Tributes, and walkin' alongside the coffin and weepin'."

"You cry for dead people you don't know?"

"It's a gift," said Bits. "I hain't sayin' it comes to everyone natural-loik, but it kin be coltervated. Watch. Everyone . . . on count of three. One, two, three . . . *mourn!*"

Instead of bursting into noisy tears, each child adopted a serious expression, cast his or her lids down, and squeezed a small teardrop out of one or both eyes.

"See? Plus," explained Tig, "we dress up and show the ladies the latest mournin' fashions in minicher. Wivout that they has to vulgarly take their own clothes orf to try 'em on. They doan wanna be bare nakid, even though Mr. Tristesse does lay on a nice coal fire for us all."

"A great shop of that nature exclusively for mourning vestments?" Renzo marveled.

Tobias Putrid nodded. "It's a queer lash-up, I know. But Queen Vic—rest her mean ole soul—set the fashion. You know she were a-grievin' forty year an' more for her Albert. Wouldn't wear nuffink 'cept the strictest black mourning, an' all her gewgaws was black too. Well, wot Her Madge doed, the nobility doed, an' what the nobs do, then the jumped-up shopkeepers do too. It's been like this ever since Her Madge became a widder. If you asks me, this whole town's one big mourning emporium, that's wot it is."

He held up an arm clad in ribbons of black, like a dilapidated crow's wing. "Black crepe from Norwich! You kint get no finer 'n that."

Teo reached out an inquisitive finger. The fabric was the dullest- and stiffest-looking silk she'd ever seen.

Bits said, "And if it hain't crape then it's plain paramatta, merino wool and cashmere. S'long as it's black as the Earl of Hell's riding boots."

"So you sleep in there with all the black dresses and crepe?" asked Teo.

"And the coffins?" Renzo's tone was lugubrious.

"*In* the coffins, ackshally." Greasy smiled. "Silk-lined, an' uncommon comfortable they is too. Brass, lead, wood, wickerwork, as you loik. 'Cept for Tobias. He sleeps in an anty-room to the privy. On account of . . ." He wrinkled his nose.

Tobias looked down. "'S'quite comfortable. I loik it there. Peaceful-loik. Anyway, Greasy snores. An' the District Disgrace cries in her sleep. All that sobbin's a trouble an' a dratted nuisance for the rest of us."

The Londoners were meanwhile exchanging significant glances, followed by nods all round. Greasy spoke gruffly. "You hain't got nowheres to kip, does you?"

"No," responded Teo bluntly. "We can't go back to our boat. The officer . . ."

Renzo threw her a warning look. Mentioning the Half-Dead disease quarantine was not likely to endear them to the Mansion Dolorous inhabitants.

"And we're not going to get sick," she told herself firmly. "If we were, we would have got ill in Venice. Or on the journey."

Greasy said generously, "We's decided to let yous come in wiv us. Turtledove woan say naught agin' it, I hopes."

"Turtle . . . ?"

"He's the chief-dog-in-mourning, wot took us all into the Mansion Dolorous. He walks in front of all the grand funeral processions, innit, wiv black ostrich plumes on his head."

"So this Turtledove can talk?" Teo was pleasantly excited when Greasy nodded in a matter-of-fact way. "Turtledove speaks more helegant than we does, to tell the truth."

Teo smiled. So there *was* some magic left in London! At least London children were not immune to it, even if the adults were.

"You work for a *dog*?" A superior tone crept into Renzo's voice.

"We worked for *Miss Uish*, Renzo," Teo reminded him, before he got too much above himself.

"We works for a dog an' we's nobbut grateful for it, my treacles," Greasy reproved. "Yew comin' or not?"

34. A cunning secret entrance

a few minutes later

They shuffled through the snow that lay in dirty pillows all over the crooked, sour streets of Southwark, passing under humid railway arches that trailed dark tears of ancient moisture. Overhead, the chimneys belched beery odors and worse. As they walked, the Londoners told Teo and Renzo of their many famished goings-to-bed and belly-growling mornings before they found Turtledove and the Mansion Dolorous; of sleeping in ditches and waking with rats snoring on their heads.

"Did you have to steal?" Renzo asked shrewdly.

"Some of us used to be in that way at one time," admitted Greasy roundaboutly. "A boy must git summat warm to put across his back, and his vittuals—or he gits the hungry staggers, doan you know?—so, blunt-loik, yes, there was days when we ate pies we found on windersills an' wore wot we could reach on washin' lines. . . ."

"And now look, what helegance!" Pylorus Salt hastily held up his arms for a general inspection of his clothing, revealing quite a deal of flesh through various apertures that did not figure in the original construction of those garments. "'Strue, they's all a bit bald where they rub, but at least they's warm, an' they's ours, an' we dint 'ave to beg for 'em at the Old Clothes Exchange in Houndsditch, an' we doan has to rent 'em out by night for others to wear while we is sleeping."

"Before we met Turtledove," said Greasy, "our lives was pitiful. They called us Ravens or Nobody's Children. When we couldn't turn a penny on our reg'lar doings, we had to hide in grand door-ways so's we could leap out to open cab doors for a tip. We turned somersaults in the mud on the hope of a half-penny. We even dived into the stinkin' river for sixpences that the nobs throwed.

"Sometimes we had to walk all night because the bobbies wunt let the likes of us sleep in doorways. We couldn't hardly ever afford the three-penny lodgin' houses. We dozed all day on park benches. *Now* we gets decent grub, we sleeps in comfort, and we got an income time to time wiv the funerals." He looked hard at Renzo. "I hain't goin' to have any jumped-up sorts from Venice tell me we's not in the pink."

"Of course not," agreed Teo hastily. "And yes, we'd be grateful if you'd permit us to share your lodgings."

Renzo opened his mouth. Teo kicked his ankle, adding, "*Abjectly* grateful."

"'S our cunning secret entrance, innit, to the Mansion Dolorous."

Greasy lifted a flap to a letterbox and turned a lever in the aperture. In the middle of an ivy-covered wall, a previously invis-ible door swung aside. Greasy parted the tendrils of ivy whitened with ice. The Londoners filed in, beckoning Teo and Renzo to follow. Thrasher struck a flint to a lantern on a hook by the door. Tig pulled aside a velvet curtain and they were plunged into a delightfully warm darkness, except for the wavering light of the lantern.

"What the bucket . . . !" exclaimed Teo, and then she too was silenced by the prospect that began to emerge in front of them as the Londoners darted about like fireflies, lighting ornamented gaslamps.

"A warehouse full of mourning vestments" did not even begin to describe this Aladdin's cave of jet-black merchandise. The walls of the Mansion Dolorous undulated into towering riches warmed by glowing grates at regular intervals. Racks of dresses stretched into the distance until they congealed into a slew of blackness. There were solidly packed shelves of black-edged stationery, visiting cards and envelopes. Teo glimpsed a card that read, *You are desired to accompany the corpse of . . .* , with a blank left for a name. There were perfume bottles bedecked with black ribbons. Black gloves were neatly folded on trolleys next to rolls of black braiding trimmed with beads and sequins, black fringes, silk and jet drops. There were crisply pleated silk mourning fans mounted on ebonized sticks, black feather boas coiled in rustling black nests, and white mourning handkerchiefs embroidered with black teardrops. There were mourning cockades for coachmen's hats. An immense haberdashery cupboard was honeycombed with compartments for black hairpins, black rosettes and black armbands.

Mourning jewelry winked somberly from glass-topped cases. Renzo and Teo bent over a display of brooches made of human hair plaited and shaped into patterns and set behind glass. Other brooches showed dim daguerreotypes of sad faces. There were gold mourning rings inset with black enamel, gray and black pearls, shiny jet bracelets, scarf pins, tiaras, jeweled and feathered hair combs, lockets, pendants and cameos with white profiles etched on onyx backgrounds. There were mourning lampshades in Chinese pongee silk and mourning bookmarks embroidered with forget-me-nots and doleful poems. There were black funeral teapots and associated tea plates, and even a mourning ear trumpet in vulcanite, horribly reminiscent of a black bat. And immortal wreaths of flowers fashioned from parian and silk stood stiff and white under glass domes.

"How the English love death!" marveled Teo. "They seem to enjoy dying more than living. They must spend more money on it, anyway."

"You hain't wrong," affirmed Hyrum Hoxton. "And this hain't even the biggest mournin' emporium in London Town. You should see Jay's in Regent Street. They is our deadly rivals. We hates em loik poison."

Even the white baby clothes stocked by Tristesse & Ganorus featured smocking threaded through with stark black ribbon.

"Poor babies," thought Teo. She might have worn one of those herself when she attended her real parents' funeral in Venice, yet she had been too young to have any memory of it now. Renzo, she suddenly remembered, had not even been allowed to attend his mother's funeral. The Mayor had been in such a hurry to get rid of him. A glance at Renzo's grief-stricken face told her he was thinking the same thing.

A pure white dress of lace and satin-scalloped ribbon caught her eye, reminding her unwelcomely of Sibella. Then she noticed the dress had no back.

"Burial gown," explained Bits briefly. "The dead doan need to cover their behinds when they's lyin' in their coffins."

A whole rack of mourning capes stretched back into the dark recesses of the warehouse. Teo ran her hands down one that was studded with black beads.

"Quality jet, you know, from Whitby," Bits informed her. "None o' that cheap French himitation stuff here!"

There were even mourning sweetmeats in miniature coffers. "That's the best mourning licorice from Knaresborough." Greasy opened a box and offered it round. The Venetians also sampled some delicious aniseed comfits and dark purple crystallized mourning grapes.

Teo walked wonderingly through rows of hats, all neatly labeled and then placed according to the size of head.

Then came the mourning underwear, carefully folded elaborate black nothings all discreetly labeled: *Cambric combinations, Trimmed with Torchon Lace Insertion; Ladies' Longcloth Mourning Knickers, Superfine Cambric, Nottingham Lace; Ladies' Mourning Knickers, Plain Featherstitched, Trimmed Embroidery and Insertion, Plain; Shrewsbury Flannels; Mourning Camisoles; Black Melton Gaiters.* A flash of bright purple caught Teo's attention.

"What's that?" she asked. "I thought I saw a bit of color?"

"After a widder's done a year an' a day in total crepe, that's deepest mourning, and then she do nine month wiv only half the crepe, but always black," intoned Greasy. "However, she may add some velvet ribbons an' jet, if she loiks, doan ye know?"

Thrasher took up the account. "Then she do six months o' half-mourning, which means as she's 'lowed to wear a bit of trimmings in gray, white or purple or heliotrope. Then, gradual-loik, the amount of color grows, till she's wearing almost ordinary clothes, but she has trimmings of mourning loik these"—he held up some jet buttons—"and these"—some black belts set with glittering eyes of jet. "It's the same rules for hats an' bonnets."

He was interrupted by a cry of pleasure from Renzo: "Look, a book department!"

"It's the Improving Tomes Library," said Greasy. "Not so very cheerful readin', I's afraid."

Renzo ran an expert finger down the black morocco spines, reading aloud in mocking wonder: *"Our Childrens' Rest, or Comfort for Bereaved Mothers* by Anonymous; *Cometh Up as a Flower* by Rhoda Broughton; *Why Weepest Thou?—A Book for Mourners; The Death and Burial of Three Little Kittens; Dead Men's Shoes* by Mrs. Braddon . . . oh, and here's Mr. Ruskin's *The Stones of Venice!* But Teo," Renzo moaned, "the pages have all gone black!"

"Like the postcards," whispered Teo. "Images of Venice. He wants to destroy them all."

Replacing the blackened book, Renzo now lifted a slim volume weighed down with the title *A Token for Children: Being an Exact Account of the Conversion, Holy and Exemplary Lives and Joyful Deaths of Several Young Children,* by the Rev. J. Janeway.

"Look at this, Teo. What tosh!" Renzo did not notice the expressions of the Londoners hardening as they gathered around him in silence.

He was still leafing through *A Token for Children* when a large, hairy paw landed with a thump on his shoulder, pushing him, then pinning him to the ground on his belly.

"Yew'd trespass then, would yew, boy?" growled a voice behind Renzo's ear. "Yew'd touch what ain't yourn, ye vagabone?"

Renzo's mouth fell open, but no words came out.

"We doan take kindly to snootified trespassers at the Mansion Dolorous," snarled the voice, which was perfumed with a strong smell of raw meat. "In fact, we tends to bile 'em up and eat 'em wiv custard. Wot yew got to say for yerself, boy?"

35. 'Childer wot needs takin' in kindness an' lovin' up a bit'

five seconds after that

Turtledove was built more for inspiring awe than for speed. However, it was a speedy cuff that the brindled bulldog administered to the side of Renzo's head now, and a speedy blow with which he rolled Renzo on his back, holding him down by a paw to the throat. The fob-watch from the dog's black sateen waistcoat dangled above Renzo's terrified eyes.

"Wot we got here, me lovelies?" The dog thrust his massive muzzle into Renzo's face, his jowls visibly shaking with outrage.

"We are exceedingly sorry, we didn't intend . . . please forgive the intrusion," gabbled Renzo.

"Speak plain, boy, do. I hates an oily tongue. Shows me a slimy heart."

Despite the fury of the dog's growl, Teo was reassured by the open, generous style of the writing visible only to her above Turtledove's head.

She spoke rapidly. "We're Venetians. We've come on the floating orphanage, the *Scilla*, to escape the ice in Venice, and to look for my parents, who've been kidnapped. They may be in London.

And we believe that Venice's deadly enemy—he's a ghost called Bajamonte Tiepolo—is here or on his way here too. He killed your Melusine and Sea-Bishops—those poor creatures that were found floating dead in the Thames a few weeks ago."

"A dirty shame!" exclaimed Turtledove, removing his paw from Renzo's throat. "'Twere all over the papers, an' none of it were kind, wot they sayed about the poor beasties. Old Queen Victoria dint approve of 'em one bit. But wot's this Venetian Bajaminty thingy got to do wiv us in London, then?"

Renzo, still flat on his back, answered, "He's in league with the Pretender to the British throne, Lord Harold Hoskins. They're planning something terrible. . . ."

"You doan mean that jumped-up nob wot were sent to Orstralia?" asked Turtledove disbelievingly.

"How come you never menshoned any of this 'mazing stuff before?" Pylorus Salt interrupted. "Sounds 'ighly unloikly to me! London's the greatest city in the world. How can some old Venetian ghosty hurt us?"

Teo explained, "Baddened magic. That's what brought the ice storm to Venice. And our boat was taken over by a terrible woman who whipped and starved us. And now she's with some awful Ghost-Convicts on the *Bad Ship Bombazine*, which will doubtless shortly arrive in London and start the attack . . . just when London is at her most vulnerable, with Queen Victoria dead."

Renzo rose to his feet. "Bajamonte Tiepolo is a coward who preys only on the weakened. His friend Miss Uish is just the same. That's why we urgently need to find Venetian Incogniti—who are disguised as pumpkin-sellers. They'll take us to the mermaids who've swum here from Venice."

The boys and girls of the Mansion Dolorous stood open-mouthed.

"A female *child*-hurter?" A deep, dreadful growl vibrated in Turtledove's throat. The glimmer of a tear appeared in the corner of one fierce eye. "Yew two mites is been through all that? Yew is all on yer alonesome in London Town? In them thin clothes? And the snow's a-lyin' thick as Irish linen over the whole city? Look at the ribs stickin' out of yew! Feelin' numblish, is yew? When did yew last git somethin' good to eat?"

The kindness of his tone undid Teo. "Ages ago," she sobbed.

"And it wasn't very good either," moaned Renzo. A bit of sympathy had unbuttoned all his bravery too.

Turtledove winked. "I thought as much. Yew have that air about yew. Of childer wot needs takin' in kindness an' lovin' up a bit."

That dog had the most expressive wink Teo had ever seen. Perhaps it was because his large eyes were so wide apart above his huge snout. And now she was made to realize why the Mansion Dolorous boys and girls all had such clean faces: Turtledove proceeded to lick her face industriously, removing every trace of tears.

"Childer," he barked at the Londoners, "bring food for these little ones, do. I has been to Butcher Brown's an' me satchel's full o' goodness."

A platter of broken pie was placed in front of Teo and Renzo.

"Gie it a chew!" urged Ann Picklefinch.

"Steak an' kidney!" shouted Tobias Putrid. "Superb!"

"I'm sorry," snuffled Teo, feeling very small indeed, "I'm a vegetarian."

"A *wot*?" boomed Turtledove.

235

"I don't eat meat. I don't like animals being killed."

Given that Turtledove was, while a figure of authority, clearly an *animal*, Teo hoped her opinion might be received with approval.

But the dog growled angrily again, jutting out his fearsome jaw. "For why've yew got the teef, then? I doan hold wiv that kind of unnatural doings, girlie. Look at poor Fossy here. She'd love to chew a cutlet, but she hain't got the 'quipment 'cos o' that cursed match factory where she worked. Marg'rit's gotta soupify everythin' for her. Turnin' down good food 'cos yew's too squeamish! I doan hold wiv it."

Turtledove cocked his leg. Teo stared up at him in horror.

Pylorus Salt whispered, "He do that on things he doan approve of."

The leg inched higher as Turtledove knitted his fantastically heavy brows. But the Mansion Dolorous gang seemed to know just what to do. They clustered around the dog, speaking very fast, changing the subject, even daring to thump his broad back affectionately. Turtledove's ferocity was soon tamed to gruffness. His leg returned by quarter-inches to the floor.

"I likes yew a heap, girlie, but I still doan hold wiv that vegetatin' lark," he muttered, staring hard at Teo. "Childer need victuallin'." Now put the kettle on, Tig. We'll bile up some o' that Benger's food wot Her Late Majesty favored, for the little Eyetalian girlie."

The Londoners screwed up their faces with distaste.

"Unpalatable, ain't it? Well, skilly, then."

Skilly proved to be a kind of porridge made from Indian corn and hot water. It wasn't tasty, yet it was filling. Teo scooped up two bowlfuls, only stopping when she felt as if a warm feather quilt had taken up residence inside her. Meanwhile, Renzo helped himself to a substantial portion of pie.

"Dint touch the sides, that," noted the dog approvingly.

Now that he had fed Teo and Renzo, Turtledove seemed to feel that the Venetian orphans were his own. "Look at them roses bloomin' in yer cheeks!" he exulted. "Who loves yew?" he asked, cuffing them lightly with his paw. "So yew'll be joinin' us then, little 'uns? In the meantimes, I mean, while we finds yer Incogneekies and yer mermaids for yew? Magical creatures doan get thesselves easily found. They will take some lookin' for."

"Join him?" thought Teo, Miss Uish's cruelty still fresh in her feelings. "I'd like to *hug* him!"

"And the *Bombazine?*" asked Renzo.

"We'll keep on eye on the Lloyd's Register."

"She's a ghost ship. Adult Londoners will not be able to see her. Nor the Ghost-Convicts."

Teo ventured, "And we need to tell our friends on the *Scilla* what is going on. They'll be worried about us. But we can't go ourselves because the ship is in quar . . ."

Renzo broke in, "Sealed up by the customs officers."

"Of course, yew wants to tell yer friends yew's safe," said Turtledove reassuringly. "Nothing simpler. I'll have a word wiv Pattercake."

Pattercake, it emerged, was a barge dog on the Thames.

"He knows a bit of Eyetalian. He works nights in an Eyetalian restaurant. He'll run a message to yer friends on the *Scilla*. Customs officers won't bovver '*im*."

"How does a dog work in a restaurant?"

"He's a washer-up. Dogs is very handy that way. Can lick a

plate clean quicker 'n an 'ooman can wash it. Yew two good for readin' an' writin'? Good. Write a letter. Pattercake will deliver it."

Greasy offered some sheets of black-edged notepaper and a slim black pencil.

"Mourning *pencils?*" asked Teo. She began to write rapidly. Eventually, she handed Renzo the paper and he added a page of his own.

. . . And so we'll be safe here at the Mansion Dolorous, and have found a way to keep ourselves until we can find Lussa and the Incogniti. We hope that the quarantine ropes will serve to keep our enemies off the Scilla, as well as keeping you in.

Renzo smiled at Teo, and then folded the sheets, and tucked them into a black-edged envelope, which he handed to Turtle-dove. "But we also need to get food to our friends. There's nothing much aboard."

"Not to worry," said Turtledove. "Pattercake'll take care o' that. They're right generous wiv the leftovers at his restaurant. Bits, take this letter down to Pattercake at Old Compton Street, do."

As Bits departed via the secret entrance, there came the jingle of a key in the lock of the Mansion Dolorous's front door.

"Messrs. Tristesse and Ganorus!" Turtledove growled. "Are the coffins shipshape? Good. Get that grin orf yer face, Greasy. Woan suit, woan suit at all. Stand in line an' look proper miserable," he ordered, pushing his head into a masterpiece of black straw. Jauntily set on top was a heart-shaped pincushion of jet beads from which sprouted curled black ostrich feathers.

He nudged Teo and Renzo in front of him.

"Why, Turtledove, have you found us two new children?" asked one of the two tidy old gentlemen who now walked into the main hall of the mourning emporium.

The writing above his head was neat and pleasant. Teo decided to like him. "Which is Tristesse and which Ganorus?" she asked.

Turtledove did not answer, but sat demurely on his brindled haunches, his head on one side. Teo realized, "With adults, Turtledove doesn't even try to talk. London must be like Venice—the adults have lost the ability to hear animals speak."

"Not that we're not grateful for the children, dear Dog," added the second gentleman, a small dapper person seemingly stitched into a tight buttonless black waistcoat. Teo saw a more imaginative and looser script above his head. He patted Turtledove's broad back.

"These two orphans is from Venice, Italy, sirs," volunteered Tig, "so they's bound to be uncommon good at sad, hain't they? Given the ice flood an' everybody drownin' an' all on Christmas Eve loik. And they speaks the Queen's Hinglish."

Their faces bright with curiosity, the two men approached. The dapper man smoothed the hair from Renzo's forehead with a manicured hand. "Look at this, Mr. Ganorus," he twittered, "hair, mouth and eyes of an angel. You cannot by any chance sing, boy? Jay's have just got themselves a singing mourning boy, and we've heard he's surpassingly popular. Do you read notes, boy?"

He handed Renzo some sheet music entitled "Little Sister's Gone to Sleep."

In answer, Renzo raised his eyes and let loose a few soulful notes that had the District Disgrace positively shivering with delight and Pylorus Salt rolling his eyes.

Mr. Tristesse clasped his hands to his breast, bleating with pleasure. "That'll give Jay's something to think about!" he crowed. Then he cast a shrewd eye on Teo. "This one's terribly thin. Good eyes, though. Can you weep a few drops, child?" he asked Teo kindly.

Teo had only to think of Professor Marìn's death and her missing parents, and the tears spurted from her eyes in clear streams that sparkled in the lamplight.

"Highly pathetical," said Mr. Ganorus approvingly. "That girl can mourn as well as any orphan in London."

Mr. Tristesse leaned down to pat Teo and Renzo affectionately on their heads. "Greasy, find these dear children some warm mourning clothes. And I think that Numbers Two and Thirteen coffins will do nicely for them."

36. A pint of tears

Sleeping in a coffin, however softly padded, held few charms. As soon as he laid himself down, Renzo missed the roll of the sea and the rough enfolding comfort of his hammock, not to mention the sleepy late-night chatter of the crew of the *Scilla*.

Renzo was also distinctly dubious about his six-foot elm coffin, ebonized and gilded, lined inside with ruffled satin over a wool mattress.

Teo's small mahogany coffin was quite humble in contrast. Its mattress was of cotton, the shroud of linen. There was only the merest graze of fretwork on the lid and handles. Teo's most urgent concern was to make certain that the lid was firmly bolted open. Once sure of that, she enjoyed stretching out inside her voluminous black flannel nightdress. Her eyes drooped. The District Disgrace sobbed inconsolably in her sleep. Greasy snored to an ecstatic rhythm. The mourning clocks—carriage, grandfather and wristwatch—ticked soothingly.

"Teo!" Renzo whispered. "Are you awake?"

"Slightly," she yawned. "What is it, Renzo? Don't you think we've been amazingly lucky?"

"But this isn't finding the mermaids. What if they've been attacked by whatever killed the Melusine and the Sea-Bishops? What if the *Bombazine* . . . ?"

"They were prepared. And Turtledove said he'd help us find them and the pumpkin-sellers. Isn't he adorable? Much better than trying on our own. We don't know the first thing about how to get around London."

"You've got maps in your head, memorized, haven't you?"

"True, but that's just paper. And we need friends. . . ."

Before she finished speaking, sleep had overtaken both Teo and Renzo.

Suddenly, Tig was opening the black curtains on a gray London morning, and it was time for Teo and Renzo's first funeral. Dressed to the neck in crepe, and smothered in mourning hats, the two of them walked in time to Thrasher's drumbeats beside an open hearse, on which lay a white-draped coffin with a spray of white ostrich plumes nodding on top. Renzo's tender singing, accompanied by Fossy's heartbreaking violin, rose above the sound of the city traffic, causing passersby to stop and stare at the coffin with tears in their eyes.

The carriage was drawn by four splendid Flemish geldings, black as jet, rippling their magnificent manes in tidy formation. The horses wore feathers on their heads, also in the deepest black. Satin rosettes decorated their velvety ears.

Turtledove waddled in front, his muzzle held at a noble angle.

The dead man was a minor member of an aristocratic Irish family. So the hearse was followed by a dozen carriages decorated with noble crests and driven by liveried coachmen. Yet all the carriages were empty. As they passed through the salubrious suburbs of

Mayfair and Belgravia, Tig explained, "Friends of the great famblies doan attend. It hain't done. They jist send the carriages as a sign of respeck. Doan look shocked. If the famblies came thesselves, we'd be out of a job today."

"What about ordinary people? Surely they come to their loved ones' funerals?"

"They do, bless 'em, but they still hire mourning children when they can afford themselves a bit of a show. They loik us to do the picturesque weepin'."

"Hoi, there's Tobias and Bits! They're mountin' the mournin' outside the corpse's own house, to show 'tis a place of sorrow today. Doan fret, Tobias's been scrubbed with carbolic."

Both boys wore long gowns of alpaca trimmed with velvet. From the tops of their hats flowed two thick ribbons of white Irish linen, tied in a bow. They stood solemnly to attention outside the stylish house, each holding an upside-down broom wrapped in black fabric and tied with enormous black bows on the stave. As the Mansion Dolorous mourners passed, Bits and Tobias remained aloof and poker-faced, neither greeting nor smiling at their friends.

"Have we done something to offend them?" asked Teo.

"Oh no, they hain't allowed to talk or smile when they is mournin'."

At that moment, Bits dared a subtle wink.

Tig instructed, "Now work them tear-pumps, Teo! We need to show the corpse's neighbors that the fambly has paid over for the very 'ighest quality o' grief. When they pays but two pounds and tenpence we can walk quite ordinary, but for twenty pounds we has got to go all out—at least a pint of tears between us. Tristesse and Ganorus pride thesselves on a spiffin' first-class funeral."

"You mean there are second-class funerals?"

"And third-class. And paupers' funerals at unmarked pits. We doan attend those, nat'rally. An' the street children wot die—we doan do it for the likes of them. No one pays for them to be buried. Their parents leaves their bodies in the streets, for to avoid the shame of a pauper's funeral."

"But that must be most rare . . . ," pressed Teo anxiously.

"I should just 'bout think it isn't," said Pylorus Salt, from behind her shoulder. "It said on the *Times* billboard last week that one child dies of hunger in London every hour."

After the funeral, Turtledove wriggled out of his finery and disappeared, saying, "Going to find yew some o' them Eyetalian zooky-men, or a taily lady or two, childer! Dint I promise I would?"

As Turtledove departed, Pattercake, a genial collie, arrived with a letter from the *Scilla*. All was well. The guards posted at St. Mary Overie Dock were not the most vigilant specimens of the force. The night watchman slept peacefully through his shift. (Perhaps Cookie's offer of a large cup of warm rum—gladly accepted in the cold—gave him sweet dreams.) Giovanni and Emilio had slipped off the *Scilla* in the early hours and had already found day-work with the bargemen. Their Venetian marine skills were much appreciated. Meanwhile, repairs were already underway on the *Scilla*, battered from her long journey and the encounter with the colossal squid.

As soon as we can afford a plank, we'll buy it and sneak it aboard, wrote Emilio. *We're already fixing the masts. Piece by piece we'll bring the old girl back to glory.*

He added, *I never thought I'd say this, but we're actually grateful to Miss Uish for the English lessons. Without them, I'm thinking we would have starved.*

Cookie had been taken to a blacksmith who gently removed the torturing wooden casings welded to his jaws.

Sibella, Emilio reported, was desperate to get ashore to the fashionable haunts of Belgravia and Pall Mall, where she apparently knew all the best people. *She will keep on about it.* Emilio quoted: *"This low end of London is quite unknown to me, yet it is plainly detestable. I shall die of disgust."*

Teo muttered, "It's actually quite surprising that she's survived this long without a new dress."

But we're keeping her aboard, continued Emilio. *We've decided that there's something about Sibella we can't quite trust. We've been thinking about what Teo said about her and the leeches and speaking spells to them. What's more, she doesn't like cats. Sofonisba doesn't like her either.*

The next lines were in Fabrizio's slanting handwriting. *And have you noticed that Miss Uish didn't even try to get a ransom for her? As if no one wanted her back? She never talks about her family, only about her dresses. And sometimes, when she thinks I'm not watching her, I see a really odd look go across her face.*

Sibella had given all of them coral necklaces. According to Emilio, who had obviously seized the pencil back, *She said they will change color and warn you if you're sickening for something.*

They didn't believe in them, but the boys wore them anyway, just in case.

Despite the good news, Renzo's face was pinched and pale. He clenched a damp, tattered newspaper in his hand.

"Why the long nose? Woan do, woan do at all!" Teo mimicked Turtledove, "You see, they are doing famously on the *Scilla*."

Renzo held out the paper. "I just picked this up in the gutter outside."

Teo too paled on reading the *Times*'s report of violent art thefts in cities all along the western coasts of Europe. In Cádiz, Oporto, Bilbao and Bordeaux, famous paintings had been ripped off the walls. Innocent guards and curators had been killed. And the stolen masterpieces? All Canalettos, Carpaccios and Longhis. And their subjects were invariably Venice and the Venetians. Looking at the map printed alongside the story, it was clear that whoever was stealing the art was gradually making their way toward London. And in every city where the Venetian art was pillaged, so too were the prisons broken into, and thousands of prisoners melted away into the countryside, with reports that many were later seen making their way north, toward the French coast. A separate story related immense losses among flocks of coastal sheep from southern Spain to France.

Renzo asked quietly, "And how shall we know when the *Bombazine* arrives in London?"

"When people start to die."

Next morning, the Mansion Dolorous was inundated with requests for children's funerals. Sixteen children had died overnight of mysterious wounds after somehow falling in the Thames. Of course, the richer children were to be buried by Jay's of Regent Street. But the Mansion Dolorous had eight funerals to prepare, using up the entire stock of size two coffins.

Carriages arrived all day, bearing small bodies wrapped in sheets. As they came out of the embalming room, Messrs. Tristesse and Ganorus were unusually pale. They locked the door behind them.

Mr. Tristesse told the boys and girls that these funerals were to be conducted with closed coffins, and as quickly as possible. Teo and Renzo were kept busy all day, twisting artificial flowers into wreaths and polishing the coffin handles. There was no time to go out and look for the zookymen. That night, the Mansion Dolorous gang—and Teo and Renzo—slept alongside the eight sealed coffins, strangely compelled to whisper, even though their little guests were beyond hearing them.

By late morning, all the funerals had been accomplished with the maximum pathos. While the Mansion Dolorous gang departed on their various doings, Teo and Renzo took to the streets separately, searching for the hot-zooky-sellers. Teo chose the south side of the river; Renzo went north.

Walking through London was not like strolling around Venice. The cobbles were lumpily hard on Venetian feet. Teo and Renzo were frequently swept off the pavements by Londoners hastening in solid brigades toward their places of business. Knocked off course, they were in constant danger of falling under hansom cabs and four-wheeled growlers.

Teo stumbled down the stone steps of Blackfriars Bridge, desperate for a moment's peace from the rumble of traffic and the relentless march of the Londoners. She stopped for a moment on a bench, but even this was inscribed with a notice REST, BUT DO NOT LOITER. Feeling guilty, she rose and carried on. In the quiet passage below the bridge, she was instantly rewarded by a spicy whiff of hot pumpkin. She followed her nose to the forecourt of a

247

warehouse. Men clustered around a handsome man who held out a large metal tray. The Londoners were eagerly exchanging their pennies for the crusts of glowing orange, and nibbling with evident pleasure on the warm flesh of the pumpkin. The smell reminded Teo sweetly and painfully of home. Her eyes prickled with a memory of the day after the ice flood when she had carried hot spiced pumpkin to the wretched and bereaved of Venice.

She waited behind a lamppost until the warehousemen had emptied the tray and the handsome man was alone. He slotted the tray into a wheeled brazier behind him and extracted a full one. A fresh wave of pumpkin scent pulled Teo from her hiding place and over to the man, before she quite realized what had happened.

"*Bon di,*" said Teo shyly, "good day."

The man looked down at her with searching eyes. "You speak the language of home," he said gently. "Who are you, child?"

Above his head, Teo saw his words written in a clear hand with a nautical jaunt to it.

"I am . . ." Teo felt irresistibly drawn to say, "Teodora Gasperin, the Undrowned Child of the Prophecy."

Then she trembled. Was that pumpkin smell too sweet? The sweetness reminded her of the emerald-green Baja-Menta ice cream, with which Il Traditore had tried to poison the minds of the Venetians two summers before. It too had smelled delicious, hiding its horrible secret in a luscious taste. Had she been beguiled into making a terrible mistake by the rich scent of pumpkin and the homesickness it induced?

Teo agonized silently, "How do I *know* he is a true Incognito? How can I be sure he was sent here by Lussa? He could be disguised, working for Bajamonte Tiepolo, waiting to grab me and throw me to whatever's killing the children in the Thames. The pumpkin could be a trick! Why did I come here without Renzo?"

The slices of pumpkin were close enough to warm her face. Suddenly, she was feverishly hot. Her heart beat so fast that she swayed on her feet. The man bent down, putting a hand on her shoulder to steady her. Or was it to pin her down?

Had Teo betrayed Venice, the *Scilla* and the mermaids—if they were still alive—by that one careless *"Bon di"*?

37. Ghost-breath

at about the same time, on the other side of the river

Renzo could not find any pumpkin-sellers. He had marched north over London Bridge, his hands driven into his pockets and his head down against the biting wind. Across the choppy water behind him, the broken masts of the *Scilla* jostled in St. Mary Overie Dock. This was as close as he dared to go to her: the quarantine officers, he knew, must still be guarding the boat.

He looked hopefully into the Thames's dark brown swell. A few barges and a Norwegian ice boat sped past: there was no sign of a jeweled tail.

Renzo slowed his pace to a miserable shuffle. Instead of exclaiming with pleasure at the little churches tucked into niches, the extravagant ironwork, the bizarre names of the old inns, he concentrated on sniffing. But there were no pumpkin-sellers in this most businesslike part of the throbbing city. Important men in their tall black hats would not stoop to eating hot snacks in the street. And certainly not with their clever, manicured, money-counting fingers! They surely dined in their famous clubs, sitting on leather chairs at tables set with solid silver and crisp damask.

Renzo worried about Teo alone on the south of the river. Belatedly, it struck him that he had allowed her to venture into the less respectable area. He should have insisted on the south side himself. It would be easy to snatch a small girl like Teo from those winding alleys of Southwark! When he reached Blackfriars Bridge, he turned left and hurried south. It was only when he was nearly across it that he lifted his downcast head, taking in the busy warehouses below. His eye slid over yards, ropes and men rolling barrels. Something caught his attention. Yes, there was a very familiar silhouette of a girl over there, standing with a tall man. The man had placed his hand on her shoulder.

"No! I don't believe it!" Renzo broke into a run. He galloped down sooty stone steps into the labyrinth of streets that fed into the warehouse district. A faint smell of pumpkin, growing ever stronger, guided him.

He burst into the yard where Teo was still staring wordlessly at her captor.

"Uncle Tommaso!" exclaimed Renzo. "I thought you drowned in the ice flood!"

Teo collapsed to her knees in confusion.

"What's the matter, Teo?" Renzo knelt and put his arm around her. "What could be better? You've found us a hot-zooky-seller! And I've got my uncle back! And it looks like he's an Incognito as well!"

"The mermaids!" gasped Teo. "Are they all right?"

"Yes." Uncle Tommaso smiled. "Lussa and our friends have arrived, and are sheltering in a secret place from whatever killed the Melusine."

Fat tears of relief spurted from Teo's eyes.

"Was my father an Incognito too?" was Renzo's first question when all the hugging and crying was over.

"No, Renzo. And nor did he know that I was."

Renzo nodded. Not for nothing were the secret saviors of Venice called "The Unknowns." It was considered safer for them not to know one another. Only in emergencies did they come together and fight for their city, as they had in the battle to save Venice the year before last. But at that time Tommaso Antonello, a sailor by profession, had been away in the Indies on a merchant vessel.

In five minutes all had been explained—including the dramatic voyage of the *Scilla*, the murder of Professor Marìn, the colossal squid, the *Bombazine*, their arrival in London, and Renzo and Teo's new lodging at the Mansion Dolorous.

"I just heard there was a Venetian vessel in quarantine—and I was planning a discreet visit this very night!" marveled Uncle Tommaso.

Soon, half a tray of spiced pumpkin had been consumed, and Teo's hands had stopped trembling. Uncle Tommaso was still shaking his head at the discovery that his very own nephew, Lorenzo, was the Studious Son of the ancient Venetian Prophecy. And that Renzo's friend Teodora, this lost-looking crop-haired girl, was the famous Undrowned Child.

"Lussa always said that the Studious Son was a handsome, useful chap." Tommaso ruffled Renzo's hair affectionately. "But I could never have guessed it was *you*. Your mother would have been so proud. Yet I guess she never knew, either." His voice was sad.

"And now she never will," Renzo said quietly. Teo squeezed his hand.

"Peace to her memory." Tommaso wiped his eyes. "And to that of dear Professor Marìn. I cannot believe that we have lost him."

"But the other Incogniti are safely here, are they not?" urged Teo.

Uncle Tommaso explained that a network of three dozen Venetian pumpkin-sellers was now spread thinly through the whole of London. "The mermaids asked me to lead them, because I know the place already, from the time I was here with your father, Renzo. Our absence from Venice was easy to explain: we let the authorities think we were among those drowned in the ice flood on Christmas Eve. I'm sorry, Renzo. We couldn't risk telling anyone that those newspaper accounts were not true."

"So can you take us to Lussa now?" Teo begged.

"Not exactly. Nor can I tell you where she is. For safety's sake, in case we are followed, we do not meet in person. Instead, the mermaids send shells with the tide to the shingle at Blackfriars, with news of Venice from their turtleshell. I was about to check for them when I met young Teodora. The mermaids will be overjoyed to hear that you are here! But"—his face suddenly fell—"look at the river. It's been slowing down for days, clogged with ice. I fear that, now it's frozen so stiffly, the next tide will not take or bring any more shells. We must find the mermaids another way."

"What have you found out? What is happening in Venice? Are the people still dying? Do you know where my parents have been taken?" Without realizing it, Teo was wringing Uncle Tommaso's sleeve.

"Draw a breath or you'll go blue, child! Venice—there is nothing good to tell. Fields of ice have formed around the city. The Half-Dead disease has taken a third of the citizens. The wells are frozen. Our beloved Venice is turning into a ghost-town. And, Teodora, we Incogniti are searching everywhere for Alberto and Leonora Stampara. As yet, sadly, without success."

"Is Bajamonte Tiepolo here?" Renzo's voice dragged over the hated name.

"That I cannot tell you. For we do not know in what form he manifests himself these days. He may have become a man—for he has his bones back—or still be a bat. And this is evil news you bring—that Il Traditore has a new ally in the Pretender to the British throne. I can tell you that Harold Hoskins has moved from Osborne to London and is lodged in royal apartments at Kenwood House up on Hampstead Heath. The other royals want him as far away from them as possible, I suppose. This Hooroo connection of which you speak, children, will explain why we Incogniti have these last two nights observed hundreds of Ghost-Convicts with Australian accents on the streets."

"So the *Bombazine* is here," groaned Teo. "Hundreds of Ghost-Convicts and so few Incogniti."

"What about the London ghosts?" Renzo asked. "Can't they help? Lussa told me that London once had more ghosts per square mile than any other place on earth."

"And more magic per square inch too," agreed Uncle Tommaso.

Teo asked, "Are there any ghosts in-the-Cold left in London? Ones who have done some bad thing and who want to redeem themselves by saving their city?"

Uncle Tommaso smiled. "There is every sort of ghost here. Also, field after field of innocent dead—those felled by the Plague or burned alive in the Great Fire. In short, yes. We've been trying to recruit all the London ghosts to our side. But they are weak and suspicious. They've had it drummed into them that Londoners do not believe in ghosts. They have been worn away to shadows by the sheer rationality of the ruling powers. Ghostliness has become a mere entertainment here—it is not taken seriously. A few enterprising charlatans set up faked séances to conjure false spirits for money. Grieving husbands and wives will pay a fortune to hear some actor pretending to be their dead spouse and saying that all is well in Heaven."

"And where are the real ghosts?"

"The poor things have taken refuge in the railway arches."

"We've never seen a ghost and we've walked under dozens of arches," protested Renzo.

"When I say in the railway arches, I mean between the very bricks. Have you noticed how humid it is under those arches? That is ghost-breath. The trails of moisture down the walls, the white efflorescence on the bricks—all condensed ghost-breath and ghost-tears."

"What use are they, hiding up there?"

"When the time comes, I believe, London will utter her ghosts, like words, like a scream. The cold helps, for the mortar between the bricks is cracking apart, making their exit easier. In fact, Harold Hoskins may unwittingly help us with his Ghost-Convicts from Hooroo. . . . The London spirits certainly won't want colonial ghosts coming in and taking advantage of the new opportunities that will surely come on the haunting market, now that Queen

Victoria is dead and Londoners feel free to use their imaginations once more."

Teo and Renzo laughed, but Tommaso frowned. "That reminds me, do not lean against any old walls! Old London stone is so rich with history that it's denser and more concentrated than the human body. It's grown stronger too, from all the ghosts who have climbed between the cracks and become at one with its particles. So it simply absorbs the unsuspecting. We've already lost one Incognito that way. Look!"

Uncle Tommaso pointed to a bumpy stone wall. At first they could see nothing untoward. But then Renzo caught the swell of a cheek in a stone. And Teo saw the jut of a hip.

She gasped. "That was an Incognito?"

"My friend Lucio from Via Garibaldi," Tommaso replied, wiping away a tear. "He was waiting to meet me here, and I was late. He must have leaned against the wall to keep out of the wind. When I finally arrived, this is what I found. Now that the old Queen is dead, everything is rousing."

"Oh no!" Renzo pointed to a cormorant cruising down the river.

Tommaso drew them into the shadows. "You are right. It's not safe for us to be seen talking like this. Three Venetians together. Our voices will carry. Go! I shall send some Incogniti to the *Scilla*, to keep an eye on her. We'll set up a hot spiced pumpkin stall in Clink Street, close to the boat."

"And Turtledove will find Lussa for us, just see if he doesn't!" added Renzo with a smile.

"Look!" cried Teo, as they hurried back toward the Mansion Dolorous.

CHILDREN SEIZED AND SHORN IN STREET!

Renzo and Teo pulled up short in front of the billboard, bending down to read the details. Dozens of children, of all ages and degrees of poverty and affluence, had been pulled behind gates, under bridges and into hansom cabs—and relieved of their hair. The dazed boys and girls could recall nothing of their ordeal, thanks to harsh blows to the head.

"Do you remember," Teo asked Renzo, staring at the poster, "how Miss Uish shaved our heads? And how the children in the hospital two years ago had their heads shorn by that horrible nurse?"

Renzo shivered. "But what would *they* want with the children's hair?"

When Teo and Renzo arrived back at the mourning emporium, they found the Londoners in a state of outrage. It was already apparent what happened to the stolen hair. That morning, while Teo and Renzo were with Uncle Tommaso, the streets had been suddenly flooded with vendors selling mourning brooches for Queen Victoria's funeral.

The street vendors sold their mourning brooches at a shilling, a tenth of the price of the smallest pin in the Mansion Dolorous's own expensive range. The boys and girls had winced when they overheard Mr. Tristesse fretting, "If those charlatans destroy our brooch business, we'll not be able to afford so many child mourners."

"We must investigerate," barked Turtledove, when Messrs. Tristesse and Ganorus had left the building. "I'll not have me childer out on the street on account of this hairy fubbery."

Tig was despatched to buy one of the offending brooches, clutching a handkerchief of grimy pennies pooled from every member of the gang.

"I feels disloyal layin' out good money on 'em, doan I?" she protested.

"It is research," insisted Renzo.

"Doan tell me what I's doin'!" blustered Tig, trotting out of the door.

"I do most prostrately apologize." Renzo bowed his head.

Pylorus shouted, "Oooh, so sickly sweet that boy is! Pass the sick bucket! Sorry, the expectoratin' receptacle."

Renzo blushed and looked at the ground.

Turtledove barked in his most undovelike fashion, "Stand up to 'im, why doan yew, Renzo? Hain't yew got no gall or gizzard, boy? A word 'twixt yew an' me—I likes to see a bit o' cheek in me childer. Doan like to see 'em too biddable. I likes character, lashings of it! I cannot be doin' wiv polite childer. Manners is the scum wot rises up when yew bile the spirit out o' a child."

Then Turtledove pinned a heavy paw on Pylorus's shoulder and growled, "Show me yer tongue! Yes, just what I thought, all black wiv nastiness!"

"Licorice, actually," remarked Greasy dreamily, "and aniseed comfits."

"All the worse for yew; how many times 'as I told yew not to raid the comestibles here? Now, have conduct, boy! 'Pologize handsome-like to poor Renzo, do. Yew know I'll have no sarky sass, no meanness 'tween one an' t'other. Woan suit, woan suit at all. Now yew two borrow the hatchet an' make nice."

"Got one!" Tig hurtled back in. It had not proved hard for her to find a vendor. Two had had the audacity to set themselves up right outside the Mansion Dolorous. Indeed, every second street corner, as far as the eye could see, boasted a person of indeterminate sex, swaddled in scarves and wearing a strange felt hat bobbing with corks, with a small tray of brooches on his meager lap, beside a black tin can with some kind of liquid inside it.

Tig opened her handkerchief to show an oval-shaped brooch. The boys and girls passed it from hand to hand. The brooch contained very fine chestnut, blond and black hairs, intricately plaited and encased in glass. On the back of each brooch, there was a gummed label: THE HAIR OF THEIR LATE MAJESTIES PRINCE ALBERT AND QUEEN VICTORIA. NEVER FORGOTTEN.

"Well, that's not right," said Renzo officiously. "Albert was her consort. He was *never* referred to as His Majesty. It should say 'Hair of Her Majesty Queen Victoria and Prince Albert.' Not to mention that Albert died back in 1861."

"And not to mention," Teo pointed out, "that there must be thousands of these brooches for sale at the moment. From his portraits, Prince Albert had a good head of hair, but he wasn't—how would you say it in English?—*un mostro peloso*—a hairy monster. And Queen Victoria's hair must have been *white* by the time she died."

Turtledove turned the brooch over with his paw.

"That is *childer* hair, that is," he growled. "I's goin' to bite them criminables from Shoreditch to Kensington."

"What did yer vendor look loik?" demanded Greasy. "Close up?"

"Were hard to see," answered Tig. "He were that covered up, right to his eyes. An' he wore blue spectickles. Strange, though—I passed annuva two of 'em on the way back, an' they was both got up in the same rig, same black tin cans an' corky hats an' the same blue spectickles."

"What has they got to hide?" growled Turtledove.

"And they started acting awful sneaky-loik when they saw me lookin' at 'em. I saw two of 'em do the strangest thing. Those black cans wiv handles they carried—when they thought there wernt no one looking, they sprinkled somefing out of 'em against the nearest doorpost an' door handle. I saw 'em do dozens of doorknobs loik that. An' no one said nuffink or tried to stop 'em."

Teo asked, "What were their voices like?"

"They dint talk to me at all. They jest pointed. I thought they might be mutes. But when I walked away, they started jabberin' among themselves, funny words, wiv lots of swearin' in 'em. It dint even sound loik proper English. Was loik they had bees up their noses an' was yawning at the same time."

"An Orstralian accent, yew mean?" asked Turtledove. "So those were billycans they was carrying."

"The criminals from Hooroo that Harold Hoskins pardoned, that's who they are," Renzo said darkly.

"Renzo, Teo, yew's off funeral duties now. Full-time looking for taily ladies, that's what yew's doin' now. Wiv my help, nat'rally,"

Turtledove was barking when Pylorus Salt rushed in from the street with a newspaper in his hand.

"They've set the date for Queen Vic's funeral," he announced. "February second. What a crush that'll be! You woan be able to see the streets for all the people in 'em."

38. Sure as a piece of string

on the streets of London, January 27, 1901

To bury Queen Victoria with the kind of pomp and ceremony that she herself would have expected—now, that was an undertaking to rival the construction of the pyramids in Egypt.

The crowds were already gathering. There was not a hotel room to be had, nor a spare bed in anybody's house from Ealing to Wood Green.

Nor, it seemed, was there a vacant branch on any tree in London.

Everyone remarked about the sudden profusion of cormorants. They were seen not only in their usual haunts along the Thames, but in gardens and parks and on people's roofs.

Black birds for our blackest days, commented the *Times*. **Even Mother Nature sends her mourners to the world's most magnificent funeral. For was our great Queen not everybody's mother?**

Obsessed with new daily details of the funeral plans, none of the newspapers could spare a column inch for another, more domestic phenomenon that befell many Londoners over the next few days. Those people would open their front doors and exclaim, "Ugh! The doorknob's all wet. What's that smell?"

And those same people would shortly afterward begin to feel quite unwell.

In Venice, *The Key to the Secret City* had led Renzo and Teo to the mermaids, sure as a piece of string. Without the book, they had no clues. There were no buildings in London as remote and romantic as the House of the Spirits, at least none that seemed magical enough to house a hundred tousled blond mermaids and their printing press in a cavern below.

Humans should be easier to track down. Teo and Renzo inquired discreetly at the large museums for natural history and science in South Kensington: Had any of their own scientists gone missing? Where were the best scientific facilities in London? But no hints emerged as to the whereabouts of Teo's adoptive parents.

Nor did the Incogniti have any luck. "*È come se fossero sepolti sotto il mare!* It's as if they were buried under the sea!" Uncle Tommaso despaired.

That night Teo slept uneasily in her cotton shroud. In the early hours, the night-nagging dream returned, the one in which Bajamonte Tiepolo's voice whispered, "*Death to Venice and all Venetians!*" in her ear. "*Blackness to her image. Oblivion to her memory.*"

She woke up, crying "Lussa!"

LONDON CHILDREN DISAPPEAR, FOUL PLAY SUSPECTED whooped the morning headlines. Children were not simply being shaved. More than two hundred had suddenly vanished without a trace.

The Mansion Dolorous gang were confined indoors. But after they'd passed a chafing day inside the mourning emporium, Turtle-dove came back with a warm, damp package and a guest: the barge dog Pattercake.

"Fish 'n' chips and eel pie—summat to celeberbrate," the bull-dog said mysteriously, winking at Teo.

"Don't mind if I do," said Pattercake, tearing open the package and helping himself to a battered haddock. The children swarmed around the table.

But instead of smacking his lips, Renzo talked nostalgically of his favorite Venetian dish, *seppie e polenta*: slices of corn porridge in a lake of hot squid ink.

"You drink ink in Venice? Dear lordy-lordy!" Bits rolled his eyes.

"Maybe that's what makes 'im talk loik that?" asked Thrasher.

Rosibund weighed in with, "It wernt an ice flood what destroyed Venice. Renzo *bored* it to estinkshon, didna'e?"

"What's bitin' yew?" cautioned Turtledove. "Leave 'im be. Quiet, childer! Pattercake has brought t'intelligence we's been awaiting. Teodora, Renzo, yer friends, the Venetian mermaids, has finely been locatered. All this time, they's been hiding thesselves in a cavern under London Bridge, not fifteen minutes' trot from 'ere."

39. Brain fag

straight after supper, January 27, 1901

"There's Pattercake's sign."

Turtledove's broad nose nudged an unpromising door in a dank passage by the river. Five scratches, clearly inflicted by a dog's splayed paw, ran horizontally across its dilapidated surface.

Renzo, Teo and Turtledove were accompanied by the District Disgrace, who had revealed a romantic side to her nature, insisting that she must see "the bootiful mermaids" at any cost, and by Tobias Putrid, whose ease and expertise in subterranean tunnels might prove useful.

Renzo held aloft a lantern to light them down the stairs. The walls were lined with shelves, and those shelves were lined with boxes and bottles bearing extravagant labels, illustrated with chromolithographs of large-eyed ladies with long, lustrous hair and remarkably pale faces. Always happy to have long words in her mouth, Teo read the labels aloud as they descended:

"The Original Widow Welch's Female Pills.

◇◇◇◇◇◇◇◇◇

"Nurse Powell's Popular Pellets for all Female Ailments (Delay is dangerous, write at once and obtain relief).
◇◇◇◇◇◇◇◇

"LYDIA E. PINKHAM'S VEGETABLE COMPOUND
(ONLY A WOMAN CAN UNDERSTAND ANOTHER WOMAN'S ILLS).
◇◇◇◇◇◇◇◇

"ZAM-BUK
(CONTAINS THOSE SUBSTANCES WHICH NATURE HAS INTENDED FOR THE
USE OF WOMAN EVER SINCE SHE BEQUEATHED TO HER THE INSTINCT TO
RUB A PLACE THAT HURTS).
◇◇◇◇◇◇◇◇

"Dr. Brodum's Nervous Cordial and Botanical Syrup.
◇◇◇◇◇◇◇◇

**"Dr. William's Pink Pills for Pale People
(Go to the very cause of the mischief).**
◇◇◇◇◇◇◇◇

**"CHAMELEON OIL
(THE ONLY PERFECT LINIMENT)."**
◇◇◇◇◇◇◇◇

The steps flattened out at a wide landing. Teo heard waves shuffling against stone. Renzo's lantern showed a cavern clad in lavatorial white tiles. A sewer rat of dimensions that commanded respect launched itself into the black water immediately in front of them. Moonlight picked out its long crooked muzzle and a flash of yellow tooth. Then Teo caught sight of a glittering blue scale.

"Lussa!" she exclaimed, for a shaft of moonlight now revealed ranks of mermaids glimmering like fireflies at the far end of the echoing chamber, their faces all stippled in the light cast by lanterns swinging overhead. On a high ledge, the Sea Spiders were busily spinning large rectangular cocoons under the beady observation of the mermaids' parrots. The turtleshell was fixed to a mossy post.

Teo was aware of breath sharply drawn in at the sight of the mermaids. Turtledove and the Mansion Dolorous gang had not disbelieved Renzo and Teo's account of them. But actually to see the mythical creatures had a literally stunning effect upon the Londoners. Looking at their taut faces and dropped jaws, Teo remembered, with compassion, the first time she herself had encountered the mermaids in their cavern under the House of the Spirits.

"Don't worry," she whispered, squeezing the District Disgrace's hand, "they don't bite."

Turtledove advanced and bowed deeply, inquiring, "How do? How do?"

Flos called out excitedly in English, "Sink me if 'Tisn't da Undrowned Child and da Studious Son! Wiv a dawg! And a dear little Lunnun chickabiddy and a ripe codling too!"

Marsil cried, "By Neptune's Mandibles, that's a sight for sawed-off eyes!"

Teo was amused to notice that, even in English, the Venetian mermaids spoke in a dialect coarse enough to bring a lump to a pirate's throat.

Lussa's English, however, was as aristocratic as her Venetian. "Dearest Children, We thought You were still in Venice, aboard the *Scilla*, with a Field of Excluding to block our Turtleshell's Vision! What has brought You to this dangerous City? Can it be that Venice's Undrowned Child & Studious Son shall also help London against Bajamonte Tiepolo? And However did You find Us? Even the dear Incogniti know not our Hiding Place, lest

One of their Number be Captured and Tortured. Did Professor Marìn . . . ?"

"Turtledove here," Teo said, stroking the dog's head, "found you for us. But Lussa, we have to tell you . . ." She broke into a sob.

Renzo finished her sentence quietly. "Miss Uish murdered Professor Marìn at sea and turned us into pirates."

Lussa clutched her heart. "'Tis too Terrible to bear."

Regaining her composure, Lussa nodded gravely at Turtledove. "We thank You, Noble Canine, for bringing our Children. Venice thanks You."

"Pleased to meet yew, Yer Majesty, Missis Lussa." Turtledove bowed. "These young 'uns has told me all about yew ladies. Quintus Turtledove, an' my two proty-jays, the District Disgrace an' Tobias Putrid."

As the Venetian mermaids swam closer, it suddenly became clear that they were not alone.

"And something's missing," thought Teo. Then she realized what it was—the familiar smell of curry was absent. It normally hung in a pleasant fug above the mermaids. Instead, a faintly medicinal smell filled the air.

"Our London Sisters." There was an uncharacteristic coolness in her voice as Lussa introduced the unfamiliar company, which consisted of fifty wan mermaids with limp hair and languid postures. All wore black armbands, black wreaths in their hair and jet earrings identical to those stocked by Tristesse & Ganorus.

"They must be in mourning for the poor Melusine and Sea-Bishops," guessed Teo, "and for Queen Victoria too, of course."

At the sight of Turtledove and the ragged orphans, the lips of the London mermaids unanimously curled into expressions of distaste. As they murmured among themselves, Teo saw above their heads the same loopy, drunken-looking handwriting that had worried Lussa on the shells she'd received in Venice from these London mermaids.

One particularly pale mermaid cried, "Dirty street children! And a dog! Look at those sallow complexions! They're sure to have brought some dreadful disease in with them. Or some eruptive condition! A dose must be taken!"

Turtledove sneezed voluminously. "We bulldogs is very suscepterbul to damp an' cold."

"Yes!" called the pale mermaid's sisters. "A dose! A dose!" "MRS. DINSMORE'S GREAT ENGLISH COUGH AND CROUP BALSAM! Or some HALE'S HONEY OF HOREHOUND AND TAR?"

"Thankee kindly," spluttered Turtledove, "but . . ."

"Not for *you*, filthy dog! For *us*! You sneezed in our direction."

"You never know what the dirty beast might have. It's probably rabid! We should take some precautionary CHARLES FORDE'S BILE BEANS FOR BILIOUSNESS."

"Nerolia, no!" protested her lanky companion. "DR. BLAUD'S CAPSULES! They produce pure, rich blood without any disagreeable effects."

"Which is why, Gloriana, they are recommended by the medical faculty as the best remedy for bloodlessness."

"But I hain't even bitten one of yew ladies," protested Turtledove, his back leg starting to rise from the floor. He growled, "Yet . . ."

Fifty pairs of pale, thin arms reached toward the medicine shelves that lined the lower part of the cavern, and grasped at bottles similar to those that Teo had seen on the walls coming down.

As they did so, she saw that the London mermaids' waists were encumbered with stout buckled corsets with labels that read: HARNESS CONSTRICTIVE BELTS FOR THE INDELICATE: PROVIDES A SLIM FIGURE FOR EVEN THE LUMPIEST LADY.

Flos, in a voice heavy with sarcasm, explained, "Our droopy sisters seem to think dem crimpin' contrapshuns keep dere arms and tails from droppin' orf, or da like. Once da mermaids of London was famous for dere archery. Great strong forearms like a haunch of hog. *Now* look at dem!"

The arms of the London mermaids looked too delicate to lift an arrow, let alone a bow. The palest mermaid explained smugly, "Indeed, the HARNESS CONSTRICTIVE BELT prevents the buildup of unsightly muscles while preserving the feminine delicacy of the upper arm."

"Pigs' ribs!" observed Flos, under her breath. "And flapdoodle."

"In flam-sauce," agreed Catalina, with feeling.

The London mermaids swigged delicately on their bottles. One, introducing herself as Pucretia, offered Teo a paperful of ATKINSON'S INFANTS PRESERVATIVE and a bottle of DR. WILLIAM'S PILLS FOR PALE PEOPLE with an air of someone who was saving her life. Teo politely declined.

Silence fell on the cavern for a moment.

Then the Venetian mermaids broke out into a clamor. "Lackaday! *This* is what we have to help us fight Bajamonte Tiepolo and the Pretender and all their criminal tribes, human and ghostly. Weeping weasels ain't in it!"

"The poor Creatures are Deluded," murmured Lussa. "I have discreetly consulted the List of the Operative Ingredients in the Medicines that They so persistently swallow. And our Chef Catalina has analyzed Others in the Kitchen. 'Tis deeply Shocking! JAYNE'S

EXPECTORANT, DR. PIECE'S FAVORITE PRESCRIPTION—laced with sugar! AYER'S CHERRY PECTORAL—a vital Spark of caffeine. MOTHER SIEGEL'S CURATIVE SYRUP contains pure cane sugar!"

Catalina broke in, "And sugar is also the working part of SETH ARNOLD'S COUGH KILLER, and TAYLOR'S SWEET GUM AND MULLEIN COMPOUND uses the same! As for ROUTLEY'S HERBAL COMPOUND FOR LADIES, why, the very instructions read: 'One powder to be taken occasionally in tea.'"

"Tea!" echoed Lussa. "These poor London Mermaids are enslaved to its Use. This, of course, explains the Disorder in the Handwriting on their Shells & the Imbecility of their Behavior. 'Tis almost as if They suffer from the Muted Mermaid Malady, which is Akin to your Human Half-Dead disease. The Mermaids become Overexcited with Large Doses of Sugar in their Tea. Shortly thereafter, inevitably, their Spirits fall suddenly into a Sad and Languid state."

"Mashed Mermaid Malady, more like," grumbled Marsil.

Flos could not be contained any longer. "And when dem's not drinking dem debilitating medickles, dem's eatin' English cakes. Nasty pale things like dirty sea foam. Dey call dem 'Victoria sponge.' Insult to da noble sponge, what is an hadmirable sea creature. Get down 'mazin' quantities of da stuff. Sufferin' catfish!"

Catalina, her chef's hat limply at half-mast, mourned, "They will not permit us to cook our spicy foods. They say the smell of onions makes them bilious."

"Lackaday," moaned Flos, clutching her belly, which did indeed look flatter than it had before.

Lussa said abruptly, "We squander Precious Time in this Fruitless Banter! Children, the *Bad Ship Bombazine* is moored—Invisible to Humanfolk, of course—by St. Katharine Docks, scarcely a Mile distant. You must hide Yourselves at all Costs."

"I *knew* they were here. I've started to have nightmares again," Teo groaned.

"Teo and I have pretty much, ahem, *buried* ourselves," began Renzo.

"But the boys on the *Scilla* . . . ." Teo bit her lip. "They've nowhere to hide."

"All Children are at Risk in London now," Lussa informed them. "The Parrots have been abroad and report that Human Criminals & Ghost-Convicts from the Hooroo roam the Streets looking for Child Victims to press-gang into Service for their Mistress. Children without Parents are the First to go. And the Plumper the Child, the more likely 'Tis to disappear, strangely."

Turtledove emitted a low grunt. "Ain't they ashamed of thes-selves, stealing little *childer*? I is at yer service, Yer Wetness, perti-kular agin all child-hurters an' pye-rats."

Lussa nodded graciously, yet she did not appear overencouraged by Turtledove's offer. "The problem is that these Ghost-Convicts are in-the-Slaughterhouse."

Renzo quickly itemized for Turtledove the various kinds of malevolent ghost with whom they'd had to deal in the bat-tle to save Venice. The dog knitted his brows. "So, if I unner-stand correct-like, these slaughter'ouse-type pye-rats is the sort that ain't sorry for what they done in life, even though it got 'em killed?"

"To a Man, they were imprisoned or hung for Piracy & Slave-Trading, Murder & Kidnap," Lussa explained. "And They'd like Nothing Better than to continue with More of the Same. And for some Unknown, yet surely Evil Reason, They want Human Children for their Victims now."

Turtledove raised his snout and howled.

Lussa moved on to better news: Signor Alicamoussa had escaped from the Venetian jail with the help of his resourceful Irish wife, Mercer, who had sent in some tame beavers from their menagerie to gnaw a hole in the door. At the mention of the circus-master's name, the Venetian mermaids began to coo and bat their eyelids.

Even the London mermaids were not impervious to the circus-master's charms, whispering eagerly among themselves.

Lussa continued smoothly, "Yar, Signor Alicamoussa arrives in London this very Night."

The London mermaids produced hand mirrors from their Constrictive Belts and began to primp.

"But where *is* the noble *Scilla?*" asked Lussa suddenly. The turtleshell cleared to show the boat at St. Mary Overie Dock.

"So the Field-of-Excluding has faded on your Voyage. This is where You have been?" Lussa smiled. "So close to Us all these Days! We never thought to look for You Here! Well, the Circus-Master shall lodge Himself forthwith at the *Scilla* and take the remaining Boys into his Care. And You must join Them there: You & your Estimable new Allies, Turtledove & his London Children."

"But we Londoners has a perfickly good 'ome at the Mansion Dolorous," protested Turtledove, "bed, board an' steadyish employmint too."

"Who is that Duchessly Girl?" Lussa asked sharply, as Sibella, dressed in an explosion of lace, promenaded into view in the turtleshell. "This Mincing Miss is not Venetian, I detect."

"A hostage taken by Miss Uish," explained Renzo quickly. "Sibella."

"In my Opinion, that Small Female could bear watching with a Close Eye. There is something about Her. . . ."

"Renzo's eye is *very* partial to her," remarked Teo bitterly.

"Oooh, who pulled your chain?" guffawed Tobias. "Not your favorite girlie, that one?"

"Supper is served," Nerolia's voice simpered from the darkness. She reappeared, wheeling a silver trolley of fine bone china around a track beside the pool by means of a golden shepherd's crook hooked into the handle.

"Antispasmodic Tea, anyone?" offered Nerolia. She proceeded to dispense into tiny china cups a faintly yellow liquid from a squat object she proudly announced as "ROYLE'S PATENT SELF-POURING TEAPOT: 'NO MORE ACHING ARMS.' "

"Caulk me dead lights!" moaned Flos.

But the London mermaids took their teacups eagerly and immediately stuck their little fingers out at right angles to the delicate handles.

Next, bone china plates of pallid greenish mush were distributed.

"Wot you call *dat*, missis?" demanded Flos, poking her finger into it.

"The common people give it a rather amusing title," tittered Gloriana, " 'Pig-in-a-swamp,' I believe."

"Oh hie-ly amusing!" mimicked Flos. "What is it when it's at home, missis?"

"An extensively boiled potato in a lake of marrowfat peas," answered Nerolia.

"Yeeuccch! Looks like what ye'd cough up if ye had the bronchitis."

The parrots burst into a juicy chorus of coughs.

"Have some WAUKESHA ARCADIAN GINGER ALE," offered Pucretia. "It counteracts the bile, you know."

The Venetian mermaids' eyes brightened at the thought of something spicy.

"Without the ginger or the bubbles, both highly prejudicial to the digestion."

"Without, without, without . . . ," chanted the parrots.

"Ye drivelswigging bootless bladders!" Flos began, "Prithee—"

"Flos," giggled Gloriana, "you would profit from some CARTER'S LITTLE NERVE PILLS. They would render you more comfortable in yourself."

Exasperation sharpened Lussa's voice, "Ladies! You squander Priceless Time in these Perpetual Squabbles while We face the Deadliest of Enemies once more!" She turned to the London mermaids, "And yet again, I ask You, Sisters, will You not take up Arms? It is clear that your City too faces Destruction at his pitiless Hand."

But the London mermaids downed the contents of their teacups, folded their thin arms over their narrow chests and stared at Lussa with stubborn expressions.

"How's yew goin' to get 'em to fight when these pallid gels— savin' their graces—can't even lift a teapot," inquired Turtledove, "Yer Scaliness?"

Catalina and Marsil now approached, pointing to the turtle-shell. One of them whispered to Lussa, who turned to the dog with a worried expression. "I regret that even while You have been Here, your London Refuge has been Discovered."

"Discovered by whom?" Renzo asked tightly.

The two mermaids swiveled the turtleshell toward them. It turned cloudy, and then filled with a scene of dark London streets.

"I'll be dognabbed if that ain't a cunning device," Turtledove said, and sniffed admiringly. "Do it come in other flavors outside o' turtle?"

The shell began to trace the Southwark byways that led to the Tristesse & Ganorus mourning emporium. Inside, a scene of devastation was revealed. Dresses lay torn and trampled. Cabinets were smashed. Mourning brooches were shattered like crushed insects. The Improving Tomes Library lay in ruins.

"Yoiks!" remarked one of the parrots.

"Who did that deed?" growled Turtledove. "I'll tear him leg from liver! And where's me childer?"

The shell closed in on a pair of Ghost-Convicts from the *Bombazine*. They were ransacking the jewelry cabinets. Their daggers glinted in the gas-lit gloom of the Mansion Dolorous. Lussa commented scathingly, "One cannot take the Gold-Lust out of the Criminal Soul."

Now a taller Ghost-Convict in a lieutenant's hat approached the looters. He kicked both of them across the room and advanced on the nearest one, his cutlass raised. A shark's tooth was to be seen sticking out of his back. He shouted hoarsely, "What are you doing, yer prize drongoes?"

The looter lifted his scarred hand to protect his face, begging piteously: "No, no, think on me poor Mammy. . . ."

Any further words were prevented by the lieutenant cutting off the Ghost-Convict's head. But as he was already dead, the ghost simply rose and saluted toward his empty neck. As he did so, the lieutenant shouted, "Children! We're looking for children. A boy and a girl. From Venice."

"A girl," said Teo flatly. "Then they know that I am not a boy and that I am here."

She felt a tremor fork down her spine and thought she might faint.

"Hey, where did young Teodora git to?" exclaimed Turtledove.

"Nowherth. She's righth beside Renzo," affirmed the District Disgrace. Tobias nodded vigorously and pointed. Teo, feeling herself again, smiled.

"For a minute there, she was vanished into thin air," marveled the dog. "What a doings!"

"That was Teo going between-the-Linings. Between-the-Linings means she's still here, but she's not visible to ordinary adults now. Just to children, animals, mermaids and ghosts," Renzo told him. "And to the Incogniti too, of course."

"This befalls Her when It becomes too Dangerous for Teodora to be Visible," explained Lussa. "As the Undrowned Child of an antique Venetian Prophecy, She is the most Hated Object of our Enemy."

"*And me own dear childer?*" Turtledove's voice shook.

"Nearly all escaped," Lussa answered, turning back to the shell.

"Nearly?" howled Turtledove. "*Nearly*, yew say?"

40. 'Can you smell kiddies?'

a moment later

The shell showed the terrified faces of Greasy and Marg'rit as a circle of Ghost-Convicts closed in on them. This was a sight that deprived Turtledove of coherent speech. He choked and whimpered, turning around in circles in his distress.

Still speechless, he merely nodded when Lussa said, "So You see why You cannot return There. The *Scilla* awaits You, Comrades. Teodora, 'Tis for You to find and cast a Protective Spell upon the Vessel from Professor Marìn's Book *The Best Ways with Wayward Ghosts*, to keep the *Scilla* hidden from Humanfolk & Spirits alike. And Spying Birds."

Teo breathed, "The whole ship? The *Scilla* must be inaudible as well as invisible."

"Can anyone smell you," asked Tobias with interest, "between-the-Linings-loik?"

"I don't think so."

"Gardyloo!" cried Marsil. At that moment a swarm of rats rustled into the cavern and ran along the lower shelves. This had the London mermaids shrieking for their patented "verminicide," ROUGH ON RATS, as they splashed out of the cavern.

"That's terrible stuff!" exclaimed Turtledove, outraged. "I doan like rats any more than the next dog, but the trouble wiv ROUGH ON RATS is how it makes 'em die so slow an' cruel. I doan hold wiv it."

Pucretia, the last to leave of the London mermaids, pushed an ovoid box of CHARLES FORDE'S BILE BEANS FOR BILIOUS-NESS on the District Disgrace, who was still sobbing and clutching her stomach. The sight of Greasy and Marg'rit in peril, closely followed by the rats, had reduced the girl to a pitiable state.

Pucretia urged, "Bile Beans positively cure headache, constipation, despondency, fatty and waxy degeneration of the liver, debility, lack of ambition, buzzing in the head and stomach ailments."

"Don't do nuffink to save ye from Bajamonte Tiepolos, do it, though?" blustered Flos. "Ye know? Da kind what is intent on murdering Undrowned Childs and Studious Sons? And mermaids? And layin' waste to whole cities? Thought not."

Another heavy fog had descended on London while they'd been underground. Leaving the cavern, the Mansion Dolorous party caught a glimpse of two Ghost-Convicts trotting through the night mist. Deep in conversation, the ghosts did not notice the Londoners hiding behind a pilaster. Both had shark bites on their necks. One was missing his nose. An unpleasant bubbling noise issued from the blackened hole. He carried a billycan that sloshed with liquid. Both continuously brushed with their skeletal hands at the corks hanging from their hats.

The District Disgrace clung to Renzo's hand with her grimy

little fingers, and he clung right back. Turtledove growled, "I'll smash the two of 'em in one."

"Shhh. They mustn't realize we know about them," pleaded Teo. "And what about your childer? We've got to find them and take them to the *Scilla*."

"Why do they keep thwiping their handths in front of their hats like that?" asked the District Disgrace.

"I guess they're in the habit of brushing off flies," said Teo.

The scene of destruction at the mourning emporium was worse even than the turtleshell had shown.

"My childer!" howled Turtledove. "They is all took!"

A muffled violin note sounded from inside one of the coffins.

"Fossy!" cried Teo. Turtledove rushed to nudge open all the wooden lids. The Mansion Dolorous boys and girls were still cowering inside. They had hidden there from the Ghost-Convicts, who had not thought to lift the lids, being much too busy raking through the stock for anything with a bit of glitter to it.

The shaking Londoners explained how only Greasy and Marg'rit, too slow to reach the coffin showroom themselves, had bravely led their pursuers away from their friends. They had paid a terrible price for their selflessness.

Ann Picklefinch whispered, "I peeped out from under my lid. Them ghoosties put our Greasy 'n' our Marg'rit's heads in sacks and tieded them up and carried 'em off, squealin' loik little pigs. 'Twas verra bad."

No one argued about leaving the Mansion Dolorous with all possible haste.

"Them ghoosties might coom back," whimpered Rosibund. "They knows where we is, an' might coom back at any time."

The move to the *Scilla* was accomplished in less than an hour. After cleaning up as best they could, Renzo was set to writing an exquisitely regretful letter to Messrs. Tristesse and Ganorus, apologizing for their lack of attendance at funerals. Subtly, yet without actually writing any lies, he implied that a late-night raiding party from the rival Jay's might be responsible for the damage, and for driving the boys and girls themselves into hiding.

Please do not give our coffins to other children, the note concluded, at Tig's urging. *We'll be back in a few days. We promise.*

"How we goin' to git on board yon boot, then?" From behind a wall, Ann looked fearfully at the two sleepy officers slumped on a bench in front of the *Scilla*.

"The Incogniti are here to help us," said Renzo, waving at Uncle Tommaso and a handful of pumpkin-sellers standing with their braziers in Clink Street.

Uncle Tommaso winked, shouting, "Free hot zooky! Late-night special!"

The guards roused themselves and sauntered toward the trays of glowing orange pumpkin. The boys and girls slipped up the *Scilla*'s ladder undetected.

From the depths of Signor Alicamoussa's hay-scented hug, Teo noticed that Fabrizio cast a rather interested eye on the District Disgrace and that Sebastiano seemed to find a soul mate in Bits Piecer. It was good to be aboard the *Scilla* again, to feel wood beneath her feet and to smell the salt of the not-too-distant sea.

Turtledove eyed Sibella, daintily dressed in a white musquash cape with a fox boa and sable muff. "*This* is the Sibellant siren? Wot the mermaids warned us to keep an eye on? I see there ain't no bamboozable he-person can be safe when this female puts her 'come hithers' upon 'im. Look how she snicker-snackers them eyelashes! Can see why yew's a bit spoony on her, lad." He grinned at Renzo, who turned into a boy-shaped fire-hydrant.

"Ah," remarked Sibella with a smirk, "an English bulldog. A dog of breeding is not absolutely detestable."

Turtledove growled low in his throat, unable to decipher the traces of a faint compliment inside the overwhelming impression of insult. He remarked to Renzo, "Doan know why yew wants to get all snoodled up to *that*. I's not one to cast asparagus, but I'd say she ain't a truster. Yew got the smarts, son, yet I think she's one too many for yew."

Then he leaned in closer to Sibella. "Them ain't *dogskin* gloves yer a-wearin', girlie?"

She drawled, "Finest Parisian poodleskin, I believe."

"Speed the wombats!" Signor Alicamoussa was startled into saying. "That blondie girlie reminds me of someone, but feather me if I can remember who."

"Poodleskin!" howled Turtledove. "This miss has the heart of a vulture!"

"Reckon that is the kind that most makes a hash of young men's bosoms," observed Signor Alicamoussa.

There was also some accommodation to be made between Turtledove and Sofonisba, both of whom slightly lost their heads on introduction, to the extent that Sofonisba finished halfway up a repaired mast, spitting like a fishwife, and Turtledove split his black velvet waistcoat jumping after her.

The boys and girls watched in silence as the cat and dog suddenly realized the indignity of their situation.

Cool apologies were exchanged, and Turtledove bowed low. "Charmed, I'm sure."

If a cat could give a weasel's smile, Sofonisba gave one now, mewing, "Certainly you are."

"Yew know wot dogs is. Hot-heads. I blame me edikation. They allus taught us that any cat would murder yew for a fish supper."

Sofonisba conceded graciously, "I myself have known several cats who would do just that."

Tig took one look at Sofonisba and pronounced her "the most helegant creetur alive!" Thereafter Sofonisba would make a point of sleeping on Tig's hammock.

The others shyly introduced themselves. The Venetian boys' English proved adequate to express themselves, but not quite good enough to understand the varied street dialects of the Londoners. Teo and Renzo found themselves busy with simultaneous translations.

Sebastiano asked, "So are you two *Londoners* now, then?"

The awkward silence was broken by the bells of St. Mary Overie tolling ten o'clock. Then Teo was struck by inspiration: "How about some games?"

"At this hour?" Renzo asked.

"It'll warm us up quicker than anything. And it'll help everyone learn the words they need to get on! Pylorus, what do London children play in the street?"

The Londoner opted for My Lady's Coach, Knock Down Ginger and Aunt Margaret's Dead. Then the Venetians successfully conveyed the complicated rules to their *Strega*, *Bandiera* and *Campanon*, a special Venetian form of hopscotch.

Turtledove beamed approvingly. "Childer. Playin' games. Like they oughter. It chokes me up, that. Bring me a hangkerchief, Tig, do."

Not everyone was playing games. While the others laughed themselves breathless on the frozen deck, Teo was sitting cross-legged by the booby hatch, scanning *The Best Ways with Wayward Ghosts*, stored in her photographic memory, to find a spell that would protect the *Scilla* from her enemies, both natural and supernatural. From time to time, she looked up wistfully at the exuberant merriment on deck. She'd have loved to warm her toes with a quick hop at *Campanon*. But each time, she turned dutifully back to *Best Ways*, desperately seeking a solution.

"How ith you gonna make the *whole* ship invithible 'n' unhearable, Teo?" asked the District Disgrace, who had crept over to sit beside her.

"Shhh. Teo's reading," Renzo admonished, skidding to where they sat. This talent of Teo's, which he envied so much, required quiet. Teo mentally leafed through pages 150 to 280 in a few minutes, finding nothing of use except a spell for making a Ghost-Convict dance a hornpipe.

At last, on page 449, Teo found a spell that might work.

At that moment, from the crow's nest, Marco shouted, "Ghost-Convicts, six of them, marching down Clink Street. Right toward us. And cormorants, approaching from the Tower!"

Renzo cried, "Teo, you've got to do it. *Now!*"

Teo closed her eyes and recited the spell. At first nothing happened. Then a strange silence fell over the boat, as if the air was thick with chloroform. The *Scilla* shook like a wet cat and began to spin in circles, wrenching her ropes from their bitts. The narrow berth of St. Mary Overie Dock had snugly contained the *Scilla*'s dimensions when she was at rest. But now, at each lurching turn, the sides of the boat juddered noiselessly against the stone walls. Pewter mugs and coiled ropes were raining down soundlessly on everyone's heads. Teo was winded by a barrel that flew across the deck to smack her in the small of the back. Waves broke over the *Scilla*'s bows, sending jets of water high into the air. The cormorants, just arriving at the dock, departed in a flurry of feathers and squawks. But aboard the *Scilla* herself, everything remained as silent as the grave.

All the while they tumbled around, Teo kept her mind's eye firmly fixed on *The Best Ways with Wayward Ghosts*. On page 450, a paragraph flashed in front of her:

"If this spell causes your accommodation to lurch or otherwise comport itself alarmingly, it is sometimes efficacious to invoke a list of Calming Visions."

Teo thought: "The Venetian lagoon at sunset, the sound of pages turning in old books, Renzo singing . . ."

The tumbling ceased abruptly. Everyone fell down, and everything fell down on top of them. When the silent shattering of jam jars had ceased, everyone sat motionless and fearful.

Down below in Clink Street, the six Ghost-Convicts arrived at the dock, staring in all directions and sniffing suspiciously. They paused every few doors to anoint the handles with liquid from their billycans.

"Can you smell kiddies?" asked one, sniffing.

"Not a whiff, dammit," growled the other.

"It works!" exulted Teo. "They can't even smell us. And look, the cormorants haven't come back!"

Signor Alicamoussa pointed. "And all accomplished in silence! Those worm-brained guards haven't noticed a thing!"

"We'll have to stop St. Mary Overie's dock-keeper renting out the space to someone else. Or another ship will come and crush the *Scilla* to matchwood," Giovanni pointed out.

Renzo suggested, "We can say that we had to make a short voyage, but that we'll pay to keep the space reserved for the *Scilla* when she comes back."

"I'll go and find the dock-keeper," said Emilio. "He's usually at the Anchor at this hour."

Fossy played an anxious note. Tig interpreted, "How will you get past the guards?"

"Watch me!" Emilio said with a grin, climbing down the ladder.

"Where did you appear from, laddie?" shouted a surprised officer when Emilio materialized beside him. For the moment the boy let go of the *Scilla*'s ladder, he had become visible once more.

"Now doan you even *think* of going aboard this here Venetian ship, laddie."

"What Venetian ship?" asked Emilio innocently.

The guard spun around to discover that he was guarding what appeared to be an empty dock.

"Well, I'll be boiled! Slipped off, has she? Well, all to the good."

He began to remove the tape and the quarantine signs.

Turtledove busied himself inspecting the quarters for his "childer," testing the hammocks for softness and diagnosing a need for cotton-flannel blankets and black bear stoles all round. "I'll nip back to the Mansion Dolorous termorrow an' see what I can rustle up from last season's stock," he said. "Meanwhile, all this adventurizing and magicking has given me a powerful appetite. Seems like three days, not three hours, since we 'ad those fish 'n' chips! Anythin' by way of gnawing round here?"

"Reckon every echidna must have his ant, yes," Signor Alicamoussa agreed, rather impenetrably. "Second suppers all round!"

The smell of roasting meat soon floated out of the galley, along with the cheerful sound of Cookie whistling. His sea pie was an immediate success with Turtledove and the Londoners. Under its crust were layered mutton, onion, mealy potato and a fragrant gravy. Teo and Signor Alicamoussa, who pronounced himself "fanging for a feed," dined on Stilton-and-apple turnovers.

The *Scilla* accepted her new inmates with an audible groaning of her exhausted timbers. As Turtledove put it, "We's mighty put to it for room 'ere! Bandboxical, wot! Still, the snugger the better in this cold, eh!"

The boys and girls would have to sleep in turns, the Venetians gallantly offering to work the first night shift. At six a.m., it was agreed, the sleepers would arise and turn their hammocks inside out to freshen them for the next occupants. Then they would go up to swab the decks before sitting down to breakfast: cocoa with cream and sugar, and freshly baked bread with jam. After breakfast, the Londoners would disembark for their various doings, and the Venetians would continue with their dock work and repairs to the *Scilla*.

Money was as tight as space. Hyrum offered to pawn the ship's brass sextant, the chronometer and even the compass inside its binnacle, along with every other item that could be pried from the deck and turned into ready money for daily expenses.

Accustomed to living on their wits, the Londoners were fast learners when it came to the lingo and customs of the sea. They needed to be shouted at only once to take it to heart that they might not sit on an upturned bucket or mention the word "rabbit."

On January 29, newsboys ran down Clink Street at dawn, bellowing the headlines: **ZOO ANIMALS STOLEN!** and **RAID ON HARRODS!** followed by **SICK CITY—LONDON FALLS TO NEW DISEASE!**

Pylorus Salt crept ashore to buy the *Times*. Apart from Uncle Tommaso, who was out zooky-selling, the *Scilla's* entire extended crew gathered around the mess table to hear Pylorus read out the stories.

Now it was not only children, but also animals of the fattier species that were disappearing from the zoo. No one had any doubt about who was taking them.

And from Harrods, the great London department store, there had been another strange theft—the food halls ransacked not for expensive caviar, but for Halford's mutton jelly, colza oil, neat's-foot oil, lard oil, tins of minced collops, dripping, linseed oil and Batty's frying oil.

Meanwhile, the *Times* reported, the Half-Dead disease had already reduced a good proportion of the London population to mumbling, shuffling shadows of themselves. The quack doctors rushed to produce medicines that claimed to cure the shattered constitutions and depressed spirits of the sufferers.

"The same disease arrived in Venice," Teo explained, "after the ice flood. The Mayor claimed—"

Signor Alicamoussa inserted, "Not that youse'd give a cup of stonkered gnat's sweat for *his* opinion."

"The Mayor claimed that it would quickly pass and not spread to the tourists."

Renzo spoke slowly. "I think the Ghost-Convicts from the *Bombazine* brought the Half-Dead disease to Venice. Do you remember what Miss Uish said?"

Teo quoted, "That the lieutenant on the *Bombazine*, Rosebud, had 'a laboratory on board this ship that positively *manufactures* death. Or, what is worse, half-death.'"

"In other words, the Half-Dead disease."

"Ye's a canny body, Renzo," Ann pressed, "but *how* kin them Ghost-Convicts be spreadin' it to 'oomans?"

Teo consulted her memory for a book that might help. Into her head tumbled James Grant's estimable, though wordy, work, *The Mysteries of All Nations, Rise and Progress of Superstition, Laws Against and Trials of Witches, Ancient and Modern Delusions Together With Strange Customs, Fables and Tales*.

Reading the page that appeared in front of her eyes, she cried out, "In 1536 a band of witches in Italy spread a plague by smearing an ointment on the posts and doors of people's houses."

Tig groaned. "Jist zackly what I saw 'em doin', the devils! Selling mournin' brooches were jist a cover! Them Ghost-Convicts is infecting the whole of London!"

When Sibella murmured that she knew a cure, actually, no one, except perhaps Renzo, believed a word of it.

"But I do!" Sibella protested sullenly. "Not that you deserve it, seeing how mean you all are to me. Yet I could cure it if you'd come down from your high horses and allow me."

Pylorus Salt commented, "Hark at that Miss Syllabella! She speaks fluent Renzo! And she's a pain in the pinny jist loik him!"

Even the ever-gallant Signor Alicamoussa now looked at Sibella with a piquant twitch of irritation briefly creasing his exquisite features. "No more tarradiddling from you, young lady, if you please. Feather me! You are veritably getting up my goat, yes."

From below came the voice of Uncle Tommaso. He hurtled up on deck, calling, "Lorenzo! Teodora! Sargano! Desperate news!"

He was carrying the pieces of a poster torn off a wall. Fitting them together, he shouted, "Look at this! They're all over the town. You can't walk past a public house or a garden wall without seeing one of them hanging there."

Black-and-white images of Teo and Renzo's faces, with convict bandannas and eye patches superimposed on them, and parrots on their shoulders, peered out of a thicket of verbiage.

WANTED FOR PIRACY
GRAND LARCENY
And BRINGING the VENETIAN HALF-DEAD DISEASE
to LONDON TOWN,
imperiling the Health of the Populace
and Spreading Terror at Large.
Teodora Gasperin, also known as
Teodora "The Undrowned Child" Stampara

and even Teodoro Ongania
and Lorenzo "The Studious Son" Antonello,
both Known Delinquents in their Native Venice,
Juvenile Mutineers and Murderers at Sea.
SUBSTANTIAL REWARD for Any Citizen
who apprehends these Low-Lifes of the Lowest Order.

41. Most Wanted

"Them photygraphs is a libel against nature!" declared Turtledove. "Yew two is way better-looking than that, me poppets! Doan let no one say otherwise! This is some rum story got up for to addle the noodles of the public."

"How *did* they get your photographs?" wondered Tig.

Renzo answered flatly, "Those are the 'school photographs' that were done on board the *Scilla* for Miss Uish. Remember how she shouted at Peaglum to take them away, Teo? He went off in the coracle. No doubt straight to the *Bombazine*. But someone else must have added those eye patches and parrots."

"And blacked out our teeth!" noted Teo indignantly.

"They've blackened our *honor*," Renzo shouted. "They're painting us as murderers."

"Was you reely truly *pye-rats*?" breathed Sally admiringly. "And moiderers and mootineers? You niver breaved a word 'bout *that*."

"Only against our will," insisted Renzo.

"Yew childer know wot 'appens to pye-rats in these septic isles?" asked Turtledove in a quiet voice.

While Renzo and Teo were casting their minds back to the mock trial conducted by Peaglum aboard the *Scilla,* Turtledove intoned, "Drowned in a barrel of salt water an' buried in the marshes below low-tide mark. Or hanged by the neck until dead at Newgate gallows."

A shiver went through everyone on deck. Fossy uttered a somber wail on the violin.

Teo exclaimed, "There is only one way that our enemies could have found out *all* my names."

And she stared straight at Sibella.

Renzo took a step so that he stood between them. "Teo," he snapped, "for charity's sake! It's just not possible, is it?"

"What about the leeches? She chanted to those leeches in magical words! She's probably still doing it."

The boys and girls gathered in a knot around Sibella. Signor Alicamoussa interposed himself.

"House arrest," he suggested pleasantly, "a spot of house arrest for the small blondie girl, yes. Sibella, go to your cabin. From the looks on these young varmints' faces, youse'll be in the altogether safer off there. But speaking as a circus-master, I reckon those little slimy fellas of yours might go after a spot of exercise in the fresh air. Fair do's, *ragazzi?*"

Their eyes gleaming, Fabrizio and Emilio ran off to fetch Sibella's pillow box. And nothing, not even the slowness of the operation, could stop the boys from making a couple of her leeches walk the plank.

Ice knocked against the *Scilla*'s prow. The crew was kept busy breaking it up by pouring saucepans of hot water overboard. But the task was hopeless. London's great river was freezing over, just like the Grand Canal in Venice.

It was obvious to all aboard the *Scilla* that the *Bombazine*, snugly moored at St. Katharine Docks, had something to do with it. That was the first part of the Thames to be frozen solid.

And now the Ghost-Convicts poured out of the *Bombazine* on their mission to anoint every doorknob in London with the Half-Dead disease. Invisible to adults, the Ghost-Convicts went about their murderous business uninterrupted. Children who saw them went crying to their mothers, who generally slapped them for making up such outrageous lies. Or dosed them with something bitter, in the belief that they were suffering from a fever that had brought on strange imaginings.

Tobias Putrid and Bits Piecer bravely volunteered to go to the hated mendicity officers to explain the situation. An hour later, Bits came running back, choking on tears.

The two boys had not been believed.

"But you'll all die, 'orribly!" Tobias had warned.

"He were that exercised, he dint care what he sayed." Bits wrung his hands.

"'Orribly! 'Orribly!" the mendicity men had mocked Tobias. "It's the end of the world, all right!"

Bits told how Tobias had lost his temper and screamed at the officers, begging them to protect London and all the children of the metropolis.

"And for his pains poor old Tobias 'as got carted orf to Bedlam." Bits colored with shame. "I 'scaped. I should of gorn wiv him, to look after him."

Tig and Sally hastened to hug and reassure Bits. "No, you did right. Otherwise 'ow'd we of known what 'appened?"

"Bedlam?" asked Teo.

"The menthol 'orspital!" whimpered Bits. "Banged up good 'n' proper wiv all them loonyticks in there."

Signor Alicamoussa's urgent voice called from the ladder. "Come, *ragazzi*! We have no time to lose! I have been news-mongering with the Incogniti. I reckon we've bits-and-pieced together ahat's afoot-and-mouth, yes."

With everyone gathered around the mess table, Signor Alicamoussa began solemnly, "Youse all know the present posture of affairs. Everyone and his dog, every bandicoot and Bendigo dingo, is a-coming to London for the funeral of Her Late Majesty, yes. Tremenjous throngs shall come a-crowding every street like wallabies at a waterhole, all gasping for a glimpse of Queen Victoria's mortal remains going to their finial rest, bless her."

Two dozen heads nodded gravely. Fossy played a funereal note.

"Well, as we already guessed, it seems is an occasion too good to be passed up by the Pretending Hoskins, the Miss Uish and that vile creature who is flower and fungus of her withered heart, Bajamonte Tiepolo. When this city is at its fullest, groaning with citizens and visitors, is the moment when the Hooroo Horror, Il Traditore, and his honeyfugling doxy plan to make their attack."

"How do you know for sure?" asked Renzo.

"Those slit-guzzled Hooroo criminals have a wolf's appetite for hot spiced pumpkin. While serving them, our Incogniti overheard gobbets of blood-gurgling *conversazioni*. We have put the pieces together."

"The Ghost-Convicts have started *their* attack already," pointed out Teo. "With the Half-Dead disease, the Londoners will be too sick to put up much of a fight."

"Yes, the Half-Dead disease has Londoners wan and whey like albino apes. Bajamonte Tiepolo is not a real he. Is cowardly like a hyena and attacks only weakened and duffered-out prey, as we know, yes. It give me the worms to think on it!" Signor Alicamoussa clutched his shapely belly.

"But whath kind of attack will it be?" quavered the District Disgrace.

"Alas, cannot yet furnish all the perpendiculars. Ice is mentioned. And squid."

"An invasion of squid?" moaned Fabrizio.

"A lot o' clossle squid loik the one wot nearly et our Teo?" whimpered Sally.

"Your Barjaminty might of tousands of 'em tings at 'is disposal!"

"No amoont of squiddies kin eat all o' London Town," insisted Ann Picklefinch. "They lodges under the water, anyhoo."

The circus-master threw up his hands. "That is not all. Hear how the plot clots! For in-the-meanwhiles, an army of Hooroo Ghost-Convicts and escaped prisoners is amassing on the French coast at all points closest to England. Isn't a sheep left between Bordeaux and Calais! Yet are no boats for to carry the invader-izers."

"So they're planning to get to London by magic means," guessed Renzo.

"Baddened magic," Teo whispered.

296

Signor Alicamoussa agreed. "The Ghost-Convicts gossip exactly thus. And also they chatter of their secret ally, who will provide the means for their soldiers to cross the English Channel." He lowered his voice, "This bloke, they call him Signor Pipistrelly."

"The bat!" exclaimed Renzo and Teo with one voice.

Renzo produced a piece of paper from his jacket and began scribbling. Teo, biting her lip, explained, "It is as a bat that Bajamonte Tiepolo shows himself when he does not choose to be—or cannot be—human."

"So," Renzo was businesslike, "we must ask the mermaids to print warning bills on the Seldom Seen Press. We'll urge Londoners to leave the city. So at least if . . . when . . . those criminal soldiers arrive here, there will be no victims waiting for them. Here's something I drafted while we've been talking."

Everyone clustered around Renzo's piece of paper. For the benefit of those who could not read, Signor Alicamoussa tested the words in his beautiful voice.

"Clever you, Renzo," breathed Sally Twinish.

"If they'll believe it." Pylorus's voice mixed doubt with hope.

"Excellent!" Teo enthused. "I'll take it straight to Lussa. No, Renzo, you can't come." She pointed to his portrait on the **WANTED** poster. "It's not safe. You're not between-the-Linings."

Signor Alicamoussa mused, "Reckon it cannot hurt our prospects, nor those of Londoners, if they are forewarned. Give 'em a chance to shoot through, at least. Tommaso, the pumpkin-sellers can distribute the printed papers in their barrows, yes!"

The District Disgrace pleaded, "And Teo, can you askth them pretty ladies if they kin help Tobias? Tell 'em we kint do wivout him."

"Course I will."

"Run like the wind in the fur of a cheetah-cat, Teodora," implored Signor Alicamoussa, "and be careful, dearest girl. Youse'll know why."

"Why?" asked Bits. "No grown-ups can see her."

"But ghosts-in-the-Slaughterhouse can," explained Renzo. "And they're looking for her."

42. Lost heads and tempers

twenty minutes later, under London Bridge

"The water is melting! The ice, I mean!"

In the cavern's pool, all the icebergs had dissolved and a pleasant steamy atmosphere made Teo feel as if she was inside a ROYLE'S PATENT SELF-POURING TEAPOT.

Lussa looked somewhat smug, insofar as smugness was compatible with her royal demeanor. "It came to a little Altercation betwixt our Venetian Selves & our London Sisters. My own Pretty Ladies, I fear, lost their Heads & their Tempers, and They emptied all the PATENT NOSTRUMS FOR WOMEN'S WEAKNESSES into the Water."

Flos took up the story. "And da water fizzed like we'd dropt acid in! Yoiks! Ye shoulda heared dem girlies bemoaning what we'd did."

"So we dropt some more," chimed in Marsil.

And the misbehaving Venetian mermaids had in this way made a most useful discovery, as Lussa now explained. DR. WORDEN'S WATER FOR WEAK WOMEN, DR. BOWDER'S COMPOUND SYRUP OF INDIAN TURNIP and DR. WYNKOOP'S

KATHARISMIC HONDURAS had one thing in common: the ability to melt ice.

"So we can kill two birds with one stone," Teo realized. "Protect the poor human ladies of London who have been ruining their health with that rubbish, and at the same time save the Thames from freezing over!"

Lussa agreed: "So runs our own Thinking."

Teo explained Signor Alicamoussa's discoveries and Renzo's idea. "Have you fitted up the Seldom Seen Press, Lussa?"

"It is indeed assembled, yet our London Sisters are against our employing It. They claim that the Ink releases Noxious Fumes that—"

"I can guess," sighed Teo. "But *you* can print the handbills to warn London?"

Flos was already floating the beautiful press over to the walkway. Teo's heart leapt with homesickness for Venice. Only a *Venetian* printing press could look like this: an airy construction of bone, carved oyster shells and pearls. She handed Flos the piece of paper on which Renzo had written his message for London. Flos busied herself composing type with expert fingers, swearing lightly at some of Renzo's more florid grammatical constructions.

IMMENSE DANGER TO LIFE AND PROPERTY . . .
INEXORABLE FORCES OF EVIL . . . SAME WHO ATTACKED
VENICE . . . THOUSANDS MORE IN LONDON,
PERIL PROPORTIONATELY GREATER . . . THE FUNERAL
PROVIDING AN OPPORTUNITY TO CREATE
MAXIMUM CARNAGE . . .

Teo turned to Lussa, raising her voice over the clicking of bone type. "Do you remember the boy Tobias Putrid? Who came with us on our first visit here?"

"Not loikly to forget a boy who smells like dat," muttered Flos.

Teo explained his plight. The Venetian mermaids hubbubed in sympathy, "Poor laddie's cabobbled."

"Bedlam," sighed Lussa, "is beyond our Reach by Water. We dare not take to the River, for We have not yet discovered what Creatures killed the Melusine. For the Moment, Teodora, prithee take Comfort that the Insane Asylum has a fine tall Cupola, and does at least lie a little away from the Thames. Young Tobias may be Safer than any of You."

Marsil, busily ripping up rags, sighed. "And our London sisters woan help. They is took agin the boy because o' the smell on 'im. They tink he carries the cholera in his pocket. Anyways, they is foolly occupied doing what dey do best, drinking Antispasmodic Tea and eatin' sponge cakes. They say it's critomancy— divination usin' cake. S'far as I can see, it means they eat a lot of cake, they gets the bellyache, they swig down their soothin' syrops and then they gets a bit giddy and sees things. No sign of their old famoused bows 'n' arrows. No more use than a headache, any of them."

From an inner cavern came the sound of ladylike hiccupping and the clink of china.

"Ain't I tellin' ye?!" Flos glared. "I'd like to stave in da ribs of whatever cannibal quack makes his moneys selling dat droffel stuff to innocent foolish laydies!"

Teo asked, "What are you doing?"

Not just Marsil, but all the Venetian mermaids were hard at

work shredding rags and fashioning them into large nests. Stacked on the rim of their pool were the Venetian paintings they had saved and brought to London. The silken cocoons made by the Sea Spiders lay in wet heaps.

"Dem cocoons has all shriveled up in da cold," explained Flos.

"Where are the Sea Spiders?"

Flos answered indignantly, "Dem wibbling girls had conniptions 'bout da arachnids. Dey begrudged 'em even da dead flies inside this cavern—everythin's droppin' wiv da cold. We had to lodge da poor beasties in the tunnels o' da 'oomin trains, long wiv all dem squished-up ghosts what lives dere. Poor thanks for all dere hard work, says I. Dat Pucretia! Dat Gloriana! An' worst of all, dat Nerolia! *Wouldn't* I love to settle dere hash with a nice little vindaloo! But dey just shriek like the girlies dey is at da tiniest whiff of a chili."

"They're not niver gonna do nuffink," muttered Marsil. "They's about as useful as a trapdoor on a gondola."

An hour later, Teo was back at the *Scilla,* breathless from carrying the first sack of sea-scented handbills.

While the pumpkin-sellers quickly stuffed them into their jackets, Teo recounted the melting properties of patent remedies for feminine weakness to the extended crew of the *Scilla.*

Renzo was examining the handbills. "There's a spelling mistake here . . . and look . . ."

"Yer rattlin' my reefer, boy!" In the last few days, a great deal of nautical lingo had cleaved to Turtledove's fluent tongue. Now the dog's rear leg lifted itself above the deck. Renzo hastily closed his mouth. Teo continued as if he had not spoken.

"So," she concluded, "all we need to do is get our hands on all the patent feminine medicines in London, and empty them into the Thames, and . . ."

"All we have to do," repeated Pylorus Salt dryly.

"I ain't sendin' me childer out on the streets to rob the chemists," said a concerned Turtledove. "'Twouldn't be right. I dint raise a pack of thieves! An' they might git caught. It's broad daylight in Piccadilly! An' there be Ghost-Convicts abroad!"

. Fabrizio held up his hand. "We don't need to steal. To save London," he asserted, "I think we can rightfully use some of our convict treasure. We still have three gold sovereigns."

The Mansion Dolorous gang were despatched to Heppell & Co. Chemists in the Strand. Teo, accompanying them, was astonished to see the undulating glass-fronted cabinets lining the walls floor to ceiling, all packed with patent remedies for female weakness.

Three gold sovereigns effectively emptied those cabinets. The astonished assistant at Heppell & Co. kindly threw in a wheeled delivery cart as a gift. The boys and girls returned to the mermaids' cavern staggering under their load of DR. BONKER'S CELE-BRATED EGYPTIAN OIL, RAMSEY'S TRINIDAD AROMATIC BIT-TERS, BEGG'S ALOCASTER BALM AND VELVETINA, PAWNEE LONG LIFE BITTERS and THE GREAT SHOSONEES REMEDY OF DR. JOSEPHUA.

"Not enough!" barked Flos. "Ye has to go to da source."

But their first sight of the mermaids had reduced the London-ers to speechless awe.

"You mean the Farmysootical Society in Bloomsbury Square?" breathed Tig eventually. "That's ever so grand. And rich. I doan fink they needs our pye-rat money."

"Anyway," said Teo, "we've just spent the last of it."

"Den ye'll jest have to take it," attested Flos. "Da Farmysooti-cals will be saved by dis jest as much as da rest of London. I would guess as some of ye 'oomin infants knows how to get into a locked storeroom if ye has to?"

Thrasher and Pylorus hurried off.

Turtledove, in the meantime, had paid a visit to Harrods. He returned with a small metal object in his mouth.

"DR. WRINCH'S DEW DROP REVOLVING LAWN SPRIN-KLER." He grinned. "We can take it in a skiff along the Thames, de-icin' to suit."

Renzo was tired of defending his courage. Teo had done her best to stick up for him, yet everyone persisted in seeing *her* as the hero-ine and him as her somewhat foppish and useless sidekick with the unnecessary vocabulary. Renzo was fed up with skulking about the *Scilla*, hiding away like a coward. Anyway, he'd just composed an eloquent new handbill urging Londoners to empty their own medicine cabinets into the river. Why shouldn't he deliver it to the mermaids himself?

"I can take care of myself," he muttered.

Having tucked his *ferro* penknife into his shoe and pulled a black mourning beret over his head, Renzo quietly climbed down the ladder and stole into Clink Street. He pressed his back against the dank bricks, breathing in the humid air. The stone seemed to stir behind him, as if making a comfortable niche for his shape.

"Ghost-breath!" he whispered, hastily moving away.

A few of the original handbills blew down the street. Renzo saw one affixed to a lamppost. Five London children were standing beneath it, laughing.

"'Dreadful disaster coming!'" quoted one mockingly. "'Evacuate London!'"

"Wot pompous rubbish, eh! This is just the nobs' way of clearing the poor people out of London for the old Queen's funeral, hain't it? A trick. No way I'm missing *that* show!"

Renzo groaned quietly. He turned up his collar and blew on his hands.

"When I go back to the *Scilla*," he reflected, "I'm going to tell them that we must paint the parrots black. We can call them mourning birds and teach them to sing hymns, and maybe I can go and borrow some jet beads from Tristesse and Ganorus for Rosato to decorate the cages. . . . And while I'm there," he thought, "perhaps I'll just borrow some of that best mourning licorice that I tasted there, and those tasty aniseed comfits. . . ."

Renzo was embroidering on this idea when two bobbies approached him from behind. They were rather strange-looking policemen, for their skin was deeply tanned and their wrists were scarred with the rusted imprints of shackles. One was missing an ear. Neither was correctly buttoned into his stiff blue serge uniform. Both scratched and pulled at their cuffs and helmets.

Too late, Renzo caught a glimpse of them.

The suntanned bobbies were on him in a second. Renzo was bundled into a black growler that was waiting on the street corner.

Renzo struggled and kicked as ferociously as he knew how. One of the bobbies dealt him a dizzying blow to the side of the head, shouting, "Ya little bunyip!"

"Newguyte Prison!" the other bobby snarled at the driver. "Fast as ya like, mate."

43. 'How do you account for that parrot on your shoulder?'

a place of judgment, January 30, 1901

Three hours later, Renzo was led into a courtroom at the Old Bailey.

He had passed the intervening hours in a crowded cell that ran with excrement and tears. No one had given him anything to eat or drink.

He had plenty of time to ponder what had happened to him.

"Those bobbies were Harold Hoskins's criminals," he concluded. "Not ghosts, because the driver could see and hear them. But why didn't they take me straight to Bajamonte? And why all this piracy rigmarole?"

After a few minutes' thought, Renzo answered his own questions. "This must be what *he* intended all along. Il Traditore's getting someone else to do his dirty work, as usual. In this case, British justice. And it isn't enough just to kill me. Bajamonte Tiepolo knows how to hurt me in the most painful way. He wants me utterly dishonored and my name blackened, and Venice's too, before I am put to death."

"Lorenzo Antonello!" a suntanned guard shouted in a broad

Australian accent. Renzo approached the cell door apprehensively. The guard unlocked the door, grabbed his ear and propelled him into a side corridor, where three men in their underwear struggled in ropes. Their mouths were gagged with tufts of wool.

The false guard jammed Renzo against a wall. Another man, whose slashed face was barely hidden by his scarves, tied a pirate bandanna around Renzo's head, forced his lips open with a filthy hand, and blacked out two of his teeth with a piece of bitter coal. Finally, the first man clapped a patch over Renzo's eye and a worn-out-looking parrot on his shoulder. Its poor feet were wound around with cruelly biting wire, the ends of which the guard fastened under Renzo's armpit so the parrot could not fly away. Now Renzo looked horribly and humiliatingly like the **WANTED** poster.

He was dragged into a room arrayed in elegance and blazing light. The public seats were occupied by an ugly-looking mob.

A woman yodeled in a deep, coarse voice, "Speed the wombats, what a shameless bast . . . ," but was quickly hushed by her companions.

"They're Hooroo criminals, every one of them," Renzo realized. "Even the ones dressed as women!"

The face of the prosecution barrister shone with intelligence. His wig was so angular and his vivid green eyes so wide apart that he had the appearance of a praying mantis—and indeed, his black tailcoat hung stiffly, like the carapace of an insect. In front of him lay a pile of documents bound and sealed in red ribbon and wax. Renzo's name was written in stabbing capitals on the front of each one.

Renzo's own shabby lawyer hiccupped as he rose unsteadily to present his client, whose name he could not quite remember.

The judge glowered from his bench.

When asked how he pleaded, Renzo asserted sturdily, on each count, "Innocent, sir."

"If you are not a pirate," demanded the prosecution barrister, "how do you account for that parrot on your shoulder?"

"I didn't put it there. Actually, it's tied on with wire."

Renzo started to lift his arm to show the wire tied underneath, but the barrister shouted, "Do you see that? The incorrigible criminal raises his hand against our judge! So young, and yet so wicked!"

The crowd chanted, "Wicked as a rattlesnake's wattle!" and "Stump me, too right!" Amid the clamor, a peevish "Baa!" was also audible.

Renzo hastily lowered his arm. Meanwhile, the barrister continued smoothly, "The Admiralty has plentiful records of parrots correctly identifying pirates. Now, Lorenzo Antonello, do you deny that on January sixteenth of this very year you made a raid upon the *Rose la Touche,* a raid in which you inflicted savage murder on the crew while her passengers were stripped of their valuables? Call the Frenchman!"

A man shuffled into the witness dock.

"Can you identify this boy?" the barrister demanded. "Is he the one who attacked you?"

"*Oui!*" The Frenchman shuddered. "*C'était lui, certainement.*"

Renzo protested, "I was there, but . . ."

"You just stood and wrung your hands, did you? Like now?" mocked the barrister, imitating Renzo with deadly accuracy. "So you not only perpetrated the shameful act, but you are also too cowardly to admit it."

To be accused of shameful cowardice was too much for Renzo.

"You're being used!" he cried. "Someone is manipulating you into commiting a crime on his behalf."

"Contempt of court," snapped the judge. "Added to the charge sheet."

The prosecution barrister continued smoothly, "As I was saying, savage murder . . ."

"But I didn't want to attack the *Rose la Touche*. My friend Teo was noosed—"

"Yet you did. Set that down, clerk! Confession at the dock. Guilty as charged. And therefore guilty of attacks on diverse innocent French, Spanish, English and Dutch vessels. Also note that this testimony incriminates that other Venetian pirate, Teodora Gasperin. I put it to you, Lorenzo Antonello, that you two hardened criminals have come to London, intent on land-piracy upon the citizens of this city!"

Someone in the crowd shouted, "String 'im up, the little tyke!"

The judge slapped his gavel on the bench and nodded approvingly. The prosecution barrister winked at him, lightly tapping his hip pocket. The court clerk busied himself at the silent typewriting machine.

The barrister snapped, "Now, boy, what do you know about the Half-Dead disease that now rages through the innocent population of London?"

"I—I know nothing . . . ," stammered Renzo.

"Boy claims to be a cretin. No defense."

A lamb wriggled out from between the legs of a man with a corked hat and stampeded around the courtroom.

Amidst the chaos, Renzo was swiftly convicted of "piracy on the high seas" and for "contaminating the Jewel of the British Empire with a wasting disease."

The judge announced, "One week from today Lorenzo Antonello shall be taken to a place of execution to be hanged by the neck until dead. Then his corpse will be exposed to three high tides and buried in an unmarked grave, so that no trace of his wicked existence on this earth shall be left behind him."

Renzo swayed in the dock, and the parrot lost control of itself for a moment too. Looking down at the warm green splatter on his shoulder, Renzo whispered aloud, "It cannot, cannot get any worse."

44. Newgate gallows

evening, January 30, 1901

Teo climbed halfway up the ladder and threw the sack of day-old bread over the *Scilla*'s taffrail. No one called down to greet her: she guessed they were all keeping warm belowdecks. Why wasn't Renzo there waiting for her, though? He always seemed to sense when she was coming back from one of her errands ashore.

Was he playing at rhapsodomancy with Sibella?

No, he hadn't done that since Teo had mocked him for it. But something wasn't right, she thought.

A newsboy ran down Clink Street shouting, "Read all about it! Venetian pirate captured! Newgate gallows to swing for Venetian boy a week from today!"

"Gristle and guts!" cried Teo, sliding down the ladder.

One of the useful documents stored in Teo's brain was a map of London Town, published by Appleyard and Hetling of Farringdon Street, a copy of which she had once gazed at in the school library. One quick look was of course enough for Teo's photographic memory to capture its every street and street name. Newgate Prison appeared in her mind, set in a web of lanes. The map in her head propelled her through the winding streets of Southwark, toward the wide expanse of Blackfriars Bridge and the misty huddle of London's roofs beyond it.

Teo's nerves did not really catch up with her until she'd left the Embankment and was running up to the very gates of Newgate Prison. Then, at the sight of so much black iron and grizzled stone exuding such rampant wretchedness, Teo stopped short, her heart thudding with terror. Newgate was exactly as Miss Uish had so happily described it during that mock trial on the *Scilla*: brooding, malignant and windowless. And Teo now had to get herself inside it.

"I'm between-the-Linings," she reassured herself. "I can get past the guards."

And so she did, passing through the gates among a crowd of visitors. The first thing that struck her about the place was the lack of light. She felt as if she were moving through a dark, flooded cellar: flooded not with water, but with a deep, liquid-seeming misery. A few miserable lamps not so much relieved as highlighted the darkness. By listening to dismal conversations, she discovered the way to the condemned quarters.

Two minutes later, she was looking down into the pathetically bare cage of a solitary cell. Her lower lip wobbled when she noted that even in his state of utter hopelessness, the sleeping Renzo contrived to look elegant in some strange attire that reminded her of nothing so much as the rags of the Ghost-Convicts from Hooroo.

Then she noticed the parrot perched on Renzo's foot.

"What's that doing there?" she wondered.

The bird cocked his head at her and nodded, before bending down to bite Renzo gently on the toe.

The first part of Renzo's brain to awaken fully was unfortunately his sense of smell: the straw on which he lay stank of every possible vile thing. Retching, he kept his eyes screwed shut and tried to drift back to sleep.

The next thing he heard was Teo whispering through the bars at him.

"Renzo! Renzo! Wake up!"

Renzo opened his eyes. "Teo," he cried, "you have to be careful. Newgate's crawling with Hooroo criminals dressed up as guards!" His voice was not quite steady as he added, "But thank you for coming."

"If they're human, they can't see me. Of *course* I'm here."

"Well, I haven't been such a good friend to you, lately, have I? You've had every reason to turn your back on me."

Neither of them mentioned Sibella, but her shimmering presence and tinkling laugh hung in the space that separated them.

Renzo began again. "I thought you would come for me. It would be so like you to put yourself at risk."

Teo wondered silently, "Would you rather have seen Sibella's face at these bars?"

As if she'd said the words aloud, Renzo whispered, "There is no one I would rather see than you now, Teo. I would wish that your face, above all others, was the last face I saw before I died."

"You're not going to die!"

"It doesn't seem very likely that I shall still be alive next week. You know the penalty for piracy." Renzo snapped his fingers with a grim humor.

"Oi!" A guard, mercifully a real one, stumped up to the cell. Teo moved hastily out of his way. "You, Venetian pirate boy, stop talking to yesself! It hain't allowed! It'll rouse up the blood of the other prisoners. Shut yer filfy foreign mouf!"

Renzo blanched.

Teo whispered, "I'm going now, Renzo, to get help. I'll work something out. I promise."

Renzo watched Teo's narrow back retreating down the corridor. Then he looked at the three walls of his cell, and up and down the bars. There was no possible way of escaping. "Maybe if I had five years and a sharp instrument I could weaken a single bar," he groaned. "But I have nothing."

"Nothing," chirped the parrot.

Renzo stared at the bird. Now that he really looked at it, he could see that it was the most intelligent breed, an African gray. Of all the parrots they trained on the *Scilla*, the African grays were always the quickest to absorb new phrases and even whole sentences.

He laughed softly. "You have given me an idea *and* the means of carrying it out."

"Carrying it out," repeated the parrot, word-perfect.

Renzo stroked the parrot's feathers and got to work.

When Teo arrived back at the *Scilla*, she found the ship in an uproar. Somehow, despite a general understanding that she was to have an eye kept on her, Sibella had managed to slip away, taking the pillow box of her remaining leeches with her.

The boys and girls were confined to the ship. Signor

Alicamoussa and Uncle Tommaso were out on the streets searching. Turtledove and Pattercake were sniffing all roads leading away from the *Scilla*. They were desperate to find her before she could alert anyone to the existence and exact location of an invisible boat full of runaway London street urchins and juvenile Venetian mutineers at St. Mary Overie Dock.

"And it looks loik that Renzo's gorn off wiv her!" muttered Tig aggrievedly. "They prob'ly worked it all out beforehand an' met up somewhere, an' now . . . Where you bin anyway, Teo? We found the bread an' we was worried summat 'ad happened to you. We can spare that Renzo orl right, but not *you*."

Teo opened her mouth to speak, but Pylorus rushed in, "They makes a fine pair, Renzo an' Sibella. Bet they's saunterin' up Mayfair arm in arm right now, lookin' at the Paris fashions!"

"Be quiet!" screamed Teo. She put their mistake to rights in a couple of short, pointed sentences. The Londoners clutched one another.

"Newgate!" breathed Hyrum.

"The Old Bailey!" shouted Thrasher in despair.

"The beak was rotten?" Bits drew in his breath. "My pa got sent down by one o' that sort. My late pa, that is."

"Renzo's a goner," groaned Pylorus Salt. "I'm right sorry I were a bit sharp 'bout him jist now."

"He prob'ly wernt spoony on that Sibella at all," moaned Ann Picklefinch. "He were prob'ly jist keeping an oiy on 'er. To protect us all, loik. And all that while we was moongin' on about him."

"It's obvious," Giovanni spat. "Sibella's gone to the *Bombazine*, to tell Miss Uish where we are. Isn't that just what she would do?"

Teo resisted the temptation to say "I told you so," yet her face ached with the unspoken words.

316

"And our poor Greasy and Marg'rit might be on the pye-rat ship too," called Bits. "And they'll be wantin' savin', urgent. Plus whoever's got our Renzo trapped loik a rat—that villain will be on that boat."

There was a short silence, during which everyone looked at the deck, the lanterns, the mast, down Clink Street—everywhere except at each other.

"Well," sighed Teo, "I guess it's going to be me."

"To do what?" asked Fabrizio skeptically.

"Who sculls over to the *Bombazine* to see what's going on there."

"Straight as a pound o' candles, her!" chuckled Bits admiringly.

"Launch the coracle!" ordered Giovanni, and the *Scilla*'s crew rushed to undo its clove hitch and lower the boat into the Thames.

The District Disgrace quavered, "If Thignor Alicamoutha were 'ere, or if Turthledove were 'ere, or Huncle Tommy-tho, they wouldn't let our Teo go on thuch a deadly mithion. In the middle of the nighth!"

"Good thing they're not here, then," muttered Teo, already halfway down the ladder to the coracle.

"*Brava*, Teo!" blurted Sebastiano dalla Mutta in a very small, frightened voice.

45. The secret manufactory

to the Bad Ship Bombazine, *late at night, January 30, 1901*

Skimming over the black Thames, Teo dodged miniature icebergs. As she stood poling with her single oar, she was grateful to Renzo for the gondoliering lessons in Venice. The coracle was easier to manage than a gondola, but the currents of the Thames were far more dangerous than the Grand Canal's lazy swaying. The unpleasantly familiar shape of the *Bombazine* appeared ahead all too soon. Starlight showed the black ship looking distinctly worse for wear: the Sea Sorcerer's storm had broken her back and slanted her masts. The pirate flag still hung in tatters.

"I guess that's why she took so long to get to London. Must have limped all the way. But how dare she show those murderous colors?" thought Teo. Then she remembered that no adults in London could see the ghost-ship at all.

From fifty yards away, she caught a glint of the moon on the weapons carried by two guards. From twenty yards, she caught the sound of their snores and the faint baaing of sheep.

The cormorants were sleeping peacefully on the crooked masts.

Teo used a reliable midshipman's hitch to secure the coracle to a ladder at the larboard side of the *Bombazine*. She climbed aboard, tiptoed across the empty deck and pushed her shoulder against the first sliding door she saw. It ran quietly along its grooves. There was no guard there either. Unobstructed, Teo entered the forecastle of the *Bombazine* thinking, "I guess no one needs to guard an invisible ghost-ship."

Inside the first room, the feeble glow of a single lantern threw shadows upon three rows of sagging hammocks. Though a fierce draft rustled Teo's hair, those hammocks hung eerily immobile, as if they were tenanted by stones.

Gingerly, she pulled down a fold of one of the hammocks. Inside, the remains of a swan lay crumpled like a wad of white paper. The hammock to its left held the wan skin of an antelope. On the right hung a hollow baby hippopotamus, drained of all its marrowfat.

"The animals from the zoo!" Teo backed out of the room and up to the deck.

There was another sliding door on the larboard side of the mast. It was locked. Putting her ear against it, Teo heard a breathy voice singing. She pulled away, chilled to the core. There was something terribly wrong about hearing "Silent Night," the loveliest Christmas carol of all, rasped out in a voice that oozed such wickedness. And in January—a month late. What kind of creature was that? And why had Miss Uish got it locked up on the *Bombazine*?

The booby hatch gaped open. Over the dreadful whispered singing, Teo became aware of a rumbling cacophony below, a pounding noise like wooden cogs turning, the cries of children and the howling of dogs.

Not a fiber of her being wanted to go down there.

"But," Teo reproved herself, "this is why I've come."

Belowdeck, the *Bombazine*'s walls were lit by ornate lanterns inlaid with colored glass in poison green and blood-red. The walls and windows were hung with velvet curtains and ancient tapestries, slashed as if by swords. The last time Teo had seen such tattered luxury and such violent hunting scenes had been inside the ghost-palace of Bajamonte Tiepolo in Venice. And then her eye fell on a carved wooden crest painted in the Tiepolo colors of red, blue and yellow.

Trembling, Teo grasped the velvet curtain that hung between her and the source of the appalling noise. The dusty fabric crumbled like a cobweb. Peering through the hole her fist had made, Teo discovered the dreadful secret of the *Bombazine*.

In a cavernous wooden chamber, dozens of treadmills were walked by chained boys, girls and dogs. All were clearly at the final stages of exhaustion. Even as Teo watched, one dog stumbled and fell off its post, rolling to the floor, where it lay quite still. The eyes of the prisoners followed it and filled with tears, as did Teo's, as a Ghost-Convict kicked it into a corner.

A large white lump appeared at the end of a wooden chute. A hatch opened, sending freezing wind whistling through the room. Teo caught a glimpse of the Thames, and a whole fleet of icebergs bobbing away from the *Bombazine*. The newborn iceberg rolled into the water and the hatch snapped shut. A few seconds later, another lump appeared at the end of the chute.

"Gristle and guts!" thought Teo. "The *Bombazine* has an ice generator!"

This must have been how Miss Uish had made the ice that engulfed Venice. Looking more closely at the treadmills, Teo recognized Augusto, a classmate of Renzo's, who'd supposedly been drowned in the ice flood. She picked out other little Venetian faces she knew.

"Slave labor and baddened magic together!" Teo breathed. "How hideously clever. They used the ice storm to 'harvest' Venetian children for this infernal machine! The ship must have lurked in the lagoon on Christmas Eve, waiting to pick up victims. That's why there were so many missing among the children. And why they never found the bodies! All this time, Augusto and the other Venetian boys and girls have been slaves on the *Bombazine!*"

Not just Venetians: Londoners as well. Greasy Ressydew and Marg'rit Savory marched on a treadmill, already reduced to shadows of their former plump selves. More boys and girls, hands cramped and bleeding, were kneeling at low trestles, stripping tar off of old ropes. Others were bent over trays of human hair, making mourning brooches. Ghost-Convicts flogged anyone who dared look up or slow down. Miss Uish was nowhere to be seen, but her chill presence was manifest in the fear and misery of the prisoners and the sound of their tears.

Teo clapped her hand over her mouth. She'd glimpsed Sibella sitting on a silken chair, sullenly playing with her worts and leeches. Sibella would give her away as soon as look at her! Then the girl turned and gazed straight in Teo's direction. She paused in her games for a moment, yet she did not raise the alarm.

"Perhaps she did not see me after all?" hoped Teo. "And why hasn't she told them where the *Scilla* is, come to think of it?"

Even if Sibella hadn't seen her, Ghost-Convicts could. Teo wrapped herself carefully in a curtain, flattening her narrow body against the wall. And it was as well that she did, because two

Ghost-Convicts now picked up the dead dog from the treadmill and marched toward her. Passing Teo's slender velvet cocoon, they proceeded down one of the inner corridors of the *Bombazine*.

"They are taking the poor creature to be boiled," Teo guessed, following them at a discreet distance. Fortunately, there were plenty of curtains and carved pilasters to hide behind.

The Ghost-Convicts paused to unlock a door. As they opened it, Teo heard voices, beloved voices, and the familiar sounds of gurgling liquids and clattering laboratory equipment. Teo's heart jumped into her mouth. Her adoptive parents were prisoners aboard the *Bombazine* too, no doubt kidnapped at the same time as the Venetian children! All those days that the *Bombazine* had shadowed the *Scilla* and all these days here on the Thames, Teo had been but a mile away from Leonora and Alberto Stampara!

The Ghost-Convicts, minus the dog, came out of the room and slammed the door. As soon as they'd disappeared down the corridor, Teo ran to the door. She heaved against it with her shoulder, making absolutely no impression. She ran back up to the deck and dived straight into the Thames, dodging deftly between icebergs. Winded by the cold, she swam jerkily around to the porthole of the locked room. Her parents were inside, both tethered at the ankle by heavy chains. They were filthy, thin and surrounded by pots of boiling animal marrowfat. The large stateroom in which they labored, however, was fitted out with the latest equipment, much of it, she guessed, ripped from their laboratory in the Venetian lagoon. In a corner were two wretched camp beds, a washbasin and a screened chamber pot.

Teo tapped frantically at the window. Her parents did not turn.

"Oh, I'm between-the-Linings: they won't be able to see, hear or feel me."

A horrible thought entered Teo's mind and refused to go away. Were her decent, loving scientist parents being forced to manufacture the Half-Dead disease from the marrowfat of the murdered animals?

Teeth chattering, she swam back to the ladder and crept through the *Bombazine*'s corridors to wait outside the laboratory door, where she hid herself between the wall and an unpleasant tapestry of a brutal boar-hunt. Five minutes passed; then ten. Her wet clothes clung to her body. She hoped she was not making a visible damp patch in the tapestry. After twenty minutes, a pair of Ghost-Convicts arrived, struggling with four heavy pails, and unlocked the door. The familiar stink of boiled marrowfat brought Teo vividly unpleasant memories of the bad days on the *Scilla* under Miss Uish's cruel regime.

Trying not to gag on the smell, Teo stealthily followed the Ghost-Convicts into the room, hiding behind the door until they shuffled out, leaving it open. "They'll be back in a minute with more marrowfat," Teo realized. "I'll have to be quick." Her parents were bent over their microscopes and murmuring confidentially to each other in terms that would be perfectly unintelligible to anyone who was not a marine biologist. Teo's chest squeezed. How haggard they looked! She hated to see the gray shadows under her mother's eyes. Her father's back was stooped with exhaustion. Teo longed to hug them and bury her face in the rough linen of her mother's laboratory apron.

She rationed herself to kissing each of them on the cheek and stroking her mother's hair.

Quite unaware of her presence, Leonora and Alberto Stampara handed one another glass petri dishes and slides, working as ever like two parts of the same highly efficient and graceful machine.

"Marrowfat is running short," Leonora warned. "How are we going to give the *Cala-Mary* the initial burst of speed *she* wants?"

"*Cala-Mary?*" thought Teo. "As in *calamari?* Squid?"

Alberto unwittingly answered her question: "To call this evil submarine after a harmless sea creature—it is typical of our captors!"

He turned to stare with hatred at a tank of water. Teo followed his eyes.

Suspended in the water was a metallic pink object, which exactly resembled the colossal squid that had tried to kill her during their voyage to London. It had tentacles, claws and blank cruel eyes for portholes. It looked frighteningly real.

"Nothing surprising about that," she thought, with a perverse kind of pride. "It was designed by brilliant marine biologists. So at least they're not making the Half-Dead disease. It's some kind of automaton."

She climbed up the stairs to an inspection stage and looked down into the tank. The lid to the squid's carapace was open. Inside, the machine was lined with padded green velvet and carved wooden racks for holding . . . what?

Teo thought, "There is just *one* squid submarine. And it has taken all this time to build. So they can't mean to invade London with mechanical colossal squids."

Now Leonora Stampara was saying, "I'm terrified for the children on the treadmills, Alberto. They're getting so tired. They're not as productive as when they were first brought in. Can't you hear how the treadmills are running more slowly every hour? If the prisoners aren't useful . . ."

"You think Miss Uish would actually sacrifice *human children* to fuel the *Cala-Mary's* maiden voyage?"

"She hasn't got a single scruple," Leonora whispered. "You know what she told us about our Teodora. That our daughter has been taken hostage. That she will be killed and boiled and brought to us in a bucket if we do not cooperate."

"Don't torture yourself, dearest," murmured Alberto.

But Leonora's white lips whispered, "And that madman whom Uish works for? She said he hates our Teodora with the hatred of ages, whatever that means. How could anyone hate a dear innocent little girl like Teodora? It's not natural."

Teo asked herself fearfully, "Is that madman actually *aboard this boat?*"

"I fear we strayed from the realms of natural some time past. Remember"—Alberto grimaced—"what happened to Teodora's real parents, Marta and Daniele Gasperin? And the rest of her relatives. All drowned in that strange shipwreck. I keep asking myself now: could that tragedy have had something to do with this *brute* who controls Miss Uish?"

Teo raged silently, "Of course it did. That brute murdered my whole family."

"The Mayor of Venice himself assured us it was a simple accident. Mind you, I've never liked that man. It's clear that Miss Uish has got her talons into him too." Leonora visibly bristled.

"Dearest, think of something else. We must work on the improvements Uish requires for the automaton *scolopendre* this day."

Teo flinched at the name of her old enemies, the *scolopendre*, a crawling, biting kind of insect that had spied for Bajamonte Tiepolo the summer before last. The *scolopendre* had also fought against the Venetians in the mighty battle of the lagoon, swarming over the faces of the brave soldiers and blinding them with bites.

325

Her parents limped on their chained feet to a glass case, where dozens of the hideous insects were corralled in transparent drawers. The mechanical *scolopendre* were different from the brown ones Nature had created. These tiny contraptions were a dirty white color. Somehow this made them even more alarming.

"I have to admit that Uish's idea for a Russian-doll setup is ingenious," muttered Alberto. "And the white color, of course, will give them excellent camouflage on the ice and snow. I hate handling *dry* arthropods, though." He shuddered. "Give me an anemone or a real squid any day."

Teo thought, "You wouldn't say that if you'd seen what I've seen."

"Ingenious? I never thought I'd hear you say anything good about that woman." Leonora was mortally offended. "I suppose those dancing eyes and auburn curls have finally had an effect on you?"

"I just wish," attested Alberto defensively, "that Uish was working on the side of good. That brain of hers is a formidable weapon. Darling, you have to admit, it is a clever concept: if you kill the outer insect, a new insect pops out fully formed, and another . . . and another."

"And just how clever are those spore syrups she is boiling up in the galley?" asked Leonora. Alberto knitted his brows.

"Spore syrups!" Teo exclaimed. "Half-Dead disease, no doubt!"

When the next two Ghost-Convicts entered the laboratory with their slopping pails, Teo slipped out of the door. In the dark corridor, she sagged against the wall.

"I don't have to do this alone." She pulled herself upright. It was time to report to the others, to gather forces and friends.

And yet—and yet, there was one more thing she had to find out. Creeping down the next corridor, Teo saw a ribbon of light under a door that was slightly ajar. She poked her head cautiously into a beautifully warm and luxurious room. The curved wooden walls glowed with color—for fixed upon them were all the Venetian Canaletto and Carpaccio paintings that had gone missing in the Christmas Eve ice storm. And pinned to the facing wall were postcards of other famous pictures of Venice, captioned with the names of the London art galleries that owned them. Those captions also showed the height above sea level of every gallery, and a date two days hence, February 2.

"The same day as the funeral of Queen Victoria," thought Teo. "Just as we thought."

He sat so quietly that she had not noticed him before. But now Teo felt the hairs lifting at the back of her neck. A man with long greasy hair was seated at a table in the far corner, painting transparent blue over a large plan of London. His back was to Teo: she could not see his face. There was a gust of cold air behind her and Miss Uish rushed in, all swirling skirts, piled curls and flashing eyes. Gone was the cruel voice that Teo knew so well. Instead, all kinds of sweet nothings flowed from that rosebud mouth as Miss Uish advanced across the room and stroked the lank hair of the man at the desk. She showed no sign of having seen Teo.

"At least that proves she is human, sort of," thought Teo.

"Dearest sweeting," purred Miss Uish to the faceless man, "you work too hard."

The man did not acknowledge her in any way. His shoulders stiffened. His paintbrush continued to waft across the page.

"Ah, dearest, you are busy; I have come at a poor time for you,"

327

chirped Miss Uish in a desperate-to-please voice. "I just wanted to see if you have everything you need? A drink, perhaps? Some bumboo? Some rumfustian? Our cook has such a good recipe. . . . Oh, never fear, the galley is almost entirely devoted to the manufacture of the Half-Dead spore syrup. There's just the tiniest corner for some warming drinks for us, dearest!"

A haughty silence. Miss Uish, Teo realized, had taken some wine already. The fumes of it subtly suffused the room.

Miss Uish was at this moment nothing more than a trembling girl with a crush on someone stronger and more ruthless even than herself.

"Professor Marìn was right about her," thought Teo. "Her and Bajamonte Tiepolo."

Miss Uish altered now. "My love, have I done something to displease you? For you, I would do anything, you know? Shall I have one of the Venetian whelps whipped again? The boy called Augusto is already on short commons."

"Leave me alone, woman; stop your wittering."

At the sound of that voice, Teo's ears drummed and she felt pins and needles in the calves of her legs. She couldn't pretend to herself that she did not know it. The trembling in her hands confirmed it. The ancient Gothic script ripped the air above his head with sinister black letters. It was perfectly familiar to Teo, but at the same time it was foreign. Then, of course, Teodora Gasperin—the Undrowned Child—had never heard Bajamonte Tiepolo—Il Traditore—speak English before.

"And never wished to," she thought numbly.

All this time she had hoped against hope that he was dead. But he was not only not dead, he must be stronger than ever, for he had clearly evolved from his unstable, batlike form. From behind, anyway—she still had not seen anything more than the back of his head—he looked exactly like a human being.

Miss Uish clattered out, cooing, "I'll leave you to your great work, sweetest."

In the absence of Miss Uish, the room grew quiet. Now Teo noticed that the map of London was pinned to the table by a pair of daggers, the hilts of which were carved with intertwined Vampire Eels. A bell tower by the river tolled three somber notes.

Bajamonte Tiepolo lifted his head and sniffed the air.

"Is that you, Undrowned Child?" he asked.

46. A short-legged horse

three in the morning, aboard the Bad Ship Bombazine, *January 31, 1901*

Teo kept her mouth tightly shut, trying to breathe as quietly as possible. The fact that he could not see her meant Il Traditore had indeed managed to drag his spirit into an almost human body. And *that* meant that his power was not only renewed—it was greater than before. It had become stable inside human skin, and was concentrated in a being that did not change shape or lose its memory.

"How do you like London, Undrowned Child? Did you see how I took my sweet revenge upon your friends, the English Melusine and the London Sea-Bishops who thwarted me in battle? And how do you like your frozen Venice now? How shall we say it? Ah yes, half dead and *cleansed* of all her tawdry art?"

He muttered, "Christmas Eve, I had to rely on bone-headed Ghost-Convicts to steal the right paintings. I might as well have sent blind newts! Next time I shall go myself in my beautiful submarine and personally attend to the details. Have you seen my lovely *Cala-Mary*? Your parents are making a masterpiece for me. They are nearly finished—in both senses of the word. For, of course, it would be foolish of me to allow them to live once they have served my purpose. They know a little more than is convenient."

His tone was cool and amused, as if the idea of murdering Leonora and Alberto Stampara was something to be done in a lighthearted manner. Teo felt her old contempt for him flooding back undiluted. She shouted unheard, "You give villains a bad name! At least you should be passionate! You have done every bad thing that a coward can do, and nothing a brave man would."

Bajamonte Tiepolo shook his head as if there were something in his ear.

"I cannot hear you, Undrowned Child, yet I sense your impotent anger. I feel you looking at my plans for a flood in London."

"So it *is* another flood," thought Teo. "Of course. Bajamonte Tiepolo loves floods. *Much* better than a battle! Lots of death for innocent people and perfect safety for himself."

Into her mind flowed images of the graceful Houses of Parliament, the spires of Westminster Abbey, the beautiful dome of St. Paul's Cathedral and even the gilded wind vanes of Billingsgate Fish Market. There followed the grimy, hopeful faces of the Mansion Dolorous gang, and those of the busy Londoners rushing to their important appointments.

Bajamonte Tiepolo wanted to destroy all these places, all these people. Teo pictured stones and humans tumbling through another great ice flood, the destruction and the silent, tragic aftermath, just as she had seen in Venice.

"So." He pointed to the map, by now nearly covered in blue wash. "A London full to bursting with mourners is inundated by a wall of water that quickly turns to ice: the same treatment that worked so capitally in Venice. And while they are all a-drowning, I'll be safely in the *Cala-Mary* on a brief art-history excursion. No one shall stop me. They'll be too busy trying not to die.

"I can almost smell your indignation, Undrowned Child.

It has no power, however, except to amuse me, which it does."
He laughed dryly. Then he pointed to the empty spaces on the
walls. "Dry and snug inside the *Cala-Mary*, I'll be helping myself
to the paintings of Venice that shall complete my collection of
doomed art."

"*Doomed* art?" fumed Teo.

"Doomed, you're no doubt asking? Yes, for when I have every
last Venetian picture in my possession, there will be such a blaze
aboard this ship! The image of Venice shall be effaced from the
world forever. Elaborate fireworks and a glorious firestorm . . .
Oh, you wonder what shall happen to all the creatures presently
at work on the treadmills? And my other slaves, your parents? I
understand that children and scientists burn quite well, particularly when they're somewhat dehydrated from short rations and
long hours of work."

Teo gripped one hand in another, trying to calm herself.

"So much death, you ask? You'll be whimpering, why must millions of Londoners and animals and visiting dignitaries lose their
lives now? What of it? I personally might have let Queen Victoria's
funeral pass unmolested—it's nothing to me—but I needed to pla-
cate my friend from the island of Hooroo, who has promised to be
so very . . . *useful* . . . to his dear Signor Pipistrelly, as he likes to
call me. Indeed, the subjugation of London was a condition of his
cooperation. And why shouldn't Harold Hoskins be king of the
few survivors if he wants? He has a family tree that shows that he
has every right to the British throne.

"Yes, I can hear you—almost—protesting that there is the
small technicality that the old Queen's son Albert Edward has
already been sworn in as king. But"—and Il Traditore laughed

again—"Bertie was never a very strong swimmer. And he'll be riding a short-legged horse for the funeral. Poor King Bertie.

"At the last minute, of course, Harold Hoskins shall be unable to attend the funeral—a slight attack of the royal family's malady will keep him in bed, resting. In his apartments at Kenwood House high on Hampstead Heath; *very* high up, as it happens.

"It grows even more beautiful, our plot. For as soon as London is drowned, I shall freeze over the English Channel. Our army of ghosts, escaped prisoners and pardoned criminals will simply step straight across from France. Any Londoners who survive the flood will be weak with the Half-Dead disease. Our soldiers will make short work of anyone who resists.

"And Harold Hoskins—the only member of the royal family to survive the flood—will have been granted his heart's desire, assuming he has a heart, of course!" Il Traditore sniggered. "And then King Harold will repay me by turning his attention on Venice! My cormorants tell me that the frozen pathway from the mainland to Venice is almost solid now and, if a few men sink through the soft ice, there are plenty more where they came from. . . ."

For the first time, Teo thought of herself. "How am I going to get away to tell Renzo and the others? He'll be calling for his Ghost-Convicts any second. They can see me between-the-Linings, even if he can't."

Yet again, Bajamonte Tiepolo followed her thoughts with uncanny accuracy. He called out, "Get in here!" and the crunch of skeletal ghost-feet could be heard at the far end of the corridor.

He turned to Teo. "Planning to run to the Studious Son with this story? A little late for that, I fear. Farewell, Undrowned Child. Even if you evade my henchmen, the Thames may not prove as easy a path as you might wish. Vampire Eels do not thrive at this latitude, so I've recruited some sanguivorous new friends from the South Pacific. *Vampyroteuthis infernalis* has proved a most happy addition to the wildlife of this estuary. At least, *they're* happy. The London creatures have suffered somewhat. Particularly the wretched Melusine and Sea-Bishops. And a few worthless children. As will anyone who gets in the way of my new friends, especially anyone planning to tell tales and alert my victims to what is about to befall them."

"Vampyr . . ." Teo tried to consult the pages of *Lagoon Creatures—Nice or Nasty?* by Professor Marìn, but Bajamonte Tiepolo continued triumphantly.

"In Venice, it was not possible to drown the accursed Undrowned Child, but in London I'm free of that old Venetian Prophecy. Anyway, you'll be dying long before you drown."

He lifted a coil of leather tubing and whispered into it. Teo's eyes traced the tube down through a hole beneath his desk. From the echoey noise that came back, it seemed that the far end of the tube lay in the water below the boat. And an excited chittering now filled the air. Bajamonte Tiepolo resumed humming to himself and filling in the very last inch of white on his map with blue paint.

Numbed, Teo backed out of the room and pounded up to the deck. The two Ghost-Convicts who were arriving had time only to shout "The girlie!" before she slid between them. For the first time, she noticed wires and sticks of dynamite fastened at intervals to the spaces above the doors. The whole *Bombazine* was nothing more than a bomb, ready primed: as soon as her slaves had served their master, she would be destroyed along with all the Venetian art—and children—aboard.

"Oh no!" Teo's coracle had been set adrift and floated an impossible half-mile down the river. Examining the rope, she saw that it had been *gnawed* off in the water. Behind her came the sound of Ghost-Convicts clanking rapidly in her direction. One shouted, "There she is!"

Teo gulped in a huge breath and dived back into the Thames. She swam away from the *Bombazine* as fast as she knew how.

Almost immediately, she found out exactly what Bajamonte Tiepolo meant by "my new friends."

47. Vampyroteuthis infernalis

in the icy waters of the Thames, just before dawn, January 31, 1901

Teo was not twenty yards from the boat when she felt her arms brushed by something soft and flabby. Putting her head under the water, she realized that she was surrounded by unblinking pale blue eyes. Those eyes belonged to brown squid. Each squid was only about one foot long, yet there were thousands of them. A wall of squid blocked every way she looked.

Then she felt something prod her left leg. It tickled. And at that same moment Teo finally found the page stored in her memory. Professor Marìn had written, "*Vampyroteuthis infernalis*, Vampire Squid, rarely seen and harmless to man unless modified by baddened magic."

She put on a burst of speed that churned the water. A moment later, tentacles were exploring her arms and legs again.

"Il Traditore is right. If they kill me," Teo groaned, "I won't be able to warn anyone about exactly what he's planning for London. The new ice flood. The Hooroo Ghost-Convicts . . ."

A tentacle surged out of the water and slapped her across the chin.

All thought vanished from her mind except one: excruciating pain. Agony surged through her face, legs and arms, as if someone was shooting a poison arrow through her blood. Her tongue immediately swelled to fill her mouth. Teo screamed, but no noise came out.

"Now," she thought desperately, "I know what killed the Melusine and the Sea-Bishops." Even as she choked, Teo was buffeted by the wake of a passing fishing vessel. Its captain and crew were evidently frustrated by something caught in their nets.

"Oh 'eck, it's a dead seal, of all the rotten luck!" shouted one of the fishermen. "Get that peskiferous corpse *rid*!"

"What's a *seal* doing in the Thames? Thought they lived in the snowy wastes."

"Cold enough for it," said his shivering companion. "Hain't you noticed what's happening here? Thought all them white floaters was just ice cubes escaped from the champagne cooler of some fancy restaurant, did you?"

A lantern caught a gutting knife being pulled from a leather holster. Again and again it hacked at the tangled nets. Teo struggled to shout to the fishermen, but she was gagging on her swollen tongue. Anyway, she was between-the-Linings—they wouldn't hear her, or see her frantic waving in the dark water just outside the small pool of light cast by their lantern.

"Never seen so much blood!" complained the first fisherman, wiping his hand on his trousers. "There we go!"

The limp body of the seal floated free. The boat sped off. Teo looked away, forgetting her own pain for a second.

And indeed the pain ebbed. For the squid, smelling the seal's blood diffusing through the water, quickly detached their tentacles from Teo's thin arms and swam greedily toward the corpse.

"A corpse, that's what Bajamonte Tiepolo thinks I am," Teo thought. "He will be sure his beastly Vampire Squid have killed me too. That is my one advantage now."

Sensation was returning to her tongue, and she could feel its swollen cushion gradually lessening to normal proportions.

She tested it by speaking aloud. "I muth go weth. Newgate ith near the Weth End."

With an eye on the moon, she turned and swam west as quietly and quickly as she could. Crusts of ice reached into the river. Floes nudged her on either side.

"Speed will keep me warm," she thought. "Keep me alive, at least."

London's stately buildings, faintly illuminated, reared on either side of her as she made her lonely progress. They seemed to bend over her with tender concern.

As she dogpaddled, her mind dipped in and out of a thousand thoughts, each blacker than the last: the *Bombazine*, her cruel cargo, the ice generator, the *Cala-Mary*, Renzo languishing in filthy straw, but, worst of all, how she had felt in the presence of Il Traditore, hearing his hated voice, listening to his evil plans, and knowing that this city, full of people she loved, was now doomed, just like Venice.

A London depleted by a million citizens—all drowned by Bajamonte Tiepolo—could put up only a feeble defense when the enemy soldiers—supernatural and criminal—came pouring in over the frozen English Channel.

A tall black obelisk loomed, its unlikely silhouette jolting her thoughts. Cleopatra's Needle! She called up her Appleyard and Hetling map for consultation. Sure enough, Newgate Prison was almost due east of the obelisk on the Embankment.

338

Using Cleopatra's Needle as her compass, Teo swam toward the shore. Dawn was breaking. Dirty streaks of light showed her empty streets.

She ran barefoot in her wet clothes to Newgate, pausing only when she caught sight of her own shocked face in a shop window. As soon as she stopped running, she felt a burning like acid on her skin. The stings from the Vampire Squid had raised weals all over her face, legs and arms. Her teeth were chattering, but her tongue was now back to its own size. She galloped on, all the way to Newgate, where she shadowed a guard opening the gates for the early-morning coal delivery. She retraced her steps all the way to Renzo's cell.

"Renzo!" she cried. "Il Traditore . . ."

The words died on her lips. Renzo's cell was empty; a few parrot feathers eddied across the floor like autumn leaves.

48. Thousands upon thousands

at Buckingham Palace, London, just after midnight, January 31, 1901

"Preparations for the funeral are all in order, dear Bertie?" the Pretender asked the new King of England over their after-supper brandies.

"Well, it's all in the hands of the best people," said Bertie defensively. "What could possibly go wrong?"

"Couldn't possibly think . . . ," hummed the Pretender. "I mean, I can't imagine. How many people are expected to turn out?"

"Thousands upon thousands," replied the King. "Everyone wants to be a part of it. And we'll be putting on a jolly fine show. Superb, in fact. The streets will be thick with all our armed services. Every square inch of London will be covered with mourners and military. Touching, isn't it? All those nice people gathered in the hope of a glimpse of poor Mama."

"Lovely stuff." Harold Hoskins smiled and drained his glass.

"I only wish it wasn't so cold for all the poor creatures," sighed King Bertie. "I worry for their health."

49. A Strangle-snare knot

Eighteen months before, Teo had run through the labyrinth of the Palazzo Tiepolo in Venice, looking for Renzo, who had fallen into the cruel wooden hands of some animated statues called Brustolons. Now she hurtled through the long passageways of Newgate Prison, equally terrified of what she would find.

How low to the ground the cells were! How dark! No natural light penetrated. Her way was lit by guttering candles in smudged black lanterns. When Bajamonte Tiepolo sent in his new ice flood, Teo realized, the prisoners down here would be drowned in minutes.

She passed a cell full of boys and girls her own age and younger. They stirred and stretched in their rags. Being children, they could see and hear Teo, even though she was between-the-Linings. Stopping, she shouted to them, "What has happened to the Venetian boy? Do you know?"

The Londoners stared at the red weals on her arms and legs with sympathy.

"Someone got at you good, dint they?" a small girl observed.

341

"A Vampire Squid or fifty," muttered Teo. Urgently, she demanded, "What about Renzo Antonello? Where is he?"

"He'll be dancing on air shortly," a boy said solemnly.

"But they said he had a week!"

"They's been told to git all the hangin's out o' the way before Queen Vic's funeral. Crammin' 'em in, they are."

"When? When?" shrieked Teo. "What time is Renzo's hanging?"

"Just after seven."

"But 'e won't die zackly on the stroke of seven, miss," whispered the solemn boy, "worse luck. This *new* hangman's a devil. He likes to let 'em dangle. We hears 'em screamin' and chokin' for quarter-hours on end."

"Which way is the execution yard?" demanded Teo.

A garden of grimy fingers pointed to a corridor on the left.

It was the sound of chanting that finally guided Teo to the place: a stark, ugly brick shed in a corner of the yard. The prison chaplain was quietly intoning his prayers.

Teo stumbled and stopped. Inside the shed, a boy's body was being cut off the rope. It had no more humanity left in it than in a sack of sticks. The face was turned to the left: she caught a glimpse of bluish skin and a tongue lolling against his cheek.

"No!" she cried. Yet it was not fury, but loneliness and sorrow that flooded Teo's heart. Renzo had been a part of her life ever since she'd found out who she really was. How empty this crowded city seemed suddenly; how desolate the whole world was. Feeling dizzy, as if someone had stolen not only Renzo's life, but the breath from her own lungs, Teo turned to leave the terrible place. Then she stopped.

She thought wildly, "No! I will steal Renzo's body and bring it back to Venice for a proper burial. He loves . . . loved . . . London. But he must come home."

"Teo!" the voice was weak. She trembled, afraid to turn.

Had Renzo come back from the dead? It happened sometimes, Teo had read, that they didn't hang people properly; that the body choked back to life after being cut down. Teo turned, her heart leaping with hope. She braced her shoulders and walked over to look the corpse full in the face.

It wasn't Renzo.

"Teo, here!"

Teo cast her eyes to the upper platform in time to see a noose being pulled over Renzo's head. His hair had been shorn again; he was dressed in a somber gray shirt. She bounded up the steps to the platform and scrambled across the old wooden stage, reaching on tiptoe to where the rope was knotted. She struggled with it, but she was too small. Only the tips of her fingers reached the knot. The rope was slippery—she simply could not get a grasp.

Renzo turned agonized eyes to hers. He whispered, "It's no use. I sent the parrot to Lussa and begged her to print an official-looking document to say . . . but it was too late. You're all wet? What hurt you, Teo? Your arms . . . ?"

"Doesn't matter."

"Turn your head away. Don't watch me die."

The chaplain concluded his prayers and cast his eyes piously upward. Below, an officer in uniform read out the charges against Renzo.

The bells of St. Sepulchre Church began to toll, deathly and hushed. For the first time, Teo saw the hangman in his black hood. Through two small slits, his eyes gleamed with visible joy.

"That's not the real executioner!" she shouted. And then she saw the noose—moving even as it lay across Renzo's neck, it was re-coiling itself into a different formation. Instead of the regular merciful gallows knot that Professor Marìn had taught them on the *Scilla*, it was now a cruel strangle-snare knot, guaranteed to prolong suffering and ensure a slow, wracking death.

"Baddened magic, that's what the executioner uses to torture the dying," she reflected. And baddened magic was what she, Teodora Gasperin, the Undrowned Child, was on this earth to fight.

"Lift me up," she cried to Renzo. "If I can get a bit higher, I could undo that knot."

A small glow of hope lit Renzo's eyes. His hands circled Teo's waist. But in the same moment, the hangman stepped forward and put his hand on the lever.

They were out of time.

Renzo whispered to her, "Just hold me, Teo. With your extra weight, at least the drop will be quicker."

There was nothing else to do. Teo wrapped her arms around Renzo. She felt his heart beating through his gray shirt, hers keeping pace. His eyes were on hers and her hand stroked his cheek for the last time.

"Goodbye, Teo," he said quietly. "You must save London and Venice on your own now."

50. Genuine London lice

a few seconds later

Teo screamed, "No! He's innocent! This is murder!"

Over her cry came the urgent patter of footsteps and a breathless shout. "Stop! In the name of the law, st-o-o-op! The Governor just found this on his desk!"

Another officer read out, "Sentence commuted for Lorenzo Antonello!"

A printed proclamation was handed around the execution chamber. Even from where she stood, Teo could smell the fishy odor of the paper and see the spatter of parrot droppings in one corner.

Teo cried, "Was that your idea, Renzo? How brilliant of you! The parrot delivered your message safely after all. Lussa must have printed it on the Seldom Seen Press and the bird brought it back. It wasn't too late."

Color slowly returned to Renzo's face.

The officer read the full proclamation: "'The sentence on Lorenzo Antonello is commuted to life imprisonment with hard labor in Backbent Castle, Scotland.'"

"I couldn't think of anything else," whispered Renzo to Teo.

The hangman's eyes glowered as he lifted the lever fully back to the wall.

Renzo nodded. Teo stood aside while a human guard untied him. She followed as he was taken back to the darkness of his cell, pulled all the way by his ear. It was an easy guess for Teo that the guard got a cut of the hangman's fee, and was disappointed to be bringing a live boy back from the execution yard.

"Stay outside the cell!" Renzo hissed to Teo in Venetian.

"Cuss me, would you, in your foreign lingo?" growled the guard, slapping Renzo's face and pushing him into the cell. As soon as the key was turned in the lock and the guard had stumped off, Teo told Renzo all she had learned on the *Bombazine*.

"So the giant squid was what the English call a red herring?" Renzo whistled quietly. "Ice and water again? I suppose he knows it works. Now . . ." And there was new resolution in his voice. "I'm no use trapped in here. Let's work on my escape plan. But first, can you get me some proper clothes? I can't wear this." Renzo gestured at his gray execution shirt. "It'll be a bit too obvious where I've escaped from."

Teo rushed back to the children who had been so helpful with information about the sadistic hangman. In her pocket she felt for the shilling she'd saved when she bought day-old bread from a baker's boy just a few hours earlier.

She sought out the least filthy boy in the cell, whose size fortunately most closely approximated Renzo's. "How much for your trousers and shirt? And that rather smart hat?"

Renzo was sitting in his cell twiddling a parrot feather in his hand as he stared up at the ceiling. In his other hand, he held the penknife that he'd hidden in his shoe.

She poked the clothes through the bars. "Put these on."

Renzo poked the smelly rags with a clenched toe. "You mean on my body? Oh! Is that a louse?"

"I do believe it is," agreed Teo, bending down to examine the tiny white grub. "Best possible camouflage for a fugitive, some genuine London lice, don't you think?"

"Speaking of fugitive," said Renzo casually, pulling the hat over his shaven head, "I've worked out how to escape. Simple, really."

"Your brush with death hasn't exactly humbled you."

"Casanova did not act *humble* to escape from the Doges' Palace in Venice, did he? Remember how he filed a hole in the *ceiling* of his cell, dressed in his best clothes and hat, and climbed up and out, returning via a window to the grand staircase? Then he had the audacity to simply stroll out of the front door, as if he was just leaving a grand ball, not a prison cell. The guard was fooled by his arrogant strut."

"Who says history can't save your life!" Teo exclaimed. The sound of scratching and tearing had already commenced.

"The guards'll come running when they hear that," warned Teo. "I'm going to ask those boys and girls to make a distraction."

"Before you go," whispered Renzo, "I've also had an idea for getting Tobias out of the lunatic asylum. Listen. . . ."

The children down the corridor were happy to oblige by

screaming, laughing, shouting and swearing ferociously. What could the guards possibly threaten them with? Penal colonies or hard labor awaited them, if not destitution on the streets. They put their all into it, while Renzo peeled off the ceiling plaster in great hunks and slices.

51. Council of war

later that day, and through the night

By the time a somewhat dusty Renzo was strolling out of Newgate with a crowd of visitors, Tobias Putrid had also been rescued from Bedlam by Signor Alicamoussa, posing as Tobias's long-lost Italian uncle, who had come to take him away to the notorious Venetian lunatic asylum on the island of San Servolo.

After explaining Renzo's idea for saving Tobias to all aboard the *Scilla*, Teo had gone straight to the cavern to tell the mermaids what had happened. The London mermaids slathered her Vampire Squid wounds with HOMOCEA, "the best remedy known for open wounds, cuts, mumps, ringworm, jellyfish stings and piles."

At least it smelled pleasantly of eucalyptus oil and beeswax; more importantly it soothed the pain.

"Of course, I wish I had some Venetian Treacle, but actually, it's not bad at all," Teo told a scowling Flos.

The London mermaids lowered their pale lashes smugly.

Back at the *Scilla*, the boys and girls had welcomed Renzo with open arms and many thumps on the back.

"That hair o' yourn'll soon grow back," soothed the District Disgrace.

A stay in the lunatic asylum had not sweetened Tobias's personal aura of sewer, but even he got his generous share of kisses on the cheek, and a lingering application of Turtledove's tongue. Then they all sat down to a tremendous high tea of soup *à la reine* (concocted from boiled mutton, ham, boned turkey, wild ducks, partridges, ground plum pudding and a drop of Madeira), followed by lashings of sea pie, with pea curry and cheddar cheese for Teo. There was a round of applause for Cookie.

That evening, Signor Alicamoussa and Turtledove called the boys and girls up to the main deck, where Emilio and Renzo had prepared charts and diagrams to outline the situation that faced them.

Joining them on deck were more than thirty soft-spoken men, the Venetian pumpkin-sellers. They'd arrived with trays of hot spiced pumpkin, which was distributed among all those attending the meeting. Uncle Tommaso had also brought a pail of strawberry ice cream, which Pylorus called hokey-pokey. In the bitter cold, not one spoonful of the ice cream melted; not one drop was wasted either.

Signor Alicamoussa began, "Thanks to vital intelligence garnered at vast personal risk by our brave Teodora, we know Il Traditore's plan of attack. Is not colossal squids."

Everyone cheered.

"Is worse than that," said Signor Alicamoussa glumly.

The boys and girls huddled together, the Venetians putting comforting arms around the shoulders of the Londoners.

"As we suspected, the Venetian Traitor, Bajamonte Tiepolo, who also goes by the name of Signor Pipistrelly, is colliding with the Pretending Harold Hoskins in this dastardly act, yes. Shall we let this happen?"

"No, we will not!" roared the boys and girls, the pumpkin-sellers, Uncle Tommaso, Turtledove and even Sofonisba.

Signor Alicamoussa turned to Turtledove. "Now my esteemed canine colleague will take over the mechanicals and logisticals of eatables, drinkables, wearables and shootables."

Turtledove pointed to a diagram of a ship shown in cross-section. "Plan is, we attacks the *Bombazine*, releases the poor childer. An' we smashes the thingamebobbity wot makes them pesky icebergs. I have . . . doingsed . . . sundry weapons from abandoned corners of 'igh-class heducational hestablishments, they all bein' closed this week as a sign of respeck for the passin' of Her Late Majesty."

He nudged open the lid of a sturdy wooden trunk, to reveal a stack of hockey sticks, wooden erasers, sticks of chalk and cricket bats.

"We're going to defeat Hooroo Ghost-Convicts and criminables wiv *those*?" Bits began. "We needs guns an' . . ."

Teo explained, "The *Bombazine* is wired up with dynamite and fireworks, so we must not use anything with a *hint* of gunpowder in it."

There was an ominous creaking outside on the dock.

"To battle stations!" cried Turtledove, with more spirit than hope, grasping a hockey stick in his jaw.

But Sebastiano dalla Mutta, who was on watch in the crow's nest, called out, "There's two pretty ladies, who seem to have fallen in the water below. *Very* pretty."

Teo and Renzo shouted simultaneously, "Mermaids!"

Then Teo paled, "What about the Vampire Squid?"

She ran up to the taffrail, crying, "Lussa, be careful!"

She was met with Flos's hearty laughter. "Turns out dem pesky varmints is scared to deaf of us *Venetian* mermaids," Flos reassured her. "Look!"

Flos reached under the water and picked up a handful of the blue-eyed brown squid, who stared at her in terror, their tentacles quivering. She flung them back into the water scornfully. "We wouldn't even stoop to kill dem, nasty little things! But prithee pardon me while I kick a few in the corybungus. Yoiks!"

A mermaid's finny kick was evidently a thing to be feared, since the water grew white with the frothing wakes of fleeing *infernalis*.

Lussa and Flos had plenty to tell. Down in the cavern, the mermaids too had been making preparations for war. Flos had conducted some experiments, after the mermaids managed to net two Ghost-Convicts who had overindulged in English beer and fallen into the water at St. Paul's Dock.

"We flunged everything at dem. Curry powder, gin, citric acid, rat droppings, ROUGH ON RATS even, but nuffink worked," explained Flos. "Dey still tried to get up and fight, jabbering 'n' bamblusterating at us like ye wouldn't believe. Yoiks! I were at my wits' end and gnawin' on my tether. When I accidentally stumbled on da answer."

Lussa chuckled. "Flos's Temper was quite naturally Exacerbated. She took a Nipkin of fermented Seaweed Juice to calm her Nerves."

"Only to discover it were completely gorn orf and stank like a drain. I were so—exacerbated—dat I threwed the whole tankard of it at dem scum-bellied Ghost-Convicts. And two seconds later, dere wernt nuffink but a bad smell and a bit of smoke, an' two corky hats, saving dere graces."

352

"Seaweed juice?" marveled Teo. "That's all it takes to kill a Ghost-Convict?"

Flos concluded triumphantly, "Ain't I tellin' yer? Rotten seaweed juice! Simple as dat. It jest dissolves 'em!"

Lussa added, "So now We are engaged upon the Gathering & Fermenting of Algae & other Marine Weeds, and in the Manufactory of Fishskin Containers with which to fling our Weapon."

Flos deftly threw up a damp sack, calling, "Empty it out, Studious Son, but careful, mind!"

When Renzo opened the sack, little balls of liquid, like black bubbles, each finishing in a curly ribbon of fishskin, cascaded on to the wood. One snagged on a splinter and burst, releasing a stink that made everyone wheeze and stand back. On closer inspection, the liquid was seen to have excavated a hole in the deck timber.

"'Ighly picturesque!" cried Turtledove enthusiastically. "But it ain't what I'd call a precision instrument, ladies. 'Magine we's all fightin' our 'earts out, an' one of yer fizzy fishskins arrives on the *Bombazine*'s deck. How's it goin' to know to hit a Ghost-Convict? What if it hits one of me childer? By which I mean me London childer an' me Venice childer, of course. What if the childer falls in the water an' gits nibbled and stinged by them little squid wot hurt our Teodora? Woan suit at all. I is flint on that point. We's got to think o' the 'elf an' safety of the childer first."

Lussa said thoughtfully, "In this World even Children must show their Mettle. But the Beast is perspicacious. Let Us refine our Ploy. We Mermaids shall supply the Juice-filled Fishskins. The Young People Themselves shall be Armed with Them to throw."

Renzo asked, "But how do we fight *her*? Miss Uish isn't a Ghost-Convict. She's not going to be dissolved by the seaweed juice."

Sofonisba hissed, flexing her long claws. "I personally have a score to settle with her, on my dear professor's behalf."

"Done," barked Turtledove. "Next item on the agenda: do yew think we should bovver at all wiv yer akshual 'oomans, I mean, draw 'em into our plans?"

"Of course! We should go to Downing Street and tell the Prime Minister what is going to happen!" urged Renzo. "The Londoners did not believe our handbills. Yet London must prepare for the worst!"

Pylorus sneered, "And do you think them in charge'll just usher the loiks of us into the Prime Minister's office? A Venetian pye-rat loik yesself or Teo? A handful of street urchins loik us? Perhaps a mermaid or two? An escaped criminable loik Signor Alicamoussa here? Turtledove?"

"Adults can't see mermaids," Renzo murmured dully, "or hear animals speak. Unless they are Incogniti like the pumpkin-sellers."

"The pumpkin-sellers can go," suggested Teo.

Renzo's voice was quiet. "Is the Prime Minister going to believe a group of street vendors from foreign parts?"

"Ghosts! That's what we need," exclaimed Teo. She turned to the Incogniti. "We need to drag those London ghosts out of those stones in the railway arches right now. We need Roman soldiers, medieval minstrels, Roundheads and Cavaliers . . . there must be thousands of those in-the-Cold because of bad deeds, who want and need to redeem themselves. . . ."

"And those Egyptian mummies from the British Museum," added Renzo, "who put curses on the archaeologists and keepers."

". . . and thieving chimney sweeps, robbing boatmen, pickpockets . . ." continued Teo. "Of course, all the ghosts will be feeling stronger in themselves since Queen Victoria died."

"Plenty of them about," confirmed Uncle Tommaso. "We just need to convince them that we believe in them. We'll need some children to come with us, to act very, very scared. . . ."

"You mean like this?" asked Thrasher, shaking all over like a baby's rattle.

"And this?" Tig uttered a bloodcurdling scream.

"Or . . . ?" Hyrum slicked up his hair so it stood on end.

"*Perfettissimo.*" Uncle Tommaso beckoned, and the Mansion Dolorous gang followed him off the boat.

Turtledove grunted, "Meanwhile, a tiny gem of an idea 'as inserted itself in me 'ead. I's orf to the parks an' back gardens to raise me an army."

"What can the bold Beast mean by That?" asked Lussa.

Teo insisted, "Trust him. He hasn't had a bad idea yet."

The mermaids departed for their cavern, shaking their pretty heads.

Even Teo's confidence was shaken when Turtledove returned a few hours later with the most obese collection of animals that ever waddled across a manicured lawn. There were corpulent sewer rats and almost rectangular foxes. There were even overweight otters, weasels like great furry cushions and heavy-hipped squirrels.

Sofonisba surveyed this army with characteristically eloquent disgust. "Even a dog should be capable of detecting the obvious military uselessness of such great beefs on sticks."

Turtledove was not the tiniest bit discouraged, growling, "Desprit times is desprit times, Feline."

All the otters, rats, squirrels, weasels and foxes looked adoringly up at Turtledove, who shouted, "Childer, clear the deck!"

The fat animals assembled ponderously in the empty space.

"Slower than a dinged-up dodo." Signor Alicamoussa frowned. "War Weasels? Fighter Squirrels? Reckon we're in strife."

"Eyes right!" shouted Turtledove. Furry, fleshy necks turned effortfully in the direction of where, a mile away, the dim hull of the *Bombazine* lurked in the Thames, truly visible only by a stretch of the imagination as it dipped in and out of the fog.

"Yew see that there boat?" Turtledove whispered, almost tenderly. "We's goin' to have them scoundrels aboard it for BREAKFAST."

At the word "breakfast" the stomachs of the creatures audibly rumbled.

"But NOT UNTIL you's IN SHAPE!" shouted Turtledove. "Niver seen such a collection of WALLOWIN' BLUBBER-BELLIES! Couldn't beat a CARPET! LEFT turn! RIGHT turn! WRIGGLE! NIP!"

The animals heaved themselves about willingly enough, but they weren't any too nimble.

Turtledove glanced up at the gallery of boys and girls watching the operation. "Wot yew staring at? Get on wiv it! We needs an ark. Coracle, cricket bats, hockey sticks—raw materials or wot? Surely there's a toolbox on this here boat? I unnerstand young Rosato knows what to do wiv a drawin' board, a saw an' some nails. What more do yew want?"

Renzo laughed out loud, "Brilliant! A Trojan ark! We'll take all these fat animals over to the *Bombazine*. Miss Uish won't be able to resist taking them aboard . . . she'll think she can boil them down to fuel the squid submarine, and then . . ."

Some of the fat foxes began to look a bit furtive, and moved themselves to the far edge of the assembled force.

"Whereupon," continued Teo, "they will secretly break out of the ark and . . ."

"Lie in their blubber till they are boiled for tallow," said Giovanni glumly.

At this, the squirrels showed the whites of their eyes and the two furtive foxes sneaked behind the water barrel.

"Ye of little faith! Not while I is breathing will that child-hurter an' animal killer touch a hair on yer chins!" shouted Turtle-dove. "By this time tomorrow, they'll be a crack squad. Yew see if they ain't!"

If Teo had not cast a spell of silence on her, the *Scilla* would have seemed the noisiest ship on the Thames that night. The wintry air reverberated to Turtledove's stentorian drill, and his verbal missiles.

"LEFT! RIGHT! DODGE! TRIP!"

Turtledove had meanwhile assumed a military waistcoat with several rows of medals pinned to it. He was in his element. "For a dog of my creed, fightin' mixes business an' pleasure most agreeable-like!"

On another corner of the deck, Rosato and a team of helpers were nailing together cricket bats and hockey sticks to form a boat to hold the creatures. Somehow the vessel acquired the appearance of a dear little Swiss chalet with a pointed roof. Each window opening had a revolving balcony, on which the animals were to display themselves like the wooden birds in a cuckoo clock, so that Miss Uish would be able to see how temptingly fat they were.

"*Ciao!*" Uncle Tommaso's voice echoed from snow-blanketed Clink Street. "Room for a few more aboard?"

The boys and girls rushed to the taffrail in time to see a cloud of transparent soldiers, minstrels, sweeps, robbers and two Egyptian mummies rise up to the masts, where they settled, swinging their transparent legs over the sails and looking at the proceedings below with interest. A Roundhead soldier called, "We are not many, but we shall have the force of many!"

A Roman centurion remarked, "*Unus vir in nave pro duobus in via valet.*"

"One man aboard ship is worth two in the street," translated Teo.

A mummy shouted hoarsely but in a friendly way, "*Assa-lum-alaikum.*"

And Renzo called, "Peace be with you too, brother. *Wa-alai-kum-salam.*"

"Where'd you learn that, Mister Cyclopeedy?" breathed Pylorus Salt.

"Don't mind us!" called a ghostly young boatman. "Carry on the good work down there!"

And so they carried on. Work and exercise were stopped only by a thick pelt of snow making the deck impassable except by tunneling on the part of the smaller rodents.

"It's pittlin' down!" observed Rosibund. "I hain't niver seen snow loik that."

"Reet g-gowsty here," chattered Ann Picklefinch. "Have we got owt aboord by the way of an extra blanky?"

"That's a power of snow," Turtledove observed. "An' look at the barometer."

No mercury was visible at all.

When everyone was frozen to the skin and glassy-eyed with exhaustion, Signor Alicamoussa found a way to make the night end well.

First, he smilingly presented a barrel-shaped box labeled Huntley & Palmer: Provisions, Treats and Snacks, Good for the Morale, Yes!

The Mansion Dolorous gang positively screamed with enthusiasm and were soon arguing over Alberts, Thick and Thin Captains, Iced Gems and Metropolitan Mixed Biscuits.

The London ghosts floated down from the masts and partook with gusto, murmuring, "Don't mind if I do!" and *"Quam suavis!"* and "Odds Bods, but I wish we'd had such sweetmeats in our time!"

The *Scilla*'s crew had almost forgotten their blue fingers and toes when Signor Alicamoussa began to speak again.

"Some of youse know," he commenced, "that I learned my English from an Australian drover, and that I have a particulate fondliness for all things Antipodean. Now, I have just remembered myself of a quaint story about the Aboriginal people of that continent, yes. Is times even in the great red heart of Australia that the temperature falls low as a koala bear's toenail. And, upon my word, at the back of Bourke and beyond the Black Stump, the currency your Aboriginal uses to measure the temperature is: dogs. Or large rodents. Or any mammal, really."

359

"Whath this g-g-got to d-d-do wiv anything?" Sally asked, her teeth chattering.

"Everything, child. You see, the Aboriginal calls a medium-cold night a two-dog night, because is how many warm dogs he takes to sleep with him on that occasion. Colder is a three-dog night. Is places where your Aboriginal is required to take up to seven dogs to bed with him, and a few desert rats, to ensure that he is not froze to death by morning."

With dawning understanding, the shivering boys and girls looked at the plump squirrels, foxes and weasels panting on the deck. A large white rat poked its head up out of the snow at Teo's numbed feet, and then wrapped itself around her ankle. She instinctively recoiled. But then she looked closer, with more interest.

52. A Trojan ark

Teo awoke in a pleasant barnyard fug.

Two weasels snuggled against her ears, and a squirrel nestled on top of her head like a fur hat. Stretched over her stomach was a plump young otter, and on top of her feet lay a pair of corpulent foxes, intertwined head to toe. The white rat nestled in a fox's tail, sucking quietly on the red brush while it snored. Teo could not remember when she'd last had such a capital night's sleep.

Climbing up on deck, she could hear Sofonisba and Turtledove exchanging stiff-lipped courtesies.

"Well, I likes yer nerve!" Turtledove strained at the sides not to bark.

"Even though you despise my very intestines?" Sofonisba observed coolly.

"What's bitin' yer, Feline? Is it the fleas a-troublin' yer? Happens to even the uppitiest folk sometimes." But Turtledove's tone betrayed him. It was gruffly affectionate. Next, he turned his attention to the Trojan ark. Rosato had stayed up all night to finish it, adding finials and decorative beading to the shutters.

"Fine as fivepence!" Turtledove pronounced. "Famously done, Ros, old chap! Yew 'as been an' gorn an' done it, an' done us proud."

Rosato blushed.

"All aboard!" Turtledove commanded. Yawning and stretching, the fat animals leapt clumsily into the ark, two by two.

The floating chalet set off, towed by a coracle rowed by four of the *Scilla*'s sailors, and followed by two other coracles containing the Mansion Dolorous gang, Turtledove, Signor Alicamoussa and Uncle Tommaso. The pumpkin-sellers, armed with their tin trays, rowed a wherry, quietly singing a new Venetian folk song about the great battle in the lagoon of 1899. Somewhat less tuneful were the wherries full of London ghosts, all singing bloody war songs from their different centuries.

The Venetian mermaids swam alongside the boats. Some were armed with shields and tridents. Other mermaids waved their "noggin' boots"—old sailors' boots mounted on sticks, designed to stamp on the automaton *scolopendre* about which Teo had warned them. The parrots hovered overhead in disciplined formation.

Teo noticed that the tousled curls of the Venetian mermaids were looking particularly bouffant in the dim dawn light. Then she realized that each mermaid bore on her head one of the large Sea Spiders who had woven the protective cocoons for the Venetian paintings. Catching Teo's eye, Flos indicated the fish-bone catapult hanging around her neck on a coral chain.

"Won't that be rather cruel?" asked Teo. "To the Sea Spiders, I mean. To hurl them from catapults?"

Lussa smiled. "The Arachnids have volunteered their Services. Who are We to refuse any Aid in this desperate Moment?"

"Speaking of aid, where are the London mermaids?" asked Renzo.

"Dey've all come down with da Nervous Prostration and da Biliousness," spat Flos contemptuously. "And da Internal Wastings and da Diseased Irritability. But Nerolia sayed mayhap dey'll come when dey has finished slatherin' demselves in mentholated Vaseline and taking turns on da Oxydonor Electropoise. Don't ask."

Flos made a noise like a *scolopendra* exploding.

"Don't ask, don't ask, don't ask . . . ," suggested the parrots wisely.

"Sssh," hissed Renzo. "We're getting close to the *Bombazine*."

The Trojan ark approached the *Bombazine* from the larboard, the other boats and the mermaids quietly making their way to hide in the shadow of the stern.

"Now!" ordered Turtledove.

The animals on the ark burst into an eloquent yapping and yowling.

Miss Uish's beautiful brow and piled curls appeared promptly over the taffrail. Her eyes widened at the sight of all the plump animals carefully arranged on the decks and balconies of the ark.

To some hovering Ghost-Convicts she snapped, "Bring the creatures aboard!"

Over the silent river, her voice rang out in all its steely cruelty, with a slight slur hanging on the consonants.

Ann Picklefinch whispered in an expert voice, "Yon lady is moroculous on gin. I'll bet she's hangin' coggly on 'er feet!"

Teo was shivering, her skin remembering all the punishments ordered by that cold voice, especially when it was under the influence of rum. Her heart ached for the fat squirrels, foxes and rats, all so willing, so stouthearted—so like sacrificial victims.

But these sacrificial victims had been drilled by Turtledove, and they had no intention of ending up as marrowfat in a pail.

As soon as they were winched onto the *Bombazine*, they went into action in their different special ways. The weasels nipped the ankles of the Ghost-Convicts; the foxes bit their thighs. The squirrels took flying leaps that toppled two Ghost-Convicts at a time. Their joint strategy, brilliantly achieved, was to get the Ghost-Convicts to fall flat on the floor, where they would entangle the legs of their colleagues and become easy targets for the fishskins.

In the resultant confusion, the Incogniti, the Mansion Dolorous gang and Teo and Renzo boarded the ship. Teo looked longingly at the booby hatch. Her parents were belowdecks, not even aware that she was about to rescue them.

"But I mustn't lead the enemy down there. They are safe for the moment," she persuaded herself, turning back to the job at hand. She pulled a fishskin out of her pinafore and launched it into the thick of the thrashing heap of Ghost-Convicts, who were still struggling to rise to their feet but were perpetually tripped up by the fat animals.

All around her, Tig, Pylorus, Giovanni, Renzo and Sebastiano were doing exactly the same thing: fishskins raced straight to their targets, who were shouting "What the flaming hell?" and "'Strewth!" And then there was a gray shimmer, a vile stink and the tinkle of cutlasses and billycans falling on deck.

The next rank of Ghost-Convicts was now advancing. Fortunately, Hyrum, Thrasher and Bits already had their fishskins primed. Signor Alicamoussa was a few yards away, in hand-to-hand combat with three human Hooroo criminals at once. The pumpkin-sellers, led by Uncle Tommaso, were decapitating braces of Ghost-Convicts with swinging arcs of their metal trays.

The Ghost-Convicts began to grimace with fright. Some of them moved backward, crushing their comrades behind. In the density of ghosts, each bursting fishskin dissolved three or four of them at a time.

"Starve the lizards, what a stink!" shouted Signor Alicamoussa.

Turtledove shook a Ghost-Convict's arm out of his mouth. "Where's that child-hurting female Uish going?" he demanded.

Miss Uish was to be glimpsed disappearing below. Renzo shouted, "She's off to get Bajamonte Tiepolo!"

"I'll be on to her, then," growled Turtledove. He bounded back on deck and padded straight down the hatch. But, by the sounds that emerged from beneath them, Teo could tell that he'd been distracted from his pursuit.

"He must have seen the treadmills," she realized.

And indeed, it was clear that Turtledove had gone utterly insane with rage to see the children at their grim work. After howls of fury, and endearments to the children and dogs, came the crash of wooden machines being reduced to matchwood.

Seconds later, the wan faces of Greasy Ressydew and Marg'rit Savory appeared through the booby hatch, followed by dozens of other emaciated boys and girls, all blinking, weeping and fainting. The Haggis-munchers, Fossy and the District Disgrace, as arranged, led all the poor captives to safety, guiding their weakened legs down the ladders to the tenders that the mermaids had "borrowed" from bigger vessels along the river. The mermaids swam their frail cargo to shore, where they were revived with small spoonfuls of curry, hot lime juice and warm black blankets from the mourning emporium.

Sibella was escorted on deck by Massimo and Emilio. "Where shall we put the prisoner?" they asked Signor Alicamoussa.

"Out of harm's way," he answered briefly. "Youse just tie her securely, yes. Somewhere below, but within cooee of the main deck. Need to be talking to her later."

And then he went back to smashing suntanned criminals between the blades of his twin rapiers, like a textbook illustration of "our handsome hero's derring-do."

The London ghosts fought with their various weapons: Round-heads and Cavaliers with their muskets ("Now die like the dog you are, sirrah!"), chimney sweeps with their brushes ("Take that, yew scum!") and Roman soldiers with their swords (*"Dabis, improbe, poenas!"*).

Rosato was meanwhile creeping about the deck with a huge pair of shears and a bucket, cutting all the wires and dousing the sticks of dynamite. All but three of the rescued children and dogs had been safely taken down the ladders when something dark flew overhead.

"Sea Spider ahoy!" called Flos from below.

One after another, the Sea Spiders allowed themselves to be hurled from the mermaids' fish-bone catapults. When they reached one of the Ghost-Convicts, the insects wrapped blinding silk around their eyes, making them easy targets for the fat little dogs and foxes, who gnawed their ankles till they fell to the ground. At

366

that point, the Venetian sailors deftly trussed them in the most devilish combinations of knots known to any navy on the face of the earth, but always including at least the monkey's fist, the carrick bend, the constrictor and the timber hitch.

Then the London ghosts carried them across the river and up into the railway arches, where they dragged their bodies deep into the stones. A sound of grinding brick echoed from the arches over to the *Bombazine*.

"They're not coming out again!" Teo noticed. "The London ghosts . . . They're staying in the stone."

Renzo lifted his telescope to his eye. "They are plugging up the walls with their own bodies!"

From below, Lussa called, "And so They shall ensure that our Enemy's Soldiers stay There as well. This is how They redeem Themselves & their Immortality."

And from under the bridge floated the voice of a Roman centurion: *"Nocte una quivis vel deus esse potest."*

"One night like this can make any man a god," Renzo translated.

There was a sudden lull in the fighting. The misty air that swirled around the deck grew colder, if possible, than it had been before. And Bajamonte Tiepolo appeared on the companionway, his expression livid, his right arm raised. In it was a cutlass dripping with a green liquid. Miss Uish stood beside him, armed with a green-tipped dagger. And next to her loomed Lieutenant Rosebud, missing an arm, but equipped with a sword in the one that was left, and with the customary shark's tooth protruding from his back. Rosebud's sword was also coated with something viscous and emerald-green. Bajamonte Tiepolo yelled menacingly, "Come and get some, Venetians!"

"Poison!" shouted Renzo. "The weapon of cowards!"

"I've been waiting some time to see you again, Studious Son," hissed Bajamonte Tiepolo. "And to hear your pathetic platitudes and your whining moralizing."

Renzo grabbed a cutlass from one of the fallen Ghost-Convicts and brandished it above his head. "Worse luck for you, then. Round two, I think?"

"I never conceded round one to you that day in Venice," sneered Bajamonte Tiepolo. "You were in pieces. I was about to have your life when the Undrowned Child started cursing me. You could never have beaten me on your own."

"And I don't require the glory of that," answered Renzo coolly. "I am happy and proud to be helped by my friends, the mermaids, these brave Londoners, my Uncle Tommaso, the Incogniti, the London ghosts and Turtledove, and especially Teo. If you were ten times as strong and twenty times as evil, we'd still have the better of you, because we have that between us."

Miss Uish advanced, murmuring, "Shall I silence the voluble little brat for you, dearest? Let this be my treat."

Everyone else on deck had frozen to the place where they were standing when Bajamonte Tiepolo had appeared.

The spell was broken when Sofonisba pounced on Miss Uish's head from high in the rigging.

"Thisss one's mi-i-i-ne!" she yowled.

The two tumbled over and over on the deck, the woman raking at the cat with her long fingernails and biting tufts of fur with her pretty white teeth. Sofonisba slashed and stabbed with her talons, ripping Miss Uish's hair with her pearly incisors.

And suddenly everyone was at war again, shrieking, slashing, punching and grabbing. Howls and dreadful Australian swearing filled the air. Renzo was dueling with Bajamonte Tiepolo; Signor Alicamoussa with Lieutenant Rosebud. Uncle Tommaso and the pumpkin-sellers were rounding up the remaining Ghost-Convicts and throwing them overboard, where Flos and the other mermaids could be heard battling with tridents and shields. The few remaining criminals had rushed to the lifeboat and were cramming it with sheep.

"Can my parents hear?" wondered Teo, flinging another fish-skin. "I hope not. They would be terrified."

Bajamonte Tiepolo shouted, "Uish! Why don't you unleash your *special* forces?"

The voice of Flos called out from below, "Ye of tepid courage, ye dog, always reliant on da devices of others! Mean as monkey's muck and twice as nasty, ye is!"

Holding Sofonisba's head down to the deck with one hand, Miss Uish shouted, "Dearest, you know that my *special forces* are somewhat . . . difficult to control. So I planned to wait and see if these clowns caused us a minute's worry. So far it has been child's play to keep them down and out."

At that moment, Sofonisba's right front paw shot out and scratched a deep, jagged weal right down Miss Uish's beautiful left cheek.

"Perhaps you are right, my darling!" she called to Il Traditore. To the nearest Ghost-Convict she shouted, "Free the insects!"

He lifted the ring of a trapdoor in the deck. Teo whispered, "Gristle and guts! The Russian-doll *scolopendre*!"

Flos, catching sight of Miss Uish's wounded face, shouted, "Oi up there, Bagger, what a fright you do look! I heard dere hiring for house hauntings in Moldavia!"

No one had time to laugh. For a sinister mist of white insects flowed from the trapdoor. They swarmed over the bodies of the pumpkin-sellers and criminals alike, running straight toward their mouths.

Too late, Teo called out, "Close your lips and your eyes! Mermaids, throw up the noggin' boots!"

A rain of boots flew over the taffrail, accompanied by the mermaids' traditional *scolopendre*-killing cry of "Yoiks!" The Londoners and Venetians seized them.

But it was too late. For the *scolopendre*'s favorite ploy was to sting the tongue so it swelled and choked their victims. Three of the pumpkin-sellers fell to the deck. The others were writhing in pain against the stanchions, and now the tide of insects headed toward the boys and girls standing horrified by the forecastle.

Sofonisba whirled away from Miss Uish to deal with this new enemy. She crunched and kicked and head-butted the *scolopendre* until just half a dozen remained, mostly those defective models that simply ran around in buzzing circles or fell on their backs with their tiny mechanical legs whirring in the air. But the pumpkin-sellers had fallen numbly silent and lay glassy-eyed on their backs. The boys and girls ran helplessly among them, smoothing their brows, wiping their faces with grimy handkerchiefs. Uncle Tommaso was among the fallen, his bloodstained face already turning blue.

"They're dyin'! Our hot-zookymen is chokin' to death," wailed Tig.

It was at this moment that the sound of refined voices was heard below. The London mermaids were to be seen swimming a ladylike breaststroke between the icebergs. On their backs were pretty straw baskets full of bottles and arrows. Slung over their shoulders were delicate bows made from the bones of fish.

"Make way!" Pucretia elevated her clipped voice. "We have a cure for all insect bites. Chameleon oil. Made from pure chameleons."

Flos paused, her slingshot held aloft. "What yer babbling about now, ye great wet? And where were ye when we called for help? Trust ye to arrive when it's all but over, ye warbling clotheslines!"

"It's not quite over, actually!" cried Emilio, manfully struggling against a Ghost-Convict who was trying to pull him into a cupboard.

Gloriana insisted, "Chameleon oil is just what you need! The only perfect liniment, you know! Please to hand it up on deck. Shake the bottle until its contents become cream-colored. And then anoint the affected parts."

Having finally pinned Rosebud to the deck with his foot, Signor Alicamoussa scratched his handsome head. "Reckon youse taily ladies might of had couple few 'plashes too many of the old cough medicine. Yet is worth a try."

A chain of boys and girls handed bottles of chameleon oil up the ladders to the rail, where others snapped them open and poured the contents on the wounds of the poor pumpkin-sellers. Below, Nerolia could be heard explaining, "Immediately the chameleon oil has been applied, it sets out upon its message of

371

discovering and healing, traveling with lightning rapidity to the seat of the trouble. This found, it restores to the affected part all that pristine freshness which pain and suffering has caused it to lose."

And indeed, the chameleon oil seemed to work just as it said on the label. The pumpkin-sellers moaned, but the color was returning to their faces. Soon they were standing up, and instantly returned to the fray.

"Bag o' nuts!" exclaimed Flos. "It works after all!"

Meanwhile the London mermaids busied themselves loading arrows into their bows. Despite their delicate arms, they proved most dextrous shots. A rain of arrows fell with deadly accuracy upon the tallest Ghost-Convicts, whose skulls were visible from the water. And when the Hooroo criminals launched their boatful of sheep and tried to sneak away, the London mermaids holed its sides in a hundred places so it sank. Fortunately, the sheeps' wool kept them afloat on their backs with their legs in the air until they could be guided to shore. And in this way they also served as useful rafts to transport the exhausted fat weasels, squirrels and rats.

Under cover of the chaos, Bajamonte Tiepolo had stopped fighting with Renzo, who was now dealing with two Ghost-Convicts. It was some minutes before anyone realized that Il Traditore had disappeared. Renzo, having pushed both his opponents into the water, ran around the deck, shouting, "Show yourself, Traditore! Give me satisfaction, you coward!"

Sofonisba paused to lick her back, shoulders and right front leg. So she did not see Miss Uish approaching her from behind, a dagger in hand. Renzo rushed forward to put himself between Miss Uish and the cat.

"Interfere with me, would you, boy?" shouted Miss Uish. "Well, you can be the first to see what happens to interfering children!"

Turning to Lieutenant Rosebud, who had raised himself from the deck and recommenced his duel with Signor Alicamoussa, she shouted, "Let's show them the spirit of Christmas past, shall we?"

Rosebud kicked Signor Alicamoussa to the ground. Winded, the circus-master cried, "Youse'd give me a porridge-stirrer in the gut, would youse, sir? Youse'll not. . . ."

But the lieutenant was striding away, burrowing in his pocket for a key. Deftly, he unlocked that mysterious door to what Teo had thought, when she first came aboard the *Bombazine*, was a cupboard, and from which she had heard that sinister voice crooning "Silent Night."

Now, out of that cupboard, flowed a shimmering tribe of heart-stoppingly ugly apparitions. They were dressed like mangy bears in shaggy fur coats. Those with bare faces had grotesquely twisted features. Others wore fearsome masks with devilish faces painted on them. Some had eyes that lit up as if on fire. Each carried a tall birch rod, and those rods were immediately employed to attack as many boys and girls as they could find. Teo crumpled to her knees as one of the creatures dealt her a blow across the shoulders. Thrasher and Hyrum were both on the deck too, their necks pinned down by filthy boots. The creatures lowered their jaws toward them. Miss Uish snarled, "Famous pedophages all of them, my sweet cupboard creatures."

373

"Child-eaters?" gasped Teo, turning to Renzo.

"Over my cadaver," shouted Signor Alicamoussa, back on his feet.

Turtledove shouted, "Wot's this? Child-hurters? I've heard about these types. Diabolical monsters wot punish childer at Christmas, instead of givin' 'em presents an' puddin' an' lovin'. *Eats* childer, yew say? I'll be havin' 'em!"

The shaggy spirits were happy to terrorize half-grown humans, but they proved none too fierce when it came to confronting a six-foot-tall sword-fighting circus-master and a large English bull-dog with his blood roused. They were soon backed into a corner, Turtledove lunging at their calloused ankles and occasionally leaping to nip one on its long, pointed nose.

"Teo," Turtledove shouted, "has yew got a spell for these bully boys in yer head-library? Use it, do. They's not awful bothersome, but they is wasting me time."

Teo was already mentally flicking though Professor Marìn's *The Best Ways with Wayward Ghosts*, speeding straight to the chapters that dealt with "Malevolent Spirits of Christmas Past." Following the professor's instructions, she shouted,

"Love! Light! And Christmas Delight!
Diminish all who trade in fright!"

A rude noise, like a balloon deflating, issued from the corner where the spirits huddled. They shrank to the size of dolls and scampered away like rats, leaping for the stanchions and throwing themselves overboard.

"Took off like ruptured ducks!" Signor Alicamoussa grinned. "Feather me!"

"Ship's rats are bigger than them now!" Teo exclaimed.

Pucretia's voice came up from the water. "And we brought with us a soda fountain, and a plentiful supply of ROUGH ON RATS."

ROUGH ON RATS proved even rougher on diminished Christmas spirits.

"Now, what about Sofonisba?" Teo cried.

Turtledove's brain was running in the same direction. "Where's that Uish woman now? Estimable Feline, I trust yew's vanquished the female child-hurter? Because now I's goin' to pulverize wot's left of her. They'll have to bury her in a hundred cardboard boxes."

Miss Uish was nowhere to be seen. Poor Sofonisba, however, lay panting on the deck, a bright ribbon of blood flowing from her side. One wing had been cut off and most of her tail lay an inch apart from her body.

Turtledove bent over her tenderly, nudging her with his soft muzzle.

"The bravest cat in the world will get the best care the quacks can provide. Yew'll soon be better," he growled. "Yew'll come back to the Mansion Dolorous and I shall treat yew as one of me own childer."

"Idiot! Fool!" hissed Sofonisba. "While you're whispering sweet nothings to me, they're getting away."

There was the sound of a splash and a glint of shining pink disappearing beneath the water.

"Wot, in the name of Unholy Cat," asked Turtledove, "were that?"

"The *Cala-Mary!*" gasped Teo. "The squid submarine! My parents must have finished it."

And then she remembered what Bajamonte Tiepolo had said when he sensed her presence in his stateroom.

"Your parents are nearly finished," he had told her, "in both senses of the word, for, of course, it would be foolish of me to allow them to live once they have served my purpose."

Bajamonte Tiepolo, Orphan-Maker.

Teo, her face bloodless and her heart almost at a standstill, ran to the booby hatch and hurtled down toward the laboratory.

53. The devil's spawn

a moment later

Teo had had many astonishing things happen to her in her life, more than the average twelve-year-old dreams about, in fact. Yet she'd never been so shocked as she was now, at the sight of her highly rational and scientific parents leaning out of a large port-hole and talking seriously to a school of mermaids in the water below.

For the first time in her life, Teo was rendered absolutely speechless.

"You can see them?" she eventually squeaked. She'd been so sure that, in the eminently sensible minds of Alberto and Leonora Stampara, modern science must have done away with mermaids, talking dogs, magical creatures and even reincarnated spirits like Bajamonte Tiepolo, explaining the sight of them as the product of a simple ganglionic imbalance or an ocular disturbance.

A dozen boys and girls poured into the laboratory, ducking their heads shyly at the sight of the unfamiliar adults. The parrots flew in behind them, taking roost on the lanterns.

"My parents," explained Teo proudly, hugging them fiercely.

She was surprised to receive twin embraces that were just as fierce in return.

"The danger must truly be over," she thought, "for I seem to have come out from between-the-Linings."

"Oh, Teodora," sobbed Leonora, "they told us they would hurt you."

"Did you build that *Cala-Mary* then?" asked Rosato admiringly.

"We're not proud of it," Leonora said gravely, over the top of Teo's head. "We had no choice."

"Course not," agreed Bits magnanimously. "You was slave labor, jist loik Greasy 'n' Marg'rit. Forced, loik."

"But now they've got away in it anyways," pointed out Pylorus in a small voice.

Alberto Stampara smiled calmly. "They won't get far."

Leonora explained, "Knowing it was to be used for evil, we built a fatal error into the submarine. Two minutes after launch, the cabin will completely fill with dark blue ink."

"Poisonous dark blue ink," added Alberto.

"And in serving Venice so against her Enemies," Lussa declared, "Leonora and Alberto Stampara have now joined the ranks of the Incogniti, Secret Protectors of Venice."

Teo cried, "Which is why they can see mermaids!"

"You mean they's made sure that old Bargyminty and that woman's goan to cark it?" cried Bits. "I hain't sayin' I wish anybody ill. But I hopes that's what you mean."

A fierce bubbling in the river answered Bits's question before Leonora and Alberto could. A sudden blush of blue crept over the icebergs juddering in the current around the *Bombazine*.

"If the ink has been released, it can only be because the cabin filled and the submarine has sunk to the bottom of the river," explained Alberto quietly.

"Hain't he got baddened magic, though, yer Traitor?" asked Pylorus. "Won't he 'scape?"

"Bajamonte Tiepolo has . . . *had* achieved a Human State again," affirmed Lussa. "So He can drown just like an ordinary Man. Like the Woman Uish, who was never More than a Very Bad Example of a Human."

Everyone's faces tightened. Yet in her heart, Teo was not a bit sorry. If anything, death by drowning in blue ink wasn't a bad-enough fate for Miss Uish. And there was no fate too terrible for Bajamonte Tiepolo.

The Venetian mermaids broke into unruly rejoicing. "He has unscrewed his billiard table!" and "Worms' night out!"

Flos shouted happily, "He's basted da poison turkey!"

Marsil cried, "And he's tied up his plum puddings!"

"Puddings! Puddings! Puddings!" screeched the parrots, though one cried "Worms!" in a wistful way.

Pucretia looked up sharply. From her quiver, Nerolia pulled a large green bottle of PATENT VERMIFUGE. The parrot whistled and looked away.

Renzo said soberly, "They will be dead, but the Pretender doesn't know it yet."

"And if yer Bargyminty and the childer-hurting wishy-woman is dead . . . ," Turtledove said slowly and regretfully, "it means we cannot interrogerate 'em as to the Hooroo plans for Venice. We is in the dark. Things ain't so rosy as we thought. . . ."

"There is someone we could ask," Teo said. "Someone who was always thick as thieves with Miss Uish. And *she's* still here."

Everyone turned to look for Sibella. She'd been safely tied to a chair in a corner of the laboratory, awaiting the judgment of the victors of the battle. She dared not struggle, of course, because of her hemophilia.

It suddenly occurred to Teo that it really was outstandingly callous of Bajamonte Tiepolo and Miss Uish to abandon Sibella to the mercies of those left on the *Bombazine*, all of whom had reasons to hate her. Yet she suppressed her pity. This was war. The fates of London and Venice hung in the balance. There were things to set straight, and this was Teo's opportunity to do so, while people were at last ready to listen to her on the subject of Sibella's treachery.

Lussa listened patiently while Teo listed her grievances against Sibella. "She spied on us. She treated us like dirt. As soon as she could, she ran to the *Bombazine* and joined our enemies. Even when we were at sea, she used her horrible leeches to send messages to them. There has always been something strange about her. And finally, who *is* she? Why does no one come to find her, or care about her? Nobody loves her, and there must be a reason for that."

"How very banal," remarked Sibella, "the case against me."

Teo felt a red haze pass in front of her eyes. In that blood-colored shimmering, Sibella's pretty face distorted. The features sharpened, lengthened. Suddenly, Sibella looked almost exactly like a miniature version of Miss Uish herself. Teo swayed, and Sibella's face changed again. Now those blue eyes seemed to darken to greenish brown, with a rim of red around them. And her pupils seemed to narrow like a snake's.

Teo's feelings rioted out of control. A fierce torrent of words rushed out of her mouth. "I know who you are, Sibella. Is it so uncommonly banal," she hissed, "that you must be the daughter of Bajamonte Tiepolo himself? And Miss Uish is no doubt your mother! You are the spawn of Venice's worst enemy and London's worst enemy!"

Silence fell on the room.

Ann Picklefinch whispered, "It's true, that Sibella hes an uncanny way aboot her."

"That is a dreadful thing to accuse her of!" exclaimed Renzo. "On what evidence?"

Signor Alicamoussa murmured, "Teodora, reckon youse is barking up the wrong dog there. . . ."

Teo shouted, "She's not denying it, is she? Remember how she came aboard the *Scilla*? We didn't capture her, not like the other prisoners. That Australian ship practically delivered her gift-wrapped. And then why did she run to the *Bombazine*, if not back to Mamma and Papà, like a good little girl?"

Sibella's face might have been etched on white marble, so unmoving were her features. She murmured, "I was not welcome on the *Scilla*."

Lussa intervened, "Teodora, your Rage is intemperate. If this Child were truly the Daughter of Il Traditore & the Uish Woman, would They really have abandoned Her here? Even if They do not love Her, She would surely be worth Something to Them. As their Heiress, at Least."

"Perhaps she's still spying! On her own account!"

Suddenly, everyone—the Venetians and the English—was shouting and waving their hands around.

Even Turtledove growled at Teo, "Is yew a few drops short of a tincture, girlie? Don't niver see them two villains as *breeders*." At which the London mermaids below tittered with their hands over their mouths.

Emilio pointed out: "She never actually told them where the *Scilla* was, did she?"

Unseen by anyone, Sibella quietly undid the ropes that bound her and edged out of the room.

Lussa's troubled voice rose above the rest, "Yet who is She? Perhaps She *is* the Daughter of Evil. Mayhap Evil even sleeps in her young Veins. But for now, She is but a Child, Friendless & Hated, and Afflicted with a rare Disease. We should pity Her, surely?"

"By the way, where *is* the girlie?" inquired Turtledove.

A shriek was heard up above. Tig Sweetiemouth came rushing into the laboratory. "Come upstairs!" she implored the company. "Everyone come on deck!"

"Sibella!" called Renzo, climbing up the hatch.

"I'm up here." A faint, bell-like voice came from high in the rigging. "And you need have no worry about how to dispose of me. I shall save you the trouble."

A piece of paper fluttered down to the deck. Signor Alicamoussa picked it up and read aloud,

"'And so I end my worthless life . . .'"

Sibella called down, "I suggest you clear the deck. I don't want to take any of you with me when I jump."

"It's only thirty yards. She might be all right, light little bundle loik that. She'll prob'ly bounce loik a feather!" whispered Greasy. "Wiv maybe a bruise or two."

"No," Renzo groaned, "her hemophilia means she will bleed to death from the slightest injury."

"Poor maid," whispered Turtledove.

"And she's so very pretty," added Tobias.

A minute later, Renzo was quietly climbing up the rigging behind Sibella.

They talked earnestly. Teo strained to read the sentences she saw above their heads. But the wind was rising noisily, blowing all the words out of shape. Sibella touched her chest and pointed south.

Turtledove patted Teo's foot with his paw. "Doan fret. Renzo ain't scrootching up to her all lovey-dovey now. It's jist a bit o' business up there."

Sibella finally smiled gravely and nodded once. Renzo offered his hand and helped her down to the deck.

There, he saluted Signor Alicamoussa. "The prisoner is delivered safely. She insists that she will not explain herself except in front of a court of her peers. We"—Renzo colored slight—"may not be considered her equals, it seems. For she says she is the natural daughter of the Pretender himself. That's why she has hemophilia, the disease of the royal family."

Signor Alicamoussa gave Sibella a considering stare. "Those eyes! That chin! That brow! Is a possible thing, I reckon, to see the features of Harold Hoskins in that tiny face, yes. Very liken, in factiest fact. Much more liken to his Nobship than to the Uish female or the Tiepolatrocity!"

Renzo said, "So she was placed on the *Scilla* not as a spy, but as a hostage—until the destruction of Venice was accomplished. Sibella constituted the *personal* and *private* bond of the Pretender to Bajamonte Tiepolo. To be held in his custody until Venice was destroyed. Now don't you see that Sibella has just been an innocent pawn in all this? I am sure any court in any land—"

"We shall take her back to Venice with us, then, yes. She can answer for herself in front of her peers there. Youse'll know what they say about Venetians?" Signor Alicamoussa smiled delightfully.

"Of course," said Renzo. "Every Venetian mother says it when she gives birth: 'Look, a lord is born in this world. We are all lords and ladies in Venice.'"

"Renzo," Teo admonished him, "why are you so happy? Just because Sibella is his daughter does not mean Harold Hoskins won't be thinking of invading Venice, now that Bajamonte Tiepolo has given him the idea. He loves power! Craves it! Venice would be a crowning jewel in his new imperial crown, wouldn't she?"

Sebastiano dalla Mutta suggested, "Or perhaps Renzo quite fancies a Queen Sibella ruling over Venice?"

"No, I do not." Renzo's voice was clear and stern. "In fact, my biggest fear is that her father will come after her."

"Easily risolverated." Signor Alicamoussa waved the piece of paper that Sibella had sent floating down to the deck. "We shall send her suiciding letter to the London bobbies and to her unfatherly father, who is colder than a billabong's bottom. He will think she has indeed carked it! In the meaningwhiles, we'll take her with us to Venice, all alivo and bucksome. And perhaps, with a little proper kindness shown to her for once, the pale girlie will come to trust us with the whole truth, yes."

A gabble of voices broke out. It was the sound of everyone on the *Scilla* changing the subject to something far more cheerfully suited to the aftermath of a victorious battle, namely the Londoners' return to the home comforts of the mourning emporium's soft-lined coffins and cozy coal fires.

"Now." Alberto Stampara smiled, hugging Teo and shaking Renzo's hand vigorously. "Tell us just how you two got all the way here from Venice, and what you are doing here on your own."

Leonora kissed the top of Teo's head. "You are changed, somehow, since we saw you last. Not just this strange hairstyle."

Renzo intervened quickly, "She has traveled now, you know. She is more cosmopolitan, perhaps?"

"No, it's not that." Leonora looked puzzled. "Teodora is more . . . sea-ish."

"Seaworthy!" maintained Renzo. "She is entirely seaworthy."

Sebastiano dalla Mutta chuckled. "Yes, if you stand close enough to Teo, you can hear the ocean. From between the ears."

Sebastiano's own ears stood in considerable danger of a pinch from Renzo at that moment, but Alberto persisted, "What were you two doing on the *Scilla*? Did your mother permit such a thing, Renzo? Teodora, we thought we left you safe with Anna. What happened?"

Teo and Renzo exchanged worried glances. Two summers before, they had agreed to spare Teo's parents the difficulty of trying to believe in mermaids, baddened magic, vengeful spirits. If they started recounting the whole truth now, then many other things would also need to be explained. And then it would come out—the painful fact that Teo now knew the identity of her real parents, that she had visited their graves, and that she wished to be like them and work in the Venetian Archives. This would be too hard on the soft hearts of Alberto and Leonora Stampara, who loved her like the kindest parents in the world. They might be Incogniti now, but they were still human, and they could be hurt.

Signor Alicamoussa saw them floundering. He winked at Teo. Then he put arms confidentially around the shoulders of Leonora and Alberto Stampara and drew them away. "Dear colleagues," he said, "is very sad news in the altogether of Renzo's Mamma. Let's not talk about it in front of the boy. And youse may not realize just what has happened to Venice in your absence."

"Saved!" sighed Renzo, as the adults moved to a sheltered part of the deck so that Leonora could sit down away from the biting wind.

"As he'd admit himself, Signor Alicamoussa could talk a dog off a meat wagon," smiled Teo.

"Did someone say 'dog'?" asked Turtledove, planting his feet on Teo's shoulders and licking her face clean of all the soot and sweat of battle.

"Not one of my favorite words." Sofonisba limped up, permitting a caress from Tig. "But I'd honor it now, after having seen you in battle, sir."

"Yew was no shabby tabby yourself, missis, when it came to the old one-two." Turtledove nudged her softly with his nose.

"Ah, but I am wrecked and mutilated now by all these adventures," Sofonisba sighed theatrically. She rolled on her back, erected a rear leg and licked at various sore spots and scratches inflicted by Miss Uish. She sported a large plaster where her wing was once tucked against her side. Her tail was neatly bandaged into a white stump, which still managed to be astonishingly communicative, rapping on the floor to emphasize its owner's words.

"I've no desire to put myself to sea again. What use is a ship's cat without a full tail? How can the young sailors learn ailuromancy without an all-expressive tail to observe? And my flying days are over. No, a new kitten must be found and trained for the *Scilla*. By the way, what happens to pensioned-off ship's cats in this country?"

Turtledove answered expertly, "Ah, they is retired to the Catswolds; 'tis a veritable heaven for cats up there. They has their own villages, like Much-Fondling-in-the-Fur and Purrington, where they lives in ease and style. The Litterbox Lanes is a wonder of modern sanitation. An' the catnip fields grow green far as the eye can see."

"Really?" asked Sofonisba. "That is not absolutely uninteresting."

Tig said enthusiastically: "Sofonisba hain't ready to retire yet! There's rats to catch in the Mansion Dolorous! And there's a dear little babby coffin all lined wiv swan's down next to mine. . . ."

Tobias edged forward shyly. His voice was thick with longing as he fixed his large gray eyes on Renzo and Teo. "There is sewers in Venice, right?"

"The most amazing and intricate sewer system, dating back to . . . ," began Renzo. Then he stopped short and shook Tobias's hand with both his own. "You are very welcome, more than welcome, isn't he, everyone?"

Emilio, Sebastiano, Rosato and all the other Venetians raised a cheer.

Renzo added hastily, "And you can sleep in the *Scilla*'s cargo store all the way home to Venice. Awfully roomy down there."

"And we *can* go back to Venice now," pressed Teo, "can't we?

We need to go home and prepare the forces of good to fight Harold Hoskins and his soldiers, if they come."

"Wot the fimble-famble? Yew wants to leave London Town right *now*," asked Turtledove, incredulous, "jist when the greatest show on earth is 'bout to start?"

54. Feasts and Farewells

the Mansion Dolorous, February 2, 1901

As ever, the old Queen preferred to snub London.

The royal funeral was to take place in Windsor, miles from her poverty-tarnished capital. Queen Victoria would pass the rest of eternity in a private chapel, lying next to her beloved Albert, as far away as possible from the vulgar public.

In her meticulous funeral plans, she had, however, conceded a procession through London.

Queen Victoria's coffin, mounted on a gun carriage and surmounted by her crown, orb and scepter, was to proceed with all possible pomp and circumstance—accompanied by Beethoven and Highland laments—from Victoria Station to Paddington via the grandeurs of the Mall, Hyde Park and Marble Arch, all of which were draped with purple cloth and white satin bows. The Mansion Dolorous gang and the crew of the *Scilla* enjoyed a splendid view from the roof of Pattercake's Soho restaurant.

The temperature outside had risen by a noticeable degree. The sun made its first appearance since the death of the Queen. Snowdrops were poking their scented heads through the softening sheaves of snow. The muted drums of the procession were accompanied by the trickle of thawed water and the tinkle of falling icicles.

The Londoners and Venetians sweltered, being all outfitted to the height of melancholy fashion in brand-new mourning outfits, after having been serially dunked in hot water in the claw-foot bath by Turtledove.

Sibella was forced to accompany the Venetians ashore—"We can't trust her alone on the *Scilla*, can we?" Fabrizio pointed out.

At the mourning emporium, where everyone had been invited for a Royal Funeral Tea, Sibella was introduced to Messrs. Tristesse and Ganorus as "a young gentlewoman fallen on hard times, who will shortly depart for Venice to take up a position as a seamstress."

At this, Sibella looked up eagerly. She seemed about to speak. Then she caught a glimpse of Teo's face and lowered her head again.

Sibella ran reverent fingers down the rolls of black moiré, black faille and black Ottoman ribbon. She was actually seen to smile when she discovered the mourning lace in all its jet-beaded glory. At the sight of the seal furs, she reached out a hand, asking, "May I have one of these, and some scissors and thread, please?"

"No harm, I suppose," replied Mr. Ganorus.

While the other boys and girls devoured their prodigious Royal Funeral Tea, Sibella sat in a corner, quietly snipping and sewing at the black fur.

Tristesse and Ganorus had done them proud: there was a roast and a boil, a raised game pie, along with three-penny Yarmouth bloaters sizzled on toasting forks and snuggled in envelopes of bread and butter, followed by a massacre of satin pralines and an apple tart (with licorice-rimmed mourning icing). There were basins of sweet tea for the boys and girls, and a hooped tankard of "Saturday Night Pertikular" for Turtledove. Sofonisba graciously condescended to nibble on a tin of boned larks, stuffed and truffled, from Harrods, pronouncing them "not uninteresting in texture and flavor."

"A tapeworm wunt believe what I's put away today." Greasy hugged his belly happily. "I've got a ways to go, though, before I's fully restored to my former glory."

At the end of the meal, Sibella produced a small, beautifully accurate black bear with button eyes and a dear little paunch.

"Pray what is that?" asked Mr. Ganorus.

"A Mourning Bear," replied Sibella.

"A toy bear? It'll never take on." Mr. Tristesse frowned. "What child in its right mind would want to hug a bear and take it to bed?"

The following days were spent outfitting and provisioning the *Scilla* for her journey home. She'd be weighed down with passengers, for most of the Incogniti were to join the voyage home. Feeding almost fifty hungry mouths seemed an impossibility: though rich with happiness and relief, the *Scilla* had no actual funds left.

"Not a brass razoo," Signor Alicamoussa had mourned.

"What about the treasure under the tree near Greenhithe?" Fabrizio asked. After all that they'd been through, the plundered goods had been far from their minds.

"It's not ours to spend," Renzo reproved.

Sebastiano said stoutly, "Surely we're entitled to a share of it—just to put us on our feet and under sail again. We shall," he insisted, "call it our wages for saving London from Bajamonte Tiepolo and the Pretender."

After much discussion, the *Scilla*—made visible and audible by a new spell—made a brief journey to Greenhithe, and a small portion of portable cash was retrieved from under the beech tree.

It was fun to walk around the dockland shops with a fat purse of coins. Teo and Emilio dipped in and out of establishments called Jack and His Mother and Jolly Jack Tar, buying all the instruments they'd had to pawn to survive in the skinny days before the battle. To their new aneroid barometers, binoculars, chronometers and charts they added ropes and cases of ship's biscuits. They bought canvas trousers, pilot coats and flannel shirts for all the sailors. At Negretti and Zambra, they purchased a smart new telescope.

Renzo insisted on a trip to Harrods, where he and Pylorus invested in such luxuries as Broadway Fine-Flavored Toothpicks and an Improved Continental Mangle & Clothes Wringer. And Renzo could not pass up a white stoneware dog-food trough for Turtledove, illustrated as it was with a fleur-de-lis, at just two shillings.

On the way home, Pylorus guided Renzo to the bookshops at Took's Court, where both were lost to literary pleasure for several hours. In gratitude, Renzo treated Pylorus to a fruit jelly at Alfred Pill's on Cheapside, followed by buns in Lombard Street. And over a plate of Ha'penny Busters, Pylorus produced an awkwardly wrapped package from his pocket. When Renzo opened it, he found a graceful white teacup with the words A PRESENT FROM LONDON below an etching of Tower Bridge.

As Renzo turned it silently in his shaking hands, Pylorus

explained, "Teo told me about your pa's gift wot that Uish female smashed. And then Bits found this in the river near Blackfriars. We thought you should 'ave it, Renzo. Aw, doan cry. You Eyetalians is godawful sentimental!"

The London mermaids also offered supplies for the *Scilla*'s return trip. They even brought gifts for the parrots—seven-pound bags of CARDIAC for poultry. "It excites a healthy action of the stomach, strengthens and invigorates young chicks."

"Excites! Excites! Excites!" shouted the parrots.

And for the Venetian sailors they had VIKING INVALID TURTLE SOUP, INVIGOROIDS and sachets of Antispasmodic Tea, all packed in a COMMODIOUS CABINET FOR PATENT NOSTRUMS, much gilded and scrolled.

"And finally," Pucretia announced, "we have MOTHERSILL'S SEASICK REMEDY!"

"None of us has been seasick in our lives," protested Giovanni. "We're Venetians! We don't know how."

For Turtledove, Nerolia flourished SPRATT'S DOG PURGING PILLS, which he gallantly swallowed and pronounced "most refreshing."

But he balked at the frowsty smell of NADIRE'S WORM POWDERS. "Not putting that up my fugo, not for nuffink. I'm full to the bung as it is, thankee kindly, ladies."

Pylorus Salt handed Renzo a small stack of magazines. "Aw, I thought you might loik somethin' to read on the voyage."

"*Boy's Own Paper!*" exclaimed Renzo, eagerly leafing through.

Pylorus enthused, "It's a real bloodcurdler! Full to burstin' wiv hangin's and robberies and adventures, all true as life 'n' twice as grisly!"

The next day Teo and Renzo left the *Scilla* one last time, walking back through the newly slushy streets to the cavern under London Bridge.

The mermaids swam a final farewell lap around the cavern, brandishing tridents and shields. Flos called out, "Dere'll be Vampire Eels to deal with yonside in Venetian waters, and dey'll not catch us napping. Dem wobble-bellied bloodsuckers'll be—"

"Utterly overcome by Flos's Forsoothery, not to mention our Tridents." Lussa smiled confidently.

"Will you come to the *Scilla* first?" Teo asked. "We're about to set sail ourselves. Everyone's there. It's time to say goodbye, really, this time."

The goodbyes were brief, because no one could bear to dwell on them. Even Fossy's violin was silent. Teo was bidding a reluctant farewell to her adoptive parents yet again. Even she could see the sense of it, however. Alberto and Leonora had undertaken to deal in person with the British authorities, informing them of the treasure at Greenhithe, the death of Peaglum and the machinations of Miss Uish, insofar as they could be contained in nonmagical accounts that would not frighten anyone, or provoke a cynical, disbelieving reaction. Then the Stamparas would take the next boat to the Continent and a train to Venice.

"We shall calibrate reality and acceptable levels of magic to a nicety," promised Alberto, "as if we measured them in a test tube."

Lussa added, "And London's own Magic is stirring again after all these Years of Suppression. I speak not just of the Ghosts coming out of the Arches to save the City. There's a Scottish Writer, one Mr. Barrie, at work upon a Tale of Mischief & Enchantment set in Kensington Gardens."

"Excellent news!" exclaimed Renzo and Pylorus simultaneously.

"But them good ghosts is goin' to stay inside the arches, hain't they?" asked Pylorus. "'Cos otherways the Ghost-Convicts would be getting out too, seeing as 'ow they is plugged in there by the good ones. I been lookin' close, and you kin see them spirits all flattened an' pressed agin the blackened bits o' the arches."

"Fortunately Humanfolk rarely look close, Pylorus," Lussa replied. "The Ghosts would be Disturbed only if London took it upon Herself to clean those dirty Arches, dislodging the Soot of Decades."

"An' after all the money wot's been spent on the funeral of Her Late Majesty," said Turtledove, "there woan be any funds for cleanin' up the town, not for an age. An' there's more good news, Yer Wetness. Pylorus, show 'em today's *Times*."

It was noted, in a small paragraph on the third page, **Harold Hoskins, cousin to the late Queen, has been escorted to a Royal Navy vessel and is returning to the island of Hooroo to resume his duties as Governor of His Majesty's penal colony. The King has been pleased to confirm that the appointment has been made "for life."**

"Then London is Safe for Life," confirmed Lussa. "And a Handful of our Incogniti shall remain in the City to ensure that All is Well."

Uncle Tommaso smiled at Renzo. "This is where I belong now."

"But is home to Venice, yes, for me," said Signor Alicamoussa. "For nothing could be sweeter or more intense than the longing I have to set eyes on my own galumptious girl again. Do you ever get the feelings that a wombat is lodged himself in your throat-parts? Is how I feel when away from my wife too long." He winked.

Turtledove embraced each of the Venetian sailors in a meaty hug that lasted almost longer than any of them could hold their breath.

55. The Commodious Compendium

homeward bound, aboard the Scilla, *February 7–18, 1901*

"**A** lovely long sea," commented Teo, looking down on the unvarying blue rollers. The wind filled the belly-parts of the sails like a light yet satisfying meal. A week of stormless weather, with a sense of anticipation and warmth in the air, had so far made for pleasant voyaging.

Yet the return journey felt so much slower than the voyage out. Without the Sorcerer's four magical winds, the *Scilla* seemed to be making inching progress.

How impatient were the young sailors to return to Venice!

But how afraid that they might not reach home alive.

For the coral necklaces around their necks were changing color. No one wanted to mention it, but all of them were slowing down. It now took Sebastiano twenty minutes to tie a simple knot. Emilio gazed at the charts for long minutes without being able to focus on them. Giovanni stirred the soup in slower and slower circles. Cookie had taken to his bunk. Most of the Incogniti lay palely on the decks, hardly able to feed themselves.

Renzo blamed the noxious fumes emanating from the bilge

water that swilled around the boat, entering through the cracks made when the *Scilla* was squeezed between the tentacles of the colossal squid. The sailors roused themselves to bail out as much of the foul liquid as they could. Yet they soon lapsed back into apathy.

Teo felt it first in her shoulders: a sense of dragging downward. It seemed too much effort even to sit up straight. She longed for her hammock. But when she got there she still felt as if the dead weight of her dissolved energy was pulling the canvas down from its hooks. It became too much trouble even to speak.

"It is the Half-Dead disease." She forced herself to face it. "We must have been infected when we fought with the Ghost-Convicts."

As it developed, the symptoms of the Half-Dead disease resembled those of scurvy, the old curse of sailors miles from shore and without fresh fruit and vegetables. Their mouths grew sore: their gums swelled around the roots of their teeth. All had the filthiest breath, no matter how often they brushed their bleeding teeth with birch twigs. Every limb ached. Their arms and feet moved feebly. Their bodies were covered with bluish and reddish spots. No one wanted to eat: it was too painful.

On the morning of February 14, Teo opened her mouth to clean her aching teeth. The first touch of the birch stick burst her gum, releasing a stream of black and putrid blood.

As Teo returned dizzily to her hammock, she wondered about Sibella.

Sibella still minced about the deck, pert and proud in her fine clothes. She alone had not succumbed to the Half-Dead disease. So did Sibella really have the cure for it, as she claimed? Or—Teo bolted upright—did the girl perhaps even cause it? Could Sibella be stealing the blood of healthy people to keep her alive? Were the leeches . . . ?

"Of course! The *leeches*!" Teo exclaimed aloud, holding her hot head. Despite Teo's vociferous misgivings, Sibella had been permitted to keep her pets and her pillow box and her private cabin. Teo herself slept down with the boys in what increasingly resembled a hospital bay.

Fabrizio had joked, "Let Sibella keep the leeches! They're her only friends, apart from Renzo. Who can she send messages to now?"

Teo rolled out of the hammock. She staggered from wall to wall all the way to Sibella's cabin. She burst in without knocking.

A wet-eyed Renzo was kneeling on the floor, as Sibella announced tragically, "But my heart is as lead."

So this was how Renzo was spending Valentine's Day!

Teo could not keep her temper any longer. "Oh, avast with all the feminine vapors, Sibella! *You* should walk the plank!" she shouted. "You're not saving us from the Half-Dead disease with your stupid necklaces!" Teo ripped hers off her burning neck and flung it against the wall. "No! It is *you* who's been spreading it! You've found a way to make your disgusting hemophilia contagious. By using your leeches and worts."

Renzo stood up unsteadily. His color was high, his eyes feverish. "Teo, you're delirious. Go back and lie down. I'll bring you a *tisana*."

Ignoring him, Teo lowered her voice dramatically. "I've worked it all out, Sibella. You want the *Scilla* to be a ship of corpses by the time it reaches Venice!

"I'll bet you creep down to our cabin in the night and put those leeches on us . . . and let them suck on us. . . ." Teo wiped droplets of sweat from her brow, but nothing, not even her dizziness, would make her stop now. "And then, and then . . . you replace our blood . . . with some kind of poison. It must be you! You have your father's bad blood. He might have gone back to Hooroo, but *you're* still acting out his dastardly plot, aren't you? Aren't you? And tell me this—*why won't you ever let me read your heart?*"

Teo jabbed a shaking finger toward Sibella's chest. The girl took a step backward, tripped over one of her fur boots, and stumbled against a low beam. She cried out, putting her hand to her head. It came away bright with red blood.

Teo was barely conscious of Renzo's hiss of intaken breath. Fabrizio had followed her into the cabin, sensing trouble. He whistled. "Will Sibella bleed to death now? I'm going to get Signor Alicamoussa!"

Renzo's voice was harsh with fear. "I don't understand you, Teo. You spared Bajamonte Tiepolo, and yet you don't scruple to cause the death of an innocent girl." He turned away from her. "Sibella," he pleaded, "is there anything that can be done for you?"

"No," replied Sibella with tragic resignation. "I await my fate. I just hope it will be quick."

Signor Alicamoussa rushed into the cabin with the London mermaids' COMMODIOUS CABINET FOR PATENT NOSTRUMS under his arm.

"*Teodora mia,*" he said regretfully, "I know you are comfoozled by her, yet was it really necessary to go the whole animal on this diseased child?"

He busied himself with the COMMODIOUS CABINET, asking Sibella, "What are your deathly symptoms? Do youse have the not-far-from-the-chamber-pots? Are youse qualmish in the belly parts?"

Teo's eyes ran blurrily over the word "COMMODIOUS" painted on the cabinet. It was at that moment that the page of the book that Teo had wanted to consult all these weeks finally flashed up involuntarily in her mind. It was page 245 of *Diseases of Childhood, 1889, a Commodious Compendium for Caring Parents*. She had memorized that book several years ago, lying in bed afflicted with the mumps.

And there it was on page 245, the one fact that revealed the great lie of Sibella's existence and identity. Teo read aloud: "'Females may carry the hemophilia gene to the next generation, yet they do not suffer from its fatal symptoms themselves.'"

"Beg yours?" whispered Signor Alicamoussa.

Fabrizio shouted, "I *knew* it! I *always* thought it was strange. Why should a girl with a dangerous blood disease want to play with leeches, of all things? It was obvious; we just couldn't see it."

Surprisingly, Teo's first emotion on hearing her own words aloud was pity for Sibella. She spoke slowly: "You were never sick. But you were told that you were by those who were supposed to take care of you, in order to keep you frightened and passive, and to make you act as a spy."

Signor Alicamoussa whispered, "Now the *gatto* is out of the *sacco!*"

Sibella sank to the floor. The blood on her hand was already dry—it had clotted perfectly well. She looked at the rusty stain on her skin, and then at Teo, and back at her hand again. She opened her mouth, but could not speak.

"I suppose," thought Teo, "it is a big thing to be given your life back."

And surprisingly, she was happy to have bestowed that gift. Even more so because now Renzo, instead of embracing Sibella, was folding Teo herself in his arms in a long, warm hug. Her dizziness returned. She felt dreadfully hot and cold, as if her skin was a glacier covering a deep vein of hot lava. Renzo too swayed, looking white as mozzarella.

From inside Renzo's arms, Teo cried, "The fact that Sibella's not a hemophiliac means she really *was* as much the victim of Miss Uish and Bajamonte Tiepolo and her horrible father as any of us!"

Renzo added in a muffled voice, "And it also means that Harold Hoskins double-crossed Il Traditore. He gave him a hostage for whom he cared absolutely nothing. The cruel hemophilia trick proves that. Harold Hoskins never intended to keep his promise to attack Venice!"

Signor Alicamoussa said wonderingly, "So the Pretender played dingo on his Signor Pipistrelly! Infamous doings all round!"

"And even more infamous," answered Renzo sadly, "is that *we* have the Pretender's vile Half-Dead disease."

"You don't have to," said Sibella.

The Venetians looked up, a faint hope stirring in their slow-beating hearts.

"Are you really an enchantress?" asked Fabrizio. Sibella shook her head.

Renzo urged, "Sibella, did they give you some secret recipe for curing the disease? In case you contracted it yourself while you were a hostage?"

She nodded. "Please bring me my leeches. And some lemons. And a mortar and pestle."

"So that's what you were doing when I saw you in your cabin?" Teo asked.

"I'd been told to make them excited before I crushed them. The blood is better aerated." Sibella screwed up her pretty face.

Now all the sailors lined up to swallow spoonfuls of the medicine Sibella prepared using extracts of leech and citrus. Within a few hours, the pink was starting to return to their cheeks and their swollen gums were less excruciating to the touch.

"Let the rest of those nice little leeches stay up on deck," suggested Teo generously. "Give them a bit of fresh air, do!"

It was then that Sibella confided her deepest ambition. "I never wanted to learn wortcunning and leechcraft at all. They made me do that . . . they threatened. . . . I don't like magic! I hate insects! I detest everything slimy! I just want to be a dressmaker. It's all I ever wanted. Yet no matter how much I begged, they never let me touch a needle, because of the hemophilia they were pretending that I had. I just wanted a haberdashery cabinet, not a pillow box, you know, with cotton reels, egg-eyed needles, *Ne Plus Ultra* pins, marking cotton, mending cotton, enamel-lined thimbles, pearl buttons . . . a crystallized metal needle mill . . ."

Sibella's voice grew dreamy. Signor Alicamoussa chortled approvingly, "Is no snoot to her at all now! A seamstress will suit nicely. And look at youse soft-hearted boys! Not a dry nose in the house!"

"There's a convent on Giudecca where the orphan girls are

403

taught exquisite needlework," Renzo said. "They make the wedding dresses for all the high society in Venice. We know the Abbess at the House of the Spirits. She will arrange everything in a moment, won't she, Teo?"

"Wedding dresses!" marveled Sibella. "With guipure lace and insertions . . . ?"

"All that." Teo smiled. "Valenciennes edging, duchesse flouncing and all the novelties in veils. Ruching of tulle and satin ribbon. Broussa brocade. Genoa velvet with a glacé frill. Plus, I think we've a new best friend for you."

"Maria?" Renzo smiled. A boarder at the Giudecca convent, Maria was every bit as interested in fashion as Sibella was, and possibly even more expert.

"So you won't hand me over to the Mayor and have me put on trial when we get to Venice?"

"Of course not," said Teo stoutly. "You've lived your trial already. It's time someone was kind to you. And no one knows how to be kind like Venetian nuns, let me tell you."

All at once, Sibella's perfect porcelain skin grew blotchy. Her lovely blue eyes screwed up. Her poised shoulders crumpled.

Teo rushed over and put her arms around the girl.

"Sibella," she observed softly, "at a moment like this, it would be detestably banal *not* to cry."

"Is there a Young Master or a Miss Alicamoussa?" asked Sibella, sewing away, seated cross-legged on the scuttlebutt.

Signor Alicamoussa looked sad, a feat he managed picturesquely. "My wife, Mercer, and myself have been blessed with infant squirrels, lion cubs and even bare-eyed cockatoo chicks, yes. Yet thus far our fecundity does not extend to human progeny of our own."

Sibella nodded toward the Venetian sailors clustered fondly around him.

"I'd say these boys would rather have no other father but you, sir. Given a choice."

"Ah," sighed Signor Alicamoussa, "that possibility is tempting as a dripping honeycomb to a spiny anteater, yes. Yet I am not adopterating any boy, not without that boy being agreeable to it."

The sailors rushed to enfold the circus-master in a wordless hug.

Signor Alicamoussa burst into tears of delight. Instead of growing red-nosed and swollen-lidded, he simply looked even more dazzling than usual: his blue eyes glowing like dewy sapphires and his skin blooming a fresh rose color. "And nor shall they have any other father," he declared. "Why, I already nourish the most hopeful hope! The Mayor shall be made to sign over these children to us."

Renzo raised his eyebrows. "The Mayor?"

"Ah, but Mercer shall see to it upon the instant. My wife has the *lingua biforcuta*, the forked tongue. If anyone razzles her ribbon, it is as well to advise everyone in the vicinity to lie down in the dry grass and watch for the fireworks. No, I do not see the Mayor presenting any difficulties when she gives him her gobful."

The sailors threw their hats in the air and cheered.

"Now," asked Signor Alicamoussa, "where's the bunting? Is it already forgotten, everything our dear Professor Marìn taught youse? Reckon that remembering him is how we'll keep the dear fellow alive! When a ship returns home victorious, she should be snickered out in every color. Let's see the *Scilla* dressed to the nines, yes!"

Renzo and Teo shared the predawn watch. The remnants of Miss Uish's clothes were festooned on every pole from the bowsprit to the sternpost. "More colorful than a corroboree frog in the mating season," as Signor Alicamoussa put it. The wind riffled through them now, so that they sparkled like tinsel in the moonlight. How the sailors had enjoyed ripping those dresses and petticoats into rags! Then Sibella had set to, sewing them into neat bunting as deftly as if she'd been born with a needle in her hand.

Teo checked the barometer—without Sofonisba to predict the weather with her tail, the *Scilla*'s sailors had to rely on the glass. The pressure was rising fast. Teo was already looking forward to interviewing a kitten for ship's cat when they arrived home. She'd been promised the choice of the most seaworthy felines.

From the way that Renzo was kicking the companionway and avoiding her eyes, Teo guessed he had something to say to her.

"Teo, you know I didn't really care for Sibella ever. Not in *that* way. I was just being a gentleman. It is a gentleman's duty . . ."

"What were you doing on your knees in Sibella's cabin on Valentine's Day then? Your duty?"

"Oh, Teo, no! It's not what you imagine at all. I was sick—as sick as you were. She'd called me in to ask me about her trial in Venice. She was suddenly terrified that her father would somehow hear about it—and of what would happen if he found out that she was alive after all, and in Venice. I found myself asking if she really loved her father. And she said no, he'd sent her away to the Swiss finishing school when she was a baby, had refused to let her know who her mother was and so, as far as he was concerned . . ."

" 'My heart is as lead,' is what she said," Teo recalled. Yet she could not resist adding, "I hate to remind you, Renzo, but *rhapso-domancy*??!"

Renzo blushed like a Sicilian tomato. "Perhaps I did lose my head *slightly*. But when I saw Sibella so composed, so lacking in any emotion . . ."

"Like a beautiful icicle?"

"I realized that I enjoyed myself more with . . ."

"Untidy, clumsy, emotional . . ."

"Argumentative . . ."

"Venetian . . ."

"*People*," concluded Renzo.

The horizon stirred with the faintest of gray light. Soon it would be dawn. Guttering night-lights spat quietly in the lanterns on the companionway. Just before the last one extinguished itself with a sigh, Renzo held out his hand and Teo took it.

The bell towers of Venice stood like pale pencils on the distant horizon as the *Scilla* plowed past the islands of the lagoon. Everyone leaned over the taffrail, eagerly breathing in the faint woody smoke of Venice's chimneys. Just an hour away were the streets where they had once played; the home of Mercer and

Sargano Alicamoussa, where they would now live; Ca' Foscari University, which Teo and Renzo hoped to attend; the Archives, where Teo one day planned to work; and the canals, where Renzo would follow his father's and *all* his grandfathers' profession of gondolier.

The lagoon in no way resembled the frozen wasteland they had left on their journey to London. The mantles of ice had slipped from the islands of the *barene*. Tips of green pushed up through the dark earth.

Over a loud quacking and flapping of wings, Giovanni called, "And look, the *alzavole* have come back! That must mean winter is nearly over."

Indeed, the ice was breaking up. The *Scilla* steered a careful clattering course between translucent sheets that were slowly melting as they drifted toward the deep sea.

Teo was worried. "If the ice is melting, then the Vampire Eels will be set free. You know they prey on . . . mermaids. What if Lussa and Flos . . . ?"

"The mermaids knew what was awaiting them in these waters," Renzo reminded her. "No more ambushes, except of the Eels by the mermaids, perhaps."

"Look, marsh marigolds are blooming!" Teo pointed to a tiny island. "The first sign of spring!"

"Don't you mean *la calta*, Teo? We are free to use the Venetian words again."

"And don't they feel good on the tongue? Can you see the *salice?*—the catkins are blossoming like white stars!" Teo turned to Renzo, "Let's stop and pick some. We'll be passing San Michele very soon. We can take them to your mother's grave."

Officer Gianni had been true to his word: he must have gone to the funeral that the Mayor had prevented Renzo from attending. For it was the little bunch of violets, carved and painted by Renzo, that helped them find his mother's tomb among the hundreds of fresh mounds of the ice flood's victims. The violets were carefully placed beside a simple stone that read *Vittoria Antonello, January 1868—Christmas 1900.*

Seeing Renzo's anguished face, Teo asked, "Do you need to be alone awhile, Renzo? To say goodbye properly?"

He nodded gratefully. Teo squeezed his shoulder. "You know where I'll be."

Walking east and then south, Teo found and then parted the bushes that hid the graves of her real parents, Marta and Daniele Gasperin, murdered by Bajamonte Tiepolo when she was still a baby. She kissed the cold stone, and laid a *calta* upon it. Then she placed her hand on the grave and pressed it there, closing her eyes and listening intently. Once, she had felt the stone heartbeat of the statue of Signor Rioba. Perhaps . . . ? But that was back when she'd had the comforting weight of *The Key to the Secret City* in her pinafore, and everything had seemed possible.

"We've lost so much," she murmured sadly, thinking of Renzo's mother, Professor Marìn, the wrecked streets of Venice, and the magical book that had led her and Renzo into and out of so many perils.

Suddenly, Renzo was at her side, his eyes still wet, but his face composed.

"What do you think it will be like, living with Signor Alicamoussa's menagerie?" he asked her in a bravely neutral tone of voice.

"Noisy," answered Teo. "But his wife, Mercer, is exceedingly clever, they say. She's writing a novel, you know. It will be fun to talk English with her. And I expect you'll travel with the menagerie. Go back to London, even. I wish I could . . ."

"Your adopted parents are not going to give you up again."

"They're Incogniti now. They'll understand if I ever have to . . ."

"Save Venice again?"

The coracle slipped back toward the *Scilla*.

They were almost alongside when Fabrizio called down from the crow's nest. "What's that, in the water? Behind you! Something swimming."

Renzo and Teo blanched. The last time something had swum toward them in this stretch of the lagoon, it had been a pack of Bajamonte Tiepolo's sharks. They stared anxiously behind them. Something was ruffling the surface of the water, just below it.

Fabrizio shouted, "I should just about think . . . but I don't believe . . . the thing is, it looks like . . . *a book*."

Teo peered down into the green-purple water. A leather-bound volume was propelling itself toward them, opening and closing its pages like a creamy butterfly.

Signor Alicamoussa's joyous face appeared over the taffrail. "I think youse'll find that's not just any old book, *ragazzi*. Pearler!"

"The Key to the Secret City!" breathed Teo. "It's found us again. It *knew* we'd come to visit your mother."

Renzo stood up, flung off his jacket and dived.

"Renzo!" screamed Teo. He was, like many Venetians, a remarkably poor swimmer, and the water was as yet only slightly less cold than solid ice. Teo kicked off her shoes and dived in after him.

Renzo, struggling to keep his head above the water, was already cradling the book in his arms. "It is *The Key*!" His teeth chattered inside his smiling mouth. "It really, really is."

"Let's get it out of the water and see what it says!"

Teo was half eager and half afraid. *The Key* had always written its very specific, though sometimes mysterious, instructions for them upon its blank pages. Those instructions had already led them into encounters with a cannibal butcher, a headless Doge and a number of hungry winged lions, not to mention Bajamonte Tiepolo himself.

"I suppose we'll open it and it'll say, 'Well done, Undrowned Child! Fine work, Studious Son! Now go and have a good long rest.' " Renzo's smile was perhaps a tiny bit smug as he hauled himself up the *Scilla*'s ladder with *The Key* under his arm.

"Only one way to see," said Teo with a grin, climbing up behind him. Seizing the book, she spread it out on top of the water barrel and opened to the first page.

"Oh, gristle and guts!" she exclaimed.

What is true, and what's made up?

Bajamonte Tiepolo

The life of Bajamonte Tiepolo, the Venetian Traitor, is explored more fully in my previous book, *The Undrowned Child* (see undrownedchild.com). After a failed conspiracy against the Venetian state in 1310, the real Bajamonte Tiepolo, a proud nobleman, was sent into perpetual exile, his *palazzo* was razed, and a Column of Infamy was erected to his eternal dishonor. He spent the rest of his life plotting against Venice. In *The Undrowned Child*, however, he is murdered by a state assassin, and his ghost returns nearly six hundred years later to wreak revenge on the city that humiliated him.

The *Scilla*

There really was a floating orphanage in Venice called the *Scilla*.

The philanthropist David Levi Morenos came up with the idea of "converting a warship into a peaceful shelter for the orphaned sons of seafarers and to educate them in the traditional profession of their family." I took the liberty of setting my story a few years earlier than the real foundation date of June 1906.

The original *Scilla* was an old gray-painted sailing ship. Boys were usually taken in at the age of seven, and "graduated" when they had learned all the skills necessary to gain employment as merchant sailors, naval mechanics or fishermen.

The first intake was just half a dozen. By 1922, there were 102 boys living on board, while seventy-two younger children were housed in dormitories on shore at San Raffaele, not far from the Zattere, where the *Scilla* was originally moored.

Aboard, the young sailors slept in double rows of hammocks hung from metal frames and poles. They rose at five-thirty a.m., winter and summer. They tidied up their hammocks and washed ten at a time in big tubs (so in reality Teo would have had problems concealing her identity!). The boys then washed their underwear in the same water.

By day they learned practical skills, such as how to climb the masts and riggings, how to unfurl and refold the sails, and how to keep watch. Or they went to the classrooms at San Raffaele for the more conventional aspects of their education.

Breakfast was bread and milk, but boys who had misbehaved were deprived of one or the other: they were allowed to choose. Lunch was served in metal mess tins, and consisted of pasta or soup and some meat. Dinner was polenta, beans and dried cod. The only drink served was water. There was no heating.

By 1920, the *Scilla* had become too dilapidated for service. She was broken up and another vessel was commissioned to replace her.

For much of the information about the *Scilla*, I am indebted to an excellent and beautifully illustrated book, *La Scuola del Mare*, edited by Samuele Costantini and published by l'Assessorato all'Educazione e all'Edilizia scolastica, Provincia di Venezia, 2009.

Nestle Tripe

Nestle Tripe or nestle-tripe is an old slang expression for the weakest fledgling in the nest; it has also been applied to human children, usually to the last-born or weakest sibling.

Queen Victoria's Life and Death

Queen Victoria was born on May 24, 1819, and died on January 22, 1901. The last few weeks of her life were very much as described in this book, although I have telescoped certain events. In fact, the first day Queen Victoria did not leave her bed at all was probably January 16, 1901.

For the purposes of this story I have overemphasized the Queen's snobbishness. No doubt Queen Victoria was once a little girl with imaginings and fears like any other. Her childhood was curtailed by the responsibilities of being a princess, which she took very seriously. And the joy went out of her life with the death of her adored husband, Albert. Queen Victoria certainly did not regard all her foreign subjects as savages. She even learned Hindustani and apparently enjoyed curry.

Queen Victoria withdrew totally from public life for only around four years after Albert's death. In 1866, she opened Parliament and thereafter attended quite a few public functions. But she loved best of all to live in retirement at Balmoral or Osborne.

Each royal residence was a knicknackatorium of funereal ornaments. The Queen would not inhabit any room without a crepe-draped portrait or somber marble bust of her darling Albert. She kept a large hand-colored photograph of his corpse above her bed wherever she slept.

The Pretender

It is true that there are people other than the current royal family with claims to the British throne. The rules of succession state that the crown must pass to a "legitimate" heir: born when his or her parents were legally married to one another.

Recently, a historian has claimed that historical documents show that Edward IV was not in fact legitimate. By that reasoning, the current claimant to the throne is Michael Abney-Hastings, fourteenth Earl of Loudoun, who emigrated to Australia in 1960. He is related to Lady Flora Hastings, a girl badly treated by Queen Victoria and those close to her, who wrongly accused the unmarried lady-in-waiting of a secret pregnancy. Flora Hastings died soon afterward of cancer. The public was enraged at the court's slander of the innocent girl, and this led to an assassination attempt upon the Queen.

However, the Earl of Loudoun has specifically stated that he has no wish to pursue his claims. And, of course, the events of this story, including the Ghost-Convicts, the island of Hooroo and the whole Pretender plot against London and the British throne, are completely fictitious. Transportation of convicts to Australia had stopped by 1868.

Hemophilia

Hemophilia is a serious disease in which blood fails to clot; a wound will bleed without stopping. Consequently, sufferers can bleed to death from internal injuries caused by a very tiny impact.

Hemophilia is passed down through a family. Normally only boys inherit the disease—a mother can carry it in her blood but not actually become ill. Very rarely is a girl severely affected, and only then if both parents carry the disease in their blood.

Queen Victoria was a carrier. One of her sons, Leopold, was a hemophiliac. Three of her grandsons and six of her great-grandsons also suffered from the disease.

In 1900, hemophilia was untreatable. Early blood transfusions were dangerous, especially for children, because scientists had not yet discovered how to separate out the component that aids the clotting of the blood. Large infusions of blood easily overloaded the systems of patients and were sometimes fatal. Only in the 1960s was a means found to separate the missing hemophilia factor (known as Factor VIII) from frozen blood plasma. Within ten years, this Factor VIII concentrate was being used to treat hemophiliacs all over the world.

Heavy Winters and Floods in Venice
The Grand Canal has frozen over quite a few times. In the eighteenth century, horse races and festivals were held on the ice. The best-documented modern freeze in Venice is probably that of 1929, of which there are many photographs and even a short film (on www.youtube.com/watch?v=TFz9a66f010).

On December 1, 2008, a disastrously high tide of 160 centimeters was pushed deep into the city by a sirocco. Every part of Venice was underwater that day. People waded around San Marco in water up to their thighs. But the famous flood of 1966 came thirty centimeters higher than that and stayed longer.

The Comune of Venice has set up a website with hundreds of photographs of the terrible flood of 1966. Go to www.albumdivenezia.it and click on *L'album privato dell'alluvione*. Then click on *Sfoglia l'album* (which means "Browse the album").

Mediterranean Monk Seal

These beautiful animals are now very rare: probably just five hundred still exist in the world, in tiny scattered colonies on the coasts of Greece, Croatia, Turkey and North Africa. But once upon a time they could be found in large colonies from North Africa to the Black Sea. The largest of this breed grows to about two meters in length. They are brown or brownish-gray with lighter fur on their bellies.

Food and Drink

Some of the recipes—like Antispasmodic Tea—are adapted from *A Plain Cookery Book for the Working Classes* by Charles Elmé Francatelli, first published in 1852. Others I improvised, using old Italian recipe books. The Australian cake known as the Lamington is named after Charles Wallace Alexander Napier Cochrane-Baillie, second Baron Lamington, who was Governor of Queensland between 1896 and 1901.

A. Hoadley & Company opened a factory in Melbourne in 1889, making jams, jellies and candied peel. I would have loved to include my own childhood favorite, Hoadley's Violet Crumble Bars, in this book, but this chocolate-dipped honeycomb confection was not invented until 1913.

The Name Ongania

I chose this name for Teo because there used to be a very famous bookshop called Libreria Ongania in Venice. It published and sold excellent guidebooks about Venice.

Gold Earrings

A single gold earring was often sported by superstitious sailors in past times. It was thought to improve the eyesight, to prevent rheumatism, to make the bearer lively and to prevent drowning. It was once law in Scotland that every fisherman had to wear a gold earring, which would be used to pay for the cost of his funeral expenses if he drowned and his body was washed up far from his native shores.

The "Cat"

The cat-o'-nine-tails was a whip made of rope. If the rope tails were knotted, it was known as a thieves' cat. The whip was stored in a baize bag, so to "let the cat out of the bag" meant that someone was about to be flogged.

Nautical Knots

Anyone who is interested in knots will enjoy a visit to netknots .com, where clever animations show you how to tie most of the knots mentioned in this book.

Giant Squid

Rumors of giant squid were rife for centuries. The creatures featured in maritime legends and novels—such as Jules Verne's classic *Twenty Thousand Leagues Under the Sea.*

The first documented sighting of a giant squid was not until 1861. And the squid's existence was not scientifically confirmed until the twentieth century. Even now, very few examples have ever been caught. A ten-meter (thirty-four-foot) squid was found in 2007 near Antarctica. The colossal squid, *Mesonychoteuthis hamiltoni*, was frozen for dissection.

Colossal squid are about the same length as giant squid, *Architeuthis dux*, but are much more substantial. They have eight arms with toothed suckers for grasping and two longer tentacles for catching prey.

Mourning Emporia

Tristesse & Ganorus's Mansion Dolorous is invented, but it is very like two real London *magasins de deuil*, or mourning warehouses. Jay's London General Mourning Warehouse opened at 247 and 249 Regent Street in 1841. Peter Robinson's Court and General Mourning Warehouse was founded in the same street in the 1850s. Harrods too had a large mourning department, including coffins, gravestones and every possible item of funerary fashion.

The rules of mourning were strictly observed in society. Briefly, a widow was expected to wear mourning for two years; the mother of a dead child, or a bereaved child, twelve months. A dead sibling required six months' mourning. But the etiquette and society magazines argued obsessively about the minor details of even these matters.

Naturally, Queen Victoria's death provoked a final run on the mourning emporia. On the days after her funeral, many people wore black. On the day of the funeral itself, it was hard to see anyone not dressed in mourning "weeds" among the crowds in London and Windsor. Queen Victoria herself, however, had specified funeral decorations in purple and white.

Quack Medicines for Ladies

It's hard to believe, but the names of all the medicines used by the London mermaids were actual preparations on the market in Victorian times or earlier. The claims and catchphrases that accompanied them were also used by their manufacturers.

Dangerous drugs were often the core ingredients of medicines with innocent and picturesque names. The hazardous substances were disguised with sugar. Many people became addicted to these medicines without having the least idea that they contained intoxicating drugs or large amounts of alcohol.

Chameleon oil was advertised exactly as the London mermaids describe it, and was for sale by post from an address in London at the beginning of the twentieth century. Analysis by the British Medical Association showed that it contained oils of turpentine, camphor, mustard, pimento and spearmint in a solution of alcohol and water. No chameleons.

Corsets

Each age has contrived tortures to "improve" the natural lines of the female body. Victorian women were supposed to be shaped like hourglasses, a form painfully achieved by the use of corsets. Some quack doctors saw an opportunity for marketing corsets with "healing" properties at a higher price. The Harness Constrictive belts worn by the London mermaids in this book were actual products called Electropathic Corsets, and were extensively advertised.

Treadmills
Treadmills were banned in Great Britain by an act of Parliament in 1898.

Tower Bridge
This structure, despite its Gothic appearance, opened only in 1894. So many tall-masted ships went under it during that period that it was forced to open up 655 times in the first month, allowing tall-masted vessels into the so-called Pool of London, between Tower and London Bridges. (St. Mary Overie Dock is on the other side of the relatively low London Bridge, so technically it would have been impossible for a masted ship like the *Scilla* to get there, even with the damage she sustains. However, the *Scilla* does many things that ordinary vessels could not, so I considered this a valid liberty to take.)

Venetian Pumpkin-Sellers in London
Hot sliced pumpkin was a traditional Venetian street snack. I invented the Venetian pumpkin-sellers in London. But at the time this book is set, Londoners were accustomed to the sight of Italian street musicians, acrobats and vendors of hot potatoes, chestnuts and particularly ice cream.

The first Italians arrived in Britain in the wake of the Napoleonic wars. By the middle of the nineteenth century, they had settled in large communities in London, as well as in major Scottish cities.

In London, the two biggest clusters of Italians were to be found in Soho, where they worked in the food trades, and in the Hatton Garden/Saffron Hill area around Holborn. Here Italians rented houses that they sublet to their countrymen, cramming in as many people as possible. And it was here that the *padroni* brought the young boys and girls they recruited from the poor areas of Italy. These children came principally from Emilia and Tuscany in the early part of the Victorian period, and later, from farther south.

The most visible (and audible) occupation of the London Italians was as itinerant musicians: of the two thousand living in London in 1860, six hundred worked as organ-grinders. They strolled the streets playing hand organs, violins and harps. Some rented performing animals from their *padroni* in exchange for their day's takings. Writers recorded seeing small Italian boys with white mice, squirrels, monkeys, dancing dogs in costumes and even a porcupine.

The noise made by these street performers enraged many Londoners, particularly the inhabitants of the prosperous inner-city suburbs. Campaigns against them were launched, and even legislation. In fact, by the end of the century, more and more Italian musicians were returning to their traditional trades: as glassblowers, pictureframers, and makers of mirrors, musical instruments, barometers and thermometers. Immigrants from Tuscany were especially known for making and selling religious figurines. Others entertained with puppets called *fantoccini*.

Italians were also famous for their ice cream: in 1860 around two hundred were working in the trade, selling ice cream in small glasses (in portions called penny-licks) or in paper wraps, known as hokey-pokeys. This expression comes from the Italian *ecco un poco*—"here, [try] a bit." Unfortunately, the confections were sometimes made with unsanitary water and could cause serious sickness.

The Italian Benevolent Society was set up in 1860, to help the gangs of children brought over to London. There were instances of the *padroni* starving and beating their young charges. If found guilty of begging and vagrancy, Italian children were repatriated to Italy. There were also Italian social clubs, an Italian Free School and even an Italian newspaper, *La Gazzetta Italiana di Londra.*

Venice was never a big exporter of people to London. But, interestingly, research by Venetian historian Lucio Sponza shows that between 1900 and 1902, the number suddenly jumped from fourteen to 129. I'm happy to claim some of those extras as my Venetian pumpkin-sellers, the Incogniti.

London Ghosts

As described in this book, some Victorian spiritualists hosted profitable séances around tables at which ghosts allegedly spoke or "rapped."

When Lussa refers to the rebirth of London magic, she is, of course, alluding to J. M. Barrie's Peter Pan, who first appeared shortly after the time when this book is set. The stage play, *Peter Pan, or The Boy Who Wouldn't Grow Up,* had its debut on December 27, 1904, at the Duke of York's Theatre. The character had earlier appeared in an adult novel, *The Little White Bird,* in 1902.

London Transport

At the beginning of the twentieth century, London buses, trams and cabs were all still horse-drawn. The two-story London omnibuses were introduced in 1897. By 1901, there were over 3,700 horse-drawn omnibuses in London, each needing eleven horses a day to keep it running. The roads were crowded with all kinds of vehicles, such as hansom cabs and growlers, sometimes slowing traffic to a standstill.

An earlier Prime Minister, Benjamin Disraeli, once referred to hansom cabs as the gondolas of London.

Provisions from Harrods
All the Harrods products mentioned in this book are to be found in the Harrods Catalogue for 1895, a book as stout as the Bible, and which includes pictures.

Mendicity Officers
The London Society for the Suppression of Mendicity was formed in 1818 to combat begging in the streets. The sad stories of the London street children were all taken from research into social conditions of that time. That awful statistic of one child dying of hunger in Victorian London every hour is, very unfortunately, true.

Newgate and Executions
The French writer Flora Tristan, who visited in the 1830s, described it thus: "Newgate has a singularly repulsive appearance: it is how one would imagine a prison of the Dark Ages."

The punishments that awaited convicted pirates in London were just as described in this book. In earlier times, notorious buccaneers like Captain Kidd were hanged at Execution Dock on the Thames. Three tides were allowed to flow over their corpses before they were removed to unmarked graves, or sent off for dissection by the anatomists.

Public executions at Newgate ended in 1868, and the condemned were thereafter hanged in an enclosure. James Billington and his son William were the last Newgate executioners. Naturally, they never tried to prolong the death of a prisoner. In any case, for this story, the hooded executioner is a minion of Bajamonte

Tiepolo who has taken over the role temporarily. I imagine the poor Billingtons bound and gagged in a cellar that day. . . .

In fact, children had not been hanged at Newgate for many years. Indeed, after 1899, British children were no longer sent to adult prisons.

The last execution of an adult prisoner took place in May 1902. The prison was demolished later that year. The current Old Bailey law courts were built on the site, reusing some of the prison's stones.

Backbent Castle in Scotland is an invention.

Casanova's Escape from Prison

Giacomo Casanova—alchemist, writer, gambler, lover, violinist—was one of Venice's most famous sons. His life spanned three-quarters of the eighteenth century and the whole of Europe. Naturally, Renzo, as a Venetian, would know all about Casanova and his exploits. In the 1750s, Casanova was confined in the "Leads"—a prison above the Doges' Palace. It was so named because the roofs above the cells were made of lead, so they were sweltering in the summer and freezing in the winter. But the resourceful Casanova found that the ceiling was the cell's weak point and escaped, just as Renzo does in this book. Sadly for him, Casanova was thereafter forced to spend most of the rest of his life in exile from his beloved Venice. Renzo will be more fortunate.

English Bulldogs

No one could call the classic English bulldog beautiful. It has a strikingly massive head and heavy shoulders, ears set high up on the skull and eyes very widely spaced on either side of a deep jaw.

Despite their formidable appearance, English bulldogs are

believed to be very gentle with children. They appear to enjoy human affection and attention. They are also very good swimmers.

At the time when this story is set, the bulldog was a popular breed, with nearly two thousand registered in Great Britain. They had come to be seen as an embodiment of the indomitable and steadfast nature of the British.

Their name comes from an old practice of using them to attack tethered bulls for sport. Bulldogs were trained to jump up and attack the sensitive muzzles of the bulls. Incredibly, it was believed by some people that beef was neither soft enough nor healthy to eat unless it had been "tenderized" like this. The cruel sport was outlawed in 1835.

When I was researching a completely different book, I was charmed by the memoirs of Agnes Hunt, published in 1935. She had a bulldog called Turtledove, and since this name expresses well the unexpected gentleness of the breed, I decided to use it too.

Teddy Bears
Of course Mr. Tristesse is absolutely wrong about toy bears. From their introduction in 1903, teddy bears were to prove extremely popular. There's even a black mourning bear at the Museum of Childhood at Bethnal Green in London.

Leechcraft and Spreading Pestilence
When deciding what Sibella would do with her leeches, I found useful a book edited by Thomas Oswald Cockayne, called *Leechdoms, Wortcunning, and Starcraft of Early England*. It was published in 1866. "Leechcraft" does not necessarily refer to the slimy little creatures. The alternative meaning of the word is simply doctoring or healing. For centuries, what we call the ring finger was known

as the "leech finger"—possibly because of a vein in it that was supposed to communicate directly with the heart. But, for obvious reasons, I decided to take my leeches literally in this book.

The idea of spreading pestilence by smearing ointment on houses is not new. In *The Betrothed*, one of Italy's most famous historical novels, Alessandro Manzoni refers to the case of the "anointers" of Milan, who were horribly tortured and killed for such a crime. And in fact a Column of Infamy, like Bajamonte Tiepolo's, was erected next to the house of one of the accused, where it stayed until the late eighteenth century. Teo remembers another case, cited in James Grant's book.

Latin
Two of the Roman soldiers' comments were appropriated from Latin literature:

Nocte una quivis vel deus esse potest.
"One night like that can make any man a god."

—Propertius 2.15.40

Dabis, improbe, poenas!
"Cur, you will pay the wages of sin!"

—Virgil, *Aeneid IV*

The Boys and Girls in this Story
There are so many of them in this book that it would be impossible to tell you everything about all of them. But now that the story is finished, I thought you might be interested to know more. You can read their biographies and see some photographs on the website: michellelovric.com/children/mournemphome.htm

Acknowledgments

The first people to thank are the two who nurtured this book into a publishable form: my wonderful editors Fiona Kennedy and Jon Appleton at Orion, and my fantastic agent, Sarah Molloy of A. M. Heath.

If Fiona and Jon parented it, then this book is also well endowed with aunts and uncles, starting with its favorite aunties at the Clink Street Writers' Group: Annabel Chown, Mavis Gregson, Cheryl Moskowitz, Mary Hamer, Ann Vaughan-Williams, Carole DeVaughn, Paola de Carolis, Sarah Salway, Jane Kirwan and Sue Ehrhardt. A special round of applause must go to the poet and wicked mermaid-impersonating aunt Geraldine Paine, and a heartfelt thanks to my *madrina*, Pam Johnson.

More vital advice was offered by Louise Berridge, Jill Foulston and Jeff Cotton, whose website fictionalcities.com is the most inspiring one I know on all things to do with Venice, London and Florence.

The acclaimed London guide Diana Kelsey checked my local history and geography; Colin de Mowbray and Peter Wilson put their weather eyes to the seaworthiness of the nautical parts; Albert

Lovric kept me on the right track with hemophilia and other medical matters; Ornella Tarantola oversaw my Italian; my Latin was checked by my wonderful fellow Orion author Caroline Lawrence (see romanmysteries.com) and James Renshaw from Colet Court Preparatory School. I'm grateful to Giovanna Diana and Valter Paties at the Fondazione Cini in Venice for their aid in researching the *Scilla*. The staff at the London Library and the Wellcome Library were as helpful as ever. I am indebted to Lucio Sponza for information on Italians in London, delivered both personally and found in his fascinating book *Italian Immigrants in Nineteenth-Century Britain: Realities and Images* (Leicester University Press, 1988). My pharmaceutical history was kindly checked by William Helfand; also by Heather Maddin and Briony Hudson at the Royal Pharmaceutical Society of Great Britain. Sergio Grandesso and the whole staff of da Gino in San Vio taught me about the Venetian children's street games.

I've also profited from the enthusiasm and knowledge of Phil and Gillian Tabor, Alberto Toso Fei, Elena Romano and Rosato Frassanito, Susie and Bruno Palmarin, John-Henry and Marilyn Bowden, Wendy and Fred Oliver and Elena Nicolai. And from the encouragement and wisdom of Sybille Siegmund-Stiefenhofer and Claire Bloom.

In July 2009, Nina Douglas at Orion twittered for possible names of London mermaids in this book. So thank you to joby14 for Gloriana and mattlibrarian for Nerolia.

Any inaccuracies or exaggerations in this book are mine alone. But a great many that might have blighted it were hunted down and done away with by Kristina Blagojevitch, Pamela Norris and Meli Pinkertow.

And finally a huge hug to Tony Bird, who has twice waded through dreadful *acqua alta* to bring me succour, eye ointment and throat spray so I could finish the first draft: just one tiny symptom of his chronic rash of kindness.

Michelle Lovric
London
May 2010

Discover how it all began!

Available from Delacorte Press

About the Author

MICHELLE LOVRIC has always lived a waterbound life. She was born by the ocean in Sydney and lived for many years by the sea in Devon, England. Now she divides her time between the palazzo on the Grand Canal in Venice and a Georgian wharf on the Thames in London.

The Mourning Emporium is the companion to Michelle's debut children's novel, *The Undrowned Child*. She is already a successful author of books for adults and has compiled over one hundred anthologies on a wide range of subjects, especially cats. She runs a poetry and fiction workshop and also writes reviews, travel features, and stories . . . always about Venice, of course. You can visit her at michellelovric.com.

September 1991

To Katie —

I should be reading your book.
(Enjoy the waiting; obviously you know
while coming.)

Charlene M Baumbach

Charlene Ann Baumbich

Don't Miss Your Kids!

(they'll be gone
before you know it)

INTERVARSITY PRESS
DOWNERS GROVE, ILLINOIS 60515

InterVarsity Press is the book-publishing division of InterVarsity Christian Fellowship, a student movement active on campus at hundreds of universities, colleges and schools of nursing in the United States of America, and a member movement of the International Fellowship of Evangelical Students. For information about local and regional activities, write Public Relations Dept., InterVarsity Christian Fellowship, 6400 Schroeder Rd., P.O. Box 7895, Madison, WI 53707-7895.

All Scripture quotations, unless otherwise indicated, are from the Holy Bible, New International Version. Copyright © 1973, 1978, International Bible Society. Used by permission of Zondervan Bible Publishers.

Cover illustration: Tim Nyberg

ISBN 0-8308-1331-4

Printed in the United States of America

Library of Congress Cataloging-in-Publication Data

Baumbich, Charlene Ann, 1945-
    Don't miss your kids/Charlene Ann Baumbich.
      p.   cm.
    "Saltshaker books."
    ISBN 0-8308-1331-4
    1. Parenting—Religious aspects—Christianity. 2. Baumbich,
  Charlene Ann, 1945-   . 3. Parents—United States. I. Title.
  BV4529.B38   1991
  649'.7—dc20   90-27667
                                       CIP

15   14   13   12   11   10   9   8   7   6   5   4   3   2   1
03   02   01   00   99   98   97   96   95   94   93   92   91

"Her children arise and call her blessed"
Proverbs 31:28

Dedicated to the
memory of:

My mother
Nellie Ruth Landers Brown
who did not miss her kids.

Acknowledgments

"I thank my God every time I remember you; In all my prayers for all of you, I always pray with joy. . . ."
Philippians 1:3-4

I give paramount thanks to my husband, George, for his divine patience, support and love. Without the unselfish freedom he gave me daily to pursue this labor of love, it wouldn't have happened. God bless him for living with dust balls and eating so many haphazard meals throughout much of this book-writing experience. Truly, many of those hurried casseroles were gross.

To my sons and untiring encouragers, Bret and Brian, I extend heartfelt gratitude. It was when they started calling me "Mom, the writer," that I believed I was one. I'd also like to thank them for supplying me with such good material and bravely allowing me to share it—the good, the bad and the dubious.

Thanks to Rodney Clapp for getting this book started by asking me what was on my mind.

Grateful thanks to Don Stephenson, my "Keep Writin'!" editor, for corralling and channeling what was on my mind—no small task.

His calming approach to my hysterical phone calls, and his sensitivity to my message and struggles were grace upon grace.

Thanks also to:

My father, Victor Wilson Brown, for teaching me to joyfully explore and drink in the world around me;

Mary Gingell for her belief in me, even way back when;

Marlene Fenske for graciously suffering through—by listening to—every trial and triumph along the way;

Mary Beth Elgass for teaching me by Spirit-filled example so much about life;

Al and Barb Unger, Russ and Doris Nelson, and Micky Jackson for celebrating the small victories with me that enabled me to plod on throughout this arduous task;

Jane Scoville for nurturing a budding desire;

Arbor Hill workshop members for their continued and energizing interest in the project;

Elizabeth Cody Newenhuyse and Susan Elizabeth Phillips for their reassurance and mentoring; and

Victor Bianchi at Software City for graciously bailing me out of numerous computer snafus, never once making me feel like the computer stupid I am.

Each behind-the-scenes person at InterVarsity Press who affected this book in one way or another—from the receptionist who fielded my calls, to the artist who symbolized my message, to the person who made sure the last period was in place—has my undying appreciation.

Thanks to countless others who have unknowingly blessed me with a smile or kind word, just when I needed one the most.

To family and friends I give thanks; to God I give the glory.

•

Dear Dixie,

Thanks for the memories.

You turned out to be

the best horse I ever had the

nerve to ride bareback.

Also, you taught me a lot

of good stuff.

•

• *One* •

A Disappearing
Act

Fleeting Time

It was one of the longest mornings in history, even though I am a morning person. I was scared beyond belief. What if I called James's home and he wasn't there?

I could picture his frozen grammar-school body lying in a shallow ditch, somewhere along the two-block path that led from our house to his. Never in my wildest nightmares did I dream my son, along with his best friend, could be responsible for someone's death. "Children Who Kill!" Didn't Oprah do a program on that once?

The morning had started typically enough. I was in the kitchen by myself—always the first to rustle and rise on a Saturday—putting tea water on. It was going to be another gloomy Chicago winter day. Temperatures had dropped to about fifteen below zero during the night. I surveyed our back yard through the kitchen window and pondered how frigid everything looked. The stark, white birch branches appeared brittle, as did the frozen steel pole to the bird feeder.

But things were toasty inside. Visions of Super Mom danced in my head as I decided to make home-made pancakes for my younger son, Brian, and his two sleep-over pals, Bob and James.

I was feeling not only clever but rather perky since I'd had a good night's sleep. Unusual for a sleep-over. It doesn't take much to awaken me; the boys must have conked out early, I suspected.

George shuffled his way into the kitchen. "Boys still sleeping?" he asked.

"I heard some mumbling up there," I answered. "They'll probably be down soon. I'm gonna make pancakes for breakfast." (Tadah!) He instructed me to call him when breakfast was ready, then down the stairs he headed for his weekend rearrange-the-basement project.

It wasn't long before Bob appeared. Probably the rattling of the pans lured him out of his sleeping bag.

"Good morning, Mrs. Baumbich."

"Good morning, Bob." He eyed the box of Bisquick (okay, *almost* home-made pancakes) and the griddle, then pulled out a chair and sat down at the table.

"Sleep well?" I queried. He didn't look like it.

"Okay, I guess." End of discussion. But then how much do sixth-grade boys ever have to say to someone else's mom?

Then Brian came out of his bedroom and headed straight for the floor in front of the living room television. Cartoons. Bob whisked in behind him and draped himself across the couch. I peeked up the stairs to Brian's bedroom door. Thought I'd welcome James to

Saturday morning at the Baumbichs' house, but the door was closed. He must still be sleeping.

About twenty minutes passed and the pancakes hit the table.

"Come and get it, everyone," I hollered into the basement and around the corner, trying to override the cartoon noise. "Somebody go wake up James."

Within a minute everyone was seated at the table. Everyone except James. "Somebody go get James," I repeated.

"He's not here," Brian casually responded.

"He's not here? Where is he?" my husband asked.

"Home," Brian said.

"What in the world time did he call his mother? Before dawn?" I asked.

"He didn't call his mother. He walked home last night. Pass the pancakes," Brian said without missing a beat or batting an eye.

"Walked home! Last night?" I squeaked out. My heart was pounding. "What time? Why?"

"Because I told him to go home," Brian said flatly.

"Good grief, Brian! It's fifteen below zero!"

"So, he had a coat."

"What time did he leave?" George asked. His voice sounded somewhere near the pitch of mine.

"About twelve or one or something. Maybe it was eleven. I don't remember."

"Why did you tell him to leave?" I asked.

"Because he got boogers on my sleeping bag."

By this time I thought I was going to hyperventilate. It was time to stop this discussion and find out if James had made it home. I didn't know whether to get in the car and start cruising the ditches or pick up the phone and call Linda, James's mother.

15

"Call Linda," George said.

"Brian!" I screeched on my way to the phone. "How could you do such a thing? Did James even have a hat? He could be frozen to death somewhere. Were his parents even home?"

Bob sat silent all this while, eyes glued to the empty plate before him.

As I dialed the number, my mind churned along with my stomach. How could I have let this happen? What will Linda think when I call her and ask her if James is home when he's supposed to be at my house? What if he isn't there?

Ring. Ring. Ring. Ring. Ring.

"Hello," a groggy voice finally said.

"Hello. This is Charlene. I can't believe I'm asking you this question," I said, trying to find the courage to get out the words. "Is James home?"

"Yes. He came home in the middle of the night. Didn't you know that?"

I deserve to die, I thought. What in the world kind of mother am I. "No," I finally answered. "Oh, Linda. I'm so sorry. I had no idea. Was James okay?"

"Cold. But okay. He said Brian kicked him out."

Just shoot me right here and now, I thought. Where did I go wrong in my parenting that a son of mine could kick a child out into sub-zero temperatures in the middle of the night.

"I'm just getting the story, Linda. I'm so sorry. I'm so relieved James is okay. I cannot apologize enough," I rattled on and on.

"Everything is all okay. Don't worry," she kept assuring. But it wasn't.

"I can't believe Brian would do such a thing! I'm so sorry."

"Charlene. Everything is okay. We'll talk about it later. Right now I want to go back to bed."

"Okay. I'll call you this afternoon. Again, I'm sorry."

Brian sat pounding down pancakes like there was no tomorrow. Bob said he wanted to go home.

"I'll take you, Bob," I said. "Brian, you sit right at this table, young man, until I get back. We're going to talk!"

"About what? James is fine, right?"

"James IS fine, right?" George echoed, needing to validate James's safety.

"Yes," I pelted into the kitchen air that seemed to be choking me, "but that's hardly the point here!"

"I know," George replied. "I'll take Bob home. Brian, listen to your mother."

Great.

Brian finished his pancakes in total silence. I was afraid if I started in, I might kill him—right after I pummeled myself to death with the pancake flipper. I waited for George to return. We pow-wowed.

It was decided we should get all three boys and their parents around the table. There was more than a child's error, here. There was an opportunity to discuss friendships, safety, attitudes, common sense, yielding to authority, responsibility and the reality of a disaster that could have happened. Brian should not have kicked James out. James should not have gone in the middle of the night without informing the people responsible for him, or his parents. Bob should have done whatever he could. They had all made bad choices. And I, for one, really didn't care to discuss the boogers that started it all.

*   *   *

17

This is an example of good, bad and dubious memories rolled into one. It happened a long time ago; that sixth-grader is now a sophomore in college.

Could I lead a happy life without this memory? Yes. Did a bad situation lend an opportunity for growth, not only for the boys, but for our parenting wisdom? Yes. Is "The Night the Boogers Almost Killed James" good fodder for a horror movie? Dubious. Was knowing how to ride bareback a helpful skill in passing through this fire? You bet.

I'll explain that last statement in a minute. Right now, I want to grab you by the shoulders and shake you into awareness. Pay attention. The clock is ticking.

Before you know it, your children have grown and flown. It happens in a finger snap—even though a colicky baby's wailing can make one late afternoon seem a week long. And a stubborn three-year-old simply will not potty train, striking the fear in you that some day his bride may have to change his diapers. And you are convinced you're locked in a time warp with your mouthy adolescent (who just nearly killed someone). And your teenager is two hours late for curfew but it seems like a year because it's after midnight and raining and you're wired from numerous cups of caffeine and . . . hey! I know what it's like; I've been there.

But now I am somewhere else in my life. Oh, my address hasn't changed, but my children are gone. I'm a new empty nester—and loaded with hindsight. You know, that kind of hindsight wherein lies truth. The kind you never have a chance to utilize because the time for its payoff is gone.

A lot of things are gone for me now: first smiles, giggles, drooling kisses, rosy cheeks, first steps, rock collections, paper Valentines, Cub Scout pins, ballet recitals, filled laps. Gone.

18

Gone too are detentions, sibling quarrels, first cars, summer jobs, slamming doors (except, perhaps, for an occasional one of mine), young love, lost glasses, sleep-overs, prom-night jitters, graduation tears. . . . My children—our children—are gone in a finger snap.

There is no dress rehearsal to prepare you for an empty nest. There is only the journey, which cannot be replayed or redone. By the time your children leave, you have either basked in the essence of their lives or missed it.

What they leave behind is precious memories. All of them: the good, the bad and the dubious. All of them we are there to collect, that is.

This isn't a book meant to give you one more thing to do, one more burden to carry. Although my message is urgent, my hope is that the impact of it will lighten your load, for now and for the rest of your days. Child rearing is always with us, whether we're simply anticipating and planning for the little darlings, trying to keep our heads out of the quicksand of the terrible twos, or living with the remnants. So the way I see it, we might as well simply learn to ride bareback.

*   *   *

Being raised on a small farm, I had occasion to barrel race on a cutting horse named Dixie. I see direct similarities between raising a child and riding a beast bareback. Forget about blankets and saddles and fancy tack, just hop on and gently neck-rein the critter. Appreciate the high-spiritedness that excites you yet gives you caution. Hug real hard to keep from sliding under its belly and getting trampled. Learn to anticipate the corners and lean into them for balance. Sometimes let the horse have the reins. Know when it's time to head for the barn. Be willing to turn the horse out to pasture when it's too old for you to ride.

Yes, both bareback riding and parenting are earthy and bold adventures.

In these pages I'd like to share with you some of my memories—about our children, not Dixie. They range from "Triumph!" to "Egads!" I present them not just to hear myself rattle (although my children *and* husband tell me I occasionally have that tendency), but in hopes that through them you will see the importance of embracing these years with your children. Think about it: if I hadn't been paying attention, these pages would be empty. As empty as my heart would be.

But fortunately for me, my child-rearing days were filled with gathering every emotional keepsake I was capable of. Oh, I'm sure my two boys, Bret and Brian, participated in lots of things that my husband and I will never know about . . . thank goodness.

And don't get me wrong, all our memories are not rosy. We have served our time in the trenches, thereby earning all the super-glued trinkets, humiliating experiences and looming regrets we are entitled to. But whether exhausting or uplifting, if memorable moments were there for the taking, we grabbed them and tucked them away like the treasures they are. For that, I will be eternally grateful.

As I openly wept and waved good-bye to my baby, a five-foot, ten-inch, handsome male with a good sense of himself—despite some parental blunders along the way—I knew life would never be the same. Leaving him there without a single friend, two whole states away and in the care of an unfamiliar college, the five-hour ride home seemed like an endless bridge. A transition journey to unfamiliar territory: a home with no children. It was a scary ride.

But along with the sense of loss there welled an overwhelming thankfulness that I had not missed my children. I wanted to leap out of the car, hurl myself up on the hood with a bull horn and roar to the heavens: "Thank you! Thank you, God, that through some blessed instinct, I knew there would be plenty of time one day for me, and here it is.

"Thank you that I was raised by parents who knew how to *play* and passed on that blessing! Thank you for choices I made along the way, as difficult as many of them were. Choices that put me on the little league parade route with my camera; in front of the principal with humility; in the bleachers with gut-wrenching tension; at the YMCA with eau-de-chlorine; in the emergency room with pure fright; on a blanket in the park with a picnic basket; in a car packed to the gills with worms, hooks, bobbers and fishing poles. All those places where I will remember being *with* my children. Enduring. Celebrating. Holding my breath. Relishing. Wishing time would freeze."

But time does not freeze. Only in the truth of hindsight do you really get a grip on how quickly it passes. Each event you are experiencing—or missing—will never happen again.

When tears and prayers of thankfulness were winding down on that ride home from college, I found a pulsating, urgent message started filling the quiet.

Wake up, parents! I wanted to scream. In a finger snap your kids will be gone! You cannot get these years back! Give yourself permission to enjoy them while you can. Study and recapture for yourself your child's eagerness. Stroke and inhale the fragrance of their perfect creation. Appreciate the adult blossoming in each of them. Let your house ring with laughter. Believe that troubled times will pass, because they do; take stock and learn to value even those bumpy roads, because they, too, may be remembered as precious milestones. Know that now you are setting the groundwork for your relationship with your children when they are grown.

So many of today's parents are filled with pressure to wear so many hats, raise "gifted" and perfect children and "have it all," that they are, I am afraid, missing what is before them. Priceless, fleeting years lost in the busy shuffle. How, I wonder, will they endure the blank pages in their personal scrapbooks. They will finger snap to an empty nest, pull out their portfolio of memories and weep for its emptiness. Don't let this be you.

I once heard someone say, "Nobody on a deathbed ever wished they had spent more time at the office."

On a similar note, Dan Zedan carries in his wallet a business-size card that has become tattered from all its years of viewing. An eighty-six-year-old scoutmaster gave it to him a long time ago hoping it would perk him up; Zedan had just become a Boy Scout leader.

"In a hundred years it will not matter what my bank account was, the sort of house I lived in or the kind of car I drove," the card reads. "But the world may well be different because I was important in the life of a boy."

Although Zedan, father of five, doesn't know who wrote those words, they've penetrated his life as well as the lives of countless others he has shared them with.

Both thoughts reflect the same message: Priorities. Will they, in the long haul, lead you to fulfillment, or fill you with regrets? Now, while the children are with you, is the time to consider the options. Later, they have passed you by.

"Behold," the psalmist said, "children are a gift of the Lord," and all too soon they are gone.

•

Attention Kmart shoppers:
We have a lost mother
in the store. If you should
find her, be kind,
then point her toward home.

•

• *Two* •

In the Beginning

Disillusionment

Visions *of wonderment begin to dance in our heads when word* comes that we are "with child." Nowadays you can find out nearly minutes after conception with over-the-counter, do-it-yourself tests. Back in my child-bearing years, however, endless months, millions of anxious, strung-together moments had to crawl by before we "officially" knew that visions of wonderment could, indeed, begin to run rampant.

Baby at Mom's breast. Dad's arm around the two of them, parental heads leaning together. Tiny fingers wrapped around larger, caring ones. The sound of a music box tinkling in the background. "Essence of Baby" fragrance that always smells like baby powder. Husband and wife perched over the softened crib pondering with adoring eyes their little sleeping bundle of perfection.

The future beckons. Finger paintings mounted with the respect of a Picasso adorn the refrigerator door. Notes from school explain that Johnny is not only the smartest child in the class but also the most polite. Best batting average on the baseball team. C.E.O. Captain of a major airline who gives free passes to Mom and Dad for world travel. A six-foot-ten quarterback for the Chicago Bears who leads his team to Superbowl Victory, then grins and waves into the camera while mouthing "Hi, Mom and Dad. Thanks for the perfect life we've had!"

And then we give birth.

*   *   *

All those Lamaze classes. I couldn't stop thinking about all that "natural" stuff I was prepared to endure. Prepared? Right! I lie groggy in the recovery room. Recovering not only from birthing my second son who weighed in a healthy eight-pound, two-ounce little porker, but from a hypodermic shot, a local, an anesthesiologist holding a gas mask over my face. . . .

Oh sure, I witnessed the birth of my son, but not without pre- and post-problems. Not without screaming at my husband who was also prepared (?) for my possible (?) uncontrollable nastiness. Not without somehow feeling like I'd blown it. I'd been through this unprepared once before—weren't things supposed to be different this time?

But hey, that was behind me now. I could concentrate on re-kindling my wonderment. I could just lie here and be waited on and ooh and aah our new bundle. I could fantasize about how this little cherub would behave even better than the first, were that humanly possible. (Not only did I forget the pains of childbirth from my first son, but other things I didn't want to remember as well.) I could envision the bonding and blessings passed between parents and child and between little brothers. I could rest assured that I was older this time, wiser, more mature, more patient and in complete control.

And then we took him home.

It wasn't long before reality gripped me by the throat and, much to my horror, I wanted to grab our precious, screaming little bundle the same way! And how about that five-year-old brother of his? Wasn't it about time he settled down?

Not that we didn't have splendid moments in the beginning; we had many. We were even occasionally visited by good days. But much of that first three to four months had to be endured, plowed through and led by a frenzied brain that simply did not get enough sleep. Scenes like the following snap into view as I recollect this passage of our lives.

It is late afternoon and supper is supposed to be cooking. I am supposed to be cooking it. Instead, I am holding a baby who has been screaming for twenty minutes straight. I am rocking him back and forth, gently bouncing him up and down, and patting his back for a burp I'm sure is lodged in there sideways and simply can't escape. I am staring out the window, down the road, in the direction from which my husband's car should be appearing any moment. PLEASE!

Bret is in his bedroom where I have sent him for the eleventy hundredth time this particular day. He is grounded—and, it occurs to me, so am I.

I remind myself that this was our choice. Our vision. Our plan. Our wonderment (egads!). I remind myself I hated baby-sitting when I was a young girl. This should have been a clue. Perhaps I should have converted and joined a convent.

Too late. This is reality. Reality: elation seasoned with heavy doses of exhaustion, despair and disillusionment. Wonderment be darned!

And then I hear it. My husband's key to our home-sweet-home is slipping into the keyhole. I also hear Bret's bedroom door squeak open and I see one half of his eye, nose and mouth risking a peek.

"Get back in there!" I demand. I fly down the stairs like Scarlett O'Hara toward Rhett, except instead of a billowing skirt accompanying me, it's a bellowing kid. I reach the entryway just in time to see my husband open the door.

"Here!" I bark. "Take your son! I have got to get out of here before I explode or kill somebody!"

"Bad day, huh?" he counters, as he sets his briefcase down and takes in a deep breath.

"Bret's in his room where he should stay until he draws a pension!"

"What's wrong with my little Brian?" my husband asks as he gently peels the hysterical mass from the crazed me and cuddles him into his own calm arms.

"Your guess is as good as mine!" I can not talk normally. I can only scream. "He's nursed five times in the last two hours. I feel like nothing but a dairy cow! His pants are dry, unless, of course, he peed them in the last thirty seconds, which he probably did because that's all he's done all day!"

"Where are you going," my husband calmly asks while his massive hand gently strokes Brian's back.

"I don't know. China. The snack bar in Kmart."

"When will you be back?"

"I don't know. Maybe never."

"What's for supper?"

"Whatever you can find."

The door closes behind me.

The door re-opens in thirty seconds. It is cold. I have no coat. No purse. No car keys. I scurry around collecting them, slamming closet and cabinet doors behind me.

I notice on my way back out that the house is full of the sounds of . . . quiet. George is sitting on the couch with Brian resting on his lap. He is talking softly to him, directly to him, their faces are not a foot apart. Brian coos. Bret's door squeaks. It is obvious he was on his way down to greet a much-welcomed Dad until Mom lodged her sneak re-entry.

For a brief moment, I consider staying. But I don't.

*   *   *

Although this is hardly one of my proudest memories, yet I find it is filled with grace. Amazing, undeserved grace. I recognize it as such because one of the most valuable arts a parent can possess, in my opinion, surfaced at that heated moment like the surprise of a refreshing wind gust—and no, it was not flying the coop!

It is the art of capturing the pristine moments. Those experiences that unleash flashes of truth. Those moments that envelop us with God's presence in our children and ourselves. Crystallized flashes that imprint divine blessings on our hearts. Imprints we can call forth from memory, afterward, to carry us through the rough times.

Pure grace. We need only be still enough to receive it.

*   *   *

The Fox River silently slips by in the background. We relax at a prime-location picnic table under a grove of trees in Pottawatomie Park, St. Charles, Illinois. We *finally* relax, that is. Earlier on this Saturday we had to spring out of bed in order to start preparing and loading up for this pleasure: Weber grill, charcoal, charcoal lighter, cooking utensils, at least two coolers, disposable diapers, Frisbee, ball and bat, fishing tackle, radio, playpen, playing cards, lawn chairs, suntan lotion, mosquito repellent, board games, toilet paper (just in case), a watermelon. . . . We met our friends there at 10:30 a.m. in order to stake our claim to this fine location—our friends who brought along just as much stuff as we did, perhaps even more since they were a child up on us.

It was one of those days when you couldn't help but feel the rays of the sun penetrate and light up your very core. A slight breeze rustled the leaves and curled around our eyebrows. It was neither hot nor cold; it was perfection. And it was a miracle: the children got along all day, except for a few minor mishaps that weren't important enough to raise a voice over.

Dusk snuck up on the river; our belongings were packed and ready to go. Two meals behind us, satisfaction swelled and took a foothold.

Brian was conked out in his playpen. He slept soundly, cheek resting on the corner of his blue "blankie" with the satin edge, thumb anchored securely in his mouth, toddler lungs full up with fresh air, knees drawn up under him. I ever-so-gently stroked the side of his cheek with the back of my index finger. His grip caressed his favorite portion of the satin and he faintly suckled and grinned.

The darkened outline of Bret's skinny little form sat squat along the bank, fishing pole extended in front of him. He was far from a patient child; this moment of stillness was rare and inspiring. In his squat little shadow, in this moment of dusk, I was suddenly washed through with warmth: how fragile are his feelings. How freely he loves; how quickly he forgives. How blessed am I to be his mother.

30

George sat off to the side with Al. They were talking quietly about something. Chuckles burst and disappeared like the light of the fireflies they mingled with.

There was time to stay a while longer. And we did.

*   *   *

This was a pristine moment that fluttered upon me like the butterfly of happiness. I would have had a hard time fighting it off. But sometimes the art of capturing—let alone even seeing—those pristine moments is elusive at best. We need to aggressively seek them, condition ourselves to spot them, and cling to their sanity-saving capabilities when we find them.

In case you missed it, just before Miss Drama here made her exit to Kmart, she seized one of those moments, even though she couldn't—and I mean COULD NOT—stay to applaud it. But she, I, seized it and tucked it away. It would be what enabled me to return.

But there were other things I needed to do first. I needed to depart. I knew my children were safe and in good hands. I shot an arrow prayer up to God thanking him for such a faithful and understanding husband who allowed me to back off from the situation so I could gain some perspective. Time to calm down. Time to think. Time to remember. I needed to reverse out of my driveway so rapidly that the tires spit gravel in all directions.

Next I needed to get a grip on safe driving while crying and screaming at the same time. Then the toughest task: finding a place to go. Girlfriends' houses were out; they all have kids. Kmart would simply have to do. After intensely aiming the cart down every aisle in the store and occasionally even hurling something in, I started winding down. Eventually, I made my way to the food area. Lingering over a diet drink and french fries, I was coming to the end of what I needed to do. Had to do to keep from exploding. Perfectly normal and relatively harmless behavior for me.

And something I advise for others. Not my particular routine, perhaps; it might not work for you. But you must find your own harmless routine that calms you down. Learn to accept overwrought, emotional moments as normal periods in any parent's life. We do, after all, have feet of clay, not Novocain.

What happened while I was downing the fries and cola, however, is what allowed me to return. I pulled out that image of my husband and Brian: face to face, serene, giving love to one another. It was a reminder that all child-rearing is not screaming kids and bad behavior, including mine. In fact, if we were to graph it I'm sure those times would be in the minority.

Then I envisioned half of my older son's little face peeking at me. Hoping the dust had settled. Wanting a hug. Needing to know that I still loved him even though it had been a rough day for all of us.

I recalled first rides on merry-go-rounds, bouquets of dandelions, ripples of three-month-old smiles, the feel of the silky hair on the top of a baby's head nestling under my chin, the sweat dripping down my husband's face at the altar . . . I remembered that I loved them all, and that included their bad and dubious behavior as well as the pristine. I needed them. They needed me.

I returned to the images I held on to (lasting truth), not the disaster I had left behind (temporary). It was an anxious ride home and a humble entrance. Brian still squawked a little at bedtime and Bret had not been transformed into wonder boy, but that was okay. I was okay. We would, indeed, all be okay.

*   *   *

Daniel Taylor recently revealed in an article for *Marriage Partnership* magazine that for him and wife Jayne their fourth child, Anne, came as a surprise. Their youngest child at that time was already nine years old.

"To be honest," he wrote, "I think I have sometimes felt a mild and unfocused resentment about the whole thing. 'Resentment' is too strong, but it suggests the sense of being put upon.

" 'I shouldn't have to be doing this,' part of me says. 'I've given lots of time and energy to getting three kids off to a good start; why should I have to do it a fourth time? Why does this come along just when I thought I was going to have more time and energy to write?'

"But then I look," he continued, "really look, at our baby, Anne.

"And what do I see? I see another bit of eternity dropped into our lives. I see something that will last forever, a God-given human spirit, making its first contact with the world. And in watching her, I am drawn away from the illusory world of getting and spending and accomplishing, and back to the real world of mind and spirit and love."

So, it is in looking, really looking, and in remembering, and calling to memory, that we find the often hidden blessings of parenting. Blessings that hide behind stress. Gifts that can easily become camouflaged by disillusionment, even though disillusionment seems to be a normal part of the parental cycle. In reality, that child, that gift from God, is no less a gift when he or she is screaming in a soggy diaper than when the newly bathed infant is all cuddly and smell-good; it is rather just not the way our wonderment pictured it.

And so, as difficult as it is, we would do well to listen to the words in the epistle of James when he advises us to "consider it ALL joy." Not just the obvious pleasures, But ALL of it. "In

EVERYTHING give thanks," Paul said in Thessalonians. Every-thing—including disillusionment.

*   *   *

Sometimes I find that the "calling to memory" portion of my philosophy needs a little help. Memories have a way of blurring at the edges, softening a bit. Like the perfect behavior I wanted to remember in Bret, when I was in the hospital having Brian. The "wonderment" memory.

Other times, however, recollections have a way of flat out getting confused. Take the two monstrous boxes of photographs we have crammed in a certain closet. Very few have dates on them. Most developed roles of film have, over the years, gotten shuffled with other roles as we scrambled through them searching for "the time. . . ." And we are aghast to find we have forgotten many of the details surrounding these visual slices of life. Oh sure, we can tell one child from another, but how old, exactly, was that child? What grade was he in? Whose birthday party was this? Where in the world were we? Who are those people in the background? I'm sure I never had that dorky hairdo!

The fact of the matter is, like putting saddle soap and leather conditioner on the reins to keep them from dry rotting, so it is necessary to date and validate photographs to overcome the dry rot of memory. Trust me, where memory fails, bold print takes over. It's the same with those wonderful baby books we accept at showers with the best of intentions. "We'll write it down later," whatever "it" may be, far too often translates into writing it down wrong or never. It's unfortunate George and I didn't learn this little gem until we owned a closet full of "guesstiments."

You may think this is crazy. You may say to yourself, "How

could I ever forget this?" as you laugh your way through your latest batch of snapshots or videos. But batches of things have a way of multiplying, like slugs under a flower pot. Even though you don't think this will happen to you, you may be grateful twenty years from now when you can prove beyond a shadow of a doubt that yes indeed, one of your family members did wear his pants hiked up that high when he was four years old!

Then again, some slices of life need no photographs, no labeling or even nudges to remain forever perfectly focused in your mind. To draw them forth elicits the same emotion that surrounded them the first time.

*   *   *

Eighteen years after I left my screaming baby in the arms of my husband to seek the shelter of Kmart, that same eight-pound, two-ounce baby boy's high-school graduation day arrived. I cannot believe it. My baby graduating.

I sit in my office with the door closed, weeping and writing him a letter while he dresses for the ceremony. So much I must say to him. So much I need to say to him. So little time to capture my thoughts before we leave for the school.

"Even though I've had since the day you were born to prepare for this," I type, "I find I'm running behind."

I sit and stare at the blinking cursor. How can I sum up eighteen years of love? Eighteen years of good, bad and dubious memories? How can I express in words how proud I am?

I hear him summon his father to make sure the knot in his tie is just right, a task he can actually handle quite well alone. Flashes of photographs rip through my mind: a little boy wearing a crooked clip-on tie making it appear as if the wind is blowing when in fact

35

it is not; a nervous young man readying for his first high-school dance who wants to make sure he looks as perfect as possible. Each photograph reveals the steady and reassuring hands of a father; his child's face, very close to his own—not unlike the face-to-face vision I carried out my door that harried day. Faces that mirror the resemblances: eyebrows, chin line, nose and that beckoning smile.

Through blurred vision, walls and time I see this familiar scenario taking place in my son's room. Perhaps this is the last time it will ever be repeated. I see the mobile gently circling over his crib and study the look of awe and wonder on his baby face. I feel his tiny hand gently pummeling my breast as he nurses. I hear the faint utterances of "da-da" and "ma-ma." I celebrate that first stumbling step he took out of my arms. I pray that God will forever hold close my baby who is readying to face the world without us at his side.

Words finally fill the page—some coaxed out of a tight throat, others pouring forth unbridled. I sign the letter with my fountain pen reserved for the most important of occasions. I carefully fold these pieces of my heart and tuck them under the ribbon I have tied around a kite. A gift I bought to present to him as a rose is presented to an opera singer as a gift of appreciation and heartfelt gratitude. The watch will come later; the kite is symbolic of the little boy I don't want to become lost in a man. The little boy I hope never forgets how to play—and I've told him this in my letter.

We arrive very early at the outdoor graduation site so we can secure premium seats in the bleachers—not unlike efforts to claim that favored picnic location. It is a beautiful day. The bleachers at Glenbard West High School overlook not only the football field where the ceremony will take place, but the lovely backdrop of Lake Ellyn surrounded by picturesque trees.

My husband keeps postponing handing me the program. I find

it curious behavior but I am too busy purposefully capturing every detail of this scene to let it bother me. Finally the ceremony begins.

There are a few words of welcome and then it is announced that four voices from the choir of the Glenbard West High School class of 1989 will sing, a cappella, the national anthem. Brian steps onto the platform with three other young adults. This is the first I know of his surprise—this perfect of gifts—for his mother.

Their voices ring clearly in the stillness. My son's eyes scan the crowd and lock on mine. His lips move to the words; his bass voice is strong and pure. His eye winks. At me. Directly at me.

I am filled with wonderment. Wonderment beyond my imagination. True wonderment that is forever captured and locked in my memory. A vision I will usher forth many times during the lonely days after he has left for college.

•

Dear Diary,
Today I learned how to tie
the magic bow that
keeps a shoelace from coming
untied. Yippee! My baby's
a sophomore in high school.

•

· *Three* ·

All We Don't Know about Parenting

Incompetence

June *1979. Last day of school. This mother's delight—and torment.* Delight that the nightly homework hassle is behind us for a few months, and parts of our harried schedule can take a nap. Torment because my last day of personal freedom until fall is drawing to a close.

There's a decision to be made here: should I be busily cleaning on this last of child-free days for a while? Nah. I should be sitting in the back yard amongst the flowers, sipping tea, reading or just staring into space. And that's precisely what I do.

I ponder the fact that Bret is experiencing his final day as an eighth grader. Major transitions lie ahead, for him and for me. For Bret, manhood looms around the corner. But first he must pass through another transition fire: going from being the eighth-grade hot shot to once again ranking lowest on the totem pole in a different school. As for George and me, we must help keep his self-esteem intact during this stormy period as well as allow him some room to be an adolescent—a difficult stage for everyone involved.

It also occurs to me I can no longer simply say what grades my boys are in when queried; I must refer to them as "a third grader and a freshman in high school."

Freshman! What year is this? I prop my tea glass in the grass next to my lawn chair and head for the bathroom mirror. After a couple minutes of jowl and crows' feet inspection I decide things aren't too bad yet. Besides, why waste these precious moments worrying anyway? I resume my laid-back post.

While I am watching cloud formations, Bret is manning home plate during a softball game at school. Steve Wasnick is pitching. There is a play at the plate. Wasnick whips the ball to Bret who immediately drops it because pain shoots through his thumb the second the ball smacks into it.

The runner is safe. Bret is sent to the nurse. She deems it possibly broken. School is almost out for the day, however, so she ices it for a while, advises him to be careful of his throbbing digit and ride the bus home as usual. Of course he is to tell his mother that she, the nurse, believes his thumb should be x-rayed. Upon his arrival home he does so, abruptly ending my freedom.

Before I deal with the thumb, however, I quickly thank God for the wisdom he granted me to know when it was time to stockpile a refreshing little rest instead of scurrying around spit-shining. I just love it when daydreaming wins! Especially when it beats out ring-around-the-collar calisthenics. "Thank you, God," I say, "for this profound discovery!" Now, back to the hand in my face.

I carefully inspect his thumb, the way I have inspected dozens of other injured limbs of both my children over the years. It looks slightly swollen, but then so do his eyes. So does a sprain. So does a mosquito bite or a good wallop.

He sighs as he reads my mind, the mind he has eventually heard spoken every other time this scenario has played.

"How badly does it hurt?" I always ask them. "It's probably not broken. We'll just go sit in the clinic for hours while they shuffle us from urgent care to x-ray and back again," I whine. "Then the doctor will finally tell us nothing is wrong and we will receive a very large bill and by tomorrow you will forget it even hurt." Not once has anything actually been broken.

But we always go anyway because I don't know what a broken anything really looks like, and my conscience starts riding me, and I love my children and I don't want them to heal with crooked limbs.

For the record, it has also been proven that I do not consistently know the difference between postnasal drip and bronchitis. How many times, I wonder, has Brian snorted and snotted around, running a slight temperature on and off, keeping us (mostly me) up at night, only for us (always me) to become convinced he will surely die without some of that pink medicine. And so I sit next to my phone in the early hours with bleary eyes haunting the clock, waiting for the appointment lines to open.

Off we finally go. Sometimes we get pink medicine or a shot. During these times I commend my intuitive self. Except, of course, for the time I sent him to school after a check-up and a throat culture because he had no temperature and seemed perfectly fine but for a scratchy throat. And don't you know the lab called and said it was strep!

But other times we are informed of a mere cold, postnasal drip, or less. And we pay our bill. And I file the episode in my memory bank for the next bout. Just like I file the "nothing-is-broken" messages we've always received. Try chicken soup and Popsicles first, I tell myself. Wait a couple days and see what transpires, I coax.

But now, this last-of-eighth-grade day, Bret stands before me, thumb presented like a royal jewel to a queen. I express my sympathy and look appropriately sad. He still thinks it's broken. I soften my usual lecture. He sighs again and endures, but doesn't become dissuaded. I wear down and take him to the clinic.

After the predicted waits between shufflings, we finally watch the doctor ceremoniously mount two very large black-and-white bits of evidence on a lighted screen. He carefully studies them, moving his head between the two. Next, he pulls a ball-point pen out of his pocket.

"Right here," he says, using the pen for a pointer, "is a slight fracture. We'll get a splint on that and it should heal just fine."

Bret jumps up in the air and screams, "Did you hear that, Mom? It's broken! It's really broken!" He grins from ear to ear as he dances around me celebrating, right there in the doctor's office. A doctor, who, I might add, seems a bit puzzled at the reaction.

I can't say I was happy, but somehow I was momentarily justified as a mother. A mother who made the right move this particular day.

And there was another happy person: Steve Wasnick. The next day Bret ran into him at a carnival. When Bret confirmed the implications of the metal and green-foam splint he was wearing like a medal of honor, the two of them did a high five. Wasnick was overjoyed that he could throw a ball fast enough to break someone's thumb!

Even Brian was happy. Although he got no immediate pleasure out of the ordeal, he knew that from this day forward he would have something to remind Mom about the next time she started her "I'm-sure-it's-nothing" lecture.

*   *   *

I am convinced that all parents struggle through bouts of feeling incompetent. Why don't I know this stuff? I've asked myself on many occasions. Why are so many things that happen to us not covered in the manuals?

Why if it worked for one kid isn't it working for the other? Are my instinct mechanisms broken? Does this little episode carry enough of its own consequences, or do I need to bring in some reinforcements? Will they settle the disagreement by themselves or will they draw blood? Is he telling me the truth? What happens when we parents disagree on an approach?

Now there's no point beating ourselves up for asking these questions; we *should* ask them. By the same token, we need to be careful we don't get swept away by confusion and doubt. We can become so focused on the trial and anxiety of it all that we miss our kids.

Our sense of incompetence can bring on panic attacks which in turn produce certain hallucinations:

HEADLINE: "Five-year-old boy stays awake for three consecutive days while father has nose stuck in books reading about the advantages and disadvantages of making your children take naps."

HEADLINE: "Toddler crawls unsupervised to top of Sears Tower while mother stands in trance-like state in front of ground-floor elevator debating the advisability of exposing her child to such a swift ascent in a confined area. She was last heard mumbling something about the possible death of her intuition."

HEADLINE: "Children run around neighborhood naked and starving while parents argue about whether or not children should wear only non-synthetic fabrics and maintain tofu diets."

Why is it we think everyone will hear about our mistakes?

There are times, however, when I marvel at my spontaneous aptitude. Just the right response. The most appropriate of disciplines. A great sense of fine tuning that enables me to read behind the words. A hug that heals. At these moments, I am fervently grateful to God for building in the skills and giving me the life experiences that enable me to be a good mother.

But basically I have to rely on God's promises and grace to carry my children through, beyond, and in spite of my blind leadings.

It would be hard to imagine raising children without counting on God to guide and instruct me. Without his presence and Spirit granting me patience, endurance and acceptance of circumstances beyond my control, I would surely be bonkers by now.

I remind myself often that he, God, is Love. He loves my children more than I am even capable of understanding the word. He loves me just as much, for I am also his child. Aren't we all in wonderful hands? And so during times of utter panic when it comes to parental decisions, I claim his promises: "I can do everything through him who gives me strength" (Phil 4:13); "In this world you will have trouble. But take heart! I have overcome the world" (Jn 16:33b).

I truly believe that if God has overcome the world, he can help me overcome the evils of potty training. I can count on him to help me know when it's time to back off. He will deliver me from prideful mistakes and forgive me for foolish ones, and vice versa. He knows my heart and I pray he will help me have sense enough to give him my will . . . and my children.

We have at our fingertips the most precious of commodities.

That makes parenting a mighty responsibility!

Just watch any of the talk shows to see how many people are blaming their messed-up lives on their parents. Just check the book stores for the swelling wave of how-to volumes about parenting, so much of it guilt-producing. I say guilt-producing because there's no way any of us can do everything they tell us to. In fact, much of what we read is in conflict within the genre. There are so many armies of warnings and directions being delivered to our browsing faces that we could easily become convinced nothing about parenting is natural—or fun. We could become neurotic and gridlocked with fear. We could forget that God calls us to be joyful.

Should we become caught in the snare of expectations of perfect parenting, we would, without a doubt, be missing our kids: we would be so focused on *us* and our abilities that we would miss out on *them* and their gifts. We would not allow room for them to teach us, and their lessons are bountiful, indeed.

We would expect the same perfection from them that we require of ourselves. We would judge our parenting skills solely by our children's behavior, which we all know is sometimes totally out of line, as is our own. We would forget why Christ died: precisely because we are incapable of reaching perfection.

Yes, parenting is crazy-making. But it also is an unequalled opportunity, in my opinion, for us to celebrate the gift of life and the freedom God gives us to ride by the seat of the pants. To cling to him for dear life and trust that he knows where he's taking us and our children.

Not that seeking advice from the experts is not good sense; it is. But pray beforehand that God will reveal his personal nudging to you. Perhaps that one thing that clicks and makes life easier. Perhaps one book's advice is good for now, but not good for later.

Maybe it doesn't apply at all to your lifestyle. Keep praying and listening for answers; confirm your course on a regular basis.

What would have happened to Isaac if Abraham had decided to stop listening after God told him to sacrifice his only son? What if he just concentrated on the altar and the knife, not hearing the next instruction God gave him? The one that said, "Do not lay a hand on the boy" (Gen 22:12).

Abraham did not have to sacrifice his son. He only had to show God he was *willing* to listen and obey. Stubborn mindsets can be lethal. Sometimes we do the right thing but carry on a little too long. Sometimes we do the wrong thing and pride keeps us from admitting it. Your children are watching! Ask God what to do next; be willing to listen and obey.

*   *   *

George and I were going through a particularly difficult time with Bret right after the broken-thumb incident. My back-yard ponderings were right on target: adolescence requires about a 9.9 on the Richter scale of tolerance. Finding the right balance between allowing him room to grow (i.e., be an adolescent jerk sometimes) and keeping him in line, seemed an impossible task short of pulling out all the hairs on our heads—one at a time.

We needed suggestions and direction. We needed to know that other parents were struggling with some of the same things we were, that our trauma (and progressing baldness) was normal and should be expected.

So we signed up for a one-day workshop I saw advertised in the local paper. I honestly can't remember who was sponsoring it, but it offered all kinds of rotating classes to choose from, and several seemed to headline our concerns.

Patiently we waited for the first speaker to arrive. She finally slunk in several minutes late, looking slightly frazzled.

"I'm sorry I'm late," she apologized. "I spent most of the night bailing my teenage son out of jail."

Our chorus of gasping was partly sympathetic and partly suspicious: *this* was the expert who was going to provide us with all the answers?

She went on to explain the circumstances. The incident wasn't nearly as bad as we imagined; no charges were pressed and her son had certainly learned a valuable lesson about the parties he should choose. There was also a lesson for us: even the experts cannot depend on their "expertness" when it comes to rearing perfect children!

Decisions come in all sizes; some are more major than others. Sometimes the same dilemma can seem like nothing one day and all consuming the next.

Take the issues of pacifiers and thumb sucking. Bret never did suck his thumb—basically, his hands were not idle long enough to take root in his mouth—but he used a pacifier for about a year. One day we lost the pacifier, and that was the end of that.

Brian, however, did them all. I made sure I had a pacifier on hand before I even brought him home from the hospital. Although I had made the decision to nurse him—something that appeared to be so natural yet sure took a lot of emergency phone calls to LaLeche League mothers—I just wanted to make sure there was something to put in his mouth should my chest not be within reasonable reach.

I found the pacifier to be a wonderful thing. When he would awaken in the middle of the night, he would, for just long enough, accept the pacifier while I changed him before I nursed. It kept him peaceful and let everyone else sleep; it allowed me to put him right down after he'd nursed and fallen asleep; it worked very well. Until he would lose his pacifier. So we bought several.

There are many who disagree with pacifiers. By the time Brian was three months old, so did he. One morning I peeked in on him and the pacifier was spit aside; his thumb was doing the job very nicely, thank you very much. His little fingers were circled around the satin edge of his blue blanket, forever transforming it to "blankie." Thus started a new chapter in our lives: Will Thumb Sucking Do Something Awful to Our Son? My friend Mary Beth said she sent up a flare when her daughter "finally found her thumb and could calm herself down." Others, however, tell frightful stories about buck teeth wicked enough to scrape wallpaper off the walls. Whatever, it all became an immaterial debate in our house because there was no getting that thumb out of Brian's mouth until he entered kindergarten.

The only good thing was that he could not suck his thumb unless he had blankie in his hand. He developed a certain style, the way all thumb suckers do. He would hold the corner in his right hand while sucking his right thumb. He would rub—and sniff—the very corner of blankie under his nose. No blankie, no thumb sucking.

When he was very young I could watch an upset baby immediately be calmed by the magic of his blankie and thumb. As he grew older, sometimes he would be playing and suddenly need a fix. He would cross the room to where the usually dirty blankie was slung over the side of a chair or bundled up in the corner, grab it, take a few drags, and off he'd go. I longed for a blankie in my own life.

I especially longed for one the year Bret had three automobile wrecks in six months. No one was hurt, thank the Lord, but needless to say all our insurance was cancelled. I also could have used one the day Brian came home his freshman year in high school and told me he wanted to wrestle.

"Gross! Isn't that the sport where you put your nose in someone's armpit?" I wanted to respond. But I didn't. I rode the beast bareback and hung on for dear life. I arranged a smile on my face and encouraged him to pursue his heart's desire.

He would come home after practice with mat burns on his forehead and I would listen to every grisly detail he unfolded about "take downs," "reversals," "pins," and the dreaded upcoming "challenge match." It was like a foreign language. All I understood was that he was very sore when he came home at night.

How much sympathy should a good parent give? Would it be too much like babying him? Should I admire the battle scars? Should I cheer or groan when he tells me he's won the challenge match, and that means I actually have to go watch him do this . . . this . . . thing. A noise uncontrollably escapes my mouth, not a cheer, not a groan, a sigh-like sound somewhere in between the two.

The entire day of the first meet I had heart palpitations picturing my little darling plastered to a sweat-beaded mat, wondering how I would ever encourage him to continue. (Oh for a blue blankie!) I watched the boys in the six-minute match before Brian's wrestle themselves into exhaustion. I didn't breathe. I practically twisted my husband's arm out of its socket. I didn't have a clue as to what all the ref's spasmodic gestures were about. Points had gone on the scoreboard and I didn't know why. (Was I too old to start sucking my thumb?)

When I saw Brian enter that ring wearing the headgear, breathing so heavily, I thought I was going to toss my cookies. He looked so vulnerable yet so brave. I was hyperventilating as he and his opponent shook hands. It was slow-motion torture. I moved his every move. I felt his every mat burn. Strong against clever. Smart against quick. No room for the theatrics of channel 60 "professional" wrestlers here. Drop your concentration for a moment, and a near victory could bring swift defeat.

Brian lost that first match. But his determination and love for the sport grew. He developed a mutual liking with the coach who encouraged him and praised him with things like, "Baumbich, I think you've got a bubble in your butt because you always rise to the top." A very good thing in wrestling, believe it or not.

Watching the sport continued to be difficult for me—for all four years of high school. But I came to realize how much it meant to him, and how many lessons he was learning through this peculiar event: humility, perseverance, concentration, acceptance of self.

As the weeks went on, I cheered his every win and cheered his every loss. One on one. No one else to blame it on. No one else to share the win. All *his,* no matter what. I started looking forward to meets, and respected every single boy who took to the mats, no matter what school he was from.

I watched my son teach me many lessons about guts and sportsmanship. We both learned to overcome first appearances: many are stronger than they look; bigger does not always mean better; yes, sometimes your nose ends up in an armpit, but there's nothing gross about triumph, respect for the opponent, or learning how to handle loss, even when your back is flat to the mat.

Over all, Brian had a successful high-school wrestling career, and his mother learned a lot about toughing it out too. But first, remember, I had to dare to ride that beast bareback and hang on for dear life.

*   *   *

It's comforting to remember the Noah's ark story. God told Noah what to do. Noah did it. He didn't worry about who was going to close the door after he got all those animals on board. It's one of my favorite Scripture passages: "and the Lord closed it [the door] behind him" (Gen 7:16 NASB). The rest is history.

So pray, do what you think is best, double back when you realize an error, keep listening, and don't fret about the final outcome. God will close the door—or open it, or crack it a hair. Just pay attention so you don't miss it because you're blinded by your own fear and inadequacies.

The apostle Paul tells the believers, in Philippians 1:6, that he is "confident . . . that he who began a good work in you will carry it on to completion until the day of Christ Jesus." The Lord began two "good works" in me: Bret and Brian. And with them he also began the good work of making me a parent. A parent capable of passing on his blessings. And just think, it's his job to perfect it all. Yea, God!

•

Dear Ex-Boss,
I can't come back to work;
my children need me.
Besides, I have a set of keys
to all my neighbors' houses
because I'm the only one
they know would be
home should they
lock themselves out.

•

· *Four* ·

Why I Can't Go Back to Work

Validation for Stay-at-Homes

"Keepers *of the Big Wheel Brigade." A title justly earned by Mary* Gingell and myself one summer when her son Noah and my Brian were about three. It wasn't the only title we bore, nor the grandest, I suppose, but nevertheless we wore it proudly.

Mary, Hugh and their two children lived right across the street from us—a blessing I continue to thank God for. Although we have lived far away from one another for many years now, when we do have occasion to get together, it is like we've never been apart. We bask in the familiarity of each other, never having to explain whence we've come. I do believe that women who have survived preschoolers together form an unbreakable bond.

I can picture us vividly. Mary's Dr. Scholl's sandals clip-clopping along Gingells' blacktop driveway. Noah's pants that simply did not ever stay slung above the top of the crease in his slimmer-than-slim buttocks. Brian always, but always, wearing a baseball cap with his ears tucked inside. He also hiked his pants up a little too high and wore his belts a little too tight—a habit, thank goodness, which he outgrew before the word "geek" came along. And me, well, I usually had a dish towel thrown over my shoulder and Mary had to remind me about it.

In retrospect, the fact that part of my "mommy" uniform was a dish towel was peculiar. During those busy years I honestly did not see the point in washing dishes that often, nor did I own a dishwasher. All everybody did was dirty them again. So I let them stack up into fairly large piles sometimes. There were just more important (or fun) things to do. By some mystery, however, the dish towel managed to ride my shoulder.

Anyway, that summer Mary and Hugh built a spacious, six-inch high deck right outside their front door and stained it red. Although that sounds a little peculiar—not the red but the six inches—it totally changed the atmosphere: we parked our lawn chairs on the deck instead of the blacktop driveway.

We spent a portion of almost every day on that deck watching the boys careen their Big Wheels at very high speeds toward the front end of the driveway, slam on the brakes, do a donut and roar back toward us—memories number 5,003 through 6,003. We experienced this racing duo at Gingells' house because our driveway was gravel and there were no sidewalks.

Day after day, time after time, Mary and I would take turns stopping our chatter mid-sentence to lunge after one of the boys who simply could not remember we told them NOT TO DRIVE TOO CLOSE TO THE STREET! I'm talking weeks of launching ourselves. Actually months.

Although it probably wasn't bad for our cardiovascular systems, the electrifying zap that rushes through a mother when she fears her child could meet with peril before she can reach him surely could be stroke-inducing. But we endured and even managed to solve world problems, as well as catch a few rays, between launches.

Then one day, life as we knew it was altered in a flash. A flash of inspiration. One of us, and I honestly can't remember who (but I hope it was me) was struck with a revelation: it was possible for us to sit at the front end of the driveway, thereby eliminating the need to live like astronauts.

We were stunned! It was so simple. So obvious. What took us so long to figure it out? Were we brain dead from being out of the working world so long?

No, we finally determined; we'd heard our husbands talk about plenty of business-world bloopers. In fact, we had each encountered doses of "business bonkers" in our own working-for-money worlds before children. So, after hashing it over a while we decided to give ourselves a break and celebrate our new and more relaxed lifestyle with giant ice teas and Popsicles all around.

*   *   *

That night as I lay in bed reading—husband dozing on the couch, boys long tucked in—something about the day gnawed at me. Not the discovery; it was grand, indeed. But our initial reaction to it.

After all, we were each committed to our choice. Content. Fulfilled. Convinced that our children deserved the best we could give them, and that was us. Happy to be free of corporate claws. Single-minded about our role. Grateful to be in a financial position that enabled us to stay home. Involved in clubs, crafts and miscellaneous volunteer projects that kept us sharp and well-rounded. So where did that reaction come from?

Other voices. Other voices that were starting to speak loudly about that time. A feminist movement that seemed to swing against some women, and eventually induced those women to start swinging back. There is nearly a full-fledged war going on now between many stay-at-home moms and career moms, and it grieves me deeply.

Who are we to judge one another when God specifically tells us time and again in the Scriptures that judgment is his job? How can we possibly know God's plan for another's life when we so often haven't a clue about our own? And why do we forget that the operative word here is "moms"? It is a title career moms and stay-at-home moms wear together.

Aren't we all just trying to do the best we can? Arming our children to enable them to fight the lures of today's world takes energy enough. Fighting each other is like clubbing your own team—and family. Who will win then? Certainly not the children who are left stranded on the bases while stay-at-homes balk at running interference for the career mom who can't take a turn in the car pool, and career moms demean the stay-at-homes, lowering their self-esteem. The children are stationed on the battlefield while we sling the mud.

Because I've walked in both sets of shoes—and believe me, neither of them walks an easy path—I'd like to present a little of each in hopes that each group may gain some insight into the other's role. The main thing is: the children need us, and we need each other.

I'll start this chapter by waving the apron, so to speak, for the home team because that is where my heart lies. But stay with me, working moms; the next chapter's for you.

When George and I married we talked about all the opportunities and options that were available to us. George lovingly took over the daily fathering responsibilities for Bret, the four-year-old son I brought into the marriage. There was no doubt in my mind that I had missed much of Bret in his early years as his natural father and I struggled to make ends meet while trying to hold together a failing relationship. Bret's and my difficult years continued alone for two years after the divorce.

Yes, there was no question that he needed more of me now, especially as we were entering a new marriage. It was a scary time for him.

George and I were also in total agreement that motherhood was a full-time job, and we wanted more children. I welcomed the opportunity to give concentrated energy to setting up a new nest. I filed myself in the ranks of the stay-at-homes and it came naturally to me.

My parents lived what used to be considered the "traditional roles." Dad went to work. Hammered and nailed things around the house. Coached little league, including my all-girl softball team. He was viewed as the great protector. He enjoyed relaxing with his family and always had a hug ready and waiting.

Mom worked at home: laundry, gardening, hanging clothes on the line, cooking, baking, taxiing her kids around, applying bandages, listening, sitting poolside while her kids screamed "Watch this!" from the top of the high dive. She laughed a lot and brimmed with passion for her family.

Traditional, familiar roles. I was relieved to be where I believed with all my heart that I belonged. I slipped right into my homemaker role with an audible sigh.

It didn't take long after Brian was born before the reality of how much I'd missed with Bret started soaking in. Now I could literally spend hours if I chose coaxing smiles from a three-month-old and receiving them. Nurturing security. Dinner didn't have to be "What can I throw together quick?" although I had that option and sometimes used it, but there was time to slowly simmer and baste. Create. Eat cookie dough.

I didn't have to wonder if Bret had his hat or not. I tugged it on his head, tied the muffler around his chin and started warming the hot chocolate.

When one is caught up in survival, one doesn't have time to mourn or even be aware of what isn't happening. Sometimes only from a distance can one step back and see the broad picture—filled with holes. And now I could clearly see that Bret's young life definitely held some buckshot.

I could not re-do Bret's early years, but I could begin that very moment basking in gratefulness that I was able to start experiencing and capturing the every-day miracles children deliver.

Don't get me wrong, all was not bliss. I also received healthy doses of scut work and crazy-making. Perhaps that's why passing through the "Big-Wheel-stay-at-home-mom" self-evaluation tripped me for a moment. Maybe life should be more than this, I said to myself. Maybe I was wrong to set aside career goals. Certainly life would be a lot easier with two incomes: I wouldn't have to darn socks just because a big toe escapes; I could throw them away and buy more! I wouldn't have to explain to Bret why he had to wear neat but rather generic jeans instead of the trendiest expensive ones. I wouldn't have to be catapulting myself out of a lawn chair days on end!

But those fleeting thoughts didn't last very long as I reflected once again on why I had chosen to stay home in the first place. I wanted to know my kids. Really *know my kids.* Develop a relationship with them.

Be there when they cried for me.

Witness unrepeated first steps. Oh sure, there are always other steps, endless other steps, but never those first ones again. And taking advantage of the opportunity to stay at home upped the odds that I would be in the right place at the right time to witness all those first and perhaps one-time-only accomplishments.

"Things happen so quickly," an acquaintance of mine once said, "that if you don't just sit still and look at them, you miss them." Amen. I valued the opportunity to give my children what my mother had given me; hours on end of undivided time.

One of my mother's tasks was ironing. I loved it when she ironed; she was a captive audience for my absolutely necessary and always urgent conversations. She would sip ice tea from her sweat-coated glass, then look into my eyes and search my face—maybe brush my hair away from my forehead—while I told the "really good stuff." Then she'd tackle the arm of a shirt or the crease in a pair of pants, ponder the magnitude of my trials and tribulations—or just sometimes the funny stuff—and respond with head nods and verbal acknowledgments. The iron would hiss when it hit the sprinkled clothes, and I would feel as warm as the ironed sleeve because my mother was listening, really listening. That's what I wanted to do for my children.

I also wanted to hang clothes out on the line, and I had the time to do it, weather permitting. Relaxing on a breezy day, watching sheets flap and snap, gathering them in my arms and inhaling the universe . . . I could monitor the boys while they ran through the sprinkler, could laugh at their playfulness and at the same time capture peace with clothespins. I viewed it as part of my responsibility to keep the Norman Rockwell image of life at home alive and well.

Mom had let my brother and me absolutely destroy her kitchen with wild concoctions. Baking. Experimenting. Testing the way food colors mixed with powdered sugar; rolling out home-made egg noodle dough—and then eating all the noodles before they dried. And so, too, my children would have this opportunity for leisurely play. Creativity boosters. After all, the child in me loved an excuse for this behavior as well. Still does. My husband and boys wouldn't have recognized Thanksgiving as a holiday if noodles weren't strung around the kitchen to dry, disappearing one by one each time one of us passed through.

And messes can always be cleaned up. In fact, they present opportunities for character building and responsibility.

Some of the best days I shared with my kids were the ones which had absolutely no plans in them. We would wake up in the morning with no place to go. No shopping to do. An entire day before us to spend time together. Or alone—each in our own corner with nothing rushing us out. Unhurried time. Time for couch cushions to become walls to forts. Time for Legos to transport them to Mars and me into a quiet time zone in which to read.

* * *

One mother told me how she simply enjoyed watching her children play together. She had been an only child, and spoke of the loneliness that sometimes surrounded her as she grew up. She said she cherished the moments her children shared with each other. Oh sure, sometimes they bickered, but she knew the bond between them was much stronger than the antagonism.

Another stay-at-home mom, who referred to herself as somewhat crafty, enjoyed the opportunity to share in that with her daughter. Although her daughter is not yet four, she has shared enough cut-out time with mom to warrant her own set of "good" scissors that don't mutilate the paper. She even clips coupons for mom with them. And together they organize and plan.

Even wallpapering became fair game for sharing in one family. "I gave them their own pan of wallpaper paste," the mother boasted. I don't think I would have had the courage to do that, but Brian often pulled up a chair next to me if I was working at the kitchen sink. I would be chopping and dicing and he would be filling the sink with water and floating things in it. Or helping me dry. Or watching the squirrels play in the back yard, right by my side.

Bret, Brian and I had time not only to smell the flowers together but to plant them as well. There was time to read them stories as they cuddled in my lap. Or sat next to me, making up their own stories as they saw fit. Children who are just learning how to talk are wonderful entertainers, and how better to get them to vocalize than by being their audience. Honestly, their stories can be a lot more interesting than any soap opera.

As the children grew older, I found it even more important to be home when they busted in through the front door. Bigger kids have bigger problems and more options of places to seek solutions. I wanted that chance to hear all about it and give my input before they found another way—a scarier way—to struggle through it besides sharing it with family.

I was available to help other mothers' children as well, many working moms' children, and that was a blessing to me. Emergency runs to school for those who missed their bus after Mom or Dad left. Picking up another's sick child from school and holding a hand until a worried parent could make it home from work. Room mother. Field-trip chaperone. All duties I enjoyed and found fulfilling.

Of course, I did get scratched off one volunteer list due to an unfortunate accident. I made cupcakes for hot dog day at the grammar school. How was I to know a screw had fallen out of my mixer into the batter? I didn't *mean* for it to show up in the little boy's mouth right behind the chocolate frosting.

Before I start sounding like I believe that simply staying home with your children solves all the problems, let me set the record straight: it does not. That assumption is far from the truth. Stay-at-homes and their children can fall victim to all kinds of dangers, pitfalls and lures.

Let's start with compulsion and overindulgence. The kind of relationship with your children that can make other people want to smack you and scream, "Get a life!" The kind that smothers and oppresses and stifles the very things in our children we are trying to nurture. The kind that exhausts—both us and our children.

When you have nothing in your life but your kids, tunnel vision can encompass you. It can sneak up on you. Consume you. Leave you an empty, lifeless shell when they are gone. Full-time parents must strive for balance. Learn to see beyond the family room so they can introduce their children to the rest of the world.

We can strive so hard to be good, twenty-four-hour-a-day parents that we become confused and blind to simple reality. Children are no longer a blessing to behold and celebrate; they have become a job. A job we take so seriously and neurotically that we cannot see the truth through the facts: Yes, children are work, but they are joy and life and creativity and spontaneity and pleasure. We can be looking so hard at each little element of their lives that we miss the whole of who they are, who they are becoming.

We need to guard against losing ourselves in our children; otherwise, who will they turn to in times of trouble if we are no longer our own strong selves but rather a part of them?

I can still fall victim to compulsive "steering" occasionally, even though my boys are young men. While they are away from me, whether permanently living away or just at college for the school year, I am forced to let go, turn them out to pasture—just as working parents are forced to do during the day. Independence creates room to grow, for all parties concerned.

*   *   *

But the temptation to ride that horse with spurs the minute it's back within reach doesn't really go away. If you've become rusty at dealing with the temptation, or let your guard down, ZAP! It's got you!

I remember the first time Bret came home for a brief visit after he'd graduated and moved to Albuquerque. I busied myself for days getting everything just perfect. I even cleaned both bathrooms and (egads!) the silverware drawer.

I set aside the rest of my life for this visit. After all, he hadn't been home for fourteen months and I was overflowing with anticipation. I planned meals and pictured us sitting around talking and talking. Doing things together. Mother and son. Yucking it up and catching lunch and. . . .

Sure, those things happened, but not twenty-four hours a day. He had friends to see and places to go and ground to cover, as well he should have. I hadn't raised a slug or a hermit; what did I expect?

I became snappy and clingy and a royal pain; there's simply no way to soften the description of my behavior. I strongly suggested who he might want to call and what he might like to do with them. Then I started laying guilt trips on him because he wasn't checking in and out with me before his every move, and on and on and on.

I had set myself up to fall in the trap. My need to know I was still important in his life—although he had never given me cause to doubt it—caused me to slip gears and engage in an obsessive, overbearing, "Get-a-life!" mode.

It happens just as easily when they're young. Yes, they need you to cross the street. But they don't need you to tell them where to sit in the sandbox and whom they should invite to sit in there with them—like you, for instance.

The flip side of this behavior: the parents who choose not to work outside the home but don't stay home or pay much attention to their kids either. They're easy to spot. They've got the kids enrolled in every activity in the world and they spend most of their time dropping them off, picking them up—trying to mold and shape their children's lives by seeing they are exposed to everything. Everything but time to play with Mom and Dad. Sit. Ponder. Explore. Cuddle in their laps.

These parents honestly believe they are over-taxed and their conversations are filled with martyristic mumblings. Or they are full of boasting about all the skills their children are mastering; yet all their children really want to accomplish is getting Mom's or Dad's attention. Undivided. Not because of what they are achieving, but simply because of who they are: a fragile child.

It is easy to fall into Super Parent behavior. Room mother, Brownie leader, Sunday-school teacher—a mother to everyone's child but your own.

There are non-working mothers who spend as much time volunteering, working out, watching television and gallivanting around as their working-mom counterparts spend on the job. Just saying you're a stay-at-home doesn't make it so.

Balance. Every mom needs to find balance.

Yes, basically I rally on the side of the stay-at-home. That's because I felt so fulfilled being there, and I knew that one day, the rest of my life would resume. And so it has, with great vigor.

I shall always cherish those at-home years. As crazy as it sounds, even my two-year stint as Bret's den mother was incredibly rewarding. It was amazing how many creative outlets that offered: ingenuity, planning for every minute so you didn't lose control of the rowdy group, reacting quickly to brewing difficulties, channeling the energy of the boys. We had one of the happening-est dens in the pack, and all of us were very proud of that.

Oh sure, den mothering had its down sides too. Like the time I almost wiped out one of the eight-year-olds when we were preparing for the "Christmas around the World" pack meeting. I had him doing a dance on a Mexican sombrero—something, it turns out, he was outrageously allergic to. Severe hives consumed him within minutes.

And then there's the time the group as a whole—excluding me or my permission, of course—decided to find out just how gross it would be if they could all (eight boys) pass gas at the same time in my basement. That almost snuffed all of us out.

But on the whole, fond Cub Scout memories are captured forever. As are the days the boys and I went on spontaneous picnics or off to the zoo or Kiddieland. Kool-Aid went down by the gallon. Summer days were, in general, lazy and relaxing. Winter brought snow angels and awesome forts.

I have a picture of my boys standing next to an outhouse at one of the county parks we visited on a brisk fall day. They are standing on a blanket of leaves, one on each side of the sign that reads "Men." They are flexing their skinny little four- and ten-year-old bodies to the max, trying to live up to the sign.

And now they are men. And now they are gone. And I usher them back with full-bloomed stay-at-home memories. And I am thankful and proud to be a mother who, most of the time, enjoyed her life as an apron waver—even though sometimes it looked suspiciously like a white flag.

•

Dear Son,

Thanks for making the

wonderful centerpiece that

adorned our dinner

table tonight. Your superb

placement of three matchbox cars

and a robot was exquisite.

•

· *Five* ·

Loosening the Straitjacket

Permission for Working Moms

It's 5:10 p.m. and I'm just heading out the office door. The day-care lady's going to have my hide . . . again. But worse than that, Bret's face is going to be a mile long. He will be among the last couple of children left waiting by the door to be rescued.

I dread the guilt that is already swallowing me. Not just because I'm late, but because Bret doesn't much care for the center anyway—to put it mildly. His little three-year-old voice asks me every day if he has to go. It's affordable, it had an opening, it's on the route between work and the apartment, it's my only choice in the matter.

"Yes, son, you must go." Every day I hate telling him that. Every day he hates hearing it. Yet we each go through the motions without applying the brakes. We each do what we must.

As a perker-upper for both of us, while he pulls on his coat I tell him we'll stop on the way home at McDonald's. This doesn't elicit much response; McDonald's is becoming old hat. We stop there anyway and get carry-out. The fragrance of fries wafts up to our hungry noses. We decide to sneak a few from the bag while we sit in rush-hour traffic.

Halloween decorations are beginning to pop up around the neighborhood. He tells me there's going to be a party at school. We speculate as to what the costume of choice might be: Dracula, ghost and clown are touched on. We are both glad for the distracting thoughts, yet the conversation is not a lively one.

Upon arriving home we unwrap our burgers and dump the fries out on the edge of our makeshift plates. I grab the ketchup and pour a couple glasses of milk. We sit in the dim light of the kitchen and eat in silence. We are both exhausted.

Bret plays in the bathtub for a while. I turn on the television and try to unwind as I pick up the morning's mess left behind. Bret soon calls for me to come wrap him up in a towel. We get his "jammies" on and watch a little television together. I tuck him in. I'm not far behind; morning swings around in a hurry. Another day is chalked off our calendars.

The pattern repeats with only slight variations from day to day. Halloween draws near. A clown it will be. We have most of the makings to whip that up; cheap is always in order.

The night before the party we take the old red pillow case with white polka dots (where in the world that thing came from I have no earthly idea) and cut a head hole and two arm holes in it. I have an old white feather hair net left over from the big fad in the sixties; we decide to use it as a headpiece. Early the next morning, I spend a considerable amount of time applying my version of clown makeup: white base, lipstick around his eyes and mouth, green eye shadow here and there. Voila! A clown.

Bret takes one look in the mirror and hates it. He's not going as a clown! he declares.

"There is no time for anything else!" I reply. "Besides, you look great," I say, and I mean it. I do not convince him. He begins to cry and the makeup runs. I fuss around, making funny faces, trying to get the gist of what's wrong. He is utterly sad and I don't know why.

He will not, cannot, stop crying. This is not like him. He's always been busy and rambunctious; he has never been a crybaby. In fact, rarely does he cry. He was blessed with a chipper personality and the ability to overcome or simply grind on through the tough stuff.

But now he cries. From the depth of him, he cries. For the life of me, I do not, cannot understand what it's all about. The clock is ticking. It's time to leave for work.

I run and grab the camera to capture this little clown on film, hoping some coaxing antics will cheer him up. He has always been a ham for the camera. It does not cheer him up. I still have the picture of that little elfin face, tears mixed with white makeup around his chin. Fresh ones brimming out of his deep brown eyes over his thick, long lower lashes.

After a near all-out power struggle—not physical, but commanding—finally I drop him off at school. He is slump-shouldered and holding back another flood. He is still dressed as a clown and hating it. I kiss him good-bye and bid him to have a good time. The door closes behind me. I cry all the way to work. I cry once more as I write this story that is twenty-three years in my past.

*   *   *

This scene has never blurred or softened at the edges in my memory portfolio. It is one of those time periods I would like to do over but cannot. Today, Bret says he can't remember what the tears were all about; I am grateful for that. But he knows it happened because he's seen the photograph many times.

I believe it has vividly stuck in my mind for a couple of reasons. It was symbolic of many things that were wrong with our lives during that time. I honestly believe Bret's tears overflowed from a very deep well having nothing to do with clowns and everything to do with time, or lack of. That vivid image serves as a reminder of how easily we can miss our kids, because certainly I was, unintentionally, robbing both of us. Not because I was working, although there is no getting around the fact that work robs our children of time with us, but because I had not yet realized a few valuable lessons.

I hadn't learned to stand my ground. I hadn't realized the importance of sticking to priorities. And I hadn't given myself permission to play. Fortunately for both of us, the clown incident triggered a good long search for what was wrong.

Gradually I figured out some very important things—and I believe the Lord used them to help me make some basic attitude changes.

STAND YOUR GROUND. Lessons on standing my ground came in bundles and made life much easier once they became ingrained through practice. I needed to be firm with my workplace and myself. These lessons also apply to stay-at-home moms who find themselves slaves to volunteer work and other over-extended commitments. Here's what I learned:

Five o'clock p.m. meant go get my son. Immediately. Not after I'd jotted one more thing down or passed on one more message or dropped something in the mailbox. It meant watch the clock and start winding down ten minutes earlier. It meant not answering the phone at the stroke of five. It meant eliminating the guilt of being late. It meant no more evenings started with long faces. It meant the gaining of trust and security for and from my son. It meant GO HOME. Amazingly, life at work did not fall apart when I started this practice. Being the last one out the door, I realized, had not proven my loyalty or won me an award or more money. It simply meant I had gotten sloppy with my time somewhere along the way and set the stage for anxiety.

STICK TO YOUR PRIORITIES. "No way do I waste ten minutes in my day!" you say. Monitor yourself, then try it. There's an old saying: work expands to meet the time allotted to it. Exactly. Do not allot tardy. Ten minutes a day, five days a week borders on an hour of stress-inducing time that can be cut from your life. It doesn't matter if you are the husband or wife, mommy or daddy, you and your family deserve this respect.

Prioritize those ten minutes, or whatever your personal goal time is. Maybe you are a punctual person, but try using the car trip or the train ride home for the same purpose. Whatever, see that block of time as an opportunity to call forth a thankful spirit that this part of the day is behind you and a cherished portion is beginning.

Don't groan; give me a chance here. Remind yourself that you are going home to a precious gift. God's gift to you. Granted, this takes serious work some days! And sometimes you do your part, but then you get home and your child behaves very unlike a cherished gift! My friend Mary Beth uses a phrase during times when one of her children is being obnoxious that has really stuck with me. She audibly refers to the troublesome child as "Oh Child of God." What an awesome reminder!

PERMISSION TO PLAY. Shock yourself daily with the following announcement to your attitude: you have permission to look forward to embracing, gaining pleasure from and playing with your children.

It is oh so easy to take your tired work self and let it fall into the trap of just going through the motions. Look for opportunities for creative relaxation and enjoyment. Maybe you won't find them every time—but then again, maybe you will.

*   *   *

I remember another evening not long after the clown episode. I'm out the door at the stroke of five, talking to my attitude all the way to the day-care center—or nursery school, as they were referred to back then. Work has been very harried. I choose a classical music channel, as opposed to depressing news, and consciously free my mind, then begin picturing Bret's small frame waiting, needing to be hugged, just as I do. I ponder the fact that perhaps his day hasn't been so hot either.

He is very happy to see me. The hug says it all.

Bret and I sit in traffic; I tell him the good and bad parts about my day. He, in turn, shares some of his. We decide we deserve something special. It is simply time for the horses to graze in fresh pastures. Even a bareback rider would be too much weight this day. And so, a quick run through the supermarket turns up a package of those crackers that come with the cheese that you spread with a stick, a fresh box of raisins, a bag of carrots and two push-up ice cream bars.

Bret stands on a chair pulled up to the sink next to me. He peels the carrots; I cut them into strips; he plunks them in a glass of ice water. I remove the covers from the cheese packets; he places things on the table. I ask him to create a centerpiece while I get a candle. Just because I've never seen three matchbox cars and a robot used for a centerpiece doesn't mean it can't be done, and so it is. I pour the glasses of milk. He sprinkles some raisins on our paper plates. The candle is lit and we unwind, share and laugh together.

He plays in the tub for a while. I clean up the mess left behind from the morning rush. We eat our orange push-ups on a pink blanket in the middle of the blue living room, sitting cross-legged on the floor. I read him a story and we talk about Valentine's Day which is still about three weeks off.

I have spent a good deal of time lately trying to remember the utter importance special holidays hold for children. I think of bareback riding and anticipate a corner, leaning into it for balance. I certainly don't want to get trampled like I did Halloween. We decide to stop on the way home tomorrow evening and buy some red construction paper and paper doilies. We already have plenty of glue. There are a few people I would like to send some cards to also. I'll make mine as well. Why not?

Bret goes to bed. I'm not far behind. I must get up extra early and throw a load of clothes in the washer so I can hang them around the bathroom before we leave in the morning. Although there is much to do, peace surrounds me as I close my eyes.

Not all days after my "awakening" were like this. But more were close to it than were not. I certainly wasn't June Cleaver and Bret wasn't the Beav. There was no Ward in our home at the time. We lived in the real world. But my attitude had changed, and therefore, so had I.

*   *   *

I was discussing this whole topic recently with a close friend of mine who happens to be a social worker. She agreed that attitude can do amazing things. Then she reminded me that one has to be equipped with a reserve to dip into, in order to be able to pull out that good attitude, and sometimes we just don't have reserve.

Point well taken. It's true. We earthly humans can flat out run dry. But God never does, and he is the one who fills us up with the Holy Spirit, the Counselor, the Comforter—the healing Attitude-Changer. That's why it's so important for us to give him our reins before we come to the end of ourselves. He will lead us to, and fill us with, refreshing waters (Ps 23:2). He promises us that if we drink of the water he gives us, we will never thirst (Jn 4:13-14).

"Let us then approach the throne of grace with confidence, so that we may receive mercy and find grace to help us in our time of need," Hebrews 4:16 reads. Draw near. Drink. Mercy. Grace. Blessing upon blessing. There for the taking.

And keep this in mind when you are fretting—it's something my dad has said to me since I was small. It's amazing how many times it rings true—when I remember to let it. *Ten years from now it won't make a bit of difference. And maybe even tomorrow.*

*   *   *

It's something I wanted to say to a mother I never met—although my heart ached for her after I heard about her child, whom I also never met. I was reporting a story for a newspaper, a story about lunchroom behavior from pre-school through college. How do kids decide who to sit with? What do they talk about? What social function does the lunch period serve? It was a light story and fun. I enjoyed talking to kids, lunchroom supervisors and teachers. Never did I expect to hear something so sad.

Perhaps it impacted me so strongly because I live across the street from a day-care center. Every morning I watch mothers and an occasional father drag sleepy children out of cars—sometimes not long after seven a.m. Some are carrying blankets and other pieces of their lives. Many don't get picked up until after six p.m. It settled me some to actually visit inside a facility and see that the children are well cared for.

But I heard a disturbing story that stuck with me. Day-care workers had to teach a child how to feed itself. A child far beyond the age when most children clumsily learn this task. It seems the mother was always in a hurry, as well as tired from all the rush, and so feeding the child herself saved her not only valuable time but mess.

I wanted to track down that poor mother and say, "Ten years from now the twenty minutes you saved each day escaping clean-up won't make a bit of difference to the success of your life, and maybe even tomorrow. But it certainly will to your child."

I wanted to give her permission to re-evaluate her system. I wanted her to have memories like I do. Memories of fat little fingers and palms spread out over a gaping mouth, trying to get the tasty morsels to stay where they belong. A crooked little plastic spoon that helps a toddler wield the tipsy load in the right direction. The triumphant grin that spreads across a munchkin's face when he has hunted down an escaped pea on his highchair tray, finally picks it up and now holds it between his toothless gums grinning like a baboon.

Yes, kids learning to eat create many a mess. Often they are intentional, as in the "bombs away" game they play leaning over the side of the high chair grinning, watching milk or handfuls of applesauce splat on the floor. But it is part of what we remember for the rest of our lives. It is another step toward their independence, which comes flying at us with the speed of the first downhill slope on a roller coaster.

Take time, find time, create time to enjoy your children. Cancel some of their lessons if you have to, or sign up for something with them. Watch them pick out their own clothes for the day and ask them why they made that choice. So what if they don't match? "Ten years from now. . . ."

Sometimes put out a towel for them next to your exercise mat and work out together instead of dropping them off or leaving them behind to go to your workout. You will have all the days of your life to exercise alone after they're gone.

Give yourself a mental break: no parent is doing it all and doing it well. Don't put unfair expectations on yourself. If another mother is doing her best to give you a guilt complex when you know, beyond the shadow of a doubt, that God has called you to do what you're doing, ask God to soften her heart, as well as yours.

"Each one should use whatever gift he has received to serve others, faithfully administering God's grace in its various forms" (1 Pet 4:10). Take heart in knowing that you are following God's plan for your life. Use your own gifts for your own family—and beyond. Don't envy or imitate somebody else. What you've got is *special.*

Stay-at-home moms need to be reminded that many working moms are tending to their children: schoolteachers, YMCA instructors, dance instructors, doctors and nurses, the lady at the dry cleaner's who got the spots out of the confirmation dress, the postal employee who delivers her child's letter to Grandma, waitresses, day-care workers (babysitters), the lady who cuts her child's hair just in time for school pictures, the editor of her child's Sunday-school literature . . . all helping, in one way or another, to care for her child.

A long-term friend of mine and I were recently conversing about where we are in our lives: both empty nesters, she is now an officer in a bank and I'm a very busy writer. Both careers began after the children were in high school. We are living proof of that old adage, "It's never too late."

But we don't have much time to get together anymore, and we were bemoaning that fact. When the kids were little, she, like Mary, was another bosom buddy with whom I spent a good deal of time. Her children were a few years older than mine and seemed to be doing fine, so she naturally became one of my mentors.

Now when we get together, after updating news of our families' progress and checking off our latest achievements, the conversation always rambles its way back to "the good old days," and we begin reminiscing about the tribulations and triumphs we shared while raising the "youngens."

During this particular visit recently, our conversation danced with anecdotes as vivid as neon jogging clothes. Our children were young, and we were young, and laughter, frustration, joy and tears spilled as often as the milk at the dinner table.

And then we started talking about today's too-busy parents and our mood swung to sad. Big houses, mounds of toys, several cars, climbing the corporate ladder, day care; tired parents, single parents, overdue bills, latchkey kids.

"All their children's memories will belong to someone else," she lamented. "They will be the treasures of whoever is watching their kids." We carried on this line of conversation for some time. It was easy for a judgmental tone to hover around our comments.

After I arrived home and reflected on our conversations, it occurred to me that I had a very short memory.

Visions of a weeping clown crept into my mind.

And then I realized that "all their children's memories will belong to someone else" isn't totally true. Yes, many will. And one hopes they're not first steps or first words or dance recitals and baseball games. But working parents can collect volumes of happy memories about and with their children, simply by giving themselves permission to have, and working at, a little creative, spontaneous enjoyment. Time to play. Warm memories.

Working parents will probably collect their own clown story somewhere along the way, too. But find me any parent without one and I'll show you somebody who's really missed their kids!

•

Dear God,
When you mirrored my
torqued-up face for me
today, I learned just how
silly Stubborn looks.
Who says you
don't have a sense of humor?

•

· Six ·

When All Else Fails, Laugh

Humor

I honestly believe that a sense of humor is as vital to joy-filled memories as a pacifier is to a screaming baby's mouth, and you already know how I feel about pacifiers.

I'd like to focus here on the importance—vital importance, healing importance, saving grace importance—of finding the funny side. And there is almost always a funny side. A ludicrous ("ludicrous" as defined in Webster's New World Dictionary: "laughably absurd") element that keeps the cannon from going off and enables you to move past the moment.

Sometimes the laughably absurd side of the situation doesn't hit you until much later, thereby transforming a traumatic encounter into a hilarious memory. Other times, a snicker erupts the instant your mind translates reality into . . . into . . . the laughably absurd.

If it happens on the spot, it can save the day.

For instance, when the apostle Peter said, "But do not forget this one thing, dear friends: With the Lord a day is like a thousand years, and a thousand years are like a day" (2 Pet 3:8), he was explaining that the Lord is not slow; God's time is not our time. He was giving us the long view. I suspect, however, that among his readers during those days there was at least one parent of a defiant teenager, grounded adolescent or baby with diarrhea who snickered out loud, then hollered, "Amen! You can say that again, Buster! One day is definitely like a thousand years!" I know I've had that thought many a time.

And I had one of those "days" when Brian was about two-and-one-half years old. By total grace, a parental victory prevailed at the conclusion of this particular incident, but it was a lion's den for sure—an arena I thankfully never had to enter again. A sense of humor ultimately—and accidentally—became the weapon that allowed me to survive the war.

Brian was in need of new shoes, and he hated anything new, including the mere suggestion.

*　　*　　*

"Guess what, Brian?" I say, as chipper as humanly possible.

"What!" he declares more than answers as he sits spellbound in front of the television while Bert and Ernie do their thing.

"Today's the day you get to pick out a brand new pair of shoes!"

"No. I don't want to."

"But Brian, you are getting to be such a big boy now. Your feet have grown so much your toes are touching the ends of your shoes."

"So?"

"So, we certainly don't want your toes to get crooked and start hurting."

"I don't care if they do."

"Well, I bet you're tired of looking at those worn out-old shoes. I know I am."

He takes the end of blankie that isn't trailing from his mouth and covers his shoes with it. "I don't look at them." He also doesn't look at me during any of this conversation.

"How about this? How about we get you a pair of gym shoes?" A daring suggestion since white, square-toed, leather high-top jobbies were about all anyone's child wore back then.

"No. NO NEW SHOES."

"But new gym shoes can run fast and jump high!"

"I CAN run fast. I don't want to jump high."

"You need them, Brian," I say through tightening lips.

"I don't want to go," he replies, just as tight.

"We have to go, Honey." I have read somewhere that using terms of endearment softens the listener—and the message. "It's not a matter of whether you want to go or not, Sweetheart. This is not a discussion. You have to go."

"I'm not going."

Okay, I say to myself, control yourself and think this through.

You can pick him up and carry him to the car and into the shoe store, kicking and screaming all the while. Or you can stall the excursion a bit until his mood turns more toward the agreeable.

You've got plenty of laundry you can start on, truckloads of ironing you can perhaps make a dent in, a bag of chocolate chips that are just waiting to become cookies. You can get those kinds of things behind you before you set out on a journey. And remember, we're talking riding bareback, not breaking wild broncos. There is time in this lovely spring day to find a peaceful solution.

I'm sure of it.

"Well, I don't want to go right now, anyway," I say rather too perkily. "We won't go until after lunch. Maybe we can get an ice cream cone for dessert on the way home from getting your new shoes."

Silence.

I translate this silence as a form of truce and agreement. Oh silly me.

By the time the peanut-butter-and-honey sandwich crumbs are being whisked off the table, I find myself trying to think of an invitation to buy new shoes that can't be refused, which seems a dichotomy in itself: What normal person doesn't like new shoes anyway? But, this is Brian, exactly as God gave him to us. Our gift to treasure and love—not necessary to understand. So on with the mental gymnastics.

The ice cream cone seed has already been planted; now how to get a mention of the shoes back in there without sounding an alarm? I do, however, want to make sure the ground rules are clearly understood before we depart on this SHOE-BUYING journey. And from experience I know that the normally fun, happy and agreeable Brian has a way of digging in occasionally, to say the least. Digging himself in to the bottom of the miry pit. And today, he has already reached for the shovel.

And so, right or wrong, the challenge suddenly becomes: to use the gift of creative thinking God has given me to smooth the way and help save this kid from himself. After all, my goal is to raise a cooperative child, not an inferior subordinate.

"So, are you ready for an ice cream cone?" I ask.

"Not if I have to get shoes first."

"How about if we get the ice cream cone first?"

"Okay," he says flatly.

I smile and rumple the wispy blonde hair on top of his cute little strong-willed head. At this point in time there is nothing funny brewing. Nothing. War is in the air. My motherly intuition is sounding its alarm.

Our ice cream cones go down without incident. Like NASA, I feel the countdown begin. "T" minus a ten-second pause and counting. Nine, eight, seven . . . liftoff!

"Okay!" I say with a flurry of excitement. "Let's go get those new shoes!"

"I told you I'm not getting new shoes."

"Brian, you need new shoes and we are getting them today. We're leaving on vacation soon and this is the only chance we'll have." The excitement in my voice has dissipated for this announcement. It is replaced by an authoritative command. "You got your ice cream, now it's time to get your shoes. Get your fanny in the car! We're going to the shoe store. Now."

We throw our sticky, ice cream-residue napkins away and head for the car. The ride to the shoe store is not a long one—maybe five minutes—but seems to take an hour. I am busy making a plan for all the possibilities. But maybe I don't need one. He did get in the car, right?

Wrong. In my wildest dreams I could not have foreseen what was to transpire.

We park the car and he reluctantly dawdles his way into the shoe store. We browse around at the rather large display of children's shoes. No matter which one I suggest, he hates it. He hates them all. He doesn't want white. He doesn't like colors.

"They're dumb. They don't have any I like. Let's go home," he says. "I like my old ones."

War is past the brewing stage now. The trenches are dug, the warriors are prepared for battle. If ever I hate to be reminded of the stubborn bent I have, it is here and now. His squinted little brow mirrors mine. We stand facing each other with arms crossed in front of us.

"We're not leaving without new shoes," I say matter-of-factly. It takes every ounce of control I have to keep from throwing a major hissing fit. I muster this control, however, while I try to sort out my scrambled brain. I need a plan. A plan to make good on the announcement I just heard myself make.

I run through a battery of options:

(1) I can try to cram his foot into a shoe. I immediately rule this out because I don't have money to throw away on shoes that don't actually fit, and there will be no way to know this for sure without a good measure on cooperative toes.

(2) I can whisk him back to the car. No dice. He will have won: his "NO NEW SHOES!" announcement will have prevailed.

(3) I can spank him, causing submission. Nasty scene in a shoe store. Brian's reaction to a spanking is not usually one of submission. Isolation works best for him, but then we're back to #2 which I have already ruled out.

(4) I can admit I don't know what to do. Right.

But I do know that love is patient, and patience is a fruit of the Spirit.

I go with #4 because I truly don't know what else to do, and I hope that through patience I'll learn what to do. Exhausted sigh follows this decision.

Firmly I grip his sweet little arm and lift him into one of the chairs. Nose to nose I explain that it is time to get shoes.

He counters my oh-so-firm announcement by sitting on his feet.

92

This is *not* the point in the story where I see how humorous the situation is. Many things flash through my mind; laughter is not one of them. I grab two shoes off the display area, blow a hair off my forehead and settle in.

"Can I help you?" a salesman asks, looking directly at Brian.

"No."

"Yes," I quickly counter. "Brian needs new shoes."

"Okay, big guy, let's have a measure, here." The salesman reaches beneath the chair next to Brian and produces the familiar silver appliance. Brian stares at him and doesn't move. I try to remain calm.

"Okay, son, let's see that growing foot." The man touches Brian's knee. Brian breaks eye contact and doesn't respond.

"Why don't you give us a minute?" I say. "We seem to need a little adjusting time."

"Fine. Just give a holler when you're ready." He retreats to behind the counter where the cash register is and I see him talking to the female cashier. She laughs. I do not.

"Brian," I say through my teeth, "we are not leaving here until you get some new shoes. Why don't you just put your foot out there, let the man measure, pick out a shoe and we'll be done."

"No."

"Then we'll just sit here until you change your mind. I don't care if it takes all day." It occurs to me that it just might.

"Can I help you?" a young saleslady asks. I look at Brian. He doesn't look at me, or her.

"Not just yet," I chirp.

"Let me know if you need help," she says, and proceeds to huddle with the other two behind the counter.

Let her know if I need help? Isn't it obvious I need a miracle?

*   *   *

Brian and I continue to sit in silence for what seems like an eternity. This could take longer than I planned on, but it will finally happen, I reassure myself. In the meantime, I just need to have patience . . . patience . . . patience . . . patience to come up with a plan.

While I'm busy entertaining the idea of hanging myself with a 24″ shoelace from the display next to me (a plan I rule out as soon as I realize Brian still won't get any shoes), the salespeople smile at me as they pass by with armloads of boxes. Shoes other people and their children are buying. Some of them are getting more than one pair. Parents and their little darlings are chatting and laughing.

I am reminded of all the times laughter rings throughout our house. So much of it begins with Brian, too: his expressions, his natural bent to explore and the joy that comes with discovery, antics that delight and entertain, sweet and precious moments he gives us with kisses, hugs and uncommon stories. . . .

And then the original salesman interrupts my daydreaming by appearing before me. He doesn't speak, but he wears a look on his face that says, "Well, how about it? Are we ready now?"

I take one hopeful look at Brian and am slam-dunked out of the sounds of ringing laughter and back into reality. I shake my head in denial.

Minutes tick by. Brian's shins grow roots in the chair. Inner dialoguing runs rampant. Once a parent takes a stand, I silently tell myself, and after they have considered the rationale of the situation, if the original stand is correct, they should stick to it. That is the case here.

Waiting has become my plan.

Brian looks at me out of the corner of his eye and I swear he reads my mind. A couple more shovels of imaginary dirt can be seen flying over each of our shoulders as we dig our trenches a little deeper.

Brian has shifted several times but continues to harbor his feet under his buttocks. I'm sure his legs have fallen asleep and must be driving him nuts.

Suddenly, as he is mid-shift, I am swept with an overview of this ludicrous scene. My mind replays the laughably absurd day in its entirety and a laugh begins to rankle around in my throat. I make several attempts to swallow it down, but it bubbles and perks ever higher, until finally it erupts, startling the near-dozing Brian.

"What's so funny?" he asks.

"Oh, nothing. I was just thinking how silly it would be, sleeping here tonight. And if you'll excuse me, I need to make a couple phone calls. I've got to call Mrs. Gingell so she can let Bret know why no one will be home when he gets off the school bus. And I have to call Dad and tell him to go ahead and eat dinner on his way home, and to not expect us."

Brian's eyes nearly pop out of his head. I realize I'm on to something here. And so for good measure I add, "I'll tell Dad to bring us the sleeping bags and a flashlight. Bet it gets dark in here."

Brian says nothing. I, his mother, who has finally seen the humor in this war, sit next to him chuckling like a loony-tune. I thrash through my purse collecting change for the phone. "I'll be right back. Sit tight." I nearly lose control as this line slips out of my mouth. Like he needs a directive to do *that*? I'm hysterical. What a gas! "Sit tight," I repeat through waves of laughter. "Isn't that funny?"

Suddenly, one of Brian's legs slips out from under him. He cringes at the pain that comes from straightening out a locked joint.

Then the other leg slowly unfolds.

"Okay," he says through a pout. "I'll get the dumb shoes."

*   *   *

This is a story I wouldn't trade for anything. It was the day that Brian learned without a doubt that I meant what I said.

It had lasting effects in terms of numerous other trials. If I said we'd wait—for behavior to change, or for sit-in-the-chair-until-you-apologize-nicely time to pass—he knew I was prepared to wait forever; *I meant what I said.* And so we didn't have to; he obeyed. Almost all of the time.

Now, I could spend the rest of my days wondering if there might have been a better way to handle this. But then I would be fretting over spilled milk instead of noticing I needed to pour more. All I know is that I made measured choices, the best I was capable of at the time. Some days, simply hanging in there takes all you've got.

But that's not the point. The BIG lesson was this: it was the capacity to relax enough to allow visions of the ludicrous to dance in my head that turned a very questionable situation into a growing period for both of us.

There just is no point in hanging onto hostility, not when there's an outside possibility that humor and laughter can replace it and actually, perhaps, accomplish something. Sit back and really look at your situation. Almost anything that is extreme is bizarre. Almost any child is surprised by unexpected behavior, and ludicrous vision definitely warms the cold war or cools down the heated battle thereby altering behavior. And the best part is, it makes life easier.

There are numerous studies being done on laughter therapy. Many believe it heals not only mind and spirit, but body as well. The technique, whether it be old Three Stooges movies, cartoons

96

or whatever, is even being used in some hospitals. "Laugh and be well," Matthew Green said. Clear back in 1737 he had this wisdom.

And what a fountain of humor children are. They are funny. Not always, but truly, they are funny. Try not to shut out your kids by hanging on to yesterday's troubles, whether they were initiated by the kids or not.

Learn to use humor—which can be a hotline to joy—as a transition tool. A transition not only from anger to laughter, but from anger to forgiveness, of ourselves and those around us.

"Be kind and compassionate to one another, forgiving each other, just as in Christ God forgave you" (Eph 4:32). So many times a good laugh lightens the mood and the spirit enough to let tenderheartedness seep in. Instant forgiveness can often follow before we even knew we had it in us.

"Of manners gentle, of affections mild; In wit, a man; simplicity, a child: With native humor temp'ring virtuous rage, Form'd to delight at once and last the age," wrote Alexander Pope. Let's hope a centuries-old message takes root in our hearts.

I have always been thankful that my parents both loved to laugh. It just came naturally to them, and so it did to me, and so it does to my sons. There is a warmth that surrounds laughter and permeates an entire house. Laughter fans an atmosphere of openness and helps us be comfortable with one another. It helps keep us from taking ourselves so seriously. It is an easy thing to share. It is catching.

When we can learn to laugh at ourselves, we have not only helped our own cause, but set a good example. We have taught our children that they, too, can—and *will*—make errors and still get through it all.

One day just a couple of years ago, Brian told George and me about a terrible day he'd just had. *Everything* had gotten fouled up. Each thing he did made the situation worse.

"You know how they say we learn from our mistakes? Well, I'm a bundle of knowledge today!" he said through a laugh.

Although the situation was confusing and caused him much anxiety at the time, he could laugh at himself now, and we could each laugh with him, and share some of our own embarrassing memories. We grow through those trying times. And we grow closer to one another by laughing together about them.

Yes, the shoe-store memory is a good one all right, and we've shared it many times. I think back to it now whenever I walk into a shoe store. I'm just thankful I didn't have to find out what it's like to sleep in one.

•

Dear Mom & Dad,
I lost my new glasses
in a six-foot-deep
mud hole. You'll be glad
to know I didn't dive in
to find them; I know
how you hate me tracking
up your clean floor.

•

· Seven ·

Haircut Wars

Perspective

It started with Bret when he was three years old, this thing about hair. Up until then, it was just something that grew on his head. Oh sure, we'd had an occasional bout of entangled gooey gum wads, but other than that, hair was just something that basically took care of itself after a little washing and slicking down.

Then one day hair issues as we knew them changed.

Bret sat watching early Saturday morning cartoons—with the scissors. This was, obviously, an activity he had not checked in with Mom about. I walked around the corner just in time to see disaster strike. He had the scissors laid flat to his scalp on the very top of his head. The hinge rested just at the hairline of his forehead. The blades were open, as was his mouth. Before I could open mine, *CRUNCH!*

The scalping registered in my brain in slow motion. His trance-like state seemed to have nothing to do with the rest of his body. It was as though his arm and hand had acted on their own.

"Bret!" I screamed, but of course too late. I responded more to the horror of what had already happened than in warning. Two-inch, slick brown hairs slid down past his eyes and over his nose.

"Bret!" I repeated. "What have you done?"

"Nothing."

"Oh yes you have, you've cut a path down the top of your head!"

"No I didn't," he said, brushing the itchy telltale remnants out of his face.

"Go look in the mirror."

He strolled into the bathroom, pulled out the stool from under the sink and hopped up to mirror height. A look of terror captured his face and stayed there, thereby confirming my suspicions that his arm and hand had indeed acted on their own accord.

"My gosh, Bret, you're gonna have to get a crew cut to even that out. It's right smack down the middle!"

"I don't want to get a crew cut," he said, seeming surprised at the suggestion.

"Well, let's see what we can do then, if anything." I wet his hair and tried combing it this way and that. No matter what I did or how sopping I got it, it still wanted to flop apart at its manmade, one-inch-wide part. The fact Bret had slicker-than-slick, straight-as-a-board brown locks that always fell into bangs, no matter what, didn't help either.

"Well, I don't see much choice. Let's go into town and let the barber have a look to see if he has any suggestions." Bret wanted to try fixing it himself first. I handed over the comb. Then the brush. He finally gave up. Off to town we went.

The barber made the mistake of laughing when Bret walked in the door. I must admit, it was obvious why we were there, but Bret is a sensitive person. He was embarrassed, to say the least.

After setting him up in the chair, draping him with the striped cloth, turning him from side to side and whipping the remaining hair around a few times, the barber said there was only one alternative: crew cut. So be it. Closer to scalped was more the truth, but calling it a crew cut sounded better.

"It'll grow back soon," I said in consolation to a sick-looking little boy.

Well, Bret's hair doesn't grow very fast. It's the only time in his life he has ever worn a baseball cap with regularity, in contrast to his brother who seemed to have his head hermetically sealed by one clear through eighth grade.

Although this was a rather traumatic incident at the time, we all laugh about it now, just as the barber did the day Bret walked in to his shop. What a hilarious sight! But we weren't yet laughing. We had become temporarily blinded by the shock of it.

*   *   *

I think I'd be hard pressed to find a parent who doesn't have his or her own version of The Hair Horror Story. I even recall a couple neighbors of mine who didn't speak to each other for a while.

One daughter whacked the pony tail of the other's daughter right off at the rubber band. It had taken the victim's hair three years to grow long enough to make even that feeble pony tail. It was only five days later when it bit the dust. We're talking substantial tears at the time, although it's a warm-and-fuzzy chuckling experience when they get together and recount it now.

But hair has that wonderful way of giving one perspective: it will always grow back. No matter how terribly it's cut, colored or permed, you can always grow a fresh crop.

Yes. Perspective. A straightforward look at the reality of the situation. The notion that this, too—whatever it is—shall probably pass. It isn't usually, after all, life-threatening.

Consider all the options and outcomes. Is it something to find the funny side in, or something you should stop laughing about? Pondering the worst-case scenarios can often produce livable solutions. Bounce if off someone else. Stand back and take in the big picture. A runaway trip to Kmart does wonders for my perspective; so does a good hair story. And so Bret's hair finally did grow back. Nevertheless, I've always wondered if this, perhaps, was the incident that triggered Bret's haircut aversion. Let's just say it seemed as if from that point on he always wanted to wear his hair longer than we deemed appropriate.

"Can't I just let the back get a little longer?" he would always beg. Remember, this was in the same era as those white shoes kids wore; long hair was for hippies, not decent suburban cherubs.

Each time his hair would be hanging in his eyes or lapping over his collar, discussions about the next cut would begin. He was different from Brian, though; when the boom finally lowered, Bret would give in. Although the predicted grumbling got tiring, for several years it was still appropriate for me to tell the barber what Bret wanted.

I would stand where Bret couldn't see me because he couldn't turn his head because the barber had pushed his chin into his chest to cut the nape. Then I would hurl myself around in the background to get the attention of the barber and charade exactly what I was looking for. Bret always complained it was too short. I always said it was just right. Ah, the good old days.

Then he reached the age where showing up at the barber shop with him would have proved embarrassing for both of us. So before we would drop him off, George and I would give him lecture number 505 about how it wasn't worth the money to get only a smidgen cut off, and how he'd better come home looking as if he'd had a haircut.

Sometimes he did; sometimes he didn't. Lecture number 506 would follow about how money didn't grow on trees, then we would harrumph around a while until other things came along that just seemed more important to spend our energy on. Perspective.

We entered the next phase when Bret started driving and earning his own money from after-school, part-time jobs. What, he asked, if he paid for his own haircut? Shouldn't he have the right to get his hair cut any way he wanted if his own money paid for it? (Don't you just hate trick questions?) Also, by this time many were wearing somewhat longer hair at the nape of their necks, and so we said okay, within reason. We tried to be mature adults gaining perspective on the situation: styles had changed a little; passing math just seemed to be more important than the length of the hair on the back of his head. This doesn't mean there were never any grumblings, however.

"When I move out I'm going to grow hair three feet long," he would announce in an occasional huff.

"Fine. When you move out and are paying all your own bills, you can do whatever you want. You can sport hair down to your buttocks if you want. But not while you live in this house."

"I'm also going to drive you guys around in the back seat of my car," he would inform us, "with all the windows down and the stereo blasting." Seems hair started him on a roll that ended up encompassing all our trespasses, like requesting he not blow us to bits or start an earthquake with the volume. For Bret, his hair became symbolic of many things.

*   *   *

By the time Brian was old enough to whine about his hair, we had gained enough perspective to realize that hair just didn't matter that much in the grand scheme of things at our house. We were able to apply the "Ten years from now it won't . . ." guideline to issues of the hair. There were, I repeat, just too many more important things to save our energy for. Vital standing-our-ground concerns like curfew, alcohol, morality, grades and respect.

Besides, Brian's whining didn't come in the form of "I want to grow my hair longer." Noooo! When he was a freshman, Brian wanted a crew cut—and *flying lessons.*

To become a pilot had been this boy's goal since he could talk; a goal that never wavered then and still hasn't today. The notion scared me to death. All I could picture were airplanes spinning toward the earth to crash and burn. I could see my baby flying into an unpredicted hurricane. I could hear the newscaster reporting every detail of the tragic episode. But I am a parent. Conjuring up disaster comes naturally.

A friend of mine had a son who bought a motorcycle and she worried herself sick every time he pulled out of the driveway on it, imagining all sorts of grisly scenes.

Then one day she received a phone call. David, her nineteen-year-old man-child, had been critically wounded while water skiing, a sport he was well trained in. She'd better come to the hospital near the friend's cabin right away, the caller said. It was a several-hour trip.

David didn't survive. I cannot even imagine her grief. I could not understand how she could wake up in the morning with the knowledge her son was gone and even lift her head off the pillow. The Lord slowly nurtured her through the situation, but life will never be the same. She will never stop missing her son. And never in her wildest imaginations had she feared a freak boating accident. Her son had spent countless supervised hours as he was growing up learning the ins and outs of water safety. She feared the motorcycle.

I tell this incident because it harshly but instantly slams perspective into place. We cannot know, really, what tomorrow brings. We do not know, truly, what is in store for us and our children. No matter how much we worry, plan, maneuver, control and contrive, we cannot cover all the bases. We must not waste our valued time on this earth fretting over what doesn't matter. Perspective is imperative if we are to use our time with our children gainfully and joyfully.

Of course we will sometimes still worry, fret and mutter. We are human. We are parents. I am concerned every time Brian takes to the sky. But I realize he is fulfilling a heart's desire, something someone greater than I planted in his heart. I have considered that the drive to the airport is much more dangerous in terms of statistics than any flying time he does. (Perspective.) The day he came home with the tail of his shirt cut off—a traditional ceremony for first solo flights—was quite a celebration around this house. We were so proud, and he so fulfilled.

We cannot raise our children in a vacuum, sheltering them from the outside world. It is their right to explore enough to find out who they are and all they can be.

Please don't misinterpret what I'm saying. I am not promoting reckless living. I am simply trying to point out that perspective is easy to lose—in anger, in boredom, in fear, in narrow thinking, in lack of trust and wavering faith.

In a way, the entire purpose of this book is to help parents gain perspective. All of us as parents will experience lots of painful things, and many unforeseen blessings as well, as our children grow. A consistent effort to gain perspective—coupled with a mega-load of prayer, a sense of humor, and the freedom to allow for our own humanness—will help us to pass through the trying times, and to not miss the blessed ones.

"Finally, brothers, whatever is true, whatever is noble, whatever is right, whatever is pure, whatever is lovely, whatever is admirable—if anything is excellent or praiseworthy—think about such things" (Phil 4:8). What a balancer and reminder for our weary, worried minds. What a way to gain perspective. Who better to help us find it than God? I believe God grants perspective/wisdom through many avenues. For me, "Angel Vanessa" was one of them. And the year he sent her to me was a life-altering one.

*   *   *

Bret was nearing the end of seventh grade and had just received his latest in a long line of pep-up slips. For those not in the know, a pep-up slip is sent to parents to inform you that your daughter or son is either wasting his/her time, or missing assignments, or cutting classes, or failing tests and quizzes, or has a poor attitude, or . . . you get the picture. They are sent out so you can do whatever you can to help pep your child up, so to speak, in order that he or she will pull up to par.

Bret's offenses were in the wasting time, missing assignments, near-failing and general dinking around categories. He was, as I have mentioned before, a busy child. Not malicious or belligerent, simply busy. Certifiably, hyperactively busy.

At any rate, pep-up slip time used to send me into a tizzy. I was relating some of this to Vanessa, a woman who worked in the library at the junior high Bret attended. During both of my boys' reigns there I volunteered in the library once a week just to keep abreast of this creature called "junior higher." To be reminded that yes, kids that age are mean to each other. And yes, they all react to every little thing as a big deal. And yes, most parents are encountering many of your same woes. I learned this from the other volunteer moms.

So, like I said, I was shelving books while unloading my latest rankling to Vanessa. Now Vanessa knew Bret rather well because he also volunteered in the library several times a week during his homeroom class. He was what was referred to as an AV (audiovisual) person. If a classroom needed equipment from the library, Bret wheeled it to them and set up the projector. It not only helped the library, but helped him burn off a little energy as well. He reported directly to Vanessa.

When I was about halfway through my more-bad-grades diatribe—by no means the first she had listened to over a two-year period—the snow-white-haired Vanessa put down the book in her hands, turned to face me and grabbed me by the shoulders.

"Charlene, I have raised five children. My oldest child was a straight-A student and never gave me a lick of trouble. She is also one of the most miserable adults I know. Nothing is ever just right for her. She complains constantly. She is not a happy person.

"Bret, on the other hand, is one of the happiest people I've ever known. He is so willing to help and please. I honestly believe he's trying his hardest right now. It's just a difficult time for him.

"In the long run," she said, "what do you want for your children when they're grown? Don't you just want them to be content and happy? An impressive report card in their history isn't the key to happiness. Oh sure, it never hurts, but it isn't all that matters.

"Bret is a neat kid. I really like Bret and am always glad to see his smiling face come into the library. Lighten up, Charlene. Enjoy him. Grades aren't everything."

". . . whatever is true . . . whatever is lovely . . . whatever is admirable . . . if anything is excellent or praiseworthy . . . think about such things." Angel Vanessa bore the heavenly message in her own words. I knew God was speaking to me.

The light Angel Vanessa shed on our way helped us find perspective with our active little son. She had captured his strengths and made us look at them.

That same light kept us from breaking his loving spirit with our relentless monologues, badgering and disciplinary grounding over grades. It gently nurtured us into discovering the need Bret had for more acceptance and encouragement. Of course we continued to press for his best effort, but we had received a hearty lesson in unconditional love and balance.

We had been sorely missing many of his blessings because we were frankly too busy magnifying his shortcomings—a fruitless and shameful approach. Thank goodness the Lord wasn't missing a minute of Bret's or our needs and Angel Vanessa took the time to set us straight.

Bret's frequent, slightly-head-tilted smile and gleaming eyes seemed ever brighter from that day forward. And guess what? That happy, willing-to-please boy grew into a very responsible man. He still brings joy to those around him; he is dedicated to a good job; he is content and happy.

As a postscript to this selection from my memory portfolio, there was a time during that seventh-grade year when we felt forced to consider the possible "worst-case scenario" in an attempt to stand back and gain perspective. It just seemed good sense to do so.

What if he did flunk seventh grade? we wondered.

Then he would have to repeat it. Not life-threatening. Certainly not the worst thing that could happen to someone. We would survive. Angel Vanessa would have another year to warm his life by her delight in him.

But he did pass. Every grade thereafter. And he did move out and pay all his own bills. And he did grow his hair long; in fact he still has it. And that entire hair issue is still helping us keep things in perspective today. Even though it wouldn't be our choice in "dos" for his head, we love him no less because of it.

And as I sit and ponder his twinkly smile and his locks that are longer than mine, I become poignantly aware of perhaps an ultimate dose of perspective: his twenty-five-year-old, long, thinning crop and receding hairline make me realize that all too soon he's going to be bald.

•

Dear Anyone Who Will Listen,
I am Bret. The one
and only. I want a job,
an apartment, a roommate,
a motorcycle and
a dog. So what's all the fuss?

•

· *Eight* ·

The One
and Only

Individuality

After my boys reached about fifth grade, I often found it necessary
to communicate with the little darlings via the written word—mostly my words to them. This was usually done in an attempt to
accomplish a number of things, not the least of which was to keep
the volume down.

If there was an important issue I felt had gotten lost or layered
with the irrelevant, I found it a healthy exercise for me to talk about
it on paper because there were no extra, heated words flying
around. Only focus. Focus on the bottom line of the issue.

Sometimes spelling it all out helped me realize I had bought into
a power struggle. If it was a subject or incident that seemed to
escalate every time it resurfaced, bringing it up in a note at least
gave me a chance to express my entire side of the matter without

interruption. It kept both parties from retaliating with hasty, unwise words. It encouraged the balance of a loving, instructive, concerned delivery instead of a diatribe. Only the important got communicated on paper.

*   *   *

Such was the occasion on the day I wrote Bret an urgent note which demanded—I engaged my parental authority about as subtly as a two-by-four—that he write me a response. It was an unusual request, but what I needed that day couldn't seem to be accomplished via talking.

The letter was my attempt at getting inside Bret's head. I needed to find out what was really going on in there, and at the time, I was convinced he was trying to function on dead batteries.

It was June 1982, and Bret's junior-year report card had just arrived, confirming what we suspected. (It isn't true that life is one darn thing after another, it's the same darn thing over and over.) By the fuzzy hairs growing out of his chinny-chin-chin, he had managed to pass everything—but *barely* pass. He sure wasn't laying a good foundation for the rest of his life.

Let me point out that this was four years after Angel Vanessa taught me so much about perspective, about seeing the good side. Her lesson had slipped my mind for the moment.

A sense of urgency was sweeping me away: when was he going to trip his trigger and get with the program? Time was running out. I wrote a very brief cover note which pretty much expressed my "not-so-good foundation" worry.

Along with the cover letter I sent a mostly blank piece of paper that was to be filled out by Bret and returned to me. I wouldn't really say he was grounded, but I told him he could not exit his room until he made a sincere attempt to evaluate his own self by addressing the title I put on each side of that yellow ruled sheet.

The front side was labeled "Side I, Goals." At the top I wrote the following: "Dedicated to my mother whom I love and want to please today so she won't nag anymore." I thought that would elicit a chuckle and help us to pass through the front lines of this encounter. It did not; it coaxed out a groan.

The other side was labeled "Side II, Who I am, and what I have to do to achieve them (goals outlined on Side I)." All right, it wasn't very good grammar, but we both understood what it meant!

Bret disappeared behind his closed door to tackle the mission. I went on with daily household tasks, pretending I wasn't paying any attention to the ticking clock and my thumping headache. Within five minutes—oh, this ought to be good! I thought—he came bounding down the stairs two at a time (his usual pace) and delivered to me his responses.

As soon as I held the paper in my hands, Bret was out the front door with a brief comment as to his destination. After all, writing the note was all I had requested; waiting until I read it was never mentioned. And so as I heard the sounds of his car taking off down the street in the background, I approached "Side I." I did not need to pour a cup of tea to get me through these two pages; his entire outpouring was only two paragraphs long.

"My goals in life," he wrote on Side I, and I change not a letter, "are to get a job that I like, one that will suit my perticular needs, to get an apartment or rent a house (and then later on probably buy a house near a lake) with a roommate, preferably Paul, Joe, and/ or Tony. Buy a motorcycle and live in a warm climate. And then learn good penmanship. [His attempt at humor.] Also I want a *dog*!!!!!!" "Dog" was underlined five times.

It sounded to me like Bret was continuing that "happy" and "contented" course which Angel Vanessa had pointed out four years ago.

So far, his note wasn't bad. In fact, I was a little taken aback with his long-range plan. I don't know what I expected, but it wasn't something so . . . so . . . normal-sounding and succinct. Hard to argue with. I couldn't wait, however, to find out just how, exactly, he planned on accomplishing all this. I flipped to "Side II."

"I am Bret. The one and only. What I have to achieve them (the goals) is the willpower to achieve them. If I want something bad enough sooner or later I will get it unless it was never meant for me to have."

"The one and only." I sat dumbfounded staring at the phrase. My heart, which had previously been twisted in knots of anguish, suddenly swelled with thankfulness at a son who could recognize his "one-and-only-ness"—and could point it out to me.

It was written with such conviction! It came right out of him within five minutes. I may not have known who he was and what he was all about, but he certainly did. It was probably hard for him to imagine what all the fuss was for. I suspect he chalked it up as "Mom off the deep end—again."

To this day, I continue to keep that piece of paper in a notebook with other valued treasures.

*   *   *

Bret has pretty much mastered his list of goals, now, and some more besides. I'm proud of that. But what really pleases me is that he continues to be "the one and only." His hair and his freckled nose, his adventuresome spirit and his sense of humor belong to him and him alone. There has never been, nor will there ever be, another exactly like him. And I don't know if I could have had that point driven home the way it was without his words to me that announced this miracle.

The unique and separate being that God creates when he breathes life into each one of us is something to be valued, treasured and explored with awe. David acknowledges to God, in Psalm 139:13 (KJV), "Thou didst weave me in my mother's womb." Notice he speaks of weaving, not using a two-ton stamping press. The imagery there is so beautiful: it is one of time-consuming, careful, exacting planning and execution. Scrupulous examination of any hand-woven fabric reveals the different intricacies in warp and woof, tension and design, spinning of the yarn and dye lot. Each piece the unique outcome of the creator's vision.

Simply looking at the disciples Jesus chose to walk with him gives us a good study in the necessity, if you will, of individuality. Each came to him in a different way, and not all started out with the goodness one might expect: there was doubting and denying and deceit. There was questioning and impatience and unbelief. But each was selected for his own distinct personality to be used as the Lord saw appropriate for his works. Each a different part of "the body" with its own particular function to perform.

The very behavior patterns that led to Bret's pep-up slips and borderline grades are the same ones that allow him to bravely tackle new challenges and far horizons. The tireless energy that kept him on the move as a youth allows him, as an adult, to carry on until tasks are complete, to pursue until answers are found.

We are called to give thanks in all things. Not an easy charge. But the very things that seem so negative sometimes when the children are small can be their biggest assets when correctly channeled.

*   *   *

Take Brian. I always said about him when he was little, "He's going to be either President of the United States or a roller derby king." His stubborn, strong-willed little self seemed to leave no room for anything in between. But those traits also kept him from being swayed by peer pressure as he grew older. His cautious nature is one of my biggest "Thank you God" prayers because of the flying vocation he is pursuing. It also helped him nail a successful high-school wrestling career.

He will do nothing before his or its time. Nothing.

I have a picture of our boys that my father took when the three of them were on a fishing trip in New Mexico once. It is an outward symbol to me of how different they are from one another and how unique each of them is. It was taken during a fishing break when the boys—well, when *Bret*—decided they would go cliff diving.

They are mid-air, on their way down, down, down. Bret's body is in the shape of an arrow: straight, toes pointed, arms out and at a forty-five-degree angle back from his shoulders. His chin is tilted slightly upward as if drinking in the sky he parts. His long hair sails behind him. He is facing this dive and challenge with all he has.

Brian is to his left and slightly upward of Bret in the photograph. His short cropped hair is standing on end. His body can't quite seem to make up its mind between diving and assuming the fetal position. He is facing the challenge with reluctance, after standing on the cliff for a very long time until *he* finally decides he would be sorry if he didn't try it.

Brian is not a coward; Bret is not daft. They are both relatively brave and face life pretty straight—each at their own pace. They are simply learning how to do the best they can with what they have, as am I, as are all of us.

120

Bret's "one and only" message helped me with more than understanding him: it gave me license to tolerate and value myself and everybody else a little better. After all, I am a one and only, too.

Recently a Mother's Day ad campaign played on that sentiment. The words were always printed beside beautiful things—things they hoped the reading public would purchase for their moms, of course. But the message was super: "Mom, my one and only."

As I watched my boys grow in their individual characteristics, so, I realized, had George and I grown as parents. In a way, we are like babies when we start out with these children. Everything is new.

But we experiment, and corral our mistakes, hopefully learning from them. We function pretty much within our individual personalities, give or take several million compromises. In order for us to function as a healthy family without constant rocks in the works, all our little personality glitches need to settle into a pattern that fits, just like a 1,000-piece puzzle. Eventually, you have one big family picture.

Not only do you have the picture, but you have the results of mingled and mixed notions, stronger and weaker genes, like and unlike attributes. Variety within which, we hope, our children can find and strike a chord of balance. Just as I ushered spontaneity and zest into our family unit, so George, thank the Lord, brought steadfastness, wise caution, predictable strength, frugality and earnest stick-to-it-iveness. Our mates and children help fill in our missing links through their unique gifts.

Pondering the concept of individuality as it fits into the grand scheme of things suggests to me some added benefits of learning to ride bareback.

*   *   *

When rider and horse are free to feel the structure and essence of each other without cumbersome tack in between, they begin to respond to the slightest of adjustments: a rein drapes across the left of a neck, the horse turns to the right; a knee pressures in with the lightest touch, the horse responds to what he has been gently taught that means. They can feel the very breath of each other.

As they run together, the horse has the incredible ability to sense the difference between a rider who loves and respects him and wants to elicit the best that he has to give, and the one who wants to bully him around and make him what he should not have to be— trying to transform a plow horse into a high stepper. Or a cutting horse into a jumper.

A good match of horse and rider meshes the two, creating one moving object that can negotiate smoothly through thicket and valley. They have learned each other's foibles and strengths and know how to adapt to them.

Each may have to depend on the other one day to arrive safely at their destination. Sometimes the horse must carry the load; sometimes the rider must lead the horse through a rough passage. Sometimes one's instinct about a future obstacle is more accurate than the other's, and yielding becomes the safest choice.

Before yielding can be done with a trusting spirit, however, they have had to build that relationship. Learn each one's areas of might and limitation. Learn to compensate for the gaps and be grateful for the differences that actually strengthen their united capability.

When a rider mounts bareback and travels for any distance, he can feel the sweat of the working horse. The horse, by the same token, instinctively assesses the rider and appreciates respect. Appreciates that the rider has taken the time to learn enough about him to trust him enough to go without a saddle, and sometimes even without a rider.

The most important thing for the rider to know is this. *Each horse has to be ridden somewhat differently.*

Some will test you every time until you prove your endurance. Others need a heel-tap in the ribs to get them going. The secret is finding out who needs what. Heaven forbid you should heel-tap the one that's already bursting to gallop at breakneck speed, especially if you're heading for a cliff!

One of the differences in my boys can best be illustrated by the old draw-the-imaginary-line scenario. Here's the line, we parents would point out. Could be the line of tolerance, curfew, patience. Didn't matter; we all needed to know exactly where the line was to eliminate misunderstandings.

Bret would tap dance up to the line twenty times a day. The widest part of the side of his foot would skim that line, constantly making us aware of his presence, eliciting endless bouts of confirmation that we noticed he was approaching. When he did step on it and the boom would be lowered, he would retreat. He basically respected authority, if he knew it was issued with genuine concern for his well-being. But everyone was constantly aware of the line.

Brian, on the other hand, could go for long periods of time without even looking at the line. We could be lulled into forgetting there was one. He would happily be in his own little world, obeying and generally being an okay kid. Then suddenly, without warning, he would march up and stand smack on the line, looking us directly in the eye while cocking his hip and pretty much daring us to do something about it.

Disciplining Bret took endless wads of patience. Disciplining Brian took occasional miracles and a lot of planning ahead. We didn't want to break their fragile spirits; we wanted them to learn to trust and obey, God and us.

Right from the minute they appeared in this world the differences in their gifts—and the trials they presented—became obvious. Bret almost never wanted to nap. He preferred just closing his eyes for a while, then revving up full-steam again. He never did crawl, but was running by the time he was nine months old—before he even had a tooth in his mischievous little grin. He ate almost anything and demanded a lot of attention. He could outlast anyone at the end of the day.

Brian, on the other hand, was (aside from his dig-in moments) an easy infant. So easy, in fact, that it worried me. After all, all I had to compare him with was the very busy Bret. Why, I wondered, would Brian sit in a playpen and actually play with things? Although the happy sounds and the sitting still gave me welcome resting periods, I wondered: is something wrong with him? After all, Bret had quickly learned how to lower the sides and escape.

I decided Brian was doing okay when he sprouted a surprise tooth at four months. Then he started showing some of his true colors when he began to selectively spit out green and strained foods.

Bret wandered off in a department store when he was about three and I decided I'd teach him a lesson by letting him realize he was lost. No such luck; I followed him around for several minutes while he explored every nook and cranny in the place and chatted with everyone in his path. Brian, remember, hated everything new, including shoes, baby sitters and foreign territory. Until he got to be about five and decided the world was his to conquer.

*   *   *

It is so much fun to see the boys together now. They stand peering at one another, shaking their heads. Then they grin and start teasing or wrestling.

"Man," Bret will say, "how did this ever happen to me? How did I ever end up with a brother who's a jock? And look at that hair!" He said that the first time he saw the flat-top which Brian sports in the summer.

Brian, on the other hand, delivers the same types of teasing when it comes to his brother the "biker," with his passion for motorcycles.

I have noticed that some of their different tendencies seem to have traded places over the years. Bret, especially when it comes to engines, can now tinker around for a long time without getting restless. He truly enjoys the tinkering. Brian, although he sticks with a project until it is done, wants to get it done much faster. Conquer it, you might say.

But for the most part, their individual characteristics have remained the same, simply growing stronger as the years pass. And I would not change a one, although they were not, and are sometimes still not, always easy to comprehend. But then again, I guess *this* one-and-only isn't either.

•

Dear Mom,

Love ya!

Bri.

•

· *Nine* ·

Learning to Eat Crow

Humility

It was a tough parental decision: how do we handle our third-grade son's getting kicked off the school bus?

Disciplining wasn't the toughest part. There was also the little matter of the total embarrassment that came with the entire episode. Our son had been kicked off the bus for *spitting*. For spitting *out the bus window.* And the spittle—wouldn't you just know it— accidentally happened to land on a car.

Well, I don't need to tell you that this is something George and I weren't mentally prepared to deal with. And, there isn't a chapter on spitting in any of the parenting handbooks I've read. Personally, I would have never believed it was actually my son who had propelled the ill-fated gob, except for the small fact that he admitted to it—without batting an eye. In fact, there almost seemed to be a hint of pride in his voice. Pride in his bull's-eye delivery.

So much for a mother's "accidental" version of the story.

Thus leading to the point of this chapter. Never, and I mean never, say that your child would never . . . (fill in any awful, mischievous, malicious, destructive, dishonest thing you can think of here). I repeat, DON'T SAY IT! Especially out loud within earshot of anyone. Most of all, never, but never, allow yourself to believe it. Because as sure as you do, you will experience lesson number one in Learning to Eat Crow, a handbook that should 1) be written and 2) be mandatory reading for all parents.

The warning has already been recorded in the Psalms. Psalm 31:23, to be exact. "Love the Lord, all his saints! The Lord preserves the faithful, but the proud he pays back in full." No mincing of words there. If the divine Word of God promises it, you can bet your parental reputation that it's true. And who better to deliver the humbling blow than your children?

Be aware, if you are new to adolescent short-circuiting, that you do not have a clue, not even a particle of a hint, as to their capabilities and spur-of-the-moment possibilities.

Now I'm pretty sure—although I have just fallen into the dangerous dark hole of Parental Assumptions by even saying that— that Brian didn't lie awake the night before, scanning through the endless realm of possible disgusting behaviors he might exhibit the next day. I assume—possibly my next naive error—that it just seemed like the thing to do on the spur of the moment. There was this boring bus ride. There was this open window. There was this car. There was this spit.

Or else he was dared. Always a possibility, especially with boys.

At any rate, he did it. And he got busted. And a letter was sent home saying that he could not ride the bus for the rest of the week (two days), and that he would be allowed back on the bus the next week, assuming, of course, that his renegade spitting-raid days were over.

Well now. Do we make this third-grader walk to school about a mile and a half, crossing numerous unguarded, dangerous intersections? Do we make him hitchhike? Or, as usual, do the parents really become the burdened ones because they now have to accommodate the penalty?

You guessed it. And I lectured him once for every revolution those car tires made, not only on the way to school but on the way home as well. Home: the place where he spent a good deal of time doing extra chores.

In the meantime, this whole spitting subject took on a life of its own. "Dad spits all the time," Brian said defensively. "What's the big deal."

"That's because I have an accumulation of saliva that needs to be released," my husband countered with a near-medical tone in his voice.

"So did I," Brian said.

"Well, I think you could have swallowed it since you were on a bus," George responded, somewhat flustered and caught in his own web.

"Well, why don't you do that then, Dad? Why do you spit and make Mom disgusted?"

Silence.

Then, "Brian, I don't spit on cars."

"Dad, it accidentally landed on a car." He looks straight in his dad's eyes. A trace of dishonesty flickers across his face. He is not believed. He is told that if he ever gets in trouble again for spitting, he will walk to school, even if we have to walk with him.

(Another warning: Don't make threats you are not prepared to deliver.)

To further complicate the issue, I was reared by a father who spits. So when I fell in love with another wonderful man who also happened to have this nasty quirk, I was already somewhat numb to the rather repulsive behavior, although I did occasionally make snide comments about the barbaric and distasteful habit. But when my baby got in trouble for it, spitting in general just seemed to resurface with a new, more powerful yuckiness. The discussion still goes on today.

In fact, in retaliation and to prove a point, I decided that I would start spitting every time my husband or son did it, just to show them how disgusting and embarrassing it really is. Due to some genetic malfunction, however, I seem to have no built-in knack for delivering the goods where I am aiming, and little droplets tend to spew all over *me,* not the sidewalk or lawn. This produces nothing but hysterical laughter from my family and very peculiar glances from strangers.

At any rate, I use this spitting saga as an example of a humbling experience which was a learning one for all of us as well. Even though Brian exhibited no outward remorse at the time, the spitting barrage was never repeated. And the old adage that parents are always modeling to their children through their actions was definitely reinforced.

Although children seldom admit that consequences or rules or disciplinary actions have any effect on them, it's one of those things you thankfully learn about them in hindsight: yes, with enough repetition, things do soak in. And I'm sure (egads! parental assuming is near-impossible to avoid) that Brian was embarrassed when he was hauled into the principal's office upon arriving at school that ill-spittled day. He often used a "big-deal," chip-on-the-shoulder attitude to cover embarrassment.

George, of course, learned that children mimic our behaviors and then come back to haunt us with them. I, of course, learned that retaliation often boomerangs.

Okay. So purposefully spit out a bus window my son may have done. But shoplifting? Never! I could be sure of that.

Right.

*   *   *

It was almost dinner time when the call came. Seems Brian, now nine, and a friend were being detained by security at a local discount store within walking distance of our house. Caught red-handed. The heist attempt? A box of cigars and a lighter. ("I'm positive my boys will never smoke," I had been heard saying. "They are dead set against it.")

In the first flush of humiliation, I assumed that probably everyone I knew within a fifty-mile radius had witnessed my son being carted into the security office. I hoped he hadn't been dragged through the parking lot in handcuffs or anything. I hoped nine-year-olds were too young for this treatment. I thought about me and my reputation, not only as a parent, but as a respectable human being.

The instinct to preserve one's own reputation is quite a normal reaction, but it needs to be overcome. It is not what's of utmost importance.

"Do nothing out of selfish ambition or vain conceit," the Bible says (Phil 2:3). In fact, your own pride can be the booby trap that sinks everyone. The minute you're off on yourself and how your children have let you down and how they've disgraced your family name and how you have been affected, you have conveyed the message that *you* are what is important here, not them or their behavior.

That is not the attitude the Bible is urging us to learn. The same verse continues, "but in humility consider others better than yourselves."

And as for your kids, your prideful agitating may possibly have clammed them up, so no further explanation and no apology is likely. It has shut down the lines of communication and their willingness to listen and learn.

It has separated you from them, thereby yanking away their safety net. It has given you the opportunity to miss them when they fall.

Once I was able to move past my first selfish instinct, what flashed through my mind next was of much more importance and consequence, and I could concentrate on the relevant:

Thank goodness Brian had been caught! What if he had learned that shoplifting was easy? Getting busted, I realized, was actually an answer to a prayer I had shot up years before. It was something I learned from another mother. We hope our kids do get caught so they learn right from wrong and suffer natural consequences, she said, that can detour larger problems down the road. I'd almost forgotten that prayer.

Yes. I needed to move past myself and on to the bigger picture. The guard had asked for his father or me to come down and get him. I thought about it for a moment and said his father would be there, an outward sign of the seriousness of the offense. (Also, I wouldn't have to be seen frequenting the security office. Okay, so I wasn't totally past myself and on to the important. But I was working on it.)

Before I hung up, I told the guard that it might be at least a half-hour before someone would come. Even though we were only a two-minute drive away, I wanted Brian to have time to sit there and sweat. Think about this mess. Fantasize about the cell door closing behind him. Receive an up-close-and-personal dose of humility.

Of course this was a first offense and the police were not summoned. But the guard had scared them; that was The End of Brian's shoplifting days. He was visibly shaken when he arrived home with George. Not a speck of bravado in sight.

I highly recommend praying that children will get caught in their wrongdoings, although, of course, we hope they never do anything that warrants entrapment. But then, that's unrealistic dreaming. They all take their turns. Especially, it seems, those whose parents speak the loudest, or let their judgments on your children's behavior show in their eyes. Like some old neighbors of ours.

*   *   *

They moved in when our boys were around three and nine. They had no children at the time and immediately became good friends of our family.

But I could occasionally see it in their eyes as they watched the endless stream of incidents at our house. That look that said, "Our children are never going to. . . ." I kept myself from responding to this subtle wave of know-it-all. After all, only one who's been there recognizes it.

And so they had their first child. And she was, much to my chagrin, a near-perfect little baby. Never seemed to give them a lick of trouble. Could say the alphabet—forward and backward—way before her time. Puckered up and whimpered when quietly issued a "no." Then, did not repeat the offense, ever again. I seemed to be the one who needed to swallow the know-it-all attitude. Maybe something about our parenting skills was totally lacking if two people could produce someone as perfect as this little girl.

Then, along came their son. Same parents. Same guiding hands. Different composition entirely. A one-and-only to behold. We'll call him Direct Path To Crow-Eating for short. He came out of the chute causing trouble. I hinted that it couldn't have happened to nicer people. I secretly celebrated each wrong turn that kid made because it did, after all, make *our* family life seem more normal. Well, maybe celebrate is too strong a word. I understood their trauma, and we became all the closer for it. We were bonded by "normalcy."

Their first child's behavior, it was decided, was a fluke. Pure grace. Yet she gave them cause to brave a third child who, as it turned out, was more like the second, thus proving our theory: Normalcy Consists of Trauma.

In the meantime, our boys continued on their "normal" path as well. One humbling episode brewed over a several-year period, and we knew nothing about it. Nothing.

*   *   *

Seems Bret did a lot of early-morning eating. After breakfast at home, he would go out for a bike ride to burn off some of that steam before the confinement of a classroom. What we didn't know was that he was stopping in at the Nelsons' and eating again. We're talking 7:30 a.m. arrival here.

All those mornings, the Nelsons were under the assumption that poor Bret was never served food at his house in the morning. Of course the truth was that he garfed down great bowls of it, then immediately burned it off. He was somewhat of a bottomless pit back then, and a skinny little twig as well. And so the Nelsons would kindly give the big-eyed, drooling Bret a portion of whatever was on their table, almost every single morning of his life during that time. And here we were building a questionable reputation all the while. No visible signs of attack; just a silent assault on our parenting prowess. Also, over this time period, Bret was building a solid and mutually caring relationship with the Nelsons. Not only with two of their boys with whom Bret spent a lot of time, but with their parents as well. Four more ears to hear about his trials and tribulations. Four more eyes to greet him with a friendly look of love. Two more mouths to reinforce parental perspective.

They have been, and continue to be, a second family to Bret. I will be eternally grateful that God sent the Nelsons into his life.

Webster's New World Dictionary refers to humility as "absence of pride." That is surely something parents need to get a handle on when one of their children finds another source of guidance, solace and love. It is easy for jealousy to rear its head and strip the goodness out of something. Thankfully, only mild bouts of that occasionally swept over me when it came to the Nelsons, and they were kept in check. Somehow, as with Angel Vanessa, I managed to see their genuine affection for Bret as another of God's vessels. God's hands. Hands to guide and love and care. Indeed a humbling vision.

Sometimes more patient hands than mine. Often an easier ear to talk to than a parent's. Thankfully, we all had the same moral standards and ideas about discipline because the Nelsons certainly had an influence on him. Thankfully, Bret felt free to reach out to them when we were not available, and they, in turn, felt free to let us know of their concern for and enjoyment of our son.

They helped Bret and us through several bouts of unrest. The Nelsons were there to catch the overflow. To help Bret land on his feet. To serve as liaison.

And eventually, years down the road, we all sat and laughed at the reputation we had built at their house for sending our child out in the morning hungry. A small price to pay for encompassing love.

*   *   *

Yes, there are countless humbling experiences in our memory portfolio, but not all of them come from negative and misunderstood behavior. The most enlightening and awesomely humbling times happen when, like the power in the wand of the fairy that transformed Cinderella, God touches us, *touches us*—through our children.

As the Nelsons' hands served as hands of God to guide, nurture, teach and help Bret grow in love, so I see our children as God's same instruments for us. They are his children he has entrusted to us, yet they also serve as his vessels. These revered, humbling, grace-filled experiences our children bring to us can be delivered through the smallest of hands or the briefest of moments.

They come to us like beautiful gifts from the sea; natural pearls. Should we be there to accept them, we can string them together, affording us the most beautiful strands of memories.

*   *   *

One day several years ago I was in town running errands. Boring, tiresome tasks that left me rather weary. When I returned to my car, which was parked on a side street, I found a ripped piece of brown paper stuck under my windshield wiper. On it was scrawled a penciled note:

"Hi Mom! Love ya, Bri."

I unlocked my car and sat in the front seat clutching that piece of paper, staring at it, smiling, tearing up a bit, smiling some more. Reading it over and over. My harried day had been transformed into a moment of warm fuzzy. How blessed was I to raise a son who would take the time to touch me in that way. How wonderful was my God to perk up my tired spirit.

Of course Brian had no idea exactly how profoundly he had touched me. He had simply gone to his car on his sophomore-year lunch break, run across his mother's car on the way either to or from his venture, and decided to leave her a little note. No big deal to him. But it certainly was to me.

I not only felt the love of my son, but the love of God as well. That note hung on my refrigerator for years, perking me up every time I looked at it. It was a reminder of all the times the boys were messengers and examples of love. Students and teachers alike.

Daily our children challenge us, giving us reason to continue growing and learning; giving us cause to draw nearer to God.

George and I both spent self-indulged hours watching Brian coo and smile up at us with total trust in his eyes. What a model he served as; an example of a refreshing way for us to approach our Father, rather than always with an endless list of "Help-me-Lord" prayers.

There were so many times I needed to apologize to Bret for my impatience. "That's okay, Mommy" always followed directly and freely on the heels of my apology, modeling Christ's instant forgiveness upon repentance. Children seem to instinctively know that it is best to forgive and let go.

Both of the boys presented us with cratefuls of scribbled drawings, many totally undecipherable as to intent. But of course we treasured the sincerity of the spirit with which they were given to us. Did we realize that God was teaching us and our children about his appreciation of our heart-given attempts, no matter how feeble the results may seem?

Recently I spoke with the mother of a seven-month-old child. She was relating the stories of how many parents spend so much time complaining. "It tends to be a habit, complaining about your kids," she said. "One mother complained about all the dirty diapers, and how sore her breasts were from nursing. . . ."

"Mine is a unique situation," she said. She and her husband had spent four years trying to conceive their son Hank: infertility treatments, stress, doubt, faith. "We waited so long to have him. It was a miracle that we were finally able to conceive. Well, I cherished every dirty diaper because it meant everything about him was working properly. My breasts were sore and it was good because it meant he could suck really hard and get nourishment."

She went on to talk about some mothers who complain about getting up at night. Her experience was viewed through different eyes.

"I enjoyed Hank at night," she said, "because it was such a quiet time. He would fall asleep at my breast and I didn't put him down right away. I would inspect his fingers and toes and see how he was growing. I thank God every day. I thought after a while the shininess of this brand new miracle would wear off. But it doesn't. I get him out of the bathtub and he will be all squeaky clean and I am thrilled all over again."

Thrilled and humbled by God's goodness, this precious gift we call our child.

*   *   *

Children humble us through their unthinkably bad choices, through their precious examples, through their mere existence. But there's yet another way, and perhaps I can best show you through the following story rather than try to explain it. I think you'll get the drift. I know I sure did.

One day about five years ago Brian and I were chatting. Suddenly he responded with something that was mean and cutting. Cutting to the quick.

I stood speechless for a moment, flushed with heat. My eyes stung with tears, my throat was tight. I finally squeaked out, "Brian, that was so mean and wounding. I can't believe you said that to me."

"Mom, I hear you talking to Dad like that lately."

He used an unrelenting tone that was far from his usual friendly and warm approach to conversations.

Part of me wanted to crack him across the face. The other part, the spiritual part, stood convicted on the spot. Brian spoke Truth.

*   *   *

I have now come complete cycle on the topic of humility: George was busted for his own spitting; I was busted for my own sharp tongue. We each received a holy pie in the face, lessons sent by the Lord and delivered by no less than the hands of our children.

And in between those cultured, manmade pearls on our strands of memories we are blessed to be able to string the finest pearls of natural beauty, God's humbling gifts to parents—theirs simply for the taking.

•

Dear Dad,

I know Mom's

in there somewhere;

I saw her eyes blink.

•

· *Ten* ·

Mommyland

Survival

Now hear this, all mommies! Even though I am spending the entirety of these pages imploring you to not miss your kids, I'm here to tell you that high on the list of things you can do to insure that is to depart from them as often as necessary, even if it's only for a mind's ride to Mommyland.

If you've never heard of Mommyland, I'd volunteer to take you by the hand and lead you there right now, but each mommy has to find her own place. Her own little haven. Her own exciting or brain-dead journey—whichever is in order at the moment to help her hang on to sanity.

"When I go there," my good friend Mary Beth ("Oh child of God") said, "I am not necessarily dreaming of butterflies and soft things. Sometimes I am trying to figure out a problem and you can't do that when people are bothering you all the time, so you just sort of go there and do some problem solving or whatever needs to be done. Sometimes you just go there to concentrate on cleaning the bathroom floor without interruptions."

So there you have a little glimpse into a corner of Mary Beth's Mommyland. And she, for the record, is the one who coined that phrase. Put title to the trip. Nailed down the journey-via-osmosis.

Now in my own Mommyland, I would not allow the thought of a dirty bathroom floor. I would consider it nothing short of a violation of my personal Mommyland principles. Oh sure, I may lock myself in the bathroom to try to find Alice's hole that leads to Mommyland, but I would not push a mop while I was doing it.

For me the truth is, the bathroom has never been conducive to Mommyland, even though I've experienced numerous aborted tries at capturing it there. Incidents like the following.

*   *   *

I poured an ice-cold glass of water in preparation for my ascent. "Hold my calls and don't knock on the door," I said as I disappeared up the stairs toward the haven of The Bath, leaving my family standing speechless in the kitchen.

It had been one of those days, leading to THAT moment that triggered my plight. I absolutely needed to be where the rest of them were not. My instinctual fight-or-flee mechanism had kicked in, then gone "tilt!" Options closed. Fleeing was the only choice.

Upon entering my oasis—my envisioned route to Mommyland— I firmly closed and locked the door behind me, then leaned against it for a moment just in case anyone should be following me.

Pause. Listen. Exhale. Proceed.

I adjusted the flow of water to the perfect fog of steam and stared into the mist for a moment. Then I poured a stream of bath beads tubward to silken the water. Essence of magnolia wafted up my nose. It was delicious.

The small glow of light from a match illumined my face as I swept around the room lighting the candles I unearthed from the closet.

Like a snake's skin, my clothes were shed. I placed the sweating glass of water on the tub's edge and set my new novel within arm's reach.

As my body cut through the bubbles, I knew everything was in order; life was as it should be. I slipped my lip over the edge of the refreshing cool water and took a sip. Aaah. For two minutes, I just soaked and stared at the flickering flames of candlelight. Mommyland was just around the corner.

After that brief, life-altering pause, I was finally ready to enter. I opened the book to page one.

Being a short person, I found that by the time my feet touched the end of the tub, my head was practically submerged under the glorious bubbles. I scooted, slid and rearranged for quite a little while before grabbing one more sip. I would have to sit up if I was to read. And so I did.

About the time I got to the third paragraph, my forehead had broken out with little beads of perspiration, and my nose, too, and my glasses began fogging up and slipping off my face. When I reached to shove them up, the side of my book accidentally found its way into my tranquil water.

I tossed the soggy mass overboard. I just soaked and stared at the mesmerizing flames. Mommyland popped back into view.

My back started getting a kink. I decided since I didn't have to read anymore, I could slip back down into the tub. As long as my nose was above water, I'd be okay. Having my eyes at water level soon led me to the discovery that my bubbles had disappeared, and a sort of a milky oil slick floated in its place. I closed my eyelids and took a deep breath. I was beginning to feel ill.

Of course I was beginning to feel ill! I never *have* handled heat very well.

I bolted up in the tub as though I had been electrocuted. Deja vu. Why can't I remember hot baths aren't for me? They are not the yellow brick road to Mommyland, they are a slide straight to insanity.

In one motion I pulled the plug and turned on the shower to rinse the scum off my body. As I stood in a foot of draining water with the shower beating on my head, I tried to think this through.

Didn't Doris Day always take a bubble bath to calm her down? Don't French women do this as the epitome of luxury and relaxation? Haven't I read this scenario in countless romance novels?

Is something wrong with my hormones?

I brusquely finished showering and soon appeared downstairs with my empty glass.

"I thought you were going to take a long bubble bath," my husband said.

"Well," I snapped, "you thought wrong!"

*　　*　　*

Even though baths may be the Mommyland doorway for many, they are certainly not mine. Flickering flames, however, are. And, lucky for me, I can light a candle on my kitchen table right in the midst of chaos. All I need do is stare at it.

But what if the kids are hanging on your legs and you can't isolate yourself?

Find your own express lane to Mommyland and hop on it. Even

as the child screams and bellows, you can learn, through conditioning, to depart into the silent corner of your Mommyland. Physically, your leg may be functioning as a hanger for infant bodies, but mentally, you are gone. Zap. Disappeared. Safe. Sheltered.

Mary Beth recently took an automobile trip with her brother— and five children. The kids were carrying on as kids do in a car and Mary Beth skipped out to Mommyland, even while she was driving. Even while the volume rose.

Her brother drew her back into his world, however, whining about the noise. "Don't get involved with the kids," she told him. "Stay out of it. Stare into space. Think about other things and pretty soon you won't hear the noise. What you need to do is focus away from the kids."

Mary Beth claims Mommyland is self-preservation. An escape. "You escape to protect yourself." And sometimes you can't get there by yourself. That is when Mommyland tools come in handy. Tools like a flickering flame, or a tub, or a book, or a lawn mower.

Lawn mower? Yes. Mary Beth also finds Mommyland behind the loud—and that is the key element here—mower. The noise, she claims, blocks out all other distractions and allows her to concentrate. Personally, I find mowing in Mommyland about as appealing as mopping floors, but it works for her, and that's what counts.

Mary Beth also believes that husbands are the biggest infiltrators of Mommyland when they are around.

"I will be concentrating on a book or a problem or whatever and the kids are screaming 'Mommy! Mommy! Mommy!' trying to get my attention. But I'm successfully blocking them out. Then my husband will call my name and say, 'Mary Beth, they are trying to talk to you.' "

And so she responds to the children and then "disappears" again.

She says her mistake has been in not telling Dave she is "gone," so that he doesn't accidentally call her back.

Mary Beth started honing her technique when she was in college. She had to learn to study through dorm noise and constant interruptions. She started referring to this "place" she went to as Mommyland when she became more aware of the need for it—immediately after she became a mother, of course.

She holds the conviction, and I agree with her, that if you can't learn to find Mommyland, you have possibly left the door open for child abuse. So Mommyland is protection for your family as well.

"There is a part of me," she admits, "that feels guilty about all this Mommyland and escaping thing." Mothers are good at mustering up guilt, aren't they? Especially toward themselves. But, "I feel like there is energy being drained that I don't have at that point," she continues. And after she analyzes it for a moment, she knows it is not self-indulgent, but merely protective.

And you have to be able to go there without baggage. "A place to work things out and let things go," she says. I ditto that reasoning. If you take all the mess with you, you might as well not have left.

Lest you get a wrong picture of my friend, she deals out more hugs and has more patience than anyone I know with three children under age seven. Perhaps Mommyland is why. It is a place to be good to yourself, therefore letting you refuel so as to pass on the goodness to others.

She comes from a long line of Mommylanders. She says her mother and her grandmother used to go there, and one of her daughters already does.

Mommyland, she clarifies, is not to be confused with The Silent Treatment. The Silent Treatment, which can cause undue stress for our children, comes out of anger and shows on your face. Mommyland is motivated by a different need and appears as zoning out.

And not to worry about your children getting in trouble and going unnoticed while you've departed. "There are certain sounds your kids make that let you know they are in trouble." And we all know exactly what she's talking about. They're the ones that make you hang up the phone or run outside. They are different than argumentative, tantrum, tired or whining sounds. They possess their own built-in express lane to Mommyland.

For Mary Beth, Mommyland is a totally isolated place. "I never want anyone there. I come out of Mommyland to discuss things," she says.

As for me, Mary Beth is part of my Mommyland. As is Mary, my Keeper-of-the-Big-Wheel-Brigade partner. There are conversations we have had and continue to have that connect us and our Mommylands. Things we know about each other that need no explanation. Experiences and thoughts we have shared that need only be referred to, and we are immediately washed with oneness. My Mommyland has a need for these kinds of connections.

As of this writing, in nine days I will be flying to Oregon to visit Mary. This is a vacation we have talked about for many years. It is one I sorely need. It is one we will take together as we leave her house for a few days to stay ocean-side and ponder. Share. Sit together in silence. Perhaps enter my version of the epitome of Mommyland: an altered state in an altered state.

She has, in the last six weeks or so, sent me a series of postcards, one more beautiful than the other. The last is a picture of a giant blue-green wave crashing and exploding high into the air. It is full of movement, white foaming release. Power. Tranquility. It beckons. She knows this about me.

"Yes," She wrote on the card. "Can you hear the sound of the ocean? Come west to renew the spirit and your creative center. Can't wait to see you and share good times. Love, Mary."

I wept when I received this card. Its timing, as usual, was exact. I celebrated and praised God for sending a friend into my life who makes a connection with me that goes beyond words. My personal Mommyland would have a missing link if there weren't people in my life I could share portions of it with.

*   *   *

Now my husband and I definitely share a lot of things, but Mommyland isn't one of them. I'm sure he has his own counterpart to this place in space, but it cannot truly be Mommyland. He is barred by virtue of testosterone.

Whether your own personal Mommyland takes in others or not, I do believe that finding others who truly understand your parenting plight is imperative. Like that all-day seminar George and I attended. Just seeing all the other bleary-eyed parents wandering around looking for answers gave us heart. "I am not alone" is always a comforting discovery.

The Chicago Tribune Magazine recently ran a lengthy article entitled "No mom is an island." It covered the plight of stay-at-homes who have no one else in their neighborhood to talk to and no other children for their children to play with; and it looked at the plight of working moms trying to find those get-together times for themselves and their children.

"Mothers need to find those colleagues with whom they can swap ideas and on whom they can lean for support. As a consequence, they have been inventing new ways to re-create the coffee klatches of the past, to create family-support and parenting-education groups," wrote Florence Hamlish Levinsohn.

The article listed many formal groups that meet. People reaching out to connect any way they can. There was even a 1988 "Directory of Self-Help and Mutual Aid Groups" talked about which listed "more than 60 parent groups in the Chicago metropolitan area, including three father's groups, 26 single-parent groups and nine groups for parents under stress."

Whatever you need, reach out and find it. Don't let your endeavors as a parent become isolated ones. We need more than children in our lives; we need each other. Problems we deal with on our own are usually magnified. Answers are often found lingering over a cup of coffee.

Although some of these groups lean more toward the educational end, I personally think the informal gatherings can be more relaxing. They are not "one more thing I have to be learning." They are a place, like Mommyland, to just hang out. Tell the truth. Listen. Laugh. Look forward to.

The article covered Family Focus centers. They offer classes in child-rearing, "but their major thrust is to provide a comfortable place for mothers with children under 4 years to spend a morning chatting with other mothers while their children play in another room attended by caregivers."

I think how lucky Mary and I were, as well as many other mothers and children in our neighborhood, to simply be able to walk across the street and not pay any dues for this much-needed camaraderie. There was always someone in need of a break. We could wander from door to door saying, "Is it break time yet?" One could always find a taker. Sometimes we would sit and chat together while the kids played in the yard. Sometimes we would unburden each other from our tykes for a spell, knowing our turn would come, too, for some time off.

*   *   *

Here are a couple of things mothers had to say about their involvement with the Family Focus centers that, in their own way, paralleled my neighborhood experience.

Karen Ami MacRoberts, sculptor: "I didn't start coming until he [2-year-old son] was 18 months old. I wish I had started coming sooner. I'd probably be a little more sane now."

Jan Sokolow, designer of computer systems: "I learned to relax about teaching him [son] all kinds of things he wasn't really ready for. You've got to let them develop naturally."

Stories about other groups covered in that article pretty much proved the same point: no mom is an island. Right.

*   *   *

But sometimes we need to be *on* one. Sometimes other mothers aren't around. Sometimes we don't want them, either. Sometimes what we really need is to recharge our spiritual batteries.

Even Christ went off alone to pray. So, too, we need to be alone and focus on God, our unending source of renewal. Let God remind us that what we are doing has value and eternal results. Recapture perspective. Lay down our burdens before him.

Jesus broke away from the pressures to rest and to regain perspective. And he made time to pray, even when it wasn't very convenient or comfortable. Sometimes, that's what we've got to do. Hire a sitter, just once, and spend a morning walking in your local park. Take a Bible and notebook; sit and read. Make notes to yourself. See if it isn't worth the sitter fee.

Taking one weekend a year to go on your church's weekend

retreat for women or couples, or to attend a marriage seminar, may be the best thing you can do—*for your kids.* Yes, it'll take a lot of planning and juggling. But the richer you are as a person, the more you have to offer as a parent.

*   *   *

Other times you simply need to enter the glorious privacy of Mommyland. Often nothing more than a sixty-second burst of self-indulgence, because that's all there's time for.

For example, not only do I like flickering flames, but I find certain fragrances have a calming effect on me. Another cheap "tool" of the Mommyland trade at my house is incense. Strawberry or patchouli, to be exact. I watch the flickering flame of the match lighting the compressed, soon-to-multiply fragrance. Aaah. Something to camouflage the odor of the stopped-up garbage disposal. Something to remind me that all can become more than it seems. Like watching green vines sprout Heavenly Blue Morning Glories. Or a cricket chirping a pulsating beat. Or the call of a red-winged blackbird that reminds me of the sounds I used to listen to as I sat by the creek as a youth.

Look for joy in simple pleasures. You'd be amazed what a mini-retreat that can be. Watching the birds splatter around in the birdbath. Deciding to use the kids' nap time to lie in the grass or see if you can still climb a tree or dig out an old favorite album.

Give yourself a pedicure. Put a cool washcloth over your eyes. Make yourself a bowl of popcorn. Dig out old pictures. Keep some bubble stuff on hand and blow bubbles out your back door. Fantasize about being in the mountains, inhaling the fragrance of burning logs and watching eagles soar.

Clear your brain. Be still. Refresh. Explore Mommyland, wheth-

155

er it be for one minute or the miracle vacation like mine that lasts a week. Dust, dirty dishes, unmade beds will still be there when you return, and perhaps they won't seem as burdensome after a pause for your cause. And guess what? The same goes for your kids.

I would suggest practicing skipping in and out of Mommyland when things are calm. When you feel put together and unhassled. Get familiar with all the paths that may lead you there; don't get discouraged by the ones that don't. There are endless possibilities.

Be aware, however. There are some occasions when Mommyland just doesn't cut it. It isn't the miracle cure for everything. I wouldn't be honest if I led you to believe that.

*　　*　　*

Mary Beth's middle child, now five years of age, was diagnosed with cancer over two years ago. She and her husband have been holding the family together while their second-born, Laura Jane, undergoes chemotherapy. She has been in remission for some time and treatment should be drawing to an end soon.

Endless trips to the hospital in the city. Sickness. Fear. Anxiety. Blood transfusions. Trying to come up with last-minute babysitters during crisis. Making it through the days without sleep during the nights. Drug deliveries from UPS. Learning about central lines and what to do in case of emergency. And so on and so on and so on. They had just finished a nine-day stay in the hospital, one of their scarier stints. Finally, they were home and life could return to what had become their normal. Then, Laura Jane took a bicycle spill and broke both bones in her left forearm—the arm to which the thumb she sucks is attached. I received this news the afternoon it happened.

Ring, went my phone.

"Hello," I answered.

"Sometimes," Mary Beth said, "Mommyland just isn't far enough away."

•

Dear George,
I am thankful we hung
together and observed one
another while the
boys were growing up. Now,
in our sweet aloneness,
we can reminisce not only
about them, but about
the US they helped to evolve.

•

· *Eleven* ·

After They're Gone

Empty Nest

I just hung up the phone from a lengthy conversation. I've been chatting long distance with my dad. Notice I didn't call him the man who used to be my dad. Nor, now that I'm a grown woman with grown children of my own, do I refer to him as Victor. He has always been, is now, and will continue to be Dad to me.

Up until the time my mother died fifteen years ago, I called her Mom. Not Nellie. Mom. I cannot imagine thinking of her in any other terms. She defined the role of mother for me, and thankfully it was a happy and fulfilling one.

Not that she didn't also become a friend as I grew older—someone to laugh with, cry with, share with. But the "friend" part of our relationship could not be separated from the mother/daughter bond, nor would I have ever wanted it to be.

We never stop being Mom and Dad. Although our parenting roles, attitudes, responsibilities and viewpoints may fluctuate, diminish, rekindle and settle over time, our kids are still our children and we are still their parents.

Amy Grant, a major presence in Christian music, recently did an interview for *Today's Christian Woman* magazine. Throughout much of her discussion with author Dale Hanson Bourke, she spoke of how different life is now that she's a mother.

During one point in the interview she made the following observation: "I don't think kids can ever know their parents like other people can know them. But once you have kids of your own, your perspective on your parents changes."

By the same token, becoming a parent adds another element to who we are and influences how others see us.

"Amy is still the charming, husky-voiced star who burst onto the contemporary Christian music scene as a teen," Bourke wrote. "But being a mom defines Amy in ways that make her more beautiful and vulnerable than she's ever seemed before."

I know for a fact that bearing a child did not automatically make me physically more beautiful: stretch marks, hair that sometimes didn't have time to be washed, stress lines that attacked my face during the wee hours, then etched a permanent map around my eyes . . . but I know what Bourke spoke of. It is a flowering. An opening of things in us we didn't know were even lying dormant: a new softness, a deeper love, the literal flowing of milk through our bodies.

*   *   *

Becoming a parent has something of the same effect on fathers. I watched my six-foot-two, two-hundred-twenty-pound, size-thirteen-ring husband—whose moves have never been mistaken for a ballerina's—become transformed at the dressing table the day we brought Brian home.

Brian was born during a time when fathers were not allowed to touch their babies until they were out of the hospital. The fathers had to be in the car, for that matter, because the nurse carried the babies alongside the wheelchair and handed them over to the mother after she was safely planted in the front seat.

George chose to wait until we arrived home to try his first hands-on experience. In fact, he changed Brian's first home-soiled diaper. I stood by his side and talked him through the task. Tears welled in my eyes and an unknown corner of my heart lit up as I watched this massive man and his massive hands exhibit the feather-light, gentle and careful touch of a brain surgeon.

Okay, so the diapering job itself wasn't so hot; but the kind of love and awe that poured forth from the imposing form of my husband into the tiny baby that lay totally vulnerable at his fingertips . . . that picture, that transformation, that first bonding gesture, instantly revealed a part of George that neither of us knew was buried inside, waiting to burst forth with this magical encounter.

And this opening, this flowering, this unveiling of more than we had been, instantly became a new and beautiful part of *us*. A part of the *us* that was created and revealed after the birth of Brian. A part of the *us* that is left now that the children are gone.

And since *us,* for the most part, is all that there is now, I am acutely aware of the importance of having hung together while the children were home. Observing one another. Catching action glimpses of each other in settings that will never be repeated. Learning to share the new-found burdens. Delighting in the surprises of hidden talents. Helping each other let go.

*   *   *

So here we are now. Alone.

But not really, because there's a spoiled-rotten dog and a bird to keep us entertained. And, thank goodness, they actually do. (There used to be a gerbil but . . . may he rest in peace.)

Why, just this last month we've taken Butch, our black-and-white-looks-just-like-a-border collie-but-is-really-a-mutt dog, to the vet three times. Each time for the same condition: fleas and his allergic reaction to their bites. He also keeps us busy screaming "STAY OFF THE NEW COUCH!"

Then, of course, there are all those trips we take outside with him because he seems to have a bladder the size of a pea and a thirst that causes him a daily water intake the size of Lake Michigan. And we don't have a fenced yard. And he runs away if he's not on a leash. And so we are kept very entertained running in and out the door with him. And then giving him treats for his "good boy" duty because . . . because . . . I don't know why we ever started rewarding him for going to the bathroom. But after six years he's grown to expect one and he follows us around barking if we forget.

As for Nellie, our blue/green parakeet—whom we named after my mother, and who we didn't find out was a male until after we named him Nellie—we must spend countless hours repeating the same phrases over and over and over so he can learn to say them back to us when we walk into a room. Things like "Hello" and "Pretty girl." He's also finally mastered an incredible wolf whistle. Yea, Nellie!

Getting back to the new couch for a moment, here's something I'd like to warn you about: By the time you send your children to college or off to the military or whatever, everything in your house is in shreds and *you just can't stand it anymore.* "Our baby is twenty years old," you say to your spouse one day. "Why does it look like preschoolers still live here?"

Not only that, but you have entered your own personal mid-life crisis, thereby compounding everything but the interest on your money—which you haven't saved anyway, so not to worry.

Lest you should start thinking conditions around our house are bleak, that's not true. Although nothing above is untrue, what I haven't mentioned yet is the up-side of the empty nest: we can now have our meat loaf with onions in it again without watching some-one pick them out or tell us how disgusting they are. We can also run around the house naked. Although we don't very often because of the dog.

We spend a lot of time trucking to Kmart together. (See, I don't always go it alone.) I don't actually know why we go there so often. After all, we need less toothpaste, less soap, less shampoo. . . . Maybe it's because we have more time to read the sale flyers now, thereby becoming aware of things we didn't know we needed.

Something we found ourselves doing the first year Brian was gone, and I'm sure we'll repeat this year, is watching other people's kids wrestle and listening to other parents' children sing. After spending so many years acquiring such well-seasoned bleacher buns, it seems a shame to let them go to waste.

In terms of that extra living space empty nesters dream about, we're not quite as far ahead of the game as planned. Although the tiny bedroom is now my office, Brian still comes home several times during the year and spends summers here, so his room isn't freed up yet. And heaven forbid we should alter anything.

On the storage front, we've gained no ground, although that's not all bad. We've kept the wind-up swing, the playpen, the Tonka trucks, Fisher Price toys and highchair for so long now "just in case," that we have decided we might as well hang on to them for our grandchildren.

Okay, so the basement and the attic will never be cleared out like we thought they would "when the kids leave," but somehow we believe that watching another generation wind, push and cart their parents' things around will bring more satisfaction to us than a few empty spaces.

*   *   *

On a more serious note, just as my parents will always be Mom and Dad to me, so George and I will be to our boys.

Bret recently visited for a week. He came roaring right up to the front door on his motorcycle all the way from Albuquerque, and what a welcome sight he was, dead bugs on his face and all. He was as happy to slip into our arms as ever, and we as happy and fulfilled to receive him, not to mention incredibly thankful for his safe arrival.

Since Brian had not departed for his sophomore year at college yet, all of us were once more gathered and sleeping under the same roof. Fellowship was warm, fun-filled, rejuvenating. The boys wrestled on the floor. The phone rang off the hook. The door opened and closed during all hours of the day and night.

I spent several long pauses observing, considering, testing, exploring my own emotions and pondering the actions and reactions of each of us—and all of us as a unit.

Although there were some similarities to the past, it was not like old times. It was more like the beginning of what comes next. Four relatively mature individuals coming face to face and hug to hug. No distinguishing lines between the chiefs and Indians; all equal members of the same tribe; each bearing fragments of what used to be; each learning to respect and accept what has changed.

And should an unacceptable pecking order try to sneak its way back in there, tasteful deterrence is administered. Such was the case after a rather intense phone conversation Brian and I had after he returned to school one time last year. A few days later, the following gentle yet straight-to-the-point announcement arrived in the middle of a letter.

"Don't get me wrong, I still want your advice, but in some areas, wait for me to come to you. Thanks." This was followed by a smiley face.

I am grateful for his diplomacy. It was something I needed to be reminded of. It is another of those treasured pieces of paper I keep in my special notebook. And I was particularly tickled he used one of the tools I taught him to deliver the message: the written word— without the possibility of interruption before the message gets delivered in its entirety. One of the remnants. One of the rewards. See, I told you they're paying attention even when you think they're not!

*   *   *

Of course, emergency phone calls still infiltrate our quiet. Like the one I got around dinner time from Bret one day.

"How long can you keep bratwurst before it rots?" he queried. Ah, the comforts of knowing we are still, in whatever small way, needed. And what a challenge it was trying to explain "that" smell as I passed on my motherly knowledge.

That same simple being-needed pleasure can also be agonizing, especially if the long-distance call concerns a broken heart that cannot be mended by the loving hands or words of a mother or father. I received such a call once.

"I wish you were here to hold me, Mom," the familiar voice quietly said.

I believe none of us ever gets too old to make that wish or too detached to long to fulfill it. Visions of my ninety-year-old grandmother stroking the hair of her bedridden seventy-four-year-old daughter, my aunt, come to mind. No, age has nothing to do with motherly and fatherly love.

But then there are the phone calls that come just to let you know what they've been up to, like the ones I make to and receive from my dad and our children make to and receive from us in return. Sometimes they're just news about the weather, or "I'm bored," or "I'm thinking about you," or "I'm thinking about something else and I'd like to run it by you."

Some of my favorite conversations are the funny, wait-until-you-hear-this-one! stories. But then again, not all of them are funny: Bret recently had his truck stolen. Brian recently ran out of money at school.

But life has its peaks as well:

We all shared the good news that Bret would be home for Christmas.

George finished a long, ongoing fix-it project in the kitchen.

I started up my Bible Study Fellowship classes again.

Brian logged 4.5 hours on a solo flight and everything went well, including communications.

(Another valley, but not a surprise: the flight ran Brian out of money—again.)

We pass the word from one to another, trying to repeat all the details so no one is left out of the family grapevine. George and I pass the phone back and forth, savoring the details and discussing them over dinner.

Of course many things happen in their lives which we will never know about. And that, too, is the way it should be. After all, Dad and I have our secrets!

And speaking of George and me, that *us* of a couple I spoke about earlier, we have discovered that quiet is nice. Very nice. Although the deadening silence in the beginning was hard to handle and a constant reminder of what was not any more, we have now grown to adore it.

We have discovered having the boys living elsewhere gives us more places to visit, aside from Kmart, of course.

We have survived our first summer of having a college student back home after his freshman year. And believe me, that ain't easy! I had been warned about this by many parents more experienced than myself. "Oh, you won't be crying next year when he leaves," they said, trying to console me after we dropped him off that first college year.

"Callous," I thought. "They're so callous. They must not have the kind of relationships with their children that we have with ours."

I have learned that this haughty attitude reaps rewards equal to the "My kids would never . . ." bravado. Yes, we learned to eat crow. We were happy, happy, happy to see him return to school. Although a couple of tears did slip down my cheek at the departure, before they were even dry, I was anxious to once again return to my silent and peaceful house. Except for the interruptions of the barking dog and squawking parakeet. Brian, too, was ready to return to his new-found independent lifestyle. And the 4,783 miles Bret put on his motorcycle this past summer definitely primed him for a sigh of relief when he pulled back into his driveway in Albuquerque.

We've all covered a lot of mental territory the last few years. I'm sure we will continue to grow in our new and ever-changing roles in the future.

*   *   *

It occurs to me as I examine our empty nest that preparing for it, in some ways, begins the minute the child leaves your womb. The tying off of the umbilical cord, severing mother from child, becomes the first step in the process of letting go. Then weaning. Independent steps. Kindergarten. Sock hops. First loves. Driver's license. Graduation. Departure.

The irony is that although you spend your entire life letting go in little, sometimes unaware chunks, it still ends up feeling like a smack of cold water in the face when they actually go.

But like diving into a cold creek, you eventually get used to the water until you no longer feel the cold. In fact, after a long enough time, it becomes the air that is hard to take again. And so it is with the empty nest.

How clever of God to make us so adaptable.

How gracious he is to send friends into our lives who travel our same roads. And now that all our kids are gone, I find the level of our relationships with these friends has somehow deepened. Perhaps it's because we're all getting so mellow with age. Perhaps it's because we have more time to talk to one another—and actually listen to answers—without child-related interruptions.

Of course when we get together, our children are always the first thing discussed. We ask about each one, carefully going through the list and marking their progress—or sometimes lack of.

One couple we know has a twenty-five-year-old college graduate working and living at home. Kids sure have a way of recycling today. Perhaps that's why I'm not panting over Brian's bedroom yet.

170

Another couple has the husband's mother living with them. She has Alzheimer's disease, and life is not quite what they had pictured. She moved in about the time their baby moved out.

"I was looking forward to not having to be home at a certain time or prepare meals at a certain time—just not to be on a schedule," the wife said. "But I am. So it didn't work out."

Together with our friends, we share the trials and triumphs, the unexpected. We nurture each other and try to fill in some of the gaps. We replay the old days. We look forward to what is ahead.

•

Dear Charlie Brown,
Yes, the Great Pumpkin
Lives! Don't let them
kid you. Keep
spreading the word with
your bountiful joy and
enthusiasm. Others
like ourselves are sure to believe!

•

· *Twelve* ·

Harvest Celebration

The Fruits of Our Labors

The sound of chirping crickets pierces through the crack under the overhead door and spreads across the garage floor. It lightly pulsates in our eardrums as we sit cross-legged on the cool cement. The fragrance of burning leaves—those piles of paisley colors—drifts under that same crack and up our noses, subtly announcing the season. It is a fragrance we love, and one that seems to inspire the creative genius in us as we face the blank canvas of pumpkin. Our senses are alive and heightened by the task at hand.

Newspapers cover the floor; pumpkin guts cover a couple of the headlines. A few seeds have already found their way into the colander where they await washing, salting, baking and eating. They are the perfect and annual complement to the fresh-pressed jugs of cider waiting in the fridge.

We are camped far enough apart from one another so that spying is ruled out. Heaven forbid an idea should be copied or a surprise unveiled before its time. Markers, pencils, knives and miscellaneous paraphernalia are scattered around us. We have collected these tools of the pumpkin-carving trade from about the house and yard: perhaps a few corn husks for hair, a bumpy gourd that "warts" can be extracted from, construction paper, yarn . . . implements are tossed back and forth on request.

An occasional snicker skitters through the garage as one of us erupts with enthusiasm for our oh-so-clever idea. Errant indelible black lines and incisions are followed by groans and sighs. Time passes; we are unaware. Our annual fall celebration is in progress.

There we would sit: mother, father and two sons carving their pumpkins. We carried on this behavior far beyond the age, by some standards, fit for pumpkin carving. Although finding a mutually agreeable time became more difficult over the years, enthusiasm never waned for this tradition.

Some things never changed: we always seemed to finish at the same time, thereby accommodating the Great Lighting and Unveiling. And there has always been sincere appreciation for each of our creations. We oohed and aahed at our individual visions-come-to-life. We seemed to take turns generating the most clever of ideas. Each year a new King or Queen Pumpkin Carver grinned while all agreed on the ordination.

As the boys grew older, an occasional newcomer joined us, and they usually wore mascara. It tickled me that Bret and Brian found this celebration grand enough to want to share with their truly beloveds of the time. Of course the celebration encompassed more than pumpkin carving; it included a near-choreographed routine of events. This tradition had begun for me when I was a toddler. I ushered it into my own family with reverence. The boys, in turn, grew up loving the annual trek and celebration as much as I did, and still do. George has a hard time envisioning fall without it now.

It always began with a drive to Johnson's Mound in Elburn. Always taking the same country roads. Speaking of nostalgic remembrances. Entering the winding road into the park. Watching for the carving of the Indian head that mysteriously appeared one year high up one of the trees.

Next stop: the Gould cider farm. We could hardly wait for a fresh taste of the day's pressing. We were given a sample like a fine wine, straight out of the holding barrel. There was never a doubt that a purchase would result. If we were lucky, they would be pressing when we arrived. All those crates of apples hand-dumped onto the mini-conveyor belt powered by a running tractor. Chopped in the chopper. Pressed through layers and layers of burlap. Yield: fresh cider that stifled any question as to why bees hung around the place.

On the way home, pumpkins were purchased and nestled next to the cider in the trunk, just waiting for carving and drinking.

Times have changed somewhat: thank goodness Johnson's Mound and the Gould cider place are still intact, but the country roads aren't quite as country anymore. Bret is never here for Halloween, and pumpkin carving usually takes place around the kitchen table now. We are all older, wiser, more careful, and less able and willing to sit cross-legged on the cold garage floor. Burning paisley fragrance no longer wafts up our noses, what with environmental concerns and all. I imagine that this year the ritual will take place whichever weekend Brian can make it home instead of "the" weekend. If he doesn't make it home during the season, I'm sure George and I will carry on tradition alone. I can't imagine Halloween around our home without cheery or dastardly pumpkin faces staring out from our front porch.

No, I can't imagine that at all, any more than I can imagine dropping the celebration all together, since we are a family that loves to harvest the celebratory fruits. After all, if we don't take time to ceremoniously take in the joyful moments, to in fact *make* some of those moments, what's the point of grinding through the rough times?

Let me just take a second here to define what I mean by a celebration: any conscious act to make something special out of the moment or occasion. This can be as large as an invitations-only party that requires a catering service, or as small as a verbal "Hey! What a moment!" It is a deliberate marking of time.

Children give us natural cause to celebrate. All those "firsts."

*   *   *

"Oh, sweetheart, Jenny smiled at me today!"

"You should have seen Jacob turn over! We've a gymnast in the making, I'm sure of it!"

"Come to Daddy, son. That's right, one wobbly foot in front of the other. You did it!"

"Okay. Let's see it. Yea, Kelly! You went poopoo in the potty!"

Some friends of ours have celebration dinners for good report cards. I like that idea, although I'm glad the Baumbichs didn't have to depend on that for fun. We do, however, make the most out of birthdays. Always have. And what more profound to celebrate than the gift of life?

Like the Gould cider tradition I brought to our family, so I inherited the Birthday Bonanza spirit. I was born into a Birthday Family. The Brown clan cherishes dozens of what we refer to as "puffer fish photographs." It doesn't matter how old or young my mom, dad, brother or I were turning, there we are, frozen in time. Cheeks flared out like a bellows, eyebrows scrunched together, face about one foot away from torching our hair on the candles, a dorky pointed hat perched on our head, wishes dangling in the air, the official pink-and-blue crepe-paper Happy Birthday streamer scotch-taped to the wall in the background. Birthday Heaven indeed!

It wouldn't have made a lick of sense if I didn't usher all this excitement into my own family, including spanking the birthday person one gentle swat for each year, plus "one to grow on." And so, of course, I did. What wonderful memories the array of birthday parties alone has left us.

One of the first that stands out was when Brian turned one year old. We have nearly worn out that short-playing, eight-millimeter piece of film over the years. And each time we laugh ourselves silly. Each year that memory becomes more precious.

*   *   *

There sits Brian in his yellow, flowered, vinyl-covered high chair. He is wearing only a tee shirt and disposable diaper, a big grin and of course a dorky birthday hat with an elastic strap encircling his beaming little face. George's large hand enters the right side of the frame and swiftly sets the pint-sized chocolate cake down in front of him. I used an old chicken-pot-pie tin as a cake pan for this masterpiece. One candle glows atop the extra thick chocolate frosting.

Brian studies it for a moment, then looks up into the camera because everyone over in that direction is instructing and coaxing him to blow it out—as well as charading. We constituted a puffer fish *ensemble,* you might say. Too bad the camera was facing in the wrong direction. Anyway, pretty soon he blows it out and we all clap and so does he. Next we start urging him to eat some cake.

At first he is a little cautious. One finger punctures the top of the cake like a meat thermometer. Then he gives the sticky goo a lick. Yummm. Like an industrial crane set to motion, his fat little hand engages, scoops out a giant helping, crams it into his mouth. This is where the picture starts bouncing up and down a tad. I have yet to learn how to keep laughter contained to my face.

As he chews and reshuffles the escaping bits, we see the candle start to disappear into his mouth like a sucked-up spaghetti noodle. This is where there is a gap in the film.

The closing shot captures the last morsel off the plate being crammed into an already full mouth. He is chocolate from ear to ear. His little toes are turned up and looking happy like the rest of him.

* * *

The next birthday occasion that comes to mind is Bret's second-grade party—to which silly us invited his entire class. What I re-member best about this party is that the basement housed a state of chaos for two full hours. Bret was so overwhelmed with it, it was hard to tell if he was even having a good time. We learned some-thing here: Birthday Happiness is not created by sheer numbers.

* * *

Next comes the magic-show birthday. It was the year Brian wanted to decorate his own cake and he used every cake decorating doo-dah in our house, including ten one-inch American flags. Let's just say that due to cake crowding, we experienced flag burning before it became newsworthy. Ours, of course, was accidental. This was not the magic part, however.

The magic part came right after the pizza party. Since Brian's birthday is December 30, Christmas gifts are still a novelty, and Bret had received a wonderful magic-show kit under the tree. Thus, the need for an audience—aside from his family who were, five days into around-the-clock entertainment, sick and tired of magic. And so, six six-year-olds gathered around the young magician who wore his hair in bangs. They sat spellbound—for about three minutes. Then they wanted cake. So much for the "magic" birthday.

*   *   *

I could go on and on telling birthday stories, but they are *obvious* reasons for celebrating. More important to the celebration tally of things are the less formal occasions, because they can gallop in at any unsuspecting moment. I'm talking about little out-of-the-ordinary bursts of things to be joyful about. And like most things, perhaps experiencing them has to do with attitude.

". . . the cheerful heart has a continual feast," reads Proverbs 15:15. I believe a cheerful heart is a hot wire to joy. And, "A cheerful heart is good medicine" (Prov 17:22).

In order to teach your children to have a joyful heart, you must first learn how yourself. Learn to take notice of the little things worthy of celebration.

"Even though I've made meat loaf a thousand times, this time it just seems perfect!"

"My boss bragged about my productivity at a meeting today!"

"This is a brand new permanent and I'm not devastated!"

"Look, everybody! The row of beans I planted last week is sprouting!"

"Can you believe it? I won the pie-eating contest at the Fourth of July fest! My name is going to be in the newspapers!"

Okay. So this last announcement didn't evoke quite the response I thought it would. But then it's not *my* fault they found my latest achievement embarrassing.

Usually, however, everyone perked up when the celebratory tone echoed throughout our household. It didn't matter who used it; it brought bursts of energy into otherwise routine days. A mini-celebration reminded everyone that life is more than cooking, cleaning your room, mowing, homework, raising kids. It sometimes even brought new meaning to those "ordinary" things.

Long ago, the writer of Ecclesiastes said, "I know that there is nothing better for men [and women, and children] than to be happy and do good while they live. That everyone may eat and drink, and find satisfaction in all his toil—this is the gift of God" (3:12-13). Life *is* worth celebrating, isn't it.

Take notice of the small miracles: A Popsicle that *didn't* drip all over the newly scrubbed floor. A lawn mower's sharpened blade which sheared the perfect path. A cookie recipe that honestly made as many cookies as the recipe said it would. (Okay, I'm still waiting for this one. But I believe it's possible!)

A baby who smiled on cue. Legos that snapped together into the perfect automobile. A sparkly rock that was delivered in the load of gravel. A knock-knock joke that was actually funny. A part in the school play. The smell of a bouquet of flowers—even though they were picked by tiny hands from a neighbor's yard. One brother patting the other on the back in a sign of consolation and love. A neatly folded basket of laundry. A hug when you need one.

Many of our friends have found one-on-one occasions are always cause for celebration. The night Daddy takes just one of his daughters for ice cream. The day Mom treats her middle son to miniature golf. The fishing trip a first-born spends alone with Dad or Mom. A special time when a child doesn't have to share the limelight or the parent. Dates are made and put on the calendar. Minds are cleared. Sharing is heard. These "dates" are remembered; I've heard that validated by parents and grown children alike.

*   *   *

All celebrations aren't cheery. The day Bret moved to Albuquerque isn't high up there on my list of singing and clapping times. You already know I am a weeper; we're talking rivers-full here.

But there he sat behind the wheel of his giant old green car that was packed to the gills and riding low. He was smiling, but anticipation and nervousness danced on his face. It was a look I had grown familiar with and quite attached to. It captured his face any time he brought us news that he knew would be met with mixed emotions.

I swear, I could see his heart beating in his eyes. His precious giving heart. The one I'm sure I errantly missed sometimes in the heat of the moment. But this time it couldn't be missed. And it nearly tugged mine out of my chest.

I couldn't help but crack a warm-hearted smile at his final get-ready. He hopped out of his car, rummaged through something in the trunk and produced his rebel flag that had adorned his bedroom wall for so many years. He ceremoniously unfolded it and draped it over his "stuff" in the back seat, carefully tucking it in. "The One And Only." Flying his rebel flag across the country.

"God's speed," I prayed as he backed out of the drive following about eleventy-dozen hugs.

And yet it was a celebration. The marking of time when a man followed his heart's desire.

*　　*　　*

So many markings of time. And then they're gone.

I find that I have now entered my grandmother wonderment phase. No, as of this writing there are none on the way—thank goodness, because neither son is married. Yet I find myself anxious for this passage of our lives.

You see, I collect crystal prisms that hang in my windows. Most are pieces of old chandeliers that I have picked up at antique shops or garage sales. Some are that Austrian full-leaded crystal that hangs in shopping malls, its sparkly beauty capturing my attention, then my pocketbook.

Please don't confuse this hobby of mine with the "new age" use of crystals. The attention that has been drawn to quartz crystals and their "powers" is totally removed from the simple pleasure I gain by seeing God-given light refracted through a crystal, then cast into beautiful rainbows around my house.

And I do mean "around my house." They hang from fish line in windows on nearly all sides, ever waiting to capture the sun as it moves past. I have seen a drab flower arrangement burst into colorful splendor. I have seen green, red and blue stripes perch on Butch's nose. I have watched my friend's baby stop in mid-crawl to try to scoop one of the colorful curiosities up off the floor, only to find it settling on the back of his hand.

One of my favorites took place the day I was baking lasagna. When I opened the oven door, a burst of color branded my bubbling dinner, thereby opening an entire chain of fanciful thinking:

*　　*　　*

I hope some day my grandchildren will be excited about coming to Granny's house so they can sit in her magic kitchen and eat cookies baked with rainbows inside them.

We will sit together—a sweet-smelling child on each of my knees—and simply be in wonder at slices of rainbows that gently peel off the sun's rays and land on ordinary objects, making them become extraordinary jewels kissed with the hope that All Can Become More Than It Appears. And I will use that beautiful image to tell them about my Lord, the Creator of Rainbows, and the power he has to make all this happen—and more.

Visions of wonderment dance in my head: baby at my beautiful daughter-in-law's breast. Tiny fingers wrapped around larger, caring ones. My sons looking over their beloved wives' shoulders. Finger paintings sent to Grandma and Grandpa to hang on their refrigerator door. Best batting average on the baseball team. Captain of a major airline . . .

And then they'll bring them over to visit.

And leave them screaming at the door. And they will dirty their pants. And tell me they love me. And track mud on the new carpet Grandpa and I just got. And curl in our laps while we read stories.

And we will study the similarities in the faces of our children and grandchildren, and maybe spy a slight resemblance to ourselves.

And they will have very good days and very bad days. And their parents will take them home and we will sigh with blessed relief and joy. And we will look ever so forward to their return.

And wonderment will take on a whole new meaning. And entire new volumes of memories in our old-age portfolios will be spread before our aged friends at bingo games.

And I wouldn't miss these children for the world, any more than I missed my own.